a Little too CLOSE

USA TODAY BESTSELLING AUTHOR

REBECCA YARROS

A LITTLE TOO CLOSE

Editing by Karen Grove

www.karengrove.com

Copy Editing by Jenn Wood

Cover by Sarah Hansen Okay Creations

To my brother, Matt.
Because you've always
shown up.

PROLOGUE

eston

JANUARY IN UPSTATE NEW YORK meant snow, and lots of it. Last night had dumped about three feet, but the skies were crystal blue this morning and perfect for flying over Fort Drum. I didn't even mind the time it had taken to shovel out before driving out to the flight line, not when I'd spent most of this year on a rotation in the sandbox. I'd take snow over sand any day.

The below-zero temps were something I could live without, though.

I shouldered my helmet bag and walked into the 1-10 hangar, waving at a couple guys on their way out.

"Hey, Madigan," one of the crew chiefs said as I climbed the stairs toward the locker room. "Harris is looking for you."

"Thanks." I gave him the nod and headed to the second floor, looking out over the birds we'd hangered yesterday before the storm.

I pushed through the door into the locker room, narrowly missing Carlson—another pilot—as he reached for the handle. "Shit, my bad."

"No problem." He caught the door. "Pretty sure Harris is looking for you."

"I heard something about that. Thanks." I headed for my locker.

"I think the promotion list might be out." He lifted his brows at me and backed through the door, letting it swing shut.

My stomach twisted into knots as I put my gear away and got ready for the day. If the promotion list was out…

Don't go there.

I wasn't even in the zone for promotion yet, but getting picked up below the zone would be absolutely mind-blowing. It would also mean I'd have to sign on Uncle Sam's dotted line for another two years after pinning the new rank.

But if Harris was looking for me—

My cell phone rang in my pocket, and I swiped to answer it before I looked at the caller ID.

"Hello?" I wedged the phone between my ear and shoulder as I hung up my coat on the metal hook.

"West?" Reed's voice brought me up short.

Not looking at the screen had been a mistake. I wasn't in the mood for anything my older brother had to say, not that I ever was.

"What's wrong?" I asked. If something had gone sideways with Crew, our little brother, I would have heard from him directly, which only left Dad.

I wasn't exactly sweating bullets over a guy who didn't give a shit about me or either of my brothers. His one and only love was the little Colorado ski resort that had been passed down through our family.

"Why does something have to be wrong?" Reed countered.

"Because you're calling at six a.m. your time."

"Actually"—there was a tone in his voice I recognized, the nice one he only used when he had shitty news to deliver—"it's seven o'clock."

I glanced at my watch to make sure I had the time right, and my brow furrowed. Then it hit me. "You're still in Colorado." Guess he'd stayed after all.

Good for him, but no-fucking-thank you.

"Yeah." He took a breath, as if summoning the courage for something. "Still working on the new lift and the condos and everything I sent that email to you and Crew about last month."

"Right. Good for you." I shut the metal door of my locker. "Look, unless there's something you need, I'm scheduled to fly—"

"Just let me get this out," he blurted.

I paused. Reed was flustered. Reed *never* got flustered. He was Mister Cool, Calm, and Collected at all times. Fuck, the guy hadn't even batted an eye when he'd left Crew and me to fend for ourselves after Mom died and Dad had disappeared into a bottle.

Reed had gone back to college and lived his perfect little ski racer life until a torn ACL had forced him to pivot to getting his MBA at Stanford.

And me? I'd paused my dream of big mountain skiing to help Mom when she first got sick, and then gave it up completely when she died my junior year, leaving a gaping chasm in our lives. Leaving for college? That was a luxury only Reed could afford. Someone had to be the adult around the house, and as much as Reed loved pretending it had been him, swooping in on his college breaks to play savior, it hadn't. It had been me, and only me, until I'd kept the promise I'd made to Mom and gotten Crew through high school. Only then had I given myself the permission to dream again, and eleven years later, I'd clawed my way through night and online courses for college and was living that dream as a helicopter pilot for the army.

"I'm waiting," I said, my grip tightening on the phone. To say that Reed and I didn't have the best relationship would have been the understatement of the century. I loved him, but I also really fucking loathed the load he'd left me to carry.

"We need a way to bring in high-end clientele while we're building the condo development. A new income stream since we're spending some major dollars right now."

"Not my problem. You're the one that decided to go back and work with Dad. Not me." I sighed and rubbed the bridge of my nose, telling myself I shouldn't care as I fought the pang in my heart that told me I most definitely did.

"I know that," he ground out. "And Dad is never around. It's just me and Ava running this."

"Aren't you supposed to have that fancy new lift open by November?" That was the typical opening month for Madigan Mountain.

"So you *do* read my emails. You just don't respond to them."

"Get to the point, Reed. My job doesn't take kindly to being late." It was one of the reasons I loved the army. I thrived on order and discipline.

"Okay. I'd like Madigan to start up its own heli-skiing operation. It would take the resort to an entirely new level, which is what we're looking to do with the expansion."

I sucked in a sharp breath, the possibilities whirring through my mind with the force of a hurricane. The higher peaks and ridges just behind the resort were perfect for that kind of operation. Nothing compared to Telluride or even Steamboat, but we could hold our own.

Not we. They.

"There's only one guy I can think of who knows the backcountry around here like it's his personal playground and already happens to know how to fly a helicopter."

Silence stretched between us as I forced air through my lungs. There was no way he was asking this of me. No. Fucking. Way.

"West?"

"Ask someone else." The door to the locker room opened, and I turned to see Theo Harris, my oldest friend and senior pilot, walk in, wearing a shit-eating grin on his face and waving a piece of paper in his hand.

"I don't want to ask someone else." Reed's tone took on a desperate edge. "You're family. This is our family's business, Weston. Our family's resort. Our family's—"

"I swear to God, if you say legacy, I'm going to hang up." I clenched my jaw.

Theo's dark brows lifted skyward, and he lowered the paper.

Reed sighed. "You'd have full control of your own operation. You'd just operate under the Madigan logo."

This wasn't happening. It wasn't. But as long he just *wanted* and didn't *need*, then I could turn him down. There were plenty of other pilots he could hire. Plenty of guides too. Just none that could do both sides of it like me. *I can't seriously be contemplating this.*

"What's up?" I asked Theo, needing to cling to something in my real world and not the pretend one Reed was spinning.

"You made the promotion list! Below the zone!" He held out the paper.

Holy shit. I did it.

"Don't you get what I'm saying?" Reed asked, apparently thinking I was talking to him. "I need you to come home, Weston."

Fuck. Me.

1

W eston

NINE MONTHS Later

HELICOPTERS WERE MY HAPPY PLACE. They were power, and lift, and drive—all without the constraints of runways. They weren't confined to roads, and they didn't require space to accelerate for takeoff. They simply launched into the sky from wherever they happened to be. They were *freedom*. At least they used to be. The shiny red slice of liberty I was currently signing for felt about as liberating as handcuffs. Because that's exactly what it was.

It was a three-million-dollar leash.

The office clock in the steel building just off the tarmac in

Leadville, Colorado, showed seven a.m., and my stomach churned as I debated my life choices for the millionth time since Reed called. But I signed, and signed, and signed, each signature tying me to the one place I'd spent eleven years avoiding like a prostate exam.

"You know, if I wanted to do dash-eighteen inspections at dawn, I would have stayed in the army," Theo said from the doorway, clipboard in hand, the brown skin of his forehead crinkling as he raised his brows at me. He'd been my best friend for the better part of a decade, so I knew it wasn't going to be the last time he looked at me like that.

"At least you're not in A2CU's." Personally, I would have traded my jeans and Henley for my uniform in a second, but Theo had been ready to get out, which was the only reason I'd been able to talk him into coming with me. I handed over another stack of paperwork to the broker, stretching as I stood. We'd sent Maria's husband and Theo's family ahead to Penny Ridge yesterday, then driven into Leadville late last night, and my body ached from spending hours behind the wheel. I needed a run to loosen up after two straight days of travel, but this had been the only time the seller had been able to meet us for delivery.

"Everything in order?" the broker asked Theo.

"Serial numbers match up on everything," Theo said with a nod, handing over the clipboard. "Ramos is still doing her once-over."

Thankfully, Maria Ramos had been approaching her ETS date and been able to turn in her combat boots with us for this insane little venture. It was almost like the stars had aligned, or fate had smiled, or some other cliché bullshit. Either way, she was the best crew chief we'd had in our unit and the final piece I'd needed.

We left the building and stepped out into the early October

air, where Maria was closing one of the compartments on the helicopter.

"How does it look?" I asked.

"Good," she answered. "It's well maintained. I mean, there's every chance you two assholes could still fly it into the ground, but that would be pilot error." She shrugged with a deceptively sweet smile.

We did the walk-around and I signed the last of the paperwork.

The broker reached out his hand and shook all three of ours in turn. "I wish you guys better luck than the last company that owned her."

"What happened to the last company?" Theo's brow furrowed, giving the helicopter a second look.

"Went under." The broker shrugged. "Everyone thinks they have what it takes to own and manage a heli-skiing operation here, but…well…" Another shrug.

My ribs tightened like a vise.

"Anyway, I'll go make some copies inside and then you guys are good to go." The broker headed back into the terminal.

"They went under," Maria said slowly, lifting her ball cap to tuck a strand of her brown hair back under the brim.

"Guess so." I shoved my hands into the pockets of my cargo pants. Gone were the multicam flight suits and the rank on my chest I'd worked my ass off for. I was starting over from scratch —well, not entirely since I had Theo and Maria with me, but their support also meant I was responsible for them.

"West." Theo turned and put his hands on my shoulders, looking me dead in the eye. "Look me in the eye and tell me this isn't going to fail. I did not move my wife and kids to the whitest town in America—and I am *not* talking about the snow —for this to fail."

"We're not going to fail," I assured him.

"Right. Now say it like you mean it."

"We aren't going to fail." I cracked a wry smile and stepped back, taking in the clean lines of the Bell 212 and her shiny new paint. Failure wasn't an option, not here, not with my family's name on that paperwork.

"It's not like we're starting up on our own," Maria added, zipping her jacket over her coveralls. "Scott signed for our new apartment last night, and he told me that little operation your family owns isn't quite the mom-and-pop shop you described." She tilted her head to the side. "I believe the words *boutique resort* came out of his mouth."

"My brother Reed is expanding it," I said by way of explanation. My friends knew everything they needed to for our business to succeed—my family was the owner of Madigan Mountain Resort, a small, family-oriented ski resort in Summit County, Colorado. They knew I'd been asked to open a heli-skiing operation to take Madigan Mountain up a notch. We weren't competing with Breck or even A-basin or anything, but the expansion Reed was overseeing was going to catapult us in that direction. My friends also knew that I'd walked away from the resort, and every string that came with it, eleven years ago and hadn't looked back once.

Not until Reed called nine months ago.

"You're regretting this, aren't you?" Theo asked, studying my face. "Because Jeanine is closing on a house I've never even seen before right now, and if you're having second thoughts—"

"I just signed for a three-million-dollar aircraft." I curled the brim of my hat, the only nervous gesture that eleven years in the army hadn't cleared me of. "There are no second thoughts."

"Good, because Scott is already unpacking," Maria said, shooting me a sideways glance.

"We're not going to fail," I repeated. "I know these mountains like the back of my hand, and with us"—I looked over at Theo—

"taking turns flying and guiding the backcountry tours, we're going to be just fine."

It was our love of backcountry skiing that had bonded Theo and I during the months we'd spent TDY in Europe that first year. The guy was just as good as I was, and I was damn good.

The broker came back from the terminal with a large blue folder that had his logo stamped across the front. "Paperwork is all here."

"Thank you." I took the folder. It wasn't every day someone held his life in his hands, but here I was.

"You ever fly out of Leadville before?" the broker asked, two little lines appearing between his eyes.

"Yep," I answered.

"High-altitude training," Theo explained.

"Good. Hate to be the last person you ever saw," the broker joked. "Keys are yours, metaphorically speaking, and the ones to the doors are in the folder. Pleasure working with you."

"You too."

We waved goodbye to Maria as she drove my truck from the airport, heading toward Penny Ridge, then Theo and I started the run-up and checks.

"You file the flight plan?" I asked through our headsets.

"You know I did. Smooth like butter," Theo said as the engines ran up. "And look, a full tank of gas."

"For three million, he better have filled the tank."

"How long is it going to take Ramos to get there?"

"About ninety minutes," I answered. "It'll take us about twenty to fly it."

"You're driving this time," Theo commented. "That way if something breaks, it's on you."

I scoffed but nodded as we finished the checklist. Then I took the controls, got clearance from the tower, and launched us into the sky. There was nothing quite like the sound of this hum. It was different in every helicopter, but the beats were distinct in this model, which was pretty much a jazzed-up Huey.

The rotors beat the air into submission, and we took off. The air was thin up here—Leadville was the highest airport in the nation—and the gauges showed it.

We dipped off the peak and flew along the range.

"That's some pretty blue sky you've got here," Theo said, taking in the scenery.

"Colorado blue. There's nothing quite like it anywhere else." We followed the dips and lines through the valley, which had us following the road for the most part.

"Breckenridge?" Theo asked, looking out over the terrain.

"Frisco," I answered as we veered east. "Breck's just up there."

"I can see the runs from here."

We flew past Keystone and A-basin, then headed toward Penny Ridge, which sat just beneath the Madigan Mountain Resort. From the air, Penny Ridge looked to be about the same as when I'd left—a few new buildings here and there, but nothing significant. That was the beauty of a small town that stayed small.

And the mountains? Those never changed. Not really. The hunter green of the pines gave way at the tree line to jagged gray peaks that cut into the sky like chipped knife blades. We had a couple of weeks until the snow would stick, and another few after that to build enough of a base to open for the season. Just enough time for Theo to get to know the area as well as I did.

"All of the really good skiing is over that ridge." I nodded toward the runs that were carved into the mountain, their thin strips of pale green slicing through the trees, accompanied only by the chairlift I'd helped repair too many times to count. "We'll do an area orientation flight tomorrow if Jeanine doesn't have you unpacking."

"She will," he answered with a smile, his voice softening like it always did when he talked about his wife. Those two were... iconic, enviable. That was the only way to describe their relationship. "But we'll make time."

From the air, I could see just how much the expansion was already underway. New runs had been cut in recently purchased land, and construction had begun for the new condo development, or whatever Reed was calling it.

And right there, between the existing resort and Madigan 2.0, was the building Reed had promised, along with an X-marked helipad. Not that I'd ever doubted. If Reed said he was going to do something, then it got done.

It was the shit he didn't promise that had always been our issue.

"Looks like that's all for us," Theo said. "You know, it's not every family that welcomes you home with a new hangar." He glanced over meaningfully.

"Don't go there." I maneuvered the aircraft carefully, making sure I hadn't missed any powerline construction in the last decade. "It's too early."

"My man, we are *already* going there." Theo leaned forward as we approached the helipad. "Or is that not your name on the side of that building?"

"My last name," I muttered, setting her down. And just like that, I was...here. My chest ached, and I knew it wasn't only from the lack of oxygen up here at nine thousand feet.

There wasn't much I could do about what was waiting for me outside the aircraft, so I concentrated on what was inside, starting the postflight. I cut the engines, and the rotors spun slower and slower, like a countdown to a confrontation that had been waiting the better part of a decade. I fucking hated this place, and now it was supposed to be my home again.

What the hell had I been thinking?

I kept my attention on the helicopter, deliberately looking away from the path that led toward the resort as we opened the unlocked building and got the bird onto the cart that would move it from the pad and into the hangar. Theo drove her in while I guided, my focus narrowed to getting her secured.

But then she was tucked away, and my time for self-indulgence was over.

Theo checked a text message after we got the hangar doors shut. "Jeanine is here."

"Go," I told him. "You have a whole house to unpack."

"Maria should be here with your truck in"—he checked his watch—"half an hour or so. You going to be okay?"

"Absolutely." Maria and Theo had bigger things to worry about than me.

He gave me a nod and took off through the side door of the building, leaving me alone in the hangar.

It was small but well-sized for what we needed. Packed correctly, we could probably fit another bird in here. Equipment lined one side of the building, and there were two walled-off offices along the other, both sporting windows into the hangar.

I could see the desks in one of them, where we would set up bookings and take care of the business end of the operation, and the other was empty except for the stack of plastic chairs that looked like they'd been taken straight out of the church basement. It was a good area to brief the skiers.

"It's set up exactly how you asked," a familiar voice said from behind me.

My jaw flexed with recognition. I should have locked the damn doors.

"It's great," I said, turning toward the helicopter instead of my brother. "Did you get all the equipment Ramos asked you for?"

"It's here." Reed walked over and stood at my side.

He had an inch on me, but what I lacked in height I more than made up for in muscle. He'd spent his years in boardrooms, and I'd spent mine in the gym or flying. We had the same dark hair and eyes, the same chin, and definitely got our dad's ears, but that's where the resemblance stopped.

"You look good," Reed said, giving me a once-over.

"Thanks. War was great for my complexion. You look..." I spared a glance over his slacks and Patagonia vest to his perfectly coiffed hair. "Polished."

"That doesn't sound like a compliment."

"It's not." I shrugged.

Reed scoffed. "I left the share agreement on your desk. You know, the one that gives you an increased stake for every year you're at Madigan."

I grunted. I wasn't here for the shares and we both knew it.

He tilted his head in examination as he stared at the helicopter. "I thought you'd go with something more like what they're using in Telluride. The Eurocopter—"

"Has a five-passenger limit and one engine for over two million," I countered. "This triples that capacity with two engines at just under three million. And you signed off on it, remember?" The thrum of a familiar engine filled the hangar from outside. Maria had made it.

"I did." He scratched the back of his neck. "Still, the hourly costs—"

I muttered a curse. "Am I talking to my brother or my business partner?"

His head snapped in my direction. "Will you talk to your brother? Because the only communications I've had with you for the last decade have been family business and this helicopter."

I ignored the jab. "This is a Bell 212 HP-BLR. It's been structurally overhauled and rewired within the last year, and yes, that's fresh paint. It has less than ten thousand hours on the body and comes complete with gear cage"—I pointed to the long wire basket along the fuselage—"and rescue hoist." I gestured toward the lift. "It has seating capacity for fourteen, and did I mention a second engine just in case that first one goes out?"

Reed rolled his eyes. "Weston—"

"Now the Eurocopter does have an operating cost that's down around $875 an hour, and the Bell is going to take that up to $1,508, but even if we operate only at the Eurocopter's capacity, we're still going to profit about three grand a day."

Reed opened his mouth, and I ran him over.

"Now, the Eurocopter is going to profit about $4,600 a day as long as they only book at five people. But the second they go to six, they have to take a second helicopter, and they won't just book it for that one. They have a minimum of three. So let's go with eight, just for fun." I crossed my arms in front of me. "So, for eight people, our profit is seven grand a day and theirs is— wait for it—$6,300 a day because they have to eat the hourly costs for the second helicopter, and that's before the cost of an additional pilot. We don't have that issue. Every person over three is profit for us, and we can take parties of four or five. They won't. You're not the only one in the family who can do math. Oh, and did you hear the part about the second engine? Trust me, you'd care if you were the one flying it."

Reed took a measured breath. "Damn, Weston, I wasn't saying you made a bad choice."

"No, you were just second-guessing it." Like he always did.

"It's a lot of money! And that thing is huge. Do you even think you can put it down on the ridgelines?"

"If I can put wheels down on the edge of a bombed-out building in a war zone to load up a platoon of soldiers, then I'm pretty damn sure I can handle some tourists in the snow." I turned to face my brother, looking into his eyes for the first time in years. "You're the one who asked me to come back and get this operation running. You called *me*, Reed. If you'd like to get behind the controls, then feel free, but flying up at this altitude is more complicated than the hostile takeovers you're used to—"

"That isn't even what I do—"

"Facilitating in those boardrooms of yours."

"For fuck's sake, this is getting us nowhere." He rubbed his hands over his face. "Have you always been this much of an asshole?"

"Yes." That shut him up.

A couple seconds passed in awkward silence, and we both cracked a reluctant smile.

"I guess you're not in the mood to hear, 'Welcome home'?" Reed asked slowly.

"Just tell me he's not here and I'll consider that welcome enough." Seeing Reed was one thing, but handling our father? Fuck that. Not today.

"No. He's off cruising the world for his honeymoon." Reed sucked in a breath. "You know, he's really changed these last—"

"Not interested." Dad had sealed his fate with me years ago when he'd disappeared into himself after Mom died and left me to raise Crew. Reed leaving us to fend for ourselves while he moved to Vermont for college had been a dick move, but Dad's abandonment? My fists clenched.

I resented Reed. I despised Dad. There was a difference.

"I can see you're going to make this absolutely easy on both of us," Reed muttered.

"I'm here, aren't I?"

"Yeah. You are." He grabbed something out of his pocket, and a second later, keys flew through the air. I caught them. "Seasonal lodging is full getting the new hires trained, but one of the employee housing duplexes is empty. It's unit sixteen, up the hill —"

"I know where the duplexes are. Thanks."

Reed took another deep breath and closed his eyes for a second, as though he was on the search for inner peace or something. "You could just stay up at the house with me—"

"I'd rather go back to the sandbox for a year than step foot in that house."

He sighed. "The fact that I know you mean that is something else, West. It's the house we grew up in."

"I need to unpack."

He put his hands up like he was under arrest. "At least that means you're staying long enough to do it. Welcome home." He tossed a second set of keys at me and walked away, leaving through the side door, where Maria sidestepped to get out of his way.

"How much did you hear?" I asked her as I locked up.

"Enough. I thought middle children were supposed to be the peacemakers?" We walked across the parking lot that smelled like fresh blacktop and climbed into my truck.

"I was too busy taking care of my mom that last year, then raising Crew, to give a shit about peace." And Reed had been having the time of his life on a ski team in Vermont.

Life was a lot of things, but fair wasn't one of them.

"Crew's your little brother, right? The X Games guy?"

"That's him." I put the truck into reverse and then backed out of the spot, flipping us around so I could pull out onto the road. At least this wasn't new. "Let's get you to your new place."

"I stopped on the way in and picked up a few essentials for you." She motioned to the back seat where I saw a grocery bag. "Figured you hadn't eaten, and you're kind of an ass when you're hungry. Plus, I was hoping if I got in your good graces, you wouldn't make us start today."

"You're not the first person to say that to me." A smile pulled at the corners of my mouth. "And thanks for the groceries. We're not starting until tomorrow and, even then, it's just an area orientation flight."

I got her dropped off at her new place and waved to her husband, Scott, as I pulled out.

I passed the picturesque, alpine-style resort my mother had taken so much pride in and kept driving up the mountain. Her stamp was everywhere: the heritage red accents of paint, the friendly staff that waved at me even though they didn't recognize me, and the window boxes that dripped red and white flowers that had yet to give in to fall. Except she hadn't planted those flowers, not in fifteen years since she'd passed.

There were a few new potholes as I headed up the hill, but everything else looked the same. I pulled into the cul-de-sac where the employee housing duplexes sat, then parked along the curb, my mind preoccupied with Reed's comments.

Had I chosen the wrong helicopter? Had it been a mistake to go for occupancy and the security of dual engines? Were we capable of luring that kind of clientele here while the expansion was built, or had I just doomed us to failure? I hadn't even been home for two hours and Reed was already in my head.

I slung one of my duffels over my shoulder, then lifted the grocery bag, fumbling with the car, house, and hangar keys as I walked up the path to the door. Everything depended on this first season. Maria and Theo had uprooted their entire lives for this—for me, for the opportunity to do what we loved while working for ourselves.

And as much as I wanted to beat the shit out of Reed some days, he'd called. He'd asked for help, and I'd answered. Why? Because as much as I hated this place, I was also wildly in love with it, and the thought of it slipping into some corporate sleezeball's hands if the expansion failed and Dad ended up selling wasn't something I could stomach.

I keyed open the door and didn't bother looking at the

layout as I walked through the living room and toward the kitchen. The units had been built when I was a kid, and they were all identical. An open-concept, shared space made up the rectangle of the living room, dining room, and kitchen. Every kitchen had the same model refrigerator and stove, and a washer and dryer was in a storage-style mudroom toward the back. Every unit had two identical staircases inside that framed the space, leading to separate, lockable hallways that led to separate two-bedroom units.

It seemed like a waste of space to give me a four bedroom, but I wasn't complaining. I'd never been big on having people in my space, which was probably why I'd never made a relationship work the way Theo and Maria had.

Or maybe it was just that I'd never met someone who I wanted to be around twenty-four seven.

I yanked open the fridge and grimaced, shoving the bacon and eggs Maria had picked up for me onto an empty shelf. Whoever had been here last hadn't cleaned out the fridge. Guess I knew what I'd be doing after my run. The place was colorfully decorated with throw pillows on the couch and poster-sized framed pictures on the wall of far-off locations like the Serengeti, which was odd, considering we were a ski resort, but I guess everyone got sick of snow at some point.

Climbing the staircase on the left, I took the bedroom and didn't bother to unpack more than my running gear. Everything else could wait. The pressure I was all too acquainted with was in my chest, my head, begging to be released with every doubt that Reed had shoved into my brain.

Ten minutes later, I was laced up and could finally breathe. The trails were the same. The air burned my lungs with a familiar ache. The sun hit my skin with nostalgic intensity. My feet followed the rocky paths as though they'd never left them, as if I'd been running here yesterday and not ten years ago. I turned onto the dirt road that switch-backed up the mountain to the top of the lift and ran harder, pushing myself further. Only when my body screamed for mercy—and oxygen—did I turn around and jog back down, stripping off my shirt and tucking it at the back of my gym shorts. The fifty-degree air felt fantastic on my sweat-soaked skin.

It would take me at least a month to acclimate to the altitude, and longer to rebuild the endurance I'd gained while stationed at Fort Drum in New York.

By the time I got back to the house, all I could think about was food, and I fumbled in the kitchen for the cookware all the units were issued with, starting the bacon.

It was only ten thirty. How had my life changed so drastically in three freaking hours?

Because you said yes.

The sound of sizzling bacon filled the space as I cooked, turning the bacon with a fork.

The Bell was the right choice. It had the greatest capacity. Even if we grew to taking multiple groups to multiple runs, it was the way to go. It was the safer way to go. *Then stop second-guessing yourself just because of Reed.*

The front door opened and my head shot up. What the hell?

A blond woman walked in, answering a phone that was jammed between her ear and shoulder, juggling a purple backpack and another black bag, her attention on something behind her as she looked over her shoulder.

"Hey, Ava," she said, tugging her keys from the door. "What's up?"

My jaw slackened.

She had the kind of profile that belonged in photographs—high cheekbones, pert little nose, and a mouth that made my breath catch as it curved into a smile. That *smile* was fucking gorgeous, lighting up her entire face as she pivoted, and somehow I knew her eyes were Colorado blue. A nagging sense of déjà vu chewed at the edge of my mind, like a half-recalled memory from a drunken night.

But what was she doing in my house? Had Reed sent her? I opened my mouth to ask just as a miniature version of the woman appeared, scooting past her mother. The little girl saw me within a heartbeat, her little eyes flying wide.

I blinked.

She screamed.

2

allie

SUTTON'S SHRIEK jolted my heart, and I dropped everything in my arms to sweep her behind my back. Her backpack, my phone, my keys, even my camera bag crashed to the tile floor of my little entryway as I jerked my head up to face whatever threat she'd spotted.

A clatter in the kitchen had my gaze flying across the house.

What the actual hell?

A man stood at the stove behind the kitchen island.

A very tall, very ripped, very...shirtless...man.

And that smell—

Wait, was he *cooking*? Bacon? In my kitchen?

I swallowed around the boulder of terror in my throat and retreated a step, keeping one arm locked around Sutton's torso as I maneuvered us back through the open door.

He threw his hands up, showing his palms, and the expression of complete, abject shock had me pausing at the threshold as recognition tickled my brain. Sutton had stopped screaming, freeing up a little space for logic in my mind as adrenaline surged through every vein.

The dark hair. The strong chin. That face.

Oh crap, I knew who this man was.

I owed him *everything.*

"Callie!" Ava yelled up through the speaker of my phone.

"Stay here," I told Sutton, keeping her outside on the porch while I scrambled for the phone and keys I'd abandoned to the floor. "Ava?" I asked, keeping my eyes on my intruder as I lifted my phone to my ear.

"Oh, thank goodness!" My friend sighed. "I was trying to get ahold of you because—"

"Let me guess," I interrupted. "You called to tell me there was a good chance I'd find Weston Madigan in my house." Because that's exactly who was cooking in my kitchen. Weston-freak-ing-Madigan, the middle brother of the family who owned this entire resort.

Weston's eyes flared, then narrowed slightly, and his mouth dropped along with his hands.

"Oh God. He's already there, isn't he?" Ava asked. "I'm in the car right now. I was hoping I'd be able to get there before you got back from Sutton's parent-teacher conference. It was today, right?"

"Yep, and yep. Just got here. He's standing in my kitchen." *Shirtless.* Oh man, did I need to get out on a date if that was where my head immediately went when there was a strange man in my house. Not that he was a stranger, not really.

"I'm so sorry. I'll be right there!" She hung up and I slid the phone into the back pocket of my jeans. At least I hadn't cracked the screen when I'd dropped it. A new phone was the last thing I could afford right now.

"You know who I am." His voice was really freaking deep and more than a little attractive. *Not the time, Callie.*

I nodded and took a deep breath, trying to calm my racing heart. He wasn't a threat, or someone who'd sneaked into my house to attack Sutton or me. This was just some kind of screwup that resulted in bacon and Weston Madigan in my kitchen. My stomach growled. "We met. A little over eleven years ago." Even now, I could still feel the chill of my rain-soaked clothes as I hiked up the last fifty feet of road to the resort after my car had run out of gas.

He cocked his head to the side and his brows furrowed.

"You hired me," I babbled. How long was it going to take Ava to get here and sort this out? "You probably don't remember. I mean, it was a long time ago, and you were getting ready to leave." I swallowed, glancing back over my shoulder to make sure Sutton was still on the porch. "In fact, I think you left the next day."

"I hired you," he repeated slowly.

"Yep. The only experience I had was a semester of Intro to Photography from NYU, but you hired me anyway, probably because I was pregnant, and crying, and my car—"

"Had run out of gas," he finished, recognition lighting his eyes. "It was raining."

"Exactly." My keys bit into the palm of my hand. "And you took me to get gas, and when your dad didn't show for my interview, you just...took a chance and hired me."

His jaw locked and he nodded once.

"Anyway, I'm Callie Thorne."

"Callie? I don't remember that being your name." He shook his head. "It was something uncommon."

"Calliope," I answered, heat rushing my cheeks. He remembered. "My friends call me Callie. And this"—I pointed to our surroundings—"is my house. Or at least it has been for the last five years." I heard the unmistakable sound of an engine approaching and nearly sighed in relief. "And your bacon is burning."

"My bac—" He looked down and grimaced, moving the pan to another burner and killing the gas. "Shit." Then he seemed to notice he was shirtless and cursed again, ripping a shirt out from behind him like it was a magic trick and tugging it over his naked torso.

Too bad, because the view had been scrumptious.

Yeah, I needed to get out more.

"Ava!" Sutton called out in greeting, but I didn't take my eyes off Weston, and within minutes, my friend was easing through the doorway to stand beside me.

"I'm so sorry about all this, Callie!" she started, a blush rising in her cheeks as she slid the long strands of her brown hair behind her ears. "Hi, Weston!" She strode across the floor and offered her hand, which he shook, keeping one eye on me.

Sutton squeezed her head between me and the doorframe, shoving her honey-blond hair out of her face and setting her wide blue eyes on Weston. My ten-year-old daughter's curiosity was going to be the death of me one day. I knew it.

"I'm so sorry we have to meet this way. I'm Ava, the executive manager of the resort." She tapped her name badge like she needed proof.

"Reed's fiancée," Weston added as their hands fell away.

"That's me." She looked back at me with a smile that bordered on begging. "Can I talk to you both for a second?"

Weston and I locked eyes and nodded simultaneously.

"Sutton, why don't you head upstairs and start on that questionnaire your teacher gave you?" I asked, ushering her into the house.

She puckered her face at me and shot a longing look at Weston. "But I want to know what's going on." There was a definite whiny pitch to her tone, and I wasn't having it.

"And I'll tell you as soon as I know." I lifted my brows at her.

Her sigh was downright melodramatic. "Fiiiine." She hefted her nearly empty backpack to her shoulder and refrained from stomping up the steps. Barely. The look she shot over her shoulder told me she wasn't happy about it.

There were moments where the upcoming preteen years scared the crap out of me.

Once she disappeared through the door and down the hall, I shut the front door and scooped up my camera bag. Then I prayed I hadn't broken any of my equipment as I walked past our living room with its worn couch and colorful throw pillows, and the school project-scarred dining room table to the kitchen island, where Ava was already sitting on one of the four stools that made up our breakfast area.

Weston stood on the other side of the island, his arms folded across his chest. He was big. *Really* big. Like…probably almost a foot taller than my five-four frame, and I had no business noticing the way that T-shirt stretched across his muscles. None. Nope. Not noticing.

I blinked rapidly to *stop* noticing.

Then it hit me. Weston Madigan was home. He was here. In my house. In my kitchen. Except, none of it was really mine, was it? This house, this kitchen…it was all his. My chest drew tight.

"Are you kicking us out?" I took the stool to the right of Ava and set my camera bag on the counter as my stomach rolled and pitched like I was on a freaking boat, like the very ground beneath my feet had suddenly become unstable.

Ava's jaw dropped for a second, and Weston's eyebrows hit the ceiling.

"What?" Ava shook her head. "No. Of course not. Why would you even ask that?"

"Because I'm the resort photographer but he"—I motioned to Weston—"is the *resort*."

"I'm not kicking you out." Weston leveled his dark eyes on

me and didn't look away. Whoa, that gaze was intense—captivating—and something told me it was indicative of the man himself. "I just didn't know you were here." His focus slid to Ava.

"And that is my fault." She grimaced, her nose crinkling. "Reed and I had a little mix-up this morning, and by the time I realized he'd grabbed the keys for the unit, he was driving in the zone of no service—you know, the one between the lodge and the turn at the lift?"

Weston and I both nodded. Cell phone reception was always hit or miss around here.

"I tried to call him, but anyway, he was supposed to give you the spare keys to the house. Like...the *house*, house. Our house. Well, it's your house, but you get the idea," she explained, lacing her fingers on the countertop. "Because I told him this was our only open unit, which to me meant we were out of housing because we've left the other side of Callie's duplex empty since she and Sutton moved in, but..." She shrugged. "Here we are."

My shoulders dipped in relief. This was all one huge misunderstanding. Weston would move back in with his family and I would keep the roof over Sutton's head. *Phew.*

Weston sighed and took two steps backward, leaning against the edge of the sink. "Employee housing is full?"

"Exactly." Ava nodded. "So, I brought you the keys." She reached into the pocket of her blazer and pulled out a set of silver keys that dangled from a Madigan Mountain keychain. "Reed and I are in the primary bedroom right now since Dad is on vacation, but your old room is empty down the hall." She smiled.

Weston stared at the keys as though they were an enemy that needed to be vanquished.

Guess the man wasn't keen on moving back in with his family.

Ava's smile slipped a fraction. "And I know it might be

awkward since we don't really know each other, but we're going to be family."

"I'm not sleeping in that house." Weston's statement was spoken softly, but the determination in his voice was solid steel. "Not now. Not ever."

Oh crap. My stomach rolled again.

"Oh," Ava whispered.

"Has nothing to do with you, I promise."

"I get it," she said with a forced, professional smile, picking up the keys and shoving them back into her pocket. Ava was always dressed for business, but this was family, and I of all people understood just how complicated family could be.

It wasn't like I was down for moving back in with my parents either.

"What about the dorm-style units by the lodge?" Weston asked, rubbing the back of his neck. "I don't need much."

Yeah, because *that's* where one of the Madigan brothers belonged, in one of the tiny seasonal rooms. My head started to spin.

I'd worked my way up the employee ranks for seven years before I'd called in every favor I had to score this house so Sutton and I could have our own space. Years I'd put to good use, saving every possible dollar to build up enough money for a down payment on a place of our own in Penny Ridge—a place we could never be kicked out of—and we were *so* close. Just another six months, maybe a little more if property prices kept skyrocketing, and we'd have enough for a solid, competitive bid. Right now, I could only afford to offer asking price, and we were getting laughed out of every showing.

"Even the dorm-style ones are full," Ava said slowly. "Season is starting up in four or five weeks, depending on the weather this month, and with the expansion happening, we brought the new hires in to train early on the lifts and runs. And we're almost done renovating the guest rooms in the lodge, but they won't be ready for a few weeks yet, and then we're completely booked out."

My heart galloped, my breath coming faster and faster as the edges of my vision narrowed. "You're going to kick us out," I whispered. Of course they would—they should. The Madigans owned this entire property. He owned my *house*. If he had nowhere to live, that meant Sutton and I were out on our own.

And this real estate market wasn't just tough, it was *impossible*.

"No one is kicking you out. I might be an ass, but I'm not that big of an ass," Weston promised, a glass of orange juice appearing in front of me. "Drink that. You look like you're going to pass out."

My hand trembled as I lifted the glass to my lips and took a sip.

What was I going to tell Sutton? I'd promised myself I'd give her stability, that the next house we lived in would have my name on the deed.

"Is there anything to rent in town?" Weston asked, but his voice dimmed as I took slow, steady sips of the juice, lost in the chaos that had just been dumped into my head. *Get a grip. You have to think, Callie.*

"The last place we saw was the one our staff recommended to your mechanic," Ava said. "I sent the info to her husband, Scott."

"They signed that lease two months ago," Weston muttered. "Two months early, just to be sure they had a place when we got here."

"Because that's how ludicrous the market is around here." I set the half-full glass on the counter. "The second the resort announced the expansion, properties started getting snatched up by every AirBnB manager and out-of-state vacationer with cash. The town council is thinking of passing a rule to limit the overnight rentals, but nothing yet. Prices have skyrocketed and houses are getting sold before they're even on the open market. Believe me, I know." My hair fell forward as I lowered my head. "I've been trying to buy a house in Penny Ridge for the last eight months." Every offer we put in got passed over for another one that came in with a higher appraisal gap clause or cash. The expansion had been great for the local economy, but I was getting priced out of the place I'd come to call home, and the frustration was real.

"Are you sure you don't want your old room, Weston?" Hope eked its way into Ava's tone.

I brushed my hair back and slowly looked up, but whatever optimism I had left ran screaming at the look in Weston's eyes.

"I'd rather die."

He meant it.

Ava's shoulders sagged.

Okay. This was fine. We'd have to move to A-basin, or maybe down to Keystone. It was thirty minutes away on a good day, and Sutton might have to switch schools, but it was better than going all the way to Frisco. The rent was going to devour my savings, but we'd make it work. We always did. *I'm going to lose my down payment money.*

"And like I said, it's not you, Ava," Weston continued. "I'm sure you're great. Hell, you must be some kind of saint to put up with my brother's bullshit. But I just can't live there."

"It's your home," Ava whispered.

"It hasn't been my home in fifteen years, and I haven't lived there in eleven."

Fifteen years. That was when his mother had died of Creutzfeldt-Jakob disease. I knew enough about the Madigan family saga to reference the timeframe. According to what Ava had told me the last couple of months, the only way Reed had managed to even get Weston back to Colorado was by asking him to start up the resort's new heli-skiing operation.

An idea hit me. It was absolutely absurd and unrealistic, but it was all I had.

From what I knew of Weston, he was a good guy. Rumors were treated like gospel in a small town, and though many of those rumors circulated about the Madigan brothers, I'd never heard a bad thing said about Weston other than he was pretty much Madigan's own Grinch, the silent, grumpy type.

I could deal with silent and grumpy.

And the doors locked to the separate wings upstairs, right?

Maybe there was a way to keep Sutton in her school, a way to save our down payment so I could keep house hunting.

"I might have a solution," I said with a voice that sounded way stronger than I felt.

"Okay?" Weston's gaze swung to me like a laser beam. No wonder he'd been in the military for years. He probably glared people to death.

I took a deep breath. "We could both live here."

allie

I PLACED a spiral notebook and fluorescent pink fine point Sharpie on the kitchen island, taking the same stool I had two hours ago when I'd proposed what could have been the most ludicrous idea known to man.

But he hadn't shot me down.

He'd simply stared at me with that intense look of his, the one that made me feel like he could see beneath my words and faltering smile, and suggested we meet back here in a couple hours after we'd both had a little time to think it over and come up with some ground rules if we decided to go through with it.

Ground rules? I was still stuck on my pros-and-cons list of living with an actual stranger. Every pro I'd come up with for the situation had to do with stability for Sutton, and there had been only one con: I knew next to nothing about the man I'd just propositioned to live with me. But that was something I could remedy.

If this was the only way to keep Sutton in her school and my savings healthy enough to buy a house, then we'd make it work. I just had to think about the pros of Weston himself. Would it be awkward? Probably. But this wasn't exactly the first time I'd asked him for a life-changing favor.

Weston pro number one: he's already saved you once.

The front door opened and Weston walked in, his arms full of grocery bags. He shut the door with his foot.

"Can I help?" I asked, already sliding off the stool.

"Don't worry. I've got it," he answered.

I liked that he didn't smile, didn't try to pretend this wasn't weird as hell. It felt more...genuine. I kept my gaze on him as he moved toward me, setting the bags down on the counter gently.

Pro number two: he isn't careless.

"I figured I might make us some lunch while we're talking. Club sandwiches sound good?" He took the groceries out of the bag and laid them on the counter next to the stove. Deli meat. Tomatoes. Cheese. Lettuce. Avocado. Bread. "There's plenty of leftover bacon that I didn't burn."

"You cook?" My eyebrows rose as I shifted in my seat. "I mean, that's really nice of you. Yes, please. Sorry, I tend to say the first thing that pops into my head, and I babble when I'm nervous. Not much for a filter over here." My lips tilted upward, and I clutched the bright pink pen.

"I actually prefer no filter. I'd rather know what someone is thinking over what they'd like me to think they're thinking. And I've been cooking since I was sixteen." He checked the cabinets one by one, familiarizing himself with the kitchen layout. I hadn't changed things much over the years, nor had I replaced much of the Madigan-supplied kitchenware. "Though I'm not sure I'd qualify throwing TV dinners in the microwave for Crew and me really cooking. But I've picked up a few things since then." He opened the small closet that served as a pantry. "Is cooking something you enjoy?"

"I'm...decent." I glanced from the fresh ingredients on the counter to the hodgepodge of sugary, processed foods in the pantry that Sutton and I indulged in. Pretty sure we could have survived the apocalypse on brown sugar Pop-Tarts and boxed macaroni and cheese.

"I didn't ask if you were good. I asked if you enjoyed it." He glanced over his shoulder, a corner of his mouth lifting into a half smirk that elevated my pulse.

Weston con one: he was way too attractive.

Wait. Was that really a con? Would it honestly hurt to have a ridiculously hot guy around to stare at every now and again? Not that I spent a lot of time staring at men—it had been a year since my last foray into the dating pool—but I knew a gorgeous one when I saw him, and Weston was an off-the-charts specimen of gorgeousness. And besides, that face? The chiseled abs and chest I'd walked in on earlier? Those were definitely worth staring at.

"Callie?" Weston asked, his eyebrows raised.

Shit, he'd asked me something. *Cooking.* Yep, that was right. He'd asked if I enjoyed cooking. "I'm more of a 'whatever's convenient' kind of girl," I answered.

"She burns stuff. A lot. Pretty much everything, really."

"Sutton!" My head whipped toward the little balcony that led to Sutton's and my bedrooms. My daughter stood at the railing, grinning down at us. "What did I say?"

"To stay upstairs," she answered, her hair tumbling around her face as she leaned over the railing slightly. "And I'm still upstairs. See?"

"Not if you fall over the railing." My eyebrow shot up into what I hoped was the not-right-now look.

Weston chuckled, his shoulders moving slightly as he washed his hands at the kitchen sink, then dried them. His back

was turned toward me, and I suppressed the inappropriate urge
to ask him to turn so I could see if he was smiling. That little
half smirk he'd given me hadn't been enough to satisfy my
curiosity.

"Never fallen before." Sutton gave me a daredevil grin that
had gotten her into trouble way too many times.

Weston popped a couple pieces of bread into the toaster.
"Are you hungry up there?" he asked Sutton before looking back
at me. No smile. *Pity.* "If it's okay with your mom."

"Mom?" The plea in her voice was unmistakable.

Weston took the cutting board out of the cabinet next to the
sink and put it on the island, then turned and grabbed three
faded plates from above the toaster. "I figure if she's going to
live here too, she should be in on the ground-rule conversation,
right? It's not just the two of us."

I stopped breathing.

His eyes met mine, and I struggled to keep my jaw from
falling to the floor as I forced air through my lungs. He'd put
Sutton on equal ground with a single sentence.

Never, not once in her ten years, had someone given her that
courtesy. The few men I'd dated had seen her as an obstacle or
an anchor. To the resort, she was a liability they respected
because we'd been Weston's last official decision before he left
the fold. To her school, she was the disruptive one who needed
to work a little harder at raising her hand before speaking. Even
to my friends, she was my daughter, someone they adored but
had to plan around.

*Weston pro number three: he treats Sutton like she's her own
person.*

"Come on down," I said, shooting her a wordless plea that
she mind her manners. We'd always been able to read each
other's cues pretty well—I guessed that's what happened when
you had a kid at eighteen and kept her strapped to you while
you worked until she hit preschool.

Sutton skipped down the steps and jumped the last three, shoving her hair out of her face as she came over to take the stool next to mine.

Weston reached across the island, offering his hand to Sutton. "I'm Weston Madigan. Nice to meet you."

Sutton's hand looked tiny in his. "Sutton Thorne. Nice to meet you too. Sorry for screaming earlier."

"I would have screamed if the roles had been reversed." The toast popped up and Weston replaced it with fresh bread, bringing the others to the cutting board in front of us.

"Really?" Sutton asked, her eyes narrowing slightly.

"Really. Ten-year-old girls are terrifying." He said it with a straight face, which earned him a smile from Sutton. "Why don't we start with your ground rules, first, since I'm assuming you have more of them?" He glanced up at me. "If we decide to do this, that is."

I was already leaning that direction.

"Why would you assume I have more of them?" I wrote *Ground Rules* on the top of the first blank piece of paper. My pros-and-cons list was safely tucked away in the back of the notebook.

"You have more at stake." He glanced at Sutton and started slicing tomatoes with a knife set I didn't recognize.

He was right. I did.

"Can I help?" Sutton asked him.

"Absolutely. You're on toast duty. Just keep 'em coming." He looked up at me from under his brows. "If what she says about your tendency to burn stuff is true, then I'm all for you staying on that side of the island."

I scoffed.

"It's true," Sutton proclaimed, racing around the island toward the toaster and sliding the last foot or so in her socks.

"You're up, Calliope," Weston said, nodding toward the blank sheet of paper as he finished slicing tomatoes.

It was on the tip of my tongue to remind him that I preferred to be called Callie, but...huh. I actually liked the way it sounded when he said it with that rough voice of his. There was none of the nasal pinch my mother used or the tone of disappointment my father fell into by default.

"Rule number one," I said, writing a big pink one that consumed about a line and a half. "We only share the common area. No one is allowed upstairs." I paused and waited for him to look me in the eyes, which he did. "Ever."

"Agreed." He nodded once. "Your side is yours. My side is mine."

I wrote down *No one upstairs.*

"You have two bedrooms," Sutton noted, switching out toast again. "Is someone else moving in?"

"Just my gear." The corner of his mouth quirked up. His brow furrowed as he looked at the notebook. "You don't write within the lines?"

"It's basically in the lines." I shrugged.

"What are you going to do if we need more space at the bottom?" Holy crap, he was serious.

I arched a single eyebrow. "I'll get another piece of paper."

He blinked and started on the avocado.

"Rule number two." I wrote out an especially oversized number two. "Overnight guests..." I glanced toward where Sutton's back was turned and then toward Weston to make sure he caught my meaning. "Will be neither seen *nor heard.*"

A glimmer of humor shone in his dark eyes, but he didn't so much as make a comment besides, "Agreed."

I sighed in relief. The last thing Sutton needed was a parade of morning-afters in her living room. Hell, the last thing *I* needed was to be reminded of just how much sex I wasn't getting. I wrote down *Respectful Guests.*

"Rule number three." I swallowed and my fingers trembled slightly as I wrote down the number. "If there's a minor in the common area, then there has to be two adults, and one of them is me." He could never be left alone with Sutton. He could have a reputation as a freaking angel around town, and it wouldn't matter. The number of people I trusted with Sutton could be counted on less than a hand.

He paused slicing and looked me in the eyes. "Absolutely understood."

"Thank you." My shoulders dipped as though a thousand pounds had been lifted from them.

"Nothing to thank me for." He set the knife down and started opening the deli packages as Sutton switched out toast behind him. "One, I'm not a fan of babysitting, and two, if it makes you feel any better, I have a pretty high security clearance —" His jaw tensed. "I mean, *had* one while I was still in the army. That background check is so thorough I half-expected someone to sort through my underwear drawer."

Sutton laughed, but I knew what he was saying, and I appreciated it. He'd been vetted.

I wrote down *Callie will supervise Sutton.* "And I don't mean like, if you're walking in the door from work or something," I babbled. "It's not like I expect you to call from the driveway to make sure you can access your own kitchen."

"I understand what you're saying, and I respect you for saying it."

"Rule four." My lips puckered as I thought. "You can eat whatever you want out of the fridge or pantry, but you have to replace it." The guy was massive, and I could barely afford to keep Sutton and myself fed on this budget, let alone Gigantor over there.

A corner of his mouth lifted into another half smirk. "That's not going to be a problem. I'm not really a Cocoa Pebbles kind of guy."

I wrote down *Replace what you eat.*

He took this morning's bacon from the fridge and started assembling the sandwiches. "Mayo?" he asked me.

"Please." My focus shifted to watching him work. He was methodical, the movements of his large hands concise, never wasting a single motion. I wondered if that was how he flew too —controlled and concise. Within moments, he had fully constructed a sandwich and cleanly cut through all the layers.

"Sutton?" he called over his shoulder.

Her nose crinkled.

"She's not a mayo kind of girl," I said with a smile.

"Ranch?" he offered.

"Yes!" She caught my gaze. "Please. Yes, please."

That had both corners of Weston's mouth curving upward, but it wasn't quite a full smile.

Weston con: he never fully smiles.

That was something we were going to have to change if we were going to be living together. Sutton and I had a pretty positive vibe going on, and I loved a challenge.

Weston pro: you can help him smile.

I fought a little grin as he passed two sandwiches across the island.

"Thank you," I said, my mind already tripping over the various ways I could rise to the occasion of making Weston's life a little easier. After all, I pretty much owed this guy everything. He could have kicked me out this morning. He could have rejected me that night. Could have given the job to someone who had actually been qualified. Instead, he'd opened up a unit in employee housing, signed a three-year contract so his father couldn't undo what he'd done, and helped me put gas in my car.

And just like Prince Charming, he'd disappeared at midnight. Crap, that was Cinderella...whatever. The result was the same—I hadn't seen him again until today.

Sutton joined me, and we both bit into our sandwiches at the same time. Oh, *forking hell*, it was delicious.

"Momitssogood," Sutton mumbled with her mouth full. I would have absolutely lectured her, but I was too busy scarfing down my own sandwich and nodding.

Weston had that mildly amused smirk tugging at his lips as he constructed his own sandwich. "Any other ground rules you can think of for that list?"

I shook my head and swallowed. "We're pretty easygoing." I'd be as easygoing as I needed to be in order to keep my house.

"What about you?" he asked Sutton.

She swallowed and put down her sandwich. "I've never had a slumber party."

My head whipped in her direction. "Not the time." Mom guilt hit me hard, dragging my heart to the floor.

"Okay?" Weston's brow knit as he sliced his lunch into neat triangular quarters, clearly not following ten-year-old logic.

"Mom says it's because we're lucky to live at the resort, so we can't just invite a bunch of other girls over because that's..." She sighed. "Taking advantage of our situation," she finished in her best impression of me.

Apparently, I needed to work on my *mom look*, because my child wasn't even phased by my lowered brows and death-threat eyes.

Weston paused, giving Sutton his full attention. "What are you proposing?"

Sutton glanced my way for all of a millisecond before turning those baby blues on Weston. "I really get to add a rule?"

He nodded.

"I want to be allowed to have a slumber party."

"Sutton!" I hissed. Tomorrow I would be proud I'd raised a smart, stubborn girl who wasn't afraid to ask for what she wanted. Tomorrow. Not today. Today, I was going to ground her for the rest of her natural-born life. "Forget that she said that."

He took a massive bite and chewed.

They were locked in an epic stare-down, though his gaze was more curious and hers was stubborn as hell.

Finally, he swallowed. "You want me to overrule your mom? Because I somehow think she's about to prevent that with her next rule."

I wrote down, *Callie rules all,* and showed the notebook to my daughter. This was more than a sore subject, it was *raw* from how often she poked at it. But living here was a privilege, one I wasn't about to draw attention to.

"I don't want you to overrule her. I want you to change the rules for the house."

"I'm listening." He cocked his head to the side.

"Your last name is Madigan, right?" Her chin rose a good inch.

"Yep."

"So, tell Mom it's okay to have a slumber party." She took another bite of her sandwich.

She made it sound so blissfully simple.

"You won't make me paint fingernails or anything? Because I'm absolute crap at arts and crafts," he said.

She shook her head.

He glanced at me. "No one is going to care if you choose to have a few friends over, but I'm not getting between whatever this"—he gestured between us—"is. My mother taught me way better than that."

"Mom, please?" Sutton pivoted. "He's a Madigan, and if he says it's okay, it has to be, right? Even if it's just for my birthday?" There was such hope in those eyes that I felt myself caving. "Please? We'll be so quiet, and you won't have to do a single thing, I promise. I'll even clean before *and* after."

I relented and wrote, *Sutton can have a birthday slumber party.*

After all, she was giving up just as much as I was in this awkward arrangement.

"Thank you!" She threw her arms around my neck, nearly falling off her stool in her excitement.

"Only six friends." I hugged her tight. What was the harm in agreeing if Weston did? Besides, maybe we'd have a house of our own by the time her birthday came next month.

She pulled back and grinned up at Weston. "You're awesome. Thank you!" Then she shoved the remainder of her sandwich in her mouth and took her plate to the sink before fleeing upstairs.

"You're going to regret that," I said.

He shrugged, chewing.

"Seriously, when there are six little girls in here running amok and the other employees think I'm abusing this already huge privilege—"

"It's my house, right?" he asked. "That's what you keep saying, at least."

I nodded.

"Then no one's going to say a word." He motioned to the list. "You have anything else?"

"Nope." My entire chest lightened. Maybe this was going to be easier than I thought.

"Okay, my turn." He popped the remaining quarter of his sandwich in his mouth.

"Absolutely. Whenever you're ready." I poised the pink pen over the paper and waited. He'd been so understanding with everything I'd requested, and even given Sutton what she wanted. Short of stripping off my clothes, there wasn't much I wasn't willing to do to make this arrangement work.

The muscles of his forearm rippled as he leaned over the island to peek at the list, and I rethought that last stipulation.

"Okay," he said after swallowing. "So, these might sound a little extreme, but I've been in the military for a decade, so it might take me some time to adjust."

"Noted." I stuffed another bite into my mouth. So. Good.

"Rule number seven," he said, taking his plate to the sink. "I'll share in all the housework. Dishes. Sweeping. Mopping."

"We share housework," I repeated as I wrote. Oh my *gawd*, he was every woman's wet dream.

"It's because I can't stand clutter." He put both plates in the dishwasher and turned toward the island. "Messes aren't avoidable, but there's no need to live in them." He neatly packed up the extra meat and cheese and put it into the refrigerator.

Oh boy. My hand froze as my gaze darted around the room. Everything was neat, tidy, even, but that's because I'd gone on a cleaning rampage last night after my biggest non-Madigan client no-showed their appointment for engagement photos last night. Kids and clutter kind of went hand in hand.

"I mean, I don't keep it messy—" I started, heat rising in my cheeks.

"It's fine," he said with a dismissive wave, cleaning up the rest of lunch. "There's two of us now to keep it up, and I'm sure you've been busy."

"Right." I scooted my plate closer to my body for fear he'd take it before I finished eating.

"Rule eight." He took out an actual Clorox wipe he must have just bought, because I was the queen of off-brand, and started scrubbing the island. "Let's do our best to clean up after ourselves."

"Uh huh." The guy was a neat freak. This was bad. So bad.

"Rule number nine. If what Sutton says is correct, then I'll do the cooking whenever we're home at the same time." He started on the next counter that he hadn't even used. "No need to split the grocery bill or whatever, since I know I'm the picky one. I'm happy to pick up the tab."

"Okay." I kept jotting down rules, nearing the bottom quarter of the page with my scrawling handwriting.

"Rule ten, let's respect quiet hours. I'm not sure how late you stay up working—you're still a photographer, right?" He glanced back over his shoulder as he tossed one wipe and grabbed another.

"I am."

"Cool." He wiped down the pantry door. "I'm usually up for a run at five, so I'll do my best not to wake you, if you'll do your best not to throw a kegger at one a.m.?" His lip quirked into another half smile.

He was trying to tease me.

Weston con: horrible sense of humor.

"Quiet time, it is." *Weston pro: you can help him laugh.* If it was humanly possible. I was starting to think it wasn't.

"Rule number eleven." He started in on the sink, scrubbing the faucet. "No pets."

I blinked. "We don't have any."

"Let's keep it that way. I'm not a fan of getting attached to anything." He nodded and kept scrubbing.

"And it's easier to get attached to a dog than an actual person?" I teased.

"Exactly."

Whoa.

"Rule number twelve. No shoes on the couch. It's a weird pet peeve, I know, but dirt gets everywhere during mud season and there's nothing worse than sitting down to watch the news in a pile of sand."

"Um. Okay." It was a small price to pay. *No pets. No shoes on the couch.*

"Last rule." He tossed the wipe. "If there's a company—resort —issue, then we discuss it outside. I like to keep work out of the house, and honestly, I'm probably not the person to help you solve whatever it is Reed does to piss you off."

My jaw dropped. Not once in the year that Reed had been home had he done anything that remotely upset me or jeopardized my job, but the look in Weston's eyes had me closing my mouth. There were issues there. Big issues.

"Okay," I said quietly, writing it down. *Don't bring work problems inside.*

"So, I guess, if we agree on all that, then we're officially roommates," he said, coming around the island to stand next to me.

I nodded. "Officially roommates." I could make this work.

"Deal." He put out his hand and I shook it. His grip was firm and warm, and there was more than a little shot of awareness that zinged up my spine.

"Deal."

"Excellent. Then I'll start unpacking." He walked off, pausing to pick up the jacket Sutton had thrown on the couch earlier and hang it up in the hall closet.

Oh. My. Clean. Freak. Gods.

We couldn't be more opposite if we tried.

I stared at his retreating back and let the pen hover over the list I was going to have to rewrite, then let it fly. "Rule number fourteen," I whispered as I wrote. "Remove the stick from Weston's ass."

So much for this being easy.

 eston

"WE ALREADY HAVE seven bookings for November," Maria told me as I looked over her shoulder at our computerized scheduling system. "Four parties of four or five, and the other three are seven skiers."

"It's a start," Theo said from across the room, where he was throwing a tennis ball up in the air and catching it, just like he used to do when we'd pull QRF duty. But there was nothing quick or reactionary about our jobs now. At least not at this stage.

I did the calculations in my head and muttered a curse. "We're going to need more than that to keep the payments made on the bird and pay our salaries."

"Well, aren't you Debbie Downer," Maria mumbled, pushing back from the desk.

Theo laughed. "That may as well be his nickname. Worried Weston."

"Ha." I rolled my eyes.

Stepping away to give her some space, I looked out the window, admiring the freshly fallen snow that coated the trees and ground. There was only about six inches, just enough to make the drive down the hill sporty before the road was plowed, but it was enough to change the entire atmosphere of the town. We'd already taken another flight this morning so we could orient ourselves to the landmarks now that they were covered in snow. As much as I'd skied and hiked the back-country growing up, everything looked a little different from the air.

Now we just had to see if the weather was going to let the snow stick and hope opening day would come quickly.

"We all knew we'd need some time to build up the clientele," Theo said, catching the ball again. "You don't start a business like this and have it magically book out overnight."

Logically, I knew that. Hell, we'd been here a week, and only started taking reservations about four days ago when we'd fired up our online marketing. Emotionally? I had not just my future on the line here, but Theo and Maria's too. It was a different kind of pressure from anything I'd experienced, even flying combat missions. Those were short bursts of adrenaline and stress followed by an immediate sense of relief once we landed.

Starting a business? It felt like I was back in college and the homework just wouldn't quit. There was always something I should be doing—running numbers, learning about new ways to advertise, thinking up promotions to get bookings. If I was this stressed out after a week, I wasn't sure how I was going to have any hair left after the season.

"Once the guests arrive for the opening, it will pick up," Maria promised with an encouraging smile. "From what I hear, the resort is always booked, and once people get here and realize we have this available, the word of mouth will take off."

God, I hoped that was the case, or I would have given everything up for nothing.

"If you're done glowering, I'm going to go work in the hangar." Maria stood, tying her hair up as she came around the desk.

"Do you have everything you need in there?" I asked.

"Yep." She nodded, pulling a clipboard from a hook on the wall. "Everything I asked for is here, now I just need to put it where I want it."

"Need help?" Theo caught the ball and shifted, ready to stand.

"Oh, hell no." She shook her head and leveled a stare on us. "I don't need either of you two knuckleheads telling me where you think things need to be." She gave us a two-fingered, mocking salute and disappeared into the hangar.

I sank into the chair behind the desk and drummed my fingers on the arms.

"Sitting around is going to drive you insane for the next month," Theo commented.

"If we aren't flying, and the slopes aren't open, then what the hell are we supposed to do for the next month?" I'd never taken downtime well. Or maybe I was just agitated there hadn't been any orange juice left after my run-turned-hike this morning. Or that there were definite specks of *glitter* on my boots when I pulled them out of the hall closet on my way to work. I hadn't quite fallen into a routine with Calliope and Sutton yet, and I liked routine. I thrived on routine.

Had to admit, though, I'd already discovered there were perks to living with Callie and Sutton. The house always smelled good, like someone was constantly cutting oranges. Sutton was funnier than I'd expected for a ten-year-old, and I liked the sound of Callie's laughter way more than I should have. Plus, there was an energy in the house, always someone there when I got home, which made it feel like an actual...home. Maybe not *my* home, but someone's.

I really had to find a place.

"We can put some weights in the corner of the hangar and pretend we're deployed again if you're restless." Theo threw the ball into the air and caught it. "Seriously, though. We're doing exactly what we need to right now. Getting set up, orienting ourselves to the landscape, and answering the damn phone when it rings."

"Just feels like it's not enough." I'd hated this part of the year growing up. Action had always been my thing, not anticipation.

"It's never going to feel like it's enough for you unless we're flying or skiing seven hours a day, seven days a week." He caught the ball and turned a narrowed gaze on me.

I grunted.

The front door opened, and the little bell Theo had installed chimed as Jeanine walked in with a gust of cold air and her hands full with a casserole dish. "Well, hey there," she said in her thick, southern accent. The two had met when Theo was in flight school at Ft. Rucker in Alabama, and the woman had an admirable ability to tell someone to go fuck themselves without them even realizing it. She was fantastic.

Theo and I both jumped to our feet, and he got to her first, taking the dish off her hands.

"I didn't know you were coming in," he said, leaning in to kiss her cheek.

"Hey, baby, I thought you guys might be hungry." The way they looked at each other had me glancing away, as though I'd interrupted a private moment.

"You didn't have to cook." He slid the dish onto the desk. "But I'm always happy to see you. Want a seat?"

"I'll take this one right here." Jeanine sat on the edge of the desk and turned her back on Theo, focusing on me. "Why don't you have a seat, West?"

Oh shit. I knew that look. She was about to nail me to the ground for something.

"How's it going, Jeanine?" I lowered myself carefully to the office chair. "Get the kids enrolled and everything?"

"Since Monday." She tapped her chin and tilted her head. "Funny thing about the elementary school here. It's small."

Theo pulled the lid off the casserole dish and his brow furrowed. "Honey?"

I glanced over and saw the dish held four cheeseburgers and fries from The Cheese, which happened to be the best burger joint in town. My mouth watered.

"I said I thought you were hungry. I didn't say I cooked," she replied over her shoulder before turning back toward me. "You see, Max forgot his tennis shoes since he wore his snow boots today."

"Oh?" Theo handed me a cheeseburger, and I nodded in thanks, then took a bite. Damn, I'd missed these. It seemed like every day I was back, I was rediscovering something I hadn't even realized I'd missed until I saw it or tasted it again.

"Jeanine?" Theo offered her a burger, and she shook her head, her brown eyes locked on me like a heat-seeking missile with a target.

"I was waiting at the front desk, and when Max came to get his tennis shoes, he asked me if Weston could bring a certain girl in his class over to play this weekend." She leaned in. "Sutton Thorne?"

Caught. I chewed my burger with thoughtful intensity, using every second to think of something to say that wouldn't be a lie, or have Jeanine offering me one of their bedrooms.

"What?" Theo asked, knocking on the hangar door and waving to Maria through the window. "Why would you know a ten-year-old girl, West?"

"Because he's living with her," Jeanine said, never once looking away from me.

I swallowed. "Technically, I'm living with her mother."

"What's up?" Maria poked her head in the door. "Hey, Jeanine!"

"Jeanine brought food and is currently interrogating Weston about living with a woman," Theo answered, holding out a burger. "Should be a good show."

"Ooh." Maria snatched the burger and slid into the chair across the desk. "I'm so here for this. Who's the girlfriend? And how did that happen so quickly? Is she an old flame? A love gone wrong? Someone you left scorned and longing for your return?" Her eyes sparkled.

I scoffed. "Hardly."

"So, who is she?" Jeanine shrugged out of her winter coat and tossed it at the coatrack with alarming accuracy. Guess this inquisition wasn't about to be over any time soon.

"She's someone I hired for the resort right before I left." I moved to take another bite, but the angle of Jeanine's arched eyebrow told me she wasn't satisfied with that answer. "Look, there was a mix-up, employee housing was full, and I wasn't about to kick Calliope out of her house—"

"Ooh, Calliope is a good name," Maria said between bites.

"According to Sutton, she prefers Callie," I corrected her. "So we're...roommates. It's a duplex with shared living space, but we each have our own rooms upstairs. We're just sharing the common area."

"You could have bunked with us," Theo offered, his brow furrowing in concern.

"But he didn't." Jeanine inspected me. "In all the years I've known you, Weston Madigan, you've never once lived with a woman. Hell, I don't know if you've ever let one stay longer than a weekend, and now you're shacked up with one."

"Roommates," I clarified, eyeing my burger with more than a

little interest. "And besides, you guys bought a three-bedroom house. That's one for you two." I held up two fingers. "And one room for Max, and the other for Selene." I added two more. "I wasn't about to bust into your new house and be a massive inconvenience. Not when I was the one who dragged you all out here in the first place." I turned to Maria before she could argue too. "And that apartment you guys rented is one bedroom. Don't even start with me."

She took another bite and shrugged.

"Why wouldn't you just tell us?" Jeanine asked.

"Excellent point." Theo nodded.

"Not helping, man." I shot him a look.

"I am always Team Jeanine," he responded with a shit-eating grin.

"So why wouldn't you tell us?" Jeanine repeated.

"Because I knew you would all do this." I gestured around the room. "And make some big deal out of it."

"It *is* a big deal," Jeanine argued. "Theo told me he was the only one who could tolerate bunking with you during deployments because you're such an uptight asshole who loses his mind when someone's towel is hung on the wrong peg."

"Honey." Theo let out a dramatic sigh, his head falling back against the glass window that separated this office from the classroom. "That is privileged marital information you're sharing." He grimaced and rubbed the back of his neck. "She's not wrong though. I've lived with you and you're not exactly the...easiest."

"I'm not that bad," I argued. "Fine, I like everything in its place, guilty. I'm a fan of structure, true. But there are way worse ways to be. I could be a huge slob who expects Calliope to pick up after me."

Maria snorted, covering her laugh with the back of her hand.

"Hey, you're just as particular about your tools."

"At work," Maria agreed.

"So there's nothing going on with you and Sutton's mom?" Jeanine asked, a definite sparkle in her eyes. "The girl is a pretty little thing, so I'm betting the mom is a stunner."

"She's..." Beautiful. Gorgeous. Hot as hell when she laughed. "Pretty."

Jeanine smiled like a cat who had spotted her mouse. "Uh huh." She'd been trying to set me up for years, but nothing ever worked out.

"We're just roommates." I put my hand on my chest. "Scout's honor. Now can I please devour this cheeseburger?" I brought the burger up, but Jeanine was faster, snatching my lunch.

"Sure, once you agree to bring her over for dinner." She grinned, the edges of her brown eyes crinkling.

I swung my head toward Theo. "A little help here?"

He flat-out laughed at me. "Oh man, if you're living with someone we've never met, I'm on her side. Good luck with that."

I stared at Jeanine.

She stared right back.

Finally, my stomach got the best of me. "Fine, I'll *ask* her if she's free next month."

Jeanine held my burger out of reach. "Next *week*."

"Okay. Next week."

"Excellent." She nodded and smiled, handing me back my burger and then starting in on her own.

"But no trying to set us up or anything. That house is awkward enough as is." I bit into the burger and sighed with happiness.

"I make no promises." Jeanine's smile reminded me of the Cheshire cat.

"Awesome."

Two nights later, I awoke from a dead sleep, my heart pounding. Adrenaline coursed through my veins and my palms ached. I sat up and flicked on the nightstand light. There were half-moons in my skin from clenching my fists too tight.

I took one breath, filling my lungs with clean mountain air to dispel the memory of dust and metal, then another, running my fingers over my hair. At least I wasn't soaked in sweat. It had been a good year since I'd had a nightmare that had gone that far, but I also knew I wouldn't be sleeping for a hot minute.

The clock read a little past one a.m. as I swung my feet over the side of the bed. I yanked a pair of plaid pajama pants on over my boxer briefs and shook off the anxiety that did its best to grip my throat as I walked out of my bedroom and opened the door to downstairs.

Light shone from the kitchen, and I put my back toward the wall as I crept down the staircase quietly, leaning forward incrementally until I finally saw Callie sitting on the kitchen island, her legs kicking between the stools as she ate ice cream straight from the pint.

Guess she couldn't sleep either.

"Sorry, I didn't realize you were awake," I said gently, so I wouldn't scare the shit out of her.

Her startled gaze jumped to mine, and her spoon hit the ice cream with a *thud*. "No big deal. Come on in. I have plenty to share." She gestured to the counter surrounding her, and I blinked at a dozen different pints of ice cream, their lids scattered in different directions.

"I don't really think I'm dressed for the occasion," I noted, my hand slipping over my bare chest as I took in her pajama pants and hoodie. Only the tips of her brightly painted toenails were visible. The last week had been an awkward dance of sharing the space while still respecting each other's privacy, which basically meant our exchanges had been limited to "thank you for dinner" and grunts.

"Wouldn't be the first time I've found you standing shirtless in my kitchen," she replied with a slight smirk. "Come on, grab a spoon. It's pretty apparent neither of us is sleeping."

Had to admit, there were very few things in my life I'd seen that were as appealing as the sight of Callie sitting on the counter, swinging her legs, her hair piled onto her head in a loose knot.

"I've never seen an ice cream buffet like this." I grabbed a spoon from the drawer as she cleared a spot for me on the counter.

"Come on, it's better from up here." She patted the bare space on the granite next to her. "Seriously, though. It's not half as much fun if you eat it in a chair." Her gaze fell down my body and she looked away quickly, pink staining the rise of her cheeks. "Not that it looks like you eat a lot of ice cream."

Maybe I wasn't the only one who liked what they saw.

"I don't usually," I said, picking up one of the pints that hadn't been scooped. "Pink Lemonade?"

"Figured it was worth a try." She shrugged and dug her spoon into the pint she held. Cherry Berry. She swallowed and patted the counter again. "Seriously, up here, or no ice cream for you."

I'd never woken up to a woman indulging in an ice cream buffet before, let alone one who demanded I sit on the counter, but what the hell. Bracing my palms on the edge of the granite, I hoisted myself up beside her, keeping a respectable twelve inches between us and looking up just to make sure my head wasn't flirting with the pendant light.

"There you go." She offered me a smile like she was proud of me and dug back into her pint.

"Why so many pints?" I swirled my spoon into the fresh top of the Pink Lemonade and lifted the small scoop to my mouth, taking a bite. It was tart and sweet, and it left a slight chill as it slid down my throat.

"Why not?" She put her pint down and reached to her right. "I had a shit day and stopped into Two Scoops before I picked up Sutton from school." She pointed the spoon at me. "And it didn't have anything to do with the resort, so that's not violating rule number thirteen. Anyway, they were trying out some of their new flavors before the season starts up, so I grabbed a pint of each." She stabbed her spoon into a pint of Chocolate Walnut. "Sutton nabbed the Strawberry Fritter after dinner, so that one's not available."

"And now you can't sleep?" I guessed, taking another bite of Pink Lemonade.

"Nope." She shrugged. "My mind starts racing with all of the things I should have said." She stabbed into the pint again. "And I usually come up with the most brilliant things after the fact. What about you? Crap day that doesn't break rule number thirteen?" She slid the spoon past the curve of her lips, and I turned my attention back to my ice cream.

Staring at my roommate's mouth was the worst idea in the fucking world.

Nope. Kissing her would be the worst. Staring is just...bad.

"Nightmare," I answered with a shrug.

Two lines appeared between her eyebrows as she studied me, and I felt the stare like a physical caress, worried but tentative.

"What about?" she asked, turning to ditch her current pint and pick up a new one labeled Orange Dreamsicle.

"Don't remember," I answered honestly. "I never remember my dreams, but my body somehow does." Flexing my hand, I noted the nail marks were slowly fading from my palm.

"Army stuff?"

"I really don't remember." I tilted my head. "It wouldn't surprise me, though." I set the pint down between us. "I honestly can't remember sleeping well in the last fifteen years." Not since

Mom had first shown signs of getting sick. I'd woken up to the slightest sounds ever since.

She swallowed, slowly dragging the spoon from between her lips, but she didn't ask, and I didn't offer. I more than liked the fact that she didn't push.

"Is that one good?" she asked, nodding to the Pink Lemonade.

"Tastes like June," I answered. "Like that weather that's perfect for hiking, but not as stifling as July."

"Hmm." She plucked my pint off the counter and took a bite, moaning a little as she swallowed. "Good description."

I tried to look away from her mouth. Then I tried again as the echo of that moan bounced around my brain and took hold.

"You'll like this one." She pushed the pint of Orange Dream-sicle my way. "Go on. It's not like I have cooties. Besides, we live together, so if I have them, you already do."

I hesitated a second at how completely…unsanitary it was, but shrugged again and spooned a bite, my eyes closing at the smooth citrus and cream flavor.

"That one's really good, right?" she asked, her eyes sparkling as they met mine. "Almost worth the sleepless night." Her eyebrows rose as she looked at the counter next to me. "Oooh, that one looks delicious." She discarded her current pint and leaned over me, bracing her palm in the space between us. "Brownie Batter."

The woman had no concept of personal space, but I kept that thought behind my lips because she smelled so damn *good*. What the hell kind of shampoo did she use? Bottled pheromones?

"Got it!" Her shoulder brushed against my side as she sat back up, waving the pint like a trophy.

"I would have handed it to you." I took another bite of the Orange Dreamsicle.

"It's not fun if you don't have to work for it a little." She pivoted and plucked a pint from her side. "Here, try this one."

Going Bananas was shoved into my hand.

"Are there really ten pints here?" I asked.

"Eleven," she mumbled around her spoon. "I think everything is worth trying once."

I spooned up a bite and thought that over as bananas and chocolate flooded my mouth. "Everything?"

"Yep." She nodded. "I promised myself when Sutton was born that I would give her the best of both worlds. Stability by living in one place." She motioned around us. "And adventure by saying yes as often as possible. I always look for a reason to say yes, and if it's something new"—she lifted her brows in my direction—"but safe, then I'm game. You can't know what you're good at in life, what your passion might be, if you don't try everything at least once."

"So you stayed in Penny Ridge."

"Yep." She nodded and discarded that pint, reaching across me for the one labeled Mint Madness. It was slightly out of her reach, so I brought it just close enough for her to grab it, breathing in the sugar and citrus scent of her shampoo again. "The town is small enough for Sutton to know everyone and get that real feeling of community that only small towns have, and yet we never run out of things to do." Her gaze flickered toward one of the oversized photos on the wall and lingered.

"Easter Island?" I asked, recognizing the statue in the picture.

She nodded and took another bite, dragging her gaze from the wall.

That's when it hit me. The pictures weren't part of the Madigan housing design. They were Callie's. And there wasn't a snowflake in sight. "Did you take those?" I asked, gesturing toward the wall with my spoon.

"What?" Her eyebrows flew up and she laughed. "No." She

shook her head and looked into her pint like it might offer another answer. "I wish I'd taken those," she muttered, "but no."

Shit. Maybe I was wrong, and they really were just pictures the staff had hung over the years.

"Those are some of the locations photographers with *World Geographic* get to go." She looked toward the wall, her gaze dancing across the few photographs the kitchen light made visible. "Easter Island, Galapagos Islands, the Serengeti, just to name a few. I framed them as a reminder forever ago—the start of freshman year—and they just kind of moved with me."

"Reminder of what?"

Her eyes lit up. "Every year, the magazine holds a competition for the best amateur shots and gives out a paid internship. It used to be a dream of mine." She took a bite and pondered. "It used to be *the* dream. You know, the one you always knew was out of reach, but you pined for anyway? Like being an astronaut or winning an X Games medal."

"Crew lives that dream."

"Your little brother. Right." She grinned. "Sutton has a little hero-worship in that department."

A corner of my mouth lifted. "Most kids who grow up on the slopes do when it comes to Crew. So, you don't want to go photograph the world anymore?"

"Dreams change when you have kids." She smiled softly, glancing up her staircase. "Their dreams are what become important to you. Would it be amazing to travel the world and capture those kinds of images? Absolutely. But I built a life here so Sutton could have the kind of stability she deserves." She shrugged. "And it's not like I don't get to use my camera every day."

Just not taking pictures of the things she obviously loved.

She cocked her head at me. "But what about you?"

"What about me?" I put down the Going Bananas and

reached across her this time, snagging the pint of White Chocolate Madness.

She snorted.

"What?" I took a bite. Good. It wasn't on the same level as the orange, but it was good.

"What was your astronaut dream? Come on. I shared mine." She nudged my shoulder with hers.

"I wanted to be one of the Freeride world champions. Extreme backcountry skiing. You know, real Warren Miller stuff." Now I was the one shrugging.

"What stopped you?" She dug into her pint again. "It's obviously not your genes...or the body."

I lifted my eyebrows at her, and she grinned and took another bite. "Family stuff. My mom got sick, so I stopped competing. Then my only dream became flying the hell away from here, so that's what I did once I was able—I flew."

"And you came back."

"Reed needed me to." I went back to the orange. This shit was phenomenal.

A doubting smile played across her face. "You're telling me that in the decade you've been gone, this is the only time Reed asked you to come back."

"No. But it's the only time he's *needed* me to." I focused on my pint, tucking away bigger mouthfuls.

She slowly took another bite, appraising me with those crystal blue eyes. "Huh. I can see that about you. You're the guy who shows up when he's needed."

"Everyone shows up when they're needed," I argued.

She snorted. "No, they don't. They like to think they do, but people who show up are rare."

I lifted the spoon to my mouth twice but didn't take the bite, weighing the option of asking, with the respect of, well...not. Curiosity won out. "Sutton's dad?"

"No." Surprise flared in her eyes, and she blinked rapidly,

looking away. "Not Gavin. He was always…dependable, until he wasn't."

"You don't have to tell me." And yet, I really, really wanted to know. Where had he been that night in the rain a decade ago? Where was he now? Was she doing this all on her own? We locked eyes and she swallowed.

"We live together. We might as well know the basics," she said, digging back into her pint with focus. "And I'd never want you to think Sutton wasn't loved. Gavin died our freshman year in college when I was three months pregnant with Sutton."

"I'm so sorry." My stomach hit the floor, and I immediately regretted asking. Hadn't I just been thankful she hadn't gone digging into my past? And yet here I was, asking about hers.

"Thank you," she replied softly. "We were high school sweethearts. Dated all through junior and senior year. Then we went off to USC together, and he got cancer and I got pregnant."

"Holy shit." I set my pint down on the counter.

"Yeah, it was a hell of a year." She forced a smile and hopped off the counter, putting the lids back onto their matching pints. "Did you realize I only had a freshman photography class when you hired me that night?"

I thought back to the pelting rain that had turned to hail, and the silent tears of the blonde in my truck as I'd filled up the spare gas can. "Yep. I knew."

"And yet you hired me as the resort photographer?" She lifted a brow and matched every pint but the one I was eating, then started to file them away in the freezer.

"I may have done it to fuck with my father for not keeping your appointment," I answered, wincing slightly at how that sounded. "Not that he was ever really around during those days." He'd been a raging alcoholic with a temper to match. "But mostly, I saw that you desperately needed the job, so I gave it to you. It was that simple."

She leaned back against the refrigerator and smiled, shoving her hands into the front pocket of her Madigan Mountain hoodie. "See? You're the guy who shows up when he's needed."

"I'm the guy who does what needs to be done." I shrugged. "Why did you get into my truck that night? I could have been an axe murderer."

"You're not an axe murderer."

"You didn't know that."

"While I was waiting for my interview, a little kid stumbled into the lobby all lost and helpless, and you sat her down with a blanket and cup of hot chocolate and started calling every room in the hotel to find her parents." Her expression softened. "An axe murderer would have walked off with the kid and never returned."

"Never liked kids." I shrugged.

She laughed. "We've lived together for a week, and the only person I've seen you smile for is Sutton. You know that?"

"She's funny." The kid was blunt, which I appreciated. Reminded me of Crew when he was that age.

"Well, I've decided that I'm making it my personal mission to make you smile more often. It's the least I can do for everything you've done for me." She proclaimed it like the warning it was.

"I haven't done anything besides offer you a job and invade your house." I paused and debated trying to spare her, but Jeanine was impossible to thwart when she was on a mission. "By the way, my friends want you to come over for dinner so they can tell you all my bad habits and interrogate you."

"Sounds like fun," she answered, pushing off the refrigerator. "I wondered when all your flaws were going to come to light. Well, I'm headed to bed. Good night."

"Thank you for the ice cream, and I'm really sorry you had to go through all that alone." I stumbled over my words, and she lifted her brows. Fuck, this was why I never did the emotional thing with women. "You know. Sutton. Gavin. All that."

"Oh. I'm not." Her smile was so peaceful that I believed her.

"Gavin always wanted to be a dad, and I always wanted to give that to him. We knew we had to act fast, but by the time we actually *got* pregnant, there was nothing they could really do. His treatment options were so limited." Her shoulders dipped. "I love that I can see him in her smile, though. And his parents absolutely dote on her."

"And yours?" My head reeled from the words she'd just used. *Had to act fast.*

Her laugh was anything but happy. "Now those are the people who only show up when they want to. *Need* isn't in their vocabulary." She pressed her lips in a thin line and then quickly changed the subject. "Did you find something you liked tonight?"

The pint was cold in my hands, and I nodded. "Yeah, I really did."

"Good. Me too. Good night." She gave me a little wave and then walked off toward the stairs, leaving me alone in the kitchen as the clock struck two.

Had to act fast... By the time we got pregnant...

The spoon fell out of my hands.

She'd known. She'd known that her boyfriend was dying and still committed her life to creating and raising his child—a child he'd never even meet. I couldn't decide if she was the most giving person I'd ever come across, or the most emotionally reckless.

Either way, my mom would have absolutely loved her.

I realized two things as I threw the empty pint into the trash and slipped the spoons into the dishwasher.

One, she'd never told me what had made her day complete shit.

And two, I actually wanted to know—so I could fix it.

allie

"Sure, if I had an extra million laying around," I said to Ava as I poured the next wine slushie and handed it to Raven across the kitchen island. Girls' nights were something I lived for, the rare moments when I could fully relax and be myself. I wasn't the professional photographer, or the teen mom...I was just me. "Houses have jumped so high that I can't even fathom some of these prices."

And since the curator at the local gallery told me nothing in my current portfolio was display worthy—hence the wallowing ice cream fest—it wasn't like I had a second stream of income to help get us into a house.

"It's gotten out of control," Halley agreed from one of the armchairs in the living room.

"What about this one?" Ava peered at my laptop, where it sat on her knees as she lounged on the end of the couch. "Two bedrooms, mountain views, two baths. It's a condo in a great building and—"

"Wait for it," Raven whispered, raising her eyebrows as she walked backward, facing me.

"Damn! It's one—point—two million?" She rubbed at the screen like it would change the price. "That *has* to be a typo."

"There it is!" Raven took a deep drink of her slushie, and her eyes drifted upward toward the sound of footsteps above us. "You sure Sutton is asleep?" She passed by the couch and sank into one of the armchairs that made up the seating arrangement.

"Yep." I grabbed my own drink. "It's eleven p.m. and that girl is out. Checked on her about an hour ago, just to be sure." I followed her line of sight. "I bet that's Weston."

"How's that going?" Halley asked, sharing a glance with Ava as I took the opposite end of the couch.

"It's fine." I shrugged. "We're roommates. It's taken some getting used to, but it's only been two weeks." A week of which had been awkward as hell until he found me drowning my frustrations in a dozen pints of ice cream. Now? It was just...less awkward.

"And?" Halley urged, leaning forward slightly.

They looked at me with expectation.

"He's a tough guy to get to know." I shrugged. "He makes dinner and even does the dishes while I help Sutton with her homework." *He likes Orange Dreamsicle ice cream.* A smile yanked at the corners of my mouth. "Actually, I think he likes Sutton more than me. Not in a creepy way or anything. He's just..." *Quiet. Intense. Private.* I fumbled for words and turned toward Ava. "What do you know about him?"

"Me?" Her brow furrowed. "Absolutely *nothing*. He hasn't even come up to the house, and Reed says he practically growls at him every time he goes down to the hangar. I don't think they have the best relationship..." Two lines appeared between her eyebrows. "Or *any* relationship, really. From what I know about Weston, he's a stubborn…well, asshole."

"He's not an asshole," I said quietly, but put some oomph behind the words so she'd know I meant it. "He's just really—"

As if on cue, I heard his door open, and our gazes all swung that direction as he walked downstairs, clothed in pajama pants that rode low on his hips and a black T-shirt that stretched across his broad chest. Did he always have to look so deliciously edible? Selfishly, I was glad he'd thrown on a shirt. He wasn't exactly *my* eye candy, but I wasn't about to willingly share the droolworthy sight of him shirtless, either.

Down girl, he's not yours.

Wait. Did I *want* him to be? No. That was ridiculous. Just because I was wildly attracted to the man didn't mean I wanted to date him.

"Ladies," he said, his voice dipping deep as he passed by the living room. He looked my way, and I gripped my slushie glass a little tighter. "Need anything from the kitchen?"

"No thank you," I answered for all of us and noted that Halley's brows had risen to the ceiling as she turned toward me.

Oh my god, she mouthed, fanning herself.

I sent her a look that told her to stop, but her mouth was still open when she looked back at Weston as he dug through the fridge.

He grabbed a sports drink and Halley popped her mouth closed as he shut the door and walked back through the living room on his way upstairs. "You guys okay to drive?" He glanced between Raven, Ava, and Halley. "I don't mind driving you home."

"I'm okay," Raven assured him.

"At least you already know where I live," Ava noted, lifting her glass in salute.

"True. And dropping you in the driveway wouldn't break my

vow to never go inside, so my offer still stands." His jaw flexed once, and our gazes collided.

There it was again, that swirling pit in my stomach that threatened to swallow all the air in the room if I paid too much attention to it...to him.

"Reed will come grab me if I have another one," Ava promised. "And he'll take Halley."

"Or I could just stay here," Halley muttered, eyeing Weston over her glass.

"We're good," I promised him.

"Okay. Have a good night." One last, stomach-tightening look and he walked back upstairs, shutting the door after him.

"See? He's not an asshole. He offered to drive you home," I immediately said, swinging my finger at them all.

"He's..." Ava shook her head, as if she couldn't find the words.

"Hot," Halley supplied.

Raven laughed and sipped her slushie.

"He's just a little intense." I ignored Halley's astute assessment and took a quick drink in hopes the wine would settle my stomach. Living with the guy was one thing, but getting a schoolgirl crush on him was something entirely different. He had *emotionally unavailable* practically tattooed across his forehead.

"And hot," Halley nodded with each word.

"Intense is a good description," Ava agreed.

"Did you both miss the part where he's drop-dead gorgeous?" Halley asked, her gaze swinging between all of us.

"I'm staying out of this." Raven waved her off.

My cheeks burned, and it wasn't the alcohol. I knew exactly how attractive he was.

Ava wavered. "I mean, he's not *Reed*."

"No one is Reed to you." Raven tossed a pillow at Ava, smacking into my laptop and closing the device.

"He's hotter," I said with a calm sip of my slushie.

"That is what I'm talking about!" Halley laughed. "What is with the genes on these Madigan boys?"

"They do seem to be at an advantage," Ava admitted, grinning as she took a drink.

"And you *live* with that?" Halley leaned on her armrest. "Tell me, have you applied the try-everything-once philosophy to that tree of a man? Because if not, you should abandon the motto altogether."

They all stared at me.

"You can't be serious." I leaned forward and set my slushie on the coffee table.

"Dead serious," Halley said.

I scoffed, then turned to Raven, who was casually stirring a spoon through her slushie. "And your thoughts? You grew up here, so you know him, right?"

"Yeah, but he was four years ahead of me in school, so it's not like I *knew* him, knew him. Mostly, I knew his mom." She glanced between Ava and Halley before tilting her head. "He's...Weston. He's a good guy, but it might get awkward because you both work at the same resort if something went wrong."

"The resort we *all* work at," Ava reminded her.

"How about the fact that we *live* together if it went wrong?" I shook my head. "Yeah, no thanks. I'll be keeping my hands to myself." Which was a damn shame, because I couldn't remember the last time I'd actually wanted something for myself that wasn't directly tied to what was best for Sutton. And that feeling in my stomach? It was definitely *want*.

Seconds ticked by in complete silence.

"Then do you mind if I—"

Raven threw a pillow, smacking Halley in the chest.

"Got it," Halley said as the pillow fell into her lap.

"Subject change!" Ava sat up straighter, tugging a piece of

paper out of the back pocket of her jeans and handing it to me. "I saw that today and thought of you."

I unfolded it and swallowed the knot in my throat. *World Geographic Photo Open.* Phenomenal, action-packed pictures filled half the page with wildlife and portraiture taking up the rest. They were all pictures I would have killed to have taken.

"I think you should enter," Ava said.

"I don't know how to get any of these kinds of shots," I confessed, pointing to a photo of a rock climber mid-ascent. *Or how to ask if I could bring a kid along if I ever got close to winning.*

"I know someone who can probably help you out with the shots," Raven said, pointing upstairs. "Or is he not an extreme skier with a helicopter?"

Raven's right. Weston can help.

An elephant sat on my chest.

I chewed on my bottom lip, my mind racing with all the possibilities, even as that knot in my throat slid like a stone into my stomach. What was the point of even entering?

"Come on, Callie. They can't tell you yes if you don't ask," Ava urged.

"And I just, what? Take off for a year and leave Sutton? Uproot her *if* they'd even give me the internship with a kid?" I shook my head. Neither was a possibility, which was why I'd unsubscribed from *World Geographic*'s newsletter. Wanting what you couldn't have only made it hurt more.

"We could help you figure that out," Raven promised. "Or just enter for the hell of it and turn it down if you win, just so you'd know you *chose* to stay here."

Ava scooted closer, resting her shoulder against mine. "Why don't you just think about it? And even if you don't enter, I bet Weston would kill for some shots like this to use for marketing."

I nodded, staring at the brilliant photographs of rock climbers hanging off the edge of austere cliffs and surfers cresting enormous waves.

"So, are you ready for the onslaught of students with the season firing up?" Ava asked Raven, but I didn't hear the answer as I stared at the photos.

Yeah. I could think about it, but that was the problem. I *always* thought about it.

———

"Right hand, blue!" Maria called out, the spinner between her hands as we sat in Theo and Jeanine's house after dinner that Saturday night.

Sutton, Max, Seline, and Scott—Maria's husband—all moved on the giant game board, contorting themselves into place.

I laughed as Sutton blew her hair out of her eyes.

Jeanine took the seat next to me on the couch, her brown eyes twinkling as she watched her kids play. "They're something, aren't they?"

"I wouldn't get up for a week if I tried that." I motioned toward where Max was in a full backbend.

"Pretty sure Scott is going down on the next move," Maria whispered, grinning at her husband, who held a position precariously close to a split.

"I heard that," he said over his shoulder, keeping one hand on blue and the other on green as his legs stretched the entire mat.

I tried to wrap my head around the entire scene and match it to what Weston had told me about his friends.

"What are you thinking?" Jeanine asked quietly, handing me a glass of sweet tea.

"That this is nothing like what I pictured when Weston told me you wanted to have us over for dinner." I glanced into the dining room, where Weston and Theo were currently hanging a painting.

"What did you expect?" Jeanine asked as Maria called out another position and the players switched.

"He mentioned something about an inquisition." A smile tugged at my lips.

"Oh, there's still time for that," Maria said with a smile. "We just couldn't get a word in edgewise during dinner the way West jumped in to save you with every question we asked."

"You all call him West?" I glanced over at Weston, noting the way he used a level to check that the painting had been hung perfectly square.

"As long as we've known him," Jeanine answered. "Which seems like forever. He and Theo were stationed together at Campbell and then again at Drum. They've done two deployments together, the last of which—"

"Was with me," Maria finished with a smile. "Left foot, yellow!"

The kids groaned, and Scott bit back a curse word.

"He seems too serious for a nickname," I admitted, keeping my tone low.

"Oh, that's why we make a point of calling him that," Jeanine replied with a smirk. "So now that we've got you alone..."

"Ask whatever you want." I shifted on the couch, taking a sip.

"Is he totally and completely unbearable to live with?" Maria asked, spinning again.

I almost spit out my sweet tea. "Is that what you guys think?"

They shot me side-eye from each direction.

"He can be a little...precise," Jeanine said, shooting a glance toward the guys as they worked on another piece of art in the dining room. "Don't get me wrong, I love that man like a brother. He's loyal, hard-working, and protective as hell of the people in his life."

"He's also a pain in the ass," Maria muttered, calling out the new positions.

"I have no complaints," I said honestly. "But I am on a personal mission to see if I can make him smile a little more.

Figure I owe that much to him after he hired me all those years ago."

"Good luck with that," Maria shot me a smile and spun the wheel again.

"So, Weston says you're the resort photographer?" Jeanine asked.

As if the man had superhuman hearing, Weston looked in our direction, holding one side of the painting while Theo put marks on the wall. "Tell me you're not harassing Callie, Jeanine."

"I will tell you no such thing!" she called back with a shameless grin.

"I'm fine," I assured him, waving him off when it looked like he was about to head our direction.

"We've got exactly until he gets that painting hung, if I know West," Jeanine said briskly, turning to face me.

"Then you'd better ask your questions quickly." I took another sip as the players adjusted their hands. Scott looked like he was in real pain now. "I get it. I'd want to question someone living with my friends too."

"That's good to know." Jeanine's shoulders immediately eased. "Favorite color."

"Blue." That was easier than I thought.

"Favorite song."

"'Tiny Dancer' by Elton John." Another easy one.

"Are you currently in a relationship?" she asked, her words coming faster as we heard the guys driving nails into the wall.

"Nope. I'm fully committed to my kid. Guys aren't part of that equation usually."

"Sutton's daddy?"

"Dead."

Jeanine sucked in a breath.

"Damn, Jeanine," Maria muttered.

"How was I supposed to know that?" She winced. "I'm so sorry for asking."

"Don't be." My gaze found Weston's as they slipped the painting onto the nail, and I gave him a reassuring smile. "I figured Weston told you." My chest went all warm with the knowledge he hadn't, that he'd kept what was private between us just that—private.

Jeanine shook her head. "Okay, um…favorite movie?"

"*Star Wars, Episode Six.*"

"Good choice." Maria nodded.

Weston had the level out.

"Why Penny Ridge?" Jeanine asked.

"There was a job advertisement for a photographer, and I had just enough money to make it this far." I laughed as Sutton slid her hand over a circle, nearly losing her balance.

"Do you like your job?"

"Absolutely. I love photography." My brow puckered. "But I really want to strike out for myself. Eventually. You know, maybe when Sutton graduates. Then I can focus on art photography and not just family vacations, become the next Mary Ellen Mark or Elliott Erwitt." *Maybe intern for World Geographic.* Right. Once Sutton graduated.

"Time for one more," Maria whispered.

We all looked toward the dining room, where Weston was quickly headed in our direction.

"Do you find our Weston attractive?"

I fumbled my glass, barely catching it as tea sloshed up the sides, but not over.

"Guess that answers that." Maria laughed. "Right foot, yellow!"

Seline slipped, her seven-year-old arms refusing to hold her weight as her foot strained toward the yellow circle. Theo swooped in, holding her by the waist so she could make it.

"That's cheating!" Max accused, his foot on the same circle as Sutton's. "Uncle Scott, tell him that's cheating!"

"No can do, buddy, Seline is on my team," he grunted, his foot sliding.

Seline giggled and Theo steadied her. "It's absolutely cheating," Theo agreed. "But I don't think it matters because—"

Scott fell to the ground.

"You're out, babe!" Maria blew him a kiss.

"Thank God. I couldn't take another move," he groaned, rolling out of the way as the kids laughed.

"We won!" Sutton scrambled to her feet and high-fived Max.

"We welcome all challengers!" Max said, lifting his hands into the air. "Mom?"

"Oh no. Not a chance." Jeanine shook her head.

"Mom?" Sutton looked at me with hopeful eyes.

I glanced down at my jeans and wrap-style shirt. "I'm not sure I'm dressed for it, honey."

"Please?" Her eyes lit up and I sighed. How many years did I have left before she no longer wanted me to play games with her?

"Fine," I said, standing to toe off my shoes and socks.

"Uncle West?" Max lifted his brows.

"Uhh…." Weston looked at the mat in horror.

I snorted, which earned me a narrowed glance from *West*.

"What about me?" Theo asked. "I'm right here too."

"You cheat." Max shook his head. "And Aunt Maria already said no earlier."

I lifted a brow at Weston.

"Please?" Sutton turned to him, lacing her fingers in plea. "We won't beat you too badly."

"Beat us *too* badly?" Weston's eyebrows shot up, and he pushed the sleeves of his Henley up his forearms. "Oh, you're on."

He was out of his shoes and socks in seconds, and before I knew it, we stood side by side, facing Max and Sutton across the mat.

"Oh, this is going to be good," Jeanine said from the couch as Seline slipped into her lap.

"My money is on Max," Scott remarked, leaning against the wall next to Theo.

"I never bet against Weston," Theo replied.

"You sure about this?" I asked.

"Absolutely." He rolled his shoulders as Maria spun the dial.

"Right foot, red!"

We all moved. I took the circle in front of the one Weston claimed, and my ass brushed against him. My pulse jumped. *Bad idea. This is such a bad idea.*

Weston didn't seem to notice, thank God, and within three spins, we were a contorted mess on the mat.

"I didn't know you had that kind of flexibility, West," Theo said with a laugh as Weston's foot moved to right foot blue on the circle just beneath mine.

Weston shot Theo a four-letter look.

"I'm going to seriously need some Motrin after this." I'd gotten myself into a predicament. My feet were on blue and red, and my hands were behind me, both on yellow, leaving me twisted to the side, while Weston held the same position but had done it leaning forward so part of his body hovered above mine.

"Come on, Mom, you can make it!" Sutton called from the other side of the mat.

"Oh, you're making it," Weston said from above me, pure challenge in his eyes. "We're winning."

"Competitive, aren't you?" My left shoulder was killing me.

A corner of his mouth lifted into the sexiest smirk I'd ever seen. "You have no idea."

"Right hand, red!" Maria called out.

I glared toward the couch. "You're kidding me, right?"

Sutton squealed with laughter, and I could hear the kids shifting on the mat.

"Nope." Maria chuckled, turning the spinner so we could see it.

I was going to have to throw my right hand across my body and pivot all my weight into a crab position.

Weston's brows furrowed. "You're going to have to move first. I have an idea. We can touch each other, right? Just not the mat?" he asked Maria.

"Yep," she answered, fully enjoying our situation. "And members of the same team can share the same circle."

"You go first, bend your back, and I'll go for the circle above you."

A grin pulled at my lips at the intensity of his focus. "You know it's just a game, right?"

"A game we're winning."

"A game you're losing if you don't move," Scott added.

"On three." I took a deep breath. "One. Two. Three!" I lifted my right hand and threw it toward red, landing on the second circle and somehow managing to keep my ass in the air. "Who needs CrossFit when you can play Twister?"

Weston smiled. He really, actually *smiled*, and I almost lost my balance. He was gorgeous while broody and serious, but smiling? He was beautiful. Even his eyes joined in, the tiny gold flecks of amber in those dark depths shining brilliantly.

"West, you have to move," Maria said.

"Yeah, yeah." He balanced all his weight on his left arm and then crossed his right underneath, just above my head.

It had to be illegal for a guy to smell this good. I didn't know what kind of cologne he wore, but it was definitely working for him. Was that pine? Ocean? Pheromones? His chest was only inches away from my nose, and I was happy to stay there forever, or until my legs began cramping. Whatever.

Every muscle in my body started to tremble.

"Spin, Maria!" Weston barked, as if he could feel how close I was to falling.

"Right hand, red!"

"It's already on red!" we shouted at the same time.

The kids laughed. *Flexible little fiends.*

"Right foot, yellow!"

"She's trying to kill me," I whispered.

Weston's chest shook with laughter above me, and he adjusted his stance.

Balancing my weight, I slid my right foot under my left, searching for the circle, but it was no good. My shoulder buckled, threatening to slide out of joint, and I yelped as I fell.

I never hit the mat.

Weston's arm was around me, his hand splayed out under my back, holding all my weight as my legs crossed underneath him. My chest was against his and his face was inches from mine. "You okay?"

Was I okay? The man was spread out all over the mat and still managed to hold me up, and he was asking if *I* was okay? "My shoulder gave out."

"But you're okay?" he asked, his voice dipping low, concern furrowing his brow as he held me tighter against him.

"I'm okay," I answered, my pulse skyrocketing as heat flushed every inch of my skin.

"We won!" Sutton shouted, jumping to her feet.

Weston sighed. "I guess they did. We'll never live it down," he whispered.

"We'll ask them for a rematch some other night," I promised, my gaze dropping to his mouth. It was so close to mine that I could just lean up and—

"Arms around my neck," he ordered, and I immediately complied.

He pushed off with his left hand and brought us both up to a standing position. *Holy fucking strong much?* His hands were off me before I could even process just how much I liked being pressed against him.

"We won!" Max and Sutton practically bounced with happiness.

"You did," Weston agreed, putting his hand up for a high five, which Sutton gave.

"See?" Jeanine whispered, having stood when I wasn't looking. "Protective."

I muttered something in agreement, and a whole other game started. Theo and Jeanine took to the mat against the reigning champions, and I sat back and watched, my gaze returning time and again to where Weston stood along the wall. He was so relaxed here, so…at ease.

Was it because we were with his friends? Or had coming back to Penny Ridge made him more tense than usual over the last couple weeks?

It was after ten when we finally left, piling into Weston's truck to drive home.

"I like your friends," I told him as we pulled out of their driveway.

Jeanine and Theo waved from the porch.

"They're pretty great," he agreed. "And you held your own with Jeanine." Another half smile graced his face. "She can be tough when she's defending the people she cares about."

"Funny, she said the same thing about you." We took the turn out of their neighborhood and started up the road that led to the resort. "You're different there."

"How so?" He kept his eyes on the road as we began the climb, taking the curves like he'd driven them thousands of times—because he had.

Sometimes it was easy to forget that this was just as much his home as it was mine. That while I had ten years here, he'd had over twenty before I arrived.

"You're just more relaxed." I settled back against the seat and peeked in the rearview mirror. Sutton was out cold. "It was nice to see you loosen up a little."

"When I'm with them, it's easy to feel like we're just back in New York." He swallowed and his jaw tensed.

"Easy to forget that you're here?"

His nod was quick. "Something like that."

Change the subject. We might have been roommates, but he obviously wasn't ready to dig into that topic yet. "I was hoping I might be able to ask you a favor?"

"Sure." He focused on the winding road, which made it way easier for me to find the courage to ask.

"You're basically here to open up the backcountry, right? More big mountain skiing?"

"Exactly. Starting the heli-skiing operation will bring the resort to the next level."

"Is there any chance you might take me up with you once or twice when you have a group of skiers?" I fidgeted with my hands.

"You want to ski the backcountry?" He glanced my way for a second before looking back to the road.

"No. Nothing like that. I'd like to take some landscape shots from the air. Just something out of my comfort zone." *Something that might have a shot of getting into the local gallery.* I wasn't going to say that out loud. Not yet. Then I'd end up admitting I'd been rejected, and that would be even worse than the actual rejection. It shouldn't have mattered, but I didn't want him to see me as a failure.

"No problem." We passed the resort and kept driving up the mountain. "Just let me know when and we'll make it happen."

"Thank you," I whispered. My chest tightened at just how easy it had been to ask for something, and how quickly he'd given it.

We pulled into the driveway of our house a few minutes later. We both hopped out and then stared at Sutton's sleeping frame in the back seat as Weston opened her door.

"I don't want to wake her," I admitted.

"I can carry her up for you." His gaze locked with mine and a corner of his mouth rose in a playful smile. "It will be a violation of rule number one, though."

I answered him with a smile of my own. "I can live with that. Thank you."

My stomach fluttered as I watched him scoop my daughter into his arms, carrying her like she was something precious and breakable. Then I ran ahead of them to unlock the door and stood back as he carried her inside, walking straight up my staircase, her hair falling back over his arms.

He looked like he'd done it a million times.

My heart freaking melted.

This was bad. This was so, so, *so* bad. I knew this feeling. I avoided this feeling like the plague, this sweet yet frantic pulse that screamed *teenage crush* louder than *sensible mom*.

I liked him.

eston

"You sure?" I asked Reed, balancing my phone between my ear and shoulder as I whipped up some scrambled eggs. It was ten o'clock on Saturday morning, which meant Sutton and Callie would be up at any moment.

Both girls liked to sleep in, which was something I'd learned over the last month of living with them. Reed prattled on about snowfall as I glanced at the calendar. It was Halloween, which meant, holy shit, it really had been a month since I'd moved in with them.

Since I'd moved home.

A month of me managing to keep my hands to my damn self every time Callie smiled at me, or I heard her laugh, or she walked into the room, which was becoming...an issue.

"So, with the snow accumulations for base..." Reed continued, and I switched ears.

"We should be able to open next week," I finished for him, knowing where the conversation was heading and hoping for it to get to a conclusion faster. I took the eggs off the stove as footsteps sounded upstairs.

Being home for a month hadn't done anything to lessen my resentment of Reed. If anything, it just brought the shit I'd worked hard to compartmentalize roaring to the surface. The only saving grace was that Dad wasn't due home for a couple of months.

That would put my restraint to the ultimate test. No amount of shares in Madigan was worth the price of my soul if he was still the same callous bastard he had been when I'd left. Not that I was sure I was even ready to give him a chance. Some sins were unforgivable.

"Exactly." Reed cleared his throat. "So...how are bookings for November?"

I paused, looking out the kitchen window at the fresh powder that covered what was already a decent base. "We already have eleven trips booked between the fifteenth and the thirtieth. I didn't want to offer anything sooner since I didn't know if we'd be open."

"Right." An awkward pause followed. "I mean, that was the right decision to make."

"Thanks for the approval." I scoffed.

"West—"

"Look, is there any other reason you happened to call me on a Saturday? Because all of this is something you could have brought up yesterday, you know, when it was a workday." I took out the plates and silverware.

"Damn, Weston." Reed sighed. "No, there's nothing else."

I hung up and shoved my phone into my back pocket.

"Then fuck off, Reed," I muttered to myself.

"Didn't know it was that bad," Callie said from behind me.

I whirled around and saw her standing on the other side of the kitchen island. Her hair was still mussed from sleep, and there was a little line down her face from the pillow. I could have stared at her for hours if not for the questioning look in her eyes. "I made eggs."

"I noticed." She walked around me, her pajama pants molded to the biteable curve of her ass. "Thank you. Want some coffee?"

Stop looking. You're going to hell.

"No, thanks."

"Why exactly should Reed fuck off?" she asked, leaning up on her toes to reach a fresh box of K-cups from the cabinet.

"Because he's an asshole," I answered, reaching over her to grab the box. "Here you go."

"Thanks." She took the box and turned to face me, our bodies brushing before I stepped back to give her some space. If anyone had asked me a couple of months ago, I never would have said that pajama pants and hoodies were the sexiest outfit on a woman, yet Callie was changing my mind every single morning.

Maybe it was because I wanted to peel everything off piece by piece.

"And why exactly is he an asshole?" She put her mug under the coffee maker and pressed start. The machine hissed.

There were a million reasons. Because he left. Because he *got* to leave. He took off for college and left me to handle fucking *everything*. He left me to take care of Mom, and then bury her. He left me to hold everything together, to pick up the pieces of Mom's broken pottery Dad had smashed while he fell the fuck apart. He left me to raise Crew—scratch that—to *contain* Crew, since he'd been a freshman in high school and already a reckless adrenaline junkie.

Then he dared to swoop back in on breaks like he was God's gift, just like he was doing now, moving home to Madigan last year and saving it from a corporate buyout. Perfect *fucking* Reed.

"Weston?" Callie peered up at me and something inside me cracked.

I *wanted* to tell her. The sensation was disconcerting as fuck.

"You're not going to let this go, are you?" I rubbed the back of my neck.

"Nope." She grinned as she fetched the cream and sugar. The scent of fresh coffee filled the kitchen. "So you might as well just tell me."

"Is Sutton awake?" I busied myself putting breakfast on plates.

Callie leaned back against the counter next to me, watching me with appraising eyes as she sipped her coffee. "You see, I figure it has something to do with you staying behind."

I paused for a heartbeat.

"I've been here a few years now. Long enough to put the timeline together. Your mom died," she said softly.

My gaze flew to hers, and I would have snapped that it was none of her business, but there was only compassion there. Hell, Callie knew what it was to lose someone—she'd buried Sutton's father.

"And I know Reed and Ava met at college in Vermont..." She lifted her brows, her tone indicating she wanted me to finish that sentence for her.

Too bad. I reached around her and took down two glasses. Sutton was big on orange juice in the morning.

Callie sighed with obvious frustration and angrily sipped her coffee. And yes, after living with a woman for a month, I was realizing there was an angry way to sip coffee. There was also a contented way, a happy way, a tired way, and a flustered way. I wasn't a big fan of the anger being directed at me.

"I stayed behind after I graduated to help with Crew." I poured two glasses of orange juice. "He was fourteen when

Mom died, and our father decided drinking was more important than parenting, or cooking, or cleaning, or generally
showing up." I shook my head. "Anyway, Crew was still a kid
and pretty much lost both his parents, so I stayed."

"Because he needed you."

"Whether or not he'd ever admit it." Crew was his own force
of nature. "And I don't regret staying for those two years. Never.
It was hard giving up competitive skiing and the whole go-
away-to-college experience, but I'd do it all again for Crew. I
just..." There really wasn't another word that didn't make me
sound like a petty asshole, but maybe I *was* a petty asshole. "I
just resent the hell out of Reed for getting to ski off to college
and meet his Ava, I guess. Our entire family fell apart, and he
just wiped his hands of it."

"And then he called and said he needed you to abandon your
new life for the good of the family resort after you'd already
given the first," she said softly.

I shrugged. We both already knew the answer.

She held my gaze for a breath or two, and then nodded. "I'd
be pissed at Reed too," she said quietly as footsteps skipped
down the stairs. "Good morning, sugar!"

"Hey." Sutton wiped the sleep out of her eyes. "Ooh, is that
orange juice?"

I grinned and slid the glass across the island to her as she
took a seat.

"Thank you." Sutton lifted the glass to her face and sniffed
just like her mom did with coffee.

"So, when did our little rule list become a contract?" I asked,
noticing our ground rules on the refrigerator had three signature lines. Callie had signed one and Sutton the other.

"When Sutton decided it would be fun to practice my signature." Callie stared her daughter down.

"I already told you I was sorry," Sutton argued. "And look at
how well I did!" She grinned sheepishly. "I'm getting better."

"It's not going to help you get out of trouble the next time you land in the principal's office, young lady," Callie chastised, taking one of the plates to Sutton.

I laughed, and they both looked at me like I'd lost my mind. "Sorry. It's just something Crew would have done."

We sat down to breakfast and ate, then cleaned up in a rhythm that was becoming second nature.

"What are we going to do today?" Sutton asked, peering out the window. "Are the runs open?"

"Nope," I answered. "Reed thinks we'll have some open this week and a full opening day next weekend."

"Yes!" She threw her fist in the air. "I can't wait to get back up there!" She spun, her hair flying out in a circle around her head. Then she halted, her eyes going big as she looked at me. "Wait, opening day means you won't be here much, huh?"

I shrugged. "Depends on how many weekend trips we book. But I'll probably be flying or guiding. It's hard to start up a new business. Takes a lot of nights and weekends."

Sutton's face fell.

I glanced out the window at the sky. Crystal blue. No ceiling. I looked at Callie and smiled. "I have an idea of what we should today. Grab your camera."

———

"THIS IS SO COOL!" Sutton yelled through her headset as we passed over the resort.

"You don't have to shout. We can hear you." Callie had ahold of her seat cushion with both hands, her eyes huge as we flew up the mountainside. "This is insane. Pure insanity. Certifiable."

"Sorry, but look how cool this is!" Sutton shouted, the sound nearly overpowering the rotors but not quite.

I grinned, fully in my element. My hands were steady on the

controls, my attention on the horizon, the trees, and the gauges all at once.

"I know how cool it is, and if you take off your seat belt, I'm going to make Weston land this helicopter!" Callie argued.

"You're going to have to get a little more comfortable in the sky if you want to take those pictures," I said as we crested the top of the run.

"Look at the view!" Happiness radiated from Sutton's tone.

"You're sure this is safe? You can fly this thing on your own?" Callie countered, white knuckling her seat cushion next to me, her camera bag on her lap.

"Well, if I can't, we're kind of screwed." I shot her a smile and pitched left, following the side of the peak into the backcountry.

"That's not funny." But the corners of her lips curved upward.

"This is amazing!" I saw Sutton lean forward in the seat just behind her mother. "And you get to do this every day?"

"Every other day," I answered. "Theo and I are going to trade off. One day I'll fly and he'll guide the skiers. The next day he'll fly and I'll guide."

"You can ski all of this?" Sutton motioned out over the terrain. It was flawless, crisp snow, not a track to be seen, because no one had skied it yet.

"Yep. We have a special permit from the forest service." I flew into the valley and along the base, keeping a hundred feet between us and the tips of the pine trees.

"No, I mean, *you* can actually ski all of this?"

"Been doing it since I was a kid." I glanced over at Callie, who had loosened her death grip on her seat by a fraction and was leaning toward the window slightly. "Want to take the controls?"

"I will kill you." She shot me a glare.

I laughed, and she shook her head.

"What?" We climbed out of the valley and skirted the next

ridgeline. The horizon was nothing but snow-tipped peaks as far as the eye could see. Damn, I'd missed this view. There was nothing like it in the rest of the world. Sure, the Alps were gorgeous and there was something to be said for the mountains in Afghanistan when no one was shooting at you, but nothing compared to this.

"I've never seen you smile so much in a five-minute period," Callie answered, taking her camera out of its bag.

"You've never been flying with me before." I was happy up here, where there was only my own skill and the bird.

"Can you teach me to ski back here?" Sutton asked.

My eyebrows raised under my sunglasses.

"I'm good," she promised. "Like, really, *really* good. I can handle the double black diamonds, and I was even on the racing team last year, but I'm kind of over it."

"You're over it?" I asked, following the ridge and keeping my bearings as we headed west.

"I get it, people like to go fast. But everyone takes the same path. It gets boring," Sutton said. "I keep asking Mom if I can join the big mountain team."

"And I keep saying no," Callie said over her shoulder. "You're ten—"

"Almost eleven," Sutton countered. "And the coach said I'm good enough."

"You've never even skied backcountry before," Callie argued, letting go of her death-grip on her seat to turn toward Sutton.

"Weston can teach me!"

An awkward few seconds passed with no sound other than the beat of the rotor blades above us.

"Right, Weston?" Sutton tried again, her voice quieter this time.

Callie sat back in her seat and looked at me, one hand holding her camera and the other clinging to her seat.

"I'm so not getting in the middle of this." I rolled left,

sweeping us down the mountain. "Some of the best skiing is right here," I said, hoping to change the subject.

"Are you good?" Callie asked me.

"At skiing or flying? Because it's kind of late to back out of the flying part now."

She folded her arms across her chest, but at least she wasn't strangling the seat anymore. "The skiing."

"Yes." I didn't need to explain myself with any more words than that.

She stared at me, then nodded as if she'd decided something. "Would you be willing to teach Sutton?"

"Say yes!" Sutton begged.

"Sutton!" Callie shot her another look. "There's no pressure, Weston. None. I know how busy you're about to be with the tours and everything."

I brought us through the valley, heading back toward the resort. "If you want to learn, I'll teach you, Sutton. But you have to promise that you'll listen, because the first time you do something reckless, we're done."

"Yes! Yes!" Sutton nodded, her head bobbing in my peripheral vision.

"But no big mountain team," Callie said.

"Okay!" She nodded again, obviously content with winning what she could.

"See, now that your hands are free, you could actually use your camera," I teased Callie. "Want me to put her down so you can grab some shots?"

"Like...get out of this thing? While it's..." She circled her finger, making the motions of the rotor. "No. Absolutely not."

"You'd be completely safe," I promised. "Or we can open that back door." The blood drained from her face. She really was scared. "But we can do that next time if you want. There's no rush. I'm up here almost every day."

"I'll just...shoot through the window for today." Callie lifted her camera. "You know, for practice. It really is beautiful up here."

"It's my favorite place to be." I brought us up the back of the mountain and pulled to a hover just above the top of the lift.

"I can see why." She lifted her camera and got to work, and I couldn't help but wonder if she had the same feeling I did when I was up here, like if I could just get high enough above the world—above any problem—I could figure out a solution. Everything looked different from this angle. We swept down the mountain, following the line of the run.

"Hey, Weston, isn't that your house?" Sutton asked as we passed by my parents' house.

"It's the house I grew up in," I told her. I'd never call it mine.

Even flying couldn't change the angle enough for me to view that place as anything but a mausoleum.

I took us to the helipad, then whipped the tail around to the soundtrack of Sutton's laughter, setting the bird down directly on the cart. "Stay put while I run her down," I said.

"No problem," Callie answered tucking her camera away and turning back to Sutton. "You heard him, sit tight."

I ran the bird down and then it took us a few minutes to get her hangared and put up for the day. Sutton was checking out all of Maria's tools when I saw Callie walk into the office and brace her hands on the desk.

The door swung shut behind her, and I followed her in.

"Everything okay?" I flipped my baseball cap backward. "I didn't mean to scare you up there, and if I did, I'm really sorry."

"Okay?" She turned, leaning on the edge of the desk. "That was incredible!" Her smile made every muscle in my body draw tight. *So damn beautiful.*

"I'm glad you liked it."

"I can't believe you do that for a living!" She beamed at me. "And the fact that you took us up today was just way too much, but I can't thank you enough." She was practically vibrating with joy.

"You don't have to thank me." Anyone in my position would have done the same for her.

"I do!" She rose on her tiptoes and cupped my cheeks. "Thank you. Thank you. Thank you. Sure, I was absolutely terrified for the first few minutes, but that was...." She shook her head, searching for words, and wobbled on her tiptoes.

My hands clasped her waist to hold her steady.

"That was," she repeated, softer this time, her gaze falling to my mouth.

My attention did the same, memorizing the curve of her lower lip. She ran her tongue along it, and I swallowed a groan that rumbled up through my chest. "Callie." It was a warning. Or was it, really? I was holding on to her just as tightly as she had me.

"Weston," she replied, tilting her face up toward mine.

Fuck me, I wanted to kiss her. I wanted to know what she tasted like. I tugged her closer and her breath hitched as our bodies met. The most ludicrous thought skipped through my brain—she fit against me perfectly, like every plane of my body had been made to accommodate hers.

I lowered my head.

The door burst open, and Callie and I jumped apart as Sutton sailed through, all grins, completely oblivious to what had been going on in here. Or whatever had been *about* to go on.

"That was the best time ever!" she said, spinning around. "Thank you!"

"You're welcome," I said, forcing my smile. What the hell had I almost done? Kissing Callie would be a huge mistake. Huge. It had the potential to absolutely wreck our arrangement and make everything awkward as hell at home.

"This is absolutely the best day ever!" Sutton grinned up at me. "It's Halloween too! Oh, do you want to come trick-or-treating with us?"

My gaze flew to Callie's.

She was back against the desk, her eyes wide, her breath noticeably shaky. She looked at me with the same shock and apprehension I was feeling.

"You know what, kiddo? I have plans tonight." *With myself.*

"Oh, that's okay." Sutton shrugged. "I'll grab some extra candy for you. Let's go, Mom!" She took Callie's hand and they walked out of the office, heading for the truck.

I took a deep breath and blew it out between my lips, willing my body to calm, for my thoughts to get the hell away from Callie's mouth.

I needed to put some distance between us. Fast.

allie

"ON THREE," I said, my finger poised above the shutter button. The family in front of me shifted into position, their smiles bright and their cheeks rosy from the chill. "One, two, three!" I clicked several times, making sure I captured the best images. "That's it! They'll be uploaded to the site by this evening, or tomorrow morning at the latest."

Usually, I could cram minimal edits between the time that the slopes closed at four p.m. and seven or so, but we'd never had an opening day crowd like this. Ever. I had set up just down the trail from the new lift, and the line hadn't stopped all day. It was nearing three and I hadn't even taken a break for lunch.

The family scrambled in their gear, moving away from the picturesque background, and I waved goodbye to them as they skied and boarded down the hill, motioning for the next family to come forward.

I scanned their pass so I could upload their photos.

I posed them.

I clicked.

I moved on.

I was good. I was quick. I was efficient...and I was bored out of my ever-loving mind. This definitely wasn't what I'd had in mind as a starry-eyed freshman majoring in photography. This was...monotonous. *But it pays the bills.* Mary Ellen Mark wouldn't have been caught dead in this click-and-smile routine, but she hadn't been a single mom, either.

"How's it going?" Reed asked as he came over to my side, trudging his way through the snow. He wasn't dressed for skiing, so I made the assumption he was here for resort purposes.

"Busy," I said with a smile, waving the next family into position. "Welcome to Madigan!" Reed stood by while I posed and prepped the family, then took the picture.

"You need an assistant," he noted, scanning the dozen families in line.

I blinked. "What?" Was I not moving fast enough? Was there something else I should read into that statement?

"I've seen the crowds on both lifts, and I know how quickly season passes are selling today. You're going to need an assistant." He took my scanning device and helped the next family in line.

It cut the time in half, and ten minutes later, I'd caught up.

"Thank you," I told him, taking the device back and hanging it around my neck. "I'm glad you found me."

"The bright yellow parka that says *photographer* on the back is a dead giveaway," he replied with a familiar grin.

"You look like Weston when you smile." I scrolled through the last few photos on my view screen and nodded to myself. The lighting was good, so they'd all be fast uploads, depending on if the family chose the retouching package or not. When I looked up, Reed was staring at me like he'd never seen me. "What's wrong?" I lifted my sunglasses just in case they were somehow distorting my view. "Is it going okay?"

"I've just never been told that," he replied slowly. "At least not since we were kids." He rubbed the back of his neck—the same nervous tell that Weston had. "Or maybe it's just been that long since I've seen him smile. Who knows." He kicked at the snow as another family came up for photos.

I got them through the process, and they took off down the slopes. When I turned back to Reed, he had his arms folded across his chest, his gloved fingers tapping on the arms of his Madigan-embroidered coat. "What do you want to ask, Reed?"

"I just want to know if he's happy." He took off his sunglasses and wiped the snow from them. "And yeah, I know this is as inappropriate as it gets."

"Because you could just ask him yourself." I adjusted my hat lower on my ears.

"I could do that." His jaw popped.

"But he wouldn't answer you, would he?"

Reed shook his head.

"He's..." I shrugged, looking for the right word. "Weston." We'd been living together for five weeks, which didn't exactly make me an expert, but I got to know him a little better every day. It was also becoming infinitely harder to keep my hands to myself, not that his brother needed to know that. Crap, now heat flooded my cheeks. "He doesn't have to look happy to be happy, if you get what I'm saying." I shifted my weight, my boots crunching on the snow. "He's not exactly the poster child for emotional displays."

Reed snorted. "Yeah, that's putting it lightly."

The sound of rotors filled the air, and my gaze jerked skyward as Weston's helicopter crested the peak, low enough for me to make out the details of his paint job but high enough not to blow snow over everyone. It was probably my imagination, but I could have sworn he slowed over where I stood before flying down the slope toward the helipad.

"Have to admit, that's pretty fucking cool," Reed muttered.

Incredible was a better word.

"They had two tours this morning and a private one this afternoon," I told him, noting that not only were there no more families in line but the chairlift was empty coming up the slope. We were closed for the day.

"It's a great launch for that kind of operation." Reed's gaze followed Weston until he landed all the way down the mountain. "Ride down with me?" He motioned back to the chairlift.

"Sure." I flipped the placard on the photography sign to CLOSED and walked back up the slope. We were only a hundred feet or so beyond the lift, but my legs burned and my lungs ached. I'd spent the summer filling my personal portfolio—not that it had helped me get into the local gallery—and not nearly enough time hiking.

The staff waved to Reed and me, and we stepped up to the white line as the chair approached. It was something I'd done a million times, and yet my nerves always flared at this moment that I'd trip, or fall, or lose my balance and end up on someone's TikTok as the girl who couldn't manage a chairlift.

We sat at the right time and were pulled into the air above the slope, the lone passengers on an empty lift. Awkwardness set in within the first twenty seconds. It wasn't that I didn't like Reed. He'd proven himself to be a good boss. Fair. Observant. All that. But now I didn't only view him through my eyes but through Weston's lens, which made this awkward as hell. He'd never sought me out, and I knew this had everything to do with me living with Weston.

A pang of sympathy hit me straight in the chest.

"It has to be hard," I said quietly, looking over at him. The similarities between him and Weston were easy to find in the cut of his jaw and his cheekbones, but Weston was...harder and way less approachable.

"What?"

"Having him come home after all these years and still be a stubborn, aloof, jerkface where you're concerned." Not that he didn't deserve it, but I couldn't help but wonder if Reed even knew why Weston was so angry. At some point, the brothers needed to have it out if they were ever going to move forward.

Reed laughed, but the sound wasn't happy. "Like you said, he's Weston. I just..." He looked out over the skyline and sighed so hard I thought he might bring down the lift. "I just wish I knew he was okay. I pretty much forced him into coming back."

"He's okay," I promised, thinking of the look on Weston's face last weekend when we'd been flying. Then the look of absolute horror when we'd gotten a little too close in the hangar. The attraction between us was taking on a life of its own. My body was aware of his every time he stepped into a room, humming at a frequency I only felt around him. It was like hovering my hand over one of those static electricity balls—the current was undeniable. I found myself touching him on accident all the time, grazing his hand when I reached for a glass, or brushing my hip against his when we passed by each other. The tension in the house was a live, bare wire just waiting to burn the place down.

"I hope so," Reed said.

"Have you been up with him? Flying?"

Reed shook his head. "He barely lets me in the hangar."

A small smile spread across my wind-chapped face. "You should ask him. Seeing him up there is like..." I fumbled for words that wouldn't give my attraction to him away. "He's just in his element. It's like the outer layers—the crunchy stuff—just slips away and he's...Weston."

Reed cleared his throat, and I felt heat flush my cheeks. "Ava told me you're on a one-woman mission to get the guy to smile. I don't know if I should thank you or warn you off."

"Neither is necessary." I looked him in the eye and raised my sunglasses so he could see the truth in mine. "He's a pretty great guy, Reed. He's solid, you know? Kind, even though he'll argue that point, gentle when he needs to be, and oddly dependable for someone who I've only known a little more than a month."

"Dependable." He nodded. "Yeah. Weston's always been the guy who gets it done, even when he didn't have to."

I kept my thoughts on that to myself. First, because Reed was pretty much my boss, and secondly, if there was a side to take in this little brotherly feud, then I was clearly with Weston.

The base of the lift was only a minute or so away, and the skiers beneath us became less and less frequent.

"Look, Ava was going to ask, but I figured it should be me," Reed started, his face drawing tight. "Thanksgiving is in a couple of weeks, and we'd love to have you guys over to the house."

I laughed, seeing straight through him. "In hopes that I'll bring West?"

"West?" His eyes flared. "Guess you really do know him."

My smile fell. "I can't promise he'll come," I said as we neared the exit. "But I'll see what I can do."

Relief washed over his features. "Thank you."

We hurried out of the lift, and my heart stuttered at the sight of Weston and Sutton waiting for me. His mouth was curved into a smile at something Sutton had said, and her arms gesticulated wildly as Reed and I approached.

"Hey, Mom!" Sutton waved with mitten-covered hands. She'd gone with neon pink this year, and I knew it would only be a matter of weeks until I had to replace them. She'd needed new boots, new skis, and all new winter gear this year, too, after this summer's growth spurt, but the smile on her face was worth the hit to the bank account.

Weston's smile vanished as he looked at Reed and then he turned toward me. "Figured you might want a ride home, and I found this one loitering."

"I wasn't loitering!" Sutton laughed. "I put my hot chocolate cup in the trash!"

"Loitering, not littering," Weston told her with a shake of his head. "It's when you stand around plotting shenanigans."

"How was your first day back on the slopes, Sutton?" Reed asked.

"It was great! I got some runs in with Max early in the day. He's never skied here before, so I showed him all the best paths. He's solid on the groomed trails but needs a little work in the trees." Her nose scrunched.

"Nothing like keeping it honest," Weston muttered, a smirk lifting the side of his mouth.

"And I got to Raven by ten to help with the beginners just like I promised," she told me with a nod.

Raven needed exactly zero help with ski lessons but did me a solid by keeping an eye on Sutton when she could.

"How were today's trips?" Reed asked.

"Went as scheduled," Weston replied. His tone was brusque, professional, and completely different from the one he used with me. The difference was startling. "We brought the private party down and tucked her in for the night." He glanced at me and gathered up Sutton's poles and skis. "Ready to go home?"

Translation: I'm done with Reed.

"Let's go." I held my hand out for Sutton's and she took it. "Thanks for checking on me, Reed."

"I'm serious about the assistant," he said, his brow knitting just under his hat. "And the invitation."

I nodded and we hurried after Weston, who was walking like a man on a mission to put as much distance between him and his brother as possible.

"You ride the lift down?" Weston asked, slowing as we caught up to him.

"As opposed to taking a dog sled?" I replied as we made our way through the crowd of departing skiers. The traffic was going to be at a standstill getting down from the resort, since our guests were usually split pretty equally between vacationers staying at the lodge and day and season pass holders.

"As opposed to skiing." He reached over Sutton and tucked us in close as a member of ski patrol drove by on a snowmobile. Then he switched places, crossing behind us so he was closest to the path.

It was such a small thing, and yet it made me want to kiss the crap out of him for the protective gesture. Then again, the guy could look at me and I'd want to kiss him. There was just something about his mouth that had me obsessed.

"Oh, Mom can't ski," Sutton announced as we made it to the parking lot.

"What?" Weston stopped on the blacktop, his eyebrows high above his sunglasses.

"I said Mom can't ski," Sutton repeated.

"Seriously?" Weston shoved his sunglasses to the top of his head.

"Seriously," I answered, shrugging.

"You've lived at Madigan for eleven years and can't ski?" His eyes widened.

"Nope!" Sutton answered for me. How she had so much energy after skiing all day was beyond me.

"What happened to your *try everything once* philosophy?" he asked, the gold flecks in his eyes sparkling as the afternoon sun hit them.

"Oh, I've tried it once," I assured him. "And it was *not* for me."

"She fell and rolled down the bunny bowl," Sutton said in an exaggerated whisper.

"Sutton!" I sent her a look that clearly defined her a traitor.

"What? Raven told me." She shrugged.

Weston laughed, his eyes crinkling as he shook his head at me. "You gave up after one fall?"

"It was an enormous fall," I said defensively. "And you have *no* idea how many children I took out on the way down. I was a one-woman wrecking ball. They basically had to put up signs that said, 'Danger, uncoordinated woman ahead.'"

He laughed again, and next to Sutton's first cries, it was one of the best sounds I'd ever heard. "Let's get you ladies home."

I liked the sound of that way too much.

THE NEXT DAY, Sutton and I made it home in record time, bursting through the door at four fifteen. We had to hurry. They'd be here any minute.

Weston and I had driven separately this morning, which suited me just fine since he'd been out the door by six.

No, thank you.

My phone rang as I ushered Sutton into the shower. "Hey, Ava," I said, closing the bathroom door behind me after scooping up Sutton's discarded clothes. I tossed them into the hamper at the end of our small hallway.

"Hey, Callie. We already have fourteen applicants to be your assistant," she said.

"Already?" I hurried into my room and shucked off my snow pants. "He just mentioned hiring yesterday."

"Reed doesn't mess around," she said with a smile in her voice. "Anyway, do you want to interview them personally?"

"You're sure I need an assistant? I've never needed one before." I rejected the stab of fear that I'd be easily replaced.

"We've never grown this quickly before, either. How many photos do you have to upload tonight?"

I cringed. "Hundreds. But it's opening weekend. I closed

down for a couple hours around noon too. The lighting is shit at that hour, and it gave me some time get the first session polished and uploaded."

"Right. An assistant is going to be able to do that for you. Think of all the time you'll save!"

Time. The one thing I didn't have right now.

The one thing I needed if I wanted to work on some of my own shots. I definitely needed better pictures than the ones I'd taken through the helicopter window like a nervous Nelly. But I also needed to remain valuable to Madigan. I couldn't afford to lose my job.

"What if I wanted to put that time to a different use?" An idea took shape as I pulled off my socks and wiggled my cold toes. My boots were great, but standing in the snow for hours didn't do me any favors.

"What are you thinking?"

"I was thinking about working on some marketing shots for Weston's operation." I held my breath. Asking Ava as a friend was one thing, but she was calling as the business manager, and that was entirely different.

"Really? That would be awesome!" The excitement in her voice let me exhale.

"Great! I can interview people on Mondays and Tuesdays," I told her. Those were my days off now that the season had begun, or the days I took sessions privately.

"Tuesday it is," Ava said. "Any thoughts on Thanksgiving?"

My stomach pitched. "I haven't brought it up to him yet." Given the way he'd talked about Reed, I had a feeling I was going to have to tell my friend we wouldn't be going.

"I'm just sorry Reed put you in that position. It would really help if those two had a sit-down. Oh, I'd better let you go. They're coming today, right?"

"Any minute."

"Go!" We said our goodbyes and hung up.

I cursed at the contents of my closet but settled on jeans and a V-neck long-sleeved sweater that didn't scream *budget*.

"I'm not done yet!" Sutton shouted as I opened the bathroom door, steam wafting out and clouding the mirror.

"Just grabbing my brush," I said. "You'd better hurry, sugar." I unraveled the twin braids I'd worn under my hat today and ripped a brush through my hair as the doorbell rang.

"Shit," I muttered. There was no time for makeup, so they would get me in the lone coat of mascara I'd applied before hitting the slopes this morning. Not that they'd ever cared, but I didn't want them to think I wasn't capable of caring for myself...or Sutton.

A coat of mascara isn't going to imply that.

"Coming!" I raced down the steps, my feet still bare. Taking a second to suck in a deep breath at the foot of the stairs, I composed myself and plastered a smile on my face before I opened the door.

"Callie!" Mrs. Wilson stepped through the door and pulled me into a hug, holding me just as tightly as she had when Gavin had been alive. "It's so good to see you!" She pulled back and took my face in her hands. "You look beautiful as always." Her smile was warm and reminded me so much of Gavin that my chest ached.

"You look wonderful too." I meant it. Her brown hair had faded to silver in elegant streaks, and she pulled off the winter resort look like a pro in her equestrian boots and Patagonia vest. Then again, they never came for the snow. They came for Sutton.

"Callie," Mr. Wilson greeted me with a kind smile and loose hug. "Thanks for letting us stop by." He rocked back on his heels, and I glanced away. The similarities between him and Gavin were just so strong that I wondered if that's how Gavin would look if he'd ever gotten the chance to age.

"Any time." We all knew they hadn't just stopped by. They

came every six months or so, always scheduled, always kind. I tilted my head at the sound of the shower stopping. "Sounds like she's just getting out of the shower."

"We don't mind waiting," Mrs. Wilson said, her eyes sweeping over the space.

"How was the drive?" I asked. Small talk was key here.

"Uneventful," Mrs. Wilson answered. "Hardly any traffic from the airport. And the changes to the resort are lovely." They always stayed at the resort when they came into town.

"Seems the expansion is going well," Mr. Wilson commented.

"Are you sure we can't take you to dinner with us?" Mrs. Wilson asked. "We'd love the chance to catch up with you too."

"Oh, no, but thank you. I have a whole load of work to catch up on. Opening weekend and all." A whole night of staring at Gavin's parents, wondering what my life would have been like? No thank you.

"We under—" she started.

The front door opened, and gust of cold wind accompanied Weston as he walked through, shaking snowflakes out of his hair. He saw me and blinked, his gaze skimming down my body in confusion.

Note to self: wear more than just pajamas and hoodies at home.

"It's coming down pretty heavily out there," he said, shutting the door behind him, revealing Mr. and Mrs. Wilson. His eyes flared in surprise.

Mrs. Wilson's mouth dropped.

Mr. Wilson's eyes narrowed slightly as he looked Weston over.

"Weston, this is Mr. and Mrs. Wilson," I said, shoving my hands into my back pockets. "They're Gavin's parents."

Weston's eyebrows rose for a heartbeat, but he quickly turned toward the couple. "Nice to meet you. I'm Weston Madigan." He stuck his hand out, and Mr. Wilson shook it.

"I'm Maggie and this is Paul," Mrs. Wilson said, taking Weston's hand next. "Callie is always so formal. We've told her hundreds of times to call us by our first names. We're all adults now, after all." She smiled at Weston before looking my way, curiosity in her eyes.

Adults or not, they made me feel like I was still eighteen, not by anything they did but just by being relics of a life I'd long left behind. "Weston and I are roommates," I explained quickly.

"Oh," both the Wilsons replied in tandem.

"They're here to pick up Sutton for the evening."

"Oh," Weston said, shrugging out of his coat and walking around the couple to the closet. I snagged mine off the back of the chair and tossed it at him, and he caught it mid-air, hanging it next to his.

The motion didn't go unnoticed by Mrs. Wilson. "Roommates?" she asked, a downright twinkle in her eye and a smirk playing at her lips.

"Just roommates," I assured her.

"Did you say Madigan?" Mr. Wilson asked, turning toward Weston. "As in…"

"The very same," Weston confirmed, and Mrs. Wilson stepped toward me as the guys started talking.

"You know, it would be okay if you were more than roommates," she whispered. "We'd never judge you, Callie."

Heat stained my cheeks. "I know." But I didn't. "But really, just roommates." Even if I wanted to, that was the last thing I was going to admit to Gavin's mom.

"You know, Callie, your parents asked about you when we were at the club last weekend—" Mr. Wilson started, sinking my stomach with those few words.

"Did you tell them my phone isn't broken?" I interrupted. I hadn't changed my number in the last eleven years, either.

"They're not the easiest of people," Mrs. Wilson said, squeezing one of my hands.

"I was going to say barely human," Mr. Wilson added. "They called Sutton *Sharon,* and asked if we were financing your photography hobby."

"Paul!" Mrs. Wilson hissed. "That didn't need to be repeated."

My jaw locked. *Hobby?*

"They what?" Weston snapped, coming to my side. "Callie is a great photographer. I've seen her portfolio."

I blinked, my surprised gaze swinging to his.

"You left it on the coffee table last week," he muttered in apology.

"Of course you are! We told them that you never accept our money," Mrs. Wilson gushed. "And said you've made a wonderful life for yourself up here. We're really so proud of you, Callie." Her smile turned watery.

"Grandma! Grandpa!" Sutton exclaimed from the top of the stairs.

"Sutton!" Mrs. Wilson held out her arms.

My daughter flew toward the only grandparents she'd ever known, and they hugged her tight. Then the conversation went a mile a minute, catching up on the details of Sutton's day, but I barely heard any of it.

They asked about us...or me, I guessed, since they had checked out long before I'd become an *us.*

"So is nine okay?" Mrs. Wilson asked.

I blinked.

"Maggie, I'm sure she has school tomorrow," Mr. Wilson said softly.

"Nine is fine. You guys should get every minute you can with her," I said, faking my smile so they wouldn't see that their words had shaken me.

Mom and Dad had cut me off the second I'd refused to terminate my pregnancy, and now they were *asking?* Screw them.

"Thank you," Mrs. Wilson said. "And we're okay for tomorrow?"

"Of course." I nodded. "She'll be here right after school."

Sutton kissed my cheek goodbye, and I ushered them out the door once her coat was on.

"Are you okay?" Weston asked.

"No." I shook my head.

"Want to talk about it?"

"No."

He respected my answer and left me to stew in my own frustration as I edited pictures at the dining room table. I adjusted each image methodically, distracting myself with work for hours. Edit. Upload. Repeat.

The monotony of it was as peaceful as it was depressing.

...asked if we were financing your photography hobby...

Indignation sizzled in my veins. It wasn't a hobby. It was my profession. It was how I kept us housed and clothed and fed. Was I out there scoring New York galleries and magazine covers? No, but I had a happy kid, and that was enough for me.

Is it really, though?

I ignored that little voice and slowly, surely, put my parents and the weight of all their disappointment back into the neat little box I kept them in. Between edits, I glanced up at the photographs on the wall.

I used to want to be so much...more.

There was no way I could enter that competition. Not now. Not with Sutton at such a formative age. Not that I'd even get in. My shots weren't nearly on that level, but if I did? If I had to choose between my dream internship and the stability I'd worked so hard to provide for Sutton? No. Nope. No way.

But that didn't mean I couldn't move forward and build something for myself.

Starting with getting my pictures into the local gallery.

If nothing I had was good enough now, well then, I just

needed to work harder, to take pictures that *were* good enough. I'd carve out the time, maybe focus on some of the action shots I could take if I worked with Weston. The kinds of shots on the *World Geographic* flyer.

Once it hit seven, there was no more work, and Weston stood in front of me with a pizza and a bottle of wine.

"Seemed like a pizza and movie kind of night," he said, putting them both on the table. "But I can leave you alone if you'd rather." He'd showered, his hair still damp, and had changed into lounge pants and a long-sleeved shirt he'd shoved up at the forearms. There were two worry lines between his dark eyes, and I knew he meant what he'd said. He wouldn't push. Not like I had. He'd give me space if I wanted it, and that made me crave the opposite.

"Sounds perfect." I closed my laptop. "But only if we eat on the couch."

"Deal," he said, his lips curving in a small smile.

An hour later, the pizza had been devoured, the wine was three-fourths gone, and we sat side by side on the couch while superheroes destroyed yet another city in the name of saving it.

Weston's long legs were stretched out, his feet resting on the coffee table with his ankles crossed, and he balanced a bottle of water on the armrest, sipping from it every now and again. His arm ran along the back of the couch but didn't touch me.

I put my empty wineglass on the table and leaned back, tucking my legs up under me. Maybe it was the stress of seeing the Wilsons, or knowing Sutton was out with them. Hell, maybe it was the way Weston had stepped up to my side, like he was ready to go to war for me, or maybe it was just the tension in the house, but I desperately, *desperately* wanted that arm to wrap around me.

"You really can't ski?" he asked out of the blue.

I turned slightly to face him. "You've been thinking about that since yesterday?"

"You live on a ski resort." His gaze locked with mine, and heat flooded my system. I was ninety percent sure I was blushing, and I didn't care.

"And? Are you going to ask someone who works at an NYC skyscraper why they don't BASE jump off it?" I raised a brow.

"Not the same thing." He shook his head. "Not even close. I can teach you."

"Pretty sure I am unteachable. Didn't you hear? Mauled children. Parents screaming. Me, rolling down the hill like an avalanche, taking out everyone in my path."

He chuckled. "How many years ago was this?"

"Nine. I couldn't exactly ski for the first time while pregnant, and I didn't trust anyone but Ava with Sutton for those first few years."

"You haven't tried again in nine years?" His attention slid to my mouth.

"Would you be so quick to hurry back to the slopes if you'd been a menace the first go-round?"

"Menace?" There was that smirk again.

God save me from that freaking smirk.

"Menace," I assured him.

"I've broken more than a few bones on that mountain," he said, sliding his water bottle to the end table.

"And you went back up. There are some words for that, you know." I tapped my chin. "Foolish, reckless, masochistic, for starters."

"Tenacious," he said, his voice dropping lower. "The word you're looking for is tenacious."

"Are you always *tenacious*?" I shifted closer unconsciously, like my body rejected the inches between us.

"About everything I want." The dark promise in his eyes, the heat in his gaze had me tilting back my head. In challenge? In invitation? Hell if I knew. What about what I wanted? Not for the sake of my career, or even for Sutton's benefit, but just myself?

I wanted to taste Weston, even if it was just once.

"I have a thing about wanting," I whispered.

He leaned in. "About trying everything once."

I nodded.

"Even if you think it might screw up a really good thing?" His tone was more warning than question.

"It might make it even better." I shifted my weight up onto my knees. "But that's the thing—you don't know if you don't try it once." My fingers found his shoulders.

"Callie." His hands bracketed my hips.

I gathered up every ounce of courage in my body and went for it, kissing him softly. It was nothing more than a press of our lips, but it hit me like a shot of tequila on an empty stomach, going straight to my head.

His mouth was so much softer than the rest of him, and the contrast was dizzying. He leaned in, sucking on my bottom lip, and my breath hitched.

A second later, he ripped his head back. "This is a really bad idea." But his grip tightened on my hips.

"The worst," I agreed, my hands sliding to his neck and behind, up into his hair.

"Fuck it." He slanted his mouth over mine and kissed me, his tongue parting my lips and sliding into my mouth like he owned it.

I whimpered and shifted, slipping my knee over his thighs to straddle him. He groaned in reply, kissing me deeper, stroking his tongue along mine as he explored my mouth with a hunger that matched my own. He tasted like wine and something else I couldn't quite pinpoint. Something addictive, or maybe that was just Weston. This wasn't the typical, shy kiss of a first date. This was heat and lust. This was combustible. Dangerous.

"Maybe we shouldn't," I said, yanking my mouth from his.

My chest heaved and my pulse raced as I leaned my forehead against his, struggling to find logic when all my body wanted was more.

I wasn't a stranger to sex, and I'd had boyfriends since Sutton's birth, but I'd never felt this kind of clawing, aching demand before. This was the chemistry they talked about in romance novels. This was...maddening.

"We definitely shouldn't," Weston agreed against my mouth.

We moved at the same second, our mouths colliding and opening on contact. One of his hands slid into my hair. I sucked his tongue into my mouth, and he hauled me fully against him.

Holy shit, he was hard.

For me.

From just a couple of kisses.

Holding that kind of power over him was intoxicating, and I sank into the kiss with complete abandon, slipping my tongue past his teeth to explore him the way he had me. Over and over, our mouths met, taking and giving in light brushes and deep strokes.

I rolled my hips over him, and it was like he snapped, my world spinning until I was on my back and he was above me, his weight settling between my thighs, pressing against the delicious ache coiling there.

His mouth moved along my jaw. His teeth nipped at the lobe of my ear. I arched my neck, and he took the invitation, setting his lips to my throat. I moaned, arching up for more. He may as well have found a direct map for my turn-ons, because he was flipping every single switch.

"You feel so damn good under me, Calliope." His hand stroked from the nape of my neck to my waist, his thumb skimming the side of my breast.

Just the way he said my name had me burning.

"Weston." I took that hand and slid it back to my breast. Every part of me felt hypersensitive, like fingers that had been left too long in the cold and were experiencing the first rush of heat as circulation returned.

"Such a bad idea," he murmured against my neck as his hand cupped my breast, his thumb stroking over my nipple. This sweater was too thick. I wanted his hands on my skin, his mouth and tongue on me. "But so damned good."

He brought his mouth back to mine and the kiss exploded. Our entire bodies moved with the strokes of our tongues, our hands exploring, our hips rocking like we were teenagers in the back of a car.

I wanted this man, and I wanted him *now*.

"Weston," I said against his mouth.

He lifted his head, and if his kiss hadn't done the trick, then the way he looked at me would have. There was so much heat in his eyes that I should have combusted. Our breathing was ragged, and I slid my hand down to his chest and grinned. His heart was beating just as erratically as mine was.

"Callie?" His gaze searched mine.

I ran my tongue over my swollen lower lip and his attention shifted there, a little rumble of a groan sliding past his lips.

"I want—"

Footsteps sounded outside the door and the handle turned.

Both our heads jerked that direction, and before I could so much as panic, Weston was off me. Damn, that man was fast.

There was a knock on the door.

"Mom? It's locked. Can you let me in?" I heard Sutton ask.

"Absolutely!" I called out, rolling off the couch in a graceless heap and landing on my knees.

Weston took hold of my waist and lifted me to my feet like I weighed less than a sack of flour, then steadied me so I didn't fall again. I didn't pause or wait, just scrambled toward the door, smoothing my sweater into place on the way.

I yanked open the door and plastered a smile on my face. "Hey, sugar!"

"We had such a good time!" Sutton blew right past me, her arms loaded down with bags that from past experience I knew would be full of new clothes and anything else she would have so much as glanced at while out with the Wilsons.

"Thank you so much for letting us visit with her," Mrs. Wilson said, appearing in the doorway with even more bags. "And I'm sorry, but we can't help but spoil her when we see her."

"No need to apologize." I knew they did it out of love, and more than a little grief for Gavin.

"Hopefully we're not too late." Mr. Wilson carried in more bags.

"Nope, we were just…" I turned and the words died on my lips.

Weston was gone.

eston

"THAT'S the safest fall line right there, see?" I pointed to the line that ran past the trees and down the slope. "You'd have seen it better if we had skinned our way up."

"I like the helicopter," Sutton said with a grin.

"Yeah, well, it spoils you, and I only let you get away with it because I'm already tired from being out here today." I ruffled the pom-pom on her neon pink hat.

"You thinking about coming down anytime soon?" Theo asked from the valley below, his voice coming through the radio strapped to my hip.

I unclipped the device and hit the talk button. "We'll be down in ten minutes."

"Just don't lose the daylight," he replied.

"We have hours." I rolled my eyes.

"Two, max," Theo said.

"And I just need ten minutes of it. We'll see you at the bottom." I clipped the radio back on my belt. "I've already skied this today, so I know it's safe, and it's the easiest I've seen back here," I explained to Sutton. "Now, what did we talk about?"

"Don't ski where you don't know." She pulled her goggles down over her eyes.

"Yep." I did the same. "And?"

"Absorb the impact with my knees." She bounced up and down beside me, like she needed to psyche herself up for the run.

"You got it." I put my goggles into place. "What else?"

"Make sure we can see each other at all times." Her mitten-covered hands flexed on her poles.

"Yep. And you go first," I reminded her. "Just follow the tracks that are already there."

"The point is to take a whole new path." She lifted her brows at me, a move she had to have learned from Callie, because she looked just like her when she did it.

Callie. Nope. I shut that thought down. I wasn't thinking about her...or that kiss. Not when I was up here teaching Sutton.

"The point today is seeing how you manage out here." I stared her down. "No daredevil stuff, okay? If I break you, your mother will kill me."

"No promises." She giggled.

"Sutton." I cocked my head.

"Fine, fine," she agreed. "Take the easy path today, I get it. But you've already seen me on the jumps by the slope."

I snorted. "That manufactured stuff isn't even close." I'd spent yesterday afternoon watching her on moguls, in the trees, and in the little groomed section of jumps the snowboarders favored, so I knew she could handle the run in front of her, as long as she wasn't scared. Fear up here was just as dangerous as the mountain. "Now you go down first, that way I'm not worried about leaving you up here alone in case you..." How the hell did I phrase it without insulting her?

"Chicken out?" she challenged.

"Yep. That's it." I nodded toward the gentle slope. "Now go, drop in, and remember, there's about an eight-foot drop halfway down. Knees, Sutton. Knees."

"Got it!" She gave me a thumbs-up and pushed off, dropping in.

She took the first drop like a pro, and even if it was only a five-footer, her form was good. The girl was a natural. She hooted with glee.

"Concentrate!" I shouted after her.

Crew would love her...if he ever came home.

I held my breath when she came to a fork in the tracks. The left would take her toward the bigger drops I'd led a group over this morning, and the right followed the line I'd put in just for her about an hour ago. Lucky for me, she took the right path.

She dropped out of sight, and I took off, skiing after her.

"Made it here!" she called out just as she came back into view. "Whoa, you're fast!"

I laughed. "Reed is the racer. I'm just faster than *you*."

"I don't know. This route seems pretty tame." She pointed toward the bigger drops on the left. "Did you bring me over here because you can't hit those?"

My eyebrows rose. "Are you trying to challenge me?"

"Are you challenged?" she countered.

"Your mother has her hands full," I muttered.

Sutton shrugged. "I can see the helicopter from here. You know, if you want to actually do something besides babysit me." She flat-out grinned. "I mean, unless you're scared."

"I'm not rising to the bait, kiddo, or leaving you up here. I've already skied that line today, remember?" Had to credit the girl for trying.

"How about we make a deal?" she asked. "I'll ski the rest of the way down to Theo, including that last drop, and if I don't fall, you have to take the other run."

My mouth opened, refusal on my tongue. There was no way I was letting her—

"You'll be able to see me the whole time. See?" She pointed down the short distance. "It's up to you!" She pushed off and took the gentler run, her body moving with the mountain naturally, bending and swaying with each turn she carved as she made her way down the rest of the mountain.

Thank God I'd chosen the smallest run. No doubt she would have dropped into the toughest terrain we had without batting an eyelash.

My heart stopped when she took the final drop, hanging in the air for the infinity of a millisecond, then restarted when I saw her land it and coast the rest of the way down into the valley, where Theo waited.

"Girl's got talent," Theo said through the radio.

"Girl's going to give me a heart attack," I replied once I had the radio in hand.

"Girl wants to see you take the drops!" Sutton responded. "Because girl didn't fall once!"

"Yeah, yeah." I laughed and hung the radio on my belt. Then I dropped in, cutting new tracks toward the bigger drops.

Every thought besides the terrain paused in my head. There was no Reed. No business. No Dad. Nothing but the snow under my skis, and the adrenaline in my veins. I built up speed and hit the last drop—a twenty-footer—springing into the air and flipping backward. My skis rose up over my head and blocked out the sky for a heartbeat before finding their way under me to land, my knees absorbing the impact for the second time today.

Peace. All I felt up here was peace.

"You should have seen him!" Sutton gushed to Callie as I came downstairs a couple hours later. It had taken some time to get the bird put away, but we didn't have any tours scheduled tomorrow, so I didn't mind the slightly later evening.

It would be my first day off since we'd opened a week ago.

"He was *amazing*," Sutton continued as Callie dished dinner onto three plates.

My stomach growled at the scent of the stir-fry.

"Is he?" Callie asked, her back turned toward me.

"He did a *backflip* off the last drop. It was absolutely incredible!"

"He did a what?" Callie spun, the serving spoon still in hand, and her eyes widened as our gazes locked. "Hi."

"Hey." It was the first time we'd seen each other since I'd nearly devoured her on the couch, and yes, I'd been avoiding her on purpose. I left the house before she was awake and came home once I thought she'd be upstairs in bed.

"I...um..." She gestured, behind her. "I made dinner. It's here. On the counter. Behind me. It's just stir-fry, but I knew you had Sutton with you and didn't want you to have to cook." Her cheeks turned pink as she rambled on. "And I know it's on your list." She turned again, flinging rice off the spoon. "The whole cooking thing. But, I just did it."

"Smells great. Thank you." A slow smile spread across my face. I hadn't realized until this very moment just how much I'd missed her while I'd been avoiding the hell out of her.

"Why are you being weird?" Sutton walked past Callie, grabbing two plates from the counter and taking them to the dining room table. "Stop being weird."

"From the mouths of babes," I muttered, heading into the kitchen to help.

My arm brushed Callie's, and every good intention I had

nearly flew out the window. That was all it took with her—one touch, and I was right back there on that couch. Her body was under mine, all soft and warm, and my tongue was in her mouth, learning every line behind her lips. Her breathy moans were in my ear, her breath catching every time I sucked on that little section of her neck—

"And Theo flew us back," Sutton finished, and I startled, still standing at the counter with the silverware in my hands.

I was so fucked. I couldn't even concentrate on the conversation without feeling Callie's thighs around my hips.

"Is he as good a pilot as Weston?" Callie asked as we settled in at the table.

"I think Weston is better, but we didn't die or anything." Sutton shrugged.

Callie looked across the table at me, Sutton between us.

"He's better than I am," I said honestly. "He's got a few more years' experience behind the controls."

"Thank you for taking her," Callie said, her eyes softening.

"No problem." Whatever was behind my ribs went absolutely gooey. *Shit.* There wasn't much I wouldn't do to get Callie to look at me like that.

Sutton filled every gap in the conversation, giving the details of her day and our backcountry run.

I did my best to keep my attention on my plate, but then Callie would ask a question, and I'd remember the sound of her gasps. She tucked her hair behind her ears and my hands clenched at the memory of that silk sliding through my fingers.

This was so fucking bad.

It wasn't just some generic itch I could scratch with a one-night stand with some tourist, either. I wanted Callie. It was that easy and just that tangled. She wasn't a girlfriend, or even just a friend. She was my roommate, and if we went there, it would change everything.

If she even wanted to go there. I hadn't exactly stuck around to chat about our feelings once we'd been interrupted. Thank God for the timing, or I'd have been inside her within minutes, stroking us both to orgasm, and the consequences would have been unfathomable.

We finished dinner and cleaned up together, Sutton heading off to finish her homework, which left me alone with Callie in the kitchen.

"Did you finish your edits for the night?" I asked, searching for any safe topic of conversation.

"That's a direct violation of rule number thirteen." She flashed me a smile.

"Rule number thirteen is stupid, and I made it before I knew you." *Before I cared about your day.*

She closed the refrigerator, where she'd been putting away our leftovers, and turned around, leaning against it as I finished wiping down the counters. "I was done hours ago, actually."

"Even on a Sunday?" My eyebrows shot up. We'd been busy today, and I'd never call Reed to check my estimate, but if I had to guess, I would have said we had more people today than last week at opening.

"I have an assistant now." She cocked an eyebrow at me. "Which you might know if you'd spent more than five minutes with me in the last week."

I tossed the cleaning wipe and anchored my ass against the counter opposite hers, keeping a good amount of distance between us.

"But you haven't because you've been avoiding me." She shoved her hands into the center pocket of her hoodie.

"Guilty."

She scoffed. "Why? Because I kissed you?"

I gripped the counter on either side of me to keep me right where I was. "I think I did my share of the kissing."

"I'm the one that climbed on top of you," she said quietly.

"And I more than repaid the favor." Even now, I could feel

her soft skin under my hands, the curve of her breast in my palm.

Her lips parted and she nodded her head.

"This is dangerous," I warned her.

"We can just forget it happened."

Not likely. Not even fucking possible.

I locked both my hands behind my neck and sucked in a deep breath, turning around slowly in hopes of getting some control. There were three real estate flyers on the counter. "Did you go to showings today?" There, that was a safe topic of conversation.

"Yep. But they were either too far away from town or too much work." She walked over as I pivoted to face her. "That one was pretty, though." She pointed to the flyer on top.

I noted the address. "Too far outside Penny Ridge."

"Sutton would have to change schools." She sighed. "I swear, every time I think I have enough saved up, the market jumps higher. It's like this moving goal post I can't ever reach."

"Have you thought about a fixer-upper?"

She snorted. "I might know the right way to hold a hammer, but that's about it."

It was on the tip of my tongue to offer to help, but I snapped my mouth shut, unsure if that would be overstepping. I'd worked construction in the summers before Mom died, helping with repairs around the lodge and even building a few houses on a crew the summer of my junior year before she got really sick. I had the know-how, just not the permission to extend my place in Callie's life.

"What about you?" she asked, taking the flyers out of my hand and tossing them into the recycling bin. "You looking to buy eventually?"

"Not yet." I ripped my hand over my hair.

She looked up at me, expecting an explanation.

Anyone else, I would have blown off, but not her. "It's a cognitive dissonance thing," I said slowly.

She waited for me to continue, so I did.

"I know I'm here. I'm not delusional or anything. But buying a place means I actually have to admit that I'm staying."

"I thought you already decided to stay," she replied, her tone quieting until the last word was a whisper. Her expression changed, apprehension filling her eyes.

"It's one thing to set up the operation." I took a few steps just to put some distance between us. I wasn't always the good guy, there had been plenty of women I hadn't called the next morning, but I couldn't just be the good guy here—I had to be impeccable. "Relocating Theo and his family, Maria and her husband, gambling everything was a monumental move. I get that. I did it, and I'm lucky they chose to take the leap with me. But buying a house, owning a piece of Penny Ridge or Madigan, means I have to acknowledge on every level that I'm not going anywhere, that the move is permanent, that at some point, I'm going to have to make my peace with Reed when I can barely handle speaking to him."

She swallowed. "You can always sell property. It's not a life-long commitment."

"I know that too." A wry smile tugged at my mouth. "Like I said. Cognitive dissonance." I needed to change the subject. Fast. "So, if you could pick out a dream house, what would it be? One of those big multi-million things up above Penny Ridge?"

"Nope." She smiled, and her entire face lit up. "I'm in love with all the classic architecture downtown. You know that little Victorian place on the corner of Hudson and Vine?"

I searched my memory. "The Rupert place."

She nodded. "It's about three thousand square feet and four bedrooms, which is way more than we need, but you asked about the dream, not the rational. Sutton could walk to school, and it's only about ten minutes from the lodge, so it's not like the commute is a big deal."

"Let me guess, the Ruperts won't sell." They'd lived there all my life.

"If I could even afford it." Her nose crinkled as she thought. "Oh, and I'd never actually live there, but I love the style of your parents' house. That whole chalet vibe with the open concept is to die for."

"It's a great house," I admitted, shutting down the feelings that threatened to rise with memories I didn't want to deal with. He'd thrown everything she'd owned out onto the lawn and scraped almost every part of her out of the house, leaving it a shell of what she'd made it.

"Crap," she muttered, rubbing the bridge of her nose. "I meant to ask you last week, but we were too busy avoiding each other to have a discussion—"

"You were avoiding me too?" My eyebrows shot up. My reasons had been purely for her benefit, but what were hers?

"Well...yeah." She looked up at the ceiling. "Kind of. I mean, the way you vanished like a magic act wasn't exactly a confidence booster, and I figured if you were keeping away, it was because you didn't want it to happen again, and let's face it..." Her eyes squeezed shut. "That's an embarrassing, awkward conversation I'm not really anxious to have."

I closed the distance between us and cradled the back of her head with my hands.

She sucked in a breath but kept her gorgeous eyes shut.

"Callie, look at me."

She pried open one eye.

"Both eyes." There was no stopping the smile forming on my face.

The other opened slowly.

"I nearly lost control on that couch," I told her without finesse or charm, not that I really had either of those skills. "I avoided you so I *wouldn't* lose control. Because I liked kissing you entirely too much, and the whole reason we're roommates is because there's nowhere else for either of us to live on this mountain. There's not a whole lot of room for error here."

"Oh." Her gaze lowered to my mouth and her posture relaxed, the tension draining from her muscles. It took everything I had not to lean into her, to feel her melt against me.

Slowly, I flexed my hands, releasing her head so I could step back. Sutton was upstairs. Callie was my roommate. It was inappropriate to fuck said roommate in the kitchen while her daughter was upstairs. I repeated my reasoning in my head until I'd managed to get six steps between us. "Now what was it you forgot to discuss with me?"

When in doubt, change the topic.

She cringed. "So, Reed sort of asked me to Thanksgiving."

I blinked, trying to get my brain to process that as red filled my vision. "My brother invited you to Thanksgiving?"

"He invited *us*," she said, motioning between us. "Ava and I have been friends forever, and he was just afraid that if he asked you himself, you'd say no, since they're having it at home."

My jaw locked.

"You know. *Your* home," she continued.

Anger flooded my system, racing through my veins like acid. He'd gone through Callie to get to me. He always took the easiest fucking path and never cared about putting other people out.

"The home you refuse to go to," she said, as if there was any other possibility I had a different home. Her sigh was deafening. "Honestly, I think he just wants you, and Sutton and I got the pity invite because he hoped I'd be able to talk you into it, if that makes you feel better?"

"It doesn't." The words were clipped as I yanked my cell phone from my back pocket and held up a finger to Callie before I hit Reed's contact button.

"Weston?" I heard him shifting, like he needed to sit up. "Everything okay?"

"No," I snapped. "Everything is *not* okay."

"What's wrong?"

"Did you seriously go to Callie about Thanksgiving instead of coming straight to me?"

There was a pause. "Yes. It seemed the most efficient way to extend the invitation."

"You don't use her. Do you hear me?" My grip tightened on the phone. "She's not some tool for your efficiency. She's not some conduit. She's—"

"A hell of a lot easier to talk to than you are," he retorted.

Callie chewed on her bottom lip.

"It's not my job in life to make yours easier, Reed. Those days are over." My tone sharpened.

"What is *that* supposed to mean?"

"You want me to do something? Don't corner my—" Words jumbled around my tongue. She wasn't my girlfriend. She was obviously a little more than a friend if I'd had my tongue down her throat last weekend. "My roommate," I finally managed. "When you need to get a message to me. You can call. You can text. You can email. You can walk your prissy little ass down to the hangar—"

"You barely let me get a word out before you find somewhere else to be!" he argued.

"But don't you dare put Callie in the middle of the shit between us. That's not fair to her, and you know it." I glared at the countertop so Callie didn't think any of my anger was directed at her. "Especially not when there's a huge imbalance of power where you're concerned."

"Shit," he muttered. "I didn't ask her as an employee, Weston. I asked her as the woman you live with."

"That doesn't make it better." Fuck, there was just so much fury that I didn't know where to put it, but I was clearheaded enough to know that it wasn't all about this one incident. At some point, when it came to Reed, I was going to explode.

"I'm seeing that now," he said softly. "Tell me something, brother. Was there any realistic way I could have asked without you blowing my head off?"

My jaw flexed, and I dragged my gaze to Callie's. There was nothing but compassion in her eyes. No accusation, or even rebuke at the way I'd lashed out at Reed. "Probably not," I finally admitted.

"You and me, Weston. At some point we're going to have to sit down and have a real discussion." The older brother tone was back in his voice.

"Not likely," I responded. "I have nothing to say that you'd want to hear." That was a different topic for a different decade. I had to deal with the one in front of me if I had a chance of not hating Reed forever. Baby steps and all. "Do you want to go to Thanksgiving?" I asked Callie.

She sucked her lower lip between her teeth.

"There's no wrong answer," I said, softening my tone for her. Only her.

"I think it would be fun to spend the holiday with Ava," she replied. "We used to do it all together before Reed came home."

My chest lurched. I wasn't the only one whose life had been changed by Reed coming back to Madigan. This was one thing I could fix for Callie. "We'll be there," I said to Reed.

He sighed. "Good. It will be nice to have you—"

I hung up before he could say the word *home* and tossed my phone onto the counter.

"I'm sorry I asked," Ava whispered. "I knew you and Reed aren't exactly on cozy terms, and I didn't really think about it."

"Don't be. He should have asked me." I rubbed my hand over my hair. "I'm sorry you saw that. I have a hard time not screaming at Reed every time I talk to him."

"I'd never judge you for that." She walked a few steps closer.

"Mostly because I wouldn't want you judging me for how I choose to deal with my family either."

"Never." I shook my head.

"You said yes, for me." She took the last few steps, leaned up, and kissed my cheek. "Thank you."

"We'll see if we get through dinner without me burning the place to the ground," I muttered. "Thank me then. You deserve to celebrate with your friend." I brushed her hair back, just as an excuse to touch her. I hadn't bent for me but for her, and that thought was just as unsettling as the feeling I'd had when I realized how quickly my body caught fire for hers on that couch. "We can just forget it happened."

"What?" Her brow knit.

"That's what you said about the kiss. *We can just forget it happened.*"

"Oh. Right." She shook her head and moved to step away, but I caught her waist, sliding my hand to the small of her back and pulling her closer. She inhaled swiftly, her hands bracing but not pushing at my chest.

"Did you like it?" I asked. I'd been clear as day where I stood on it, and I wasn't about to be the only one on the ledge.

She locked her eyes with mine and nodded.

Instead of feeling relieved like I thought I would, my entire body tightened. "There are a few different things we can do about that kiss."

"Such as?" The catch in her voice was so damn hot.

"Such as ignoring it," I suggested. "Which is what we should probably do considering our living arrangements."

"Right."

"We can talk about it. We can address it. We could even reenact it, although I'm pretty sure that's quite possibly the worst thing we could do to keep this house stable." I needed to back the hell away, but I couldn't get my hands to listen to reason, or talk my feet into moving, not when I had her in my arms, pressed up against me like there was nowhere else she wanted to be.

"That would be logical," she agreed, swiping her tongue over her lower lip.

I groaned. "But I'm incapable of forgetting it ever happened," I warned her. "I could live the rest of my life and recall every single detail. A week from now. A year from now, the time wouldn't matter." She swayed, and I shifted my grip to her waist, steadying her on her feet before forcing myself to step back just to prove to myself I had the control to do it. "Which is why I'm going to focus on making sure it never happens again."

I walked the hell away and just hoped I'd be able to keep doing exactly that.

allie

HAVING AN ASSISTANT WAS GREAT. Having an assistant who could shoot photos so I could take my first day off for personal time in years? That was *fabulous*.

I'd spent the early part of my morning taking a dozen new pictures—keeping the local gallery in mind—before grabbing breakfast with Halley, and then we headed back up to my house, my car loaded with decorations, snacks, and about fourteen different colors of nail polish.

"I can't believe she's already eleven," Halley said as we carried everything inside.

"Right? Me either." Sutton's birthday falling on a Friday had been kismet, according to Sutton, who had invited six little girls over for a slumber party tonight, as our contract dictated. I smiled at the sight of Weston's signature scrawling under mine —my real one, since I'd crossed out Sutton's attempt at forgery.

"You sure you don't want me to take off tonight and help out?" Halley offered. "I really don't mind."

"You'd miss out on Friday night tips," I reminded her, pulling out the long, sparkly banner I'd bought to hang in front of the kitchen. If my girl was having a slumber party, then we were going full out.

"That is true," she said with a little grimace. "But I'd do it for you."

"Thank you. Just helping me set up is more than I could hope for. Ava can't get away, and Raven has her hands full with the holiday week tourists." We climbed up on the dining room chairs and used putty to hang the banner, the kind that wouldn't peel off the paint when we cleaned up tomorrow. Weston was going to break into hives when he came downstairs in the morning, but I'd get everything back to normal by the afternoon since the girls were scheduled to be picked up by eleven.

Then again, it had been a few weeks since Weston had gone into intense cleaning mode. Maybe we were wearing him down. Or at least Sutton was.

As for me? He was heeding his own advice from last weekend and keeping his physical distance. Pretty sure he could've kept a full ski between us at all times this week.

That didn't stop his gaze from tracking me whenever we were in the same room, or keep my pulse from rising whenever our eyes would meet. And if he smiled? Forget it, I was a freaking puddle. Now that I knew how that man kissed, I had a whole new level of appreciation for his mouth.

"And what about Weston?" Halley asked.

I stumbled but caught myself before I fell off the chair, climbing down with a little more grace. "What about Weston?" Was she reading my mind?

"He's tall enough to hang this stuff without the chairs." She hopped off hers. "I mean, not quite, but you get the point."

"Oh. Right." I blinked and shook my head. "He has skiers

today. I'm pretty sure he's flying and Theo's guiding, but I don't really keep up with their schedule." Except that I remembered days where he walked in sweaty, tired, and content. Mostly because he went straight to the shower.

I thought about those showers way too often.

"They seem to be taking off over there," Halley said, breaking open the balloons.

I started on the box that held the mini tank of helium. "They are. They're booked at least four days a week and taking reservations out to spring break."

"That's incredible."

"He's working really hard," I said with more than a touch of pride as we sat in the living room and positioned everything to blow up the balloons.

Halley stared at me as I smiled wistfully. When Weston had moved in, I'd imagined him at the bar like most single guys our age, or out on dates, but he came home every single night. It was all so...domestic.

"Oh. My. God." Her brows hit the roof.

"What?" I snapped my attention back to her and killed the lever on the tank so I could tie off the balloon.

"Something happened with him." Her eyes narrowed.

"There is absolutely no reason to think that," I sputtered, losing my grip on the balloon. It flew out of my hand like a rocket, bouncing off every wall as it deflated with an indignant screech.

"Uh huh," she said, arching a single brow. "Your hair is all shiny. New conditioning treatment?"

I grabbed at my tresses. "My ends were breaking."

"And the cute little outfit you're wearing?" She gestured to my jeans and top. "The Callie I know would have met me in a hoodie and messy bun."

"I'm allowed to wear actual clothes to have breakfast with

you!" I argued, but I could feel the heat rising in my cheeks. *Stupid pale skin with my stupid obvious blushing.*

"And that whole dreamy look in your eyes when you talk about him?" She leveled me with a single look. "Don't you dare lie to me, Callie Thorne."

I opened my mouth, then shut it again.

"That's what I thought." A huge smile broke across her face. "What happened? You have to tell me. *Please God,* tell me, because I'm dying to live vicariously!"

I laughed, my cheeks flaming as I took the balloon she handed me. "We...kissed. It was nothing. We agreed it was nothing." The balloon stretched around the nozzle, and I inflated it. "I mean, we had an in-depth discussion about why it should be nothing and wouldn't happen again, and sure, he said there was no chance he'd forget it..." I turned the lever and managed to get this one tied before handing it to her for a ribbon.

"He said you were unforgettable?" She sagged back against the couch. "Total swoon."

"He didn't say that." I grabbed another balloon and started on it.

"Honey, if he said there was no chance of forgetting it, then it's pretty much the same thing." She tied an extra-long ribbon and let the neon green balloon drift to the ceiling.

"It's not the same thing." I waved her off and handed her the next balloon. "And besides, we're not in high school. If he meant something, he'd say it." I fell back against the cushions beside her. "Ugh. This feels like high school, though. I can't ever remember dissecting every word out of a guy's mouth before."

"You like him!" She tied another ribbon and let the balloon loose.

"I..." *Crap.* "I like him. Damn it, this *is* high school." I reached for the next balloon, grabbing a purple one and inflating it. "Except I live with him, so it's not like I'm waiting to see him in the hallways. Instead, I'm holding my breath for the stupid front door to open." I was so over my head. "And it's all his fault." I passed her the filled balloon.

"Right. He's just too sexy, damn him," she teased, tying the ribbon.

"It's not just that." Another balloon, more helium. I had this down to a pattern now. "He's a good guy, Halley. He's so patient with Sutton, and he's even teaching her how to backcountry ski. He bought her skins last week so she could learn how to climb up the slope herself." I sighed. "And he's a great cook too. He's neat. He's considerate. He picks up groceries. And the way he kisses? *Ugh*." I ripped the balloon off the nozzle and tied.

"That good, huh?" She grinned.

"I don't even have words," I admitted. "Scrumptious? Delicious? No. Decadent. He is pure decadence."

She tied the string to the balloon and added it to the ones streaming above us. "You're crushing on him."

Crap, we really were in high school, because that word described exactly how I felt. "This is a disaster."

"Oh yes, Callie," she teased. "Crushing on the single, hot, good-with-your-kid, considerate guy who kisses *decadently* is such a disaster. Need I remind you of the liftie you went out with a few years ago."

I grimaced. "He was cute. And that was like...five years ago."

"He was also a womanizing airhead who thought *dude* was a complete sentence. Crushing on Weston isn't just an upgrade, it's a whole other class. Let yourself enjoy it."

My stomach flipped. "And what happens when it doesn't work out?"

"Then at least he's a good kisser?" She shrugged. "I'm not saying marry the guy. I'm saying there's no shame in a little after-hours activities. You're both grown adults and obviously attracted to each other."

Attracted to each other was an understatement. We were

compatible on every physical level. I knew that without even getting our clothes off. My body turned on the second I heard his voice, and just the memory of his mouth raised my temperature.

"You're all flushed," Halley teased, bumping against my shoulder as I reached for the next balloon.

I felt all flushed, and my stomach wouldn't settle. "Subject change. Tell me about the guys you've been seeing. Let *me* live vicariously for a minute."

Her eyes brightened. "Okay, well, there's this guy I've been seeing for a few weeks. Nothing serious, but the thing he does with his tongue? It's to die for."

I laughed and shoved the nausea aside as we finished decorating for Sutton's party.

FOUR HOURS LATER, I knew it wasn't the thought of Weston that had me queasy as I leaned over the toilet, puking up everything I'd had for breakfast. It was the second time in thirty minutes. My skin was clammy, and the world spun as I held on to the porcelain bowl.

"No, no, no," I muttered to myself. "Not today. I refuse to be sick today."

My cell phone rang, and I swatted at the floor in the direction of the noise until I found it, swiping to answer as Halley's name flashed on the screen.

"Oh my God," she said slowly. "Do you feel as horrible as I do?"

"Worse," I promised. "I've thrown up twice."

"Only once here," she replied. "It has to be something we ate this morning. The sausage?"

Just the thought of it had my stomach pitching, trying to hurl itself out of my body. "That has to be it."

"Callie?" Weston's voice carried up the stairs and into my bathroom.

"Up here! Weston's here," I said into the phone. "Kill me now. No one should see the guy they're crushing on while their head is in the toilet."

"Tell that to every college freshman you know," she managed to croak out. "Good luck over there."

"Do you need anything?" I laid my cheek against the seat and begged my body to cooperate.

"Like you're in a position to help," she teased. "I'm okay. Just take care of yourself."

We hung up, the phone sliding from my hand and crashing to the floor as Weston appeared in the doorway.

His eyes flew wide. "Holy shit. Callie."

Of course he looked freaking *perfect*. His jeans were perfect. His Henley? Perfect. The way his baseball cap was turned around backward? Perfect.

"I'm fine," I assured him, even as my stomach heaved and my mouth watered. "Oh no," I groaned, forcing myself to my knees as I retched up whatever was left in my stomach.

"Shit," Weston muttered. Then he was at my side, gathering my hair back at the base of my neck. "It's okay." He rubbed my back as my body tried to force up contents that weren't there, my stomach cramping so hard that sweat broke out all over my body. His hand left my back, and I heard him rustling for something on the counter.

"You shouldn't see this," I managed to say between spasms.

"You're sick, Callie. Not committing a murder." He tied my hair back. "I've seen way worse, trust me."

"There is no worse," I mumbled, sagging against the toilet and flushing.

"I've been to war with a helicopter that has guns on it. Trust me, there's worse," he said quietly as he stood.

Good, he should go. This was the kind of stuff husbands and parents signed up for, not roommates who occasionally kissed.

He grabbed a clean washcloth from under the counter, then ran the water in the sink, soaking the cloth. "Here we go." His voice was way too soothing as he stroked the cloth over my forehead and cheek.

It felt so good that I whimpered. "I think it's something I ate."

"Selfishly glad it's not contagious," he replied. "But I'd be here anyway. What time is Sutton coming home?"

"The party!" I jolted upright and the world tilted.

"Whoa." He caught my shoulders and steadied me as he crouched down next to me in the tiny space. "Let's think about that in a second. Do you think you're done throwing up?"

I assessed the state of my body. "If I say I don't know, will you think less of me?"

"Impossible," he replied with a soft smile. "Just stay here, okay? Don't move."

"I'm not sure I could if I wanted to."

He stroked my forehead and disappeared through the door. I concentrated on breathing in through my nose and out through my mouth. I had to be done puking, right? There was nothing left in there to heave up...and Weston had seen me hurling. Man, I was a *catch*.

It felt like hours, but it was only minutes before he was back, a small glass of water in his hands. "Swish and spit," he ordered.

I did it.

He flushed. "Think you're ready to move to the bed?"

"Why sir, how highly inappropriate of you to seduce me at such a time." I cracked a smile and pushed myself into a sitting position.

"Smartass," he muttered, bending toward me.

"What are you doing?" I asked as he scooped me into his arms and stood.

"Taking you to bed, obviously." He turned sideways to get us through the door, then walked down the small hallway to my bedroom.

"Not the way I imagined it." My head fell against his shoulder.

"Oh, then I guess you've imagined it?" He turned sideways again, sliding through my doorway. I tried to see my bedroom through his eyes, the durable bedframe and sensible dresser the house had come with and the dark blue curtains I'd splurged on our first summer in the space. Was it too cluttered for him? Too generic? It certainly didn't say that I'd been living here for five years. He laid me down on the bed and pulled the covers up to my waist.

"See?" I said, curling on my side as another wave of nausea hit. "There are benefits to not making your bed. Mainly, it's always ready for you to be tucked in during the most embarrassing moment of your life."

He stroked my hair, the mattress dipping as he sat beside me. "Nothing to be embarrassed over. I brought up the stock pot too. Just in case you can't make it to the bathroom. And if you give me a minute, I'll grab some saltines and electrolytes."

My eyes burned, and suddenly I was blinking back tears.

"Hey." He took my hand in his and kept stroking my hair with the other. "It's okay."

But was it? No one had taken care of me in over a decade, and no one had ever been this nice while I was sick. This was horrible to feel so weak and yet amazing to be cared for. My eyelids felt like they weighed four hundred pounds, but I managed to force them open so I could see him.

He moved, sliding off the bed and kneeling next to me so our faces were at the same level. "Give me a few minutes. Just let me take care of you."

I nodded, and he disappeared again.

Exhaustion yanked me into sleep.

WHEN I WOKE, an hour had passed according to my alarm clock. I heard paper rustle and turned over. Weston was next to me, his back against my headboard, his legs stretched out as he read a book.

"Look who's aw—"

My stomach spasmed again and I lurched away from him.

He was at my side before I could fall from the bed. "Bathroom or pot?"

"Bathroom!" There was no way I was puking into a freaking kitchen pot in front of him. Even sickness had its limits.

He scooped me up again, carrying me down the hall. Then he carried me back again once I was done. The man was going straight to heaven.

"Hopefully it lets up soon," he said as he wiped my face with a fresh washcloth.

"Sutton should be home in an hour," I whispered, my eyes already closing again. "What are you doing home, anyway?"

"The weather's shit. We can't fly when it's dumping like this," he said, moving the washcloth to my neck. "And I figured I'd come home and see if there was anything you needed before tonight."

"The party," I groaned, leaning into the washcloth as it stroked over my cheek. "I'll be okay. I just need a few hours of sleep."

"Rest. We'll figure it out," he promised, but his voice was already fading out as I dozed off.

"IT LOOKS AMAZING!" Sutton's voice pulled me from sleep.

"Give me a second," Weston murmured, sliding off the bed.

I heard vague chatter, and then footsteps racing up the stairs.

"Mom!" Sutton appeared in the doorway, her eyes huge and worried. "Are you okay?"

"Just something I ate," I managed to say. "I'm so sorry, sugar. I know it's your birthday. I just need another hour to sleep it off, okay?"

"I'll call the girls and cancel the party," she promised. "It's no big deal."

"It's a huge deal," I replied. "Just give me another hour."

"What time is everyone showing up?" I heard Weston ask as my eyes fluttered closed.

"An hour," Sutton replied in a whisper. "But I can call everyone."

I couldn't keep conscious and faded out again.

WHEN I MANAGED to open my eyes again, it was five fifteen. I lurched to a sitting position, and my head swam.

"I'm never eating sausage again," I muttered, pawing at my nightstand for my phone.

"You're awake," Weston said from the doorway, his usual perfection leaning toward the frazzled end of the spectrum.

Then it hit me, the sound of raucous girls downstairs. "Oh no." I tried to move again, but my limbs didn't agree.

"It's fine," he assured me, smoothing back my hair. "I can handle it. It's six little girls. How much damage can they do?"

"You have no idea," I groaned. "We have to send them home. And there should be seven."

"No, *we* don't," he argued. "*You* have to sleep. *I* already warned the parents just in case it was contagious. Five of the girls stayed. I've got this."

I pried my eyes open and found his brown and gold ones staring back at me. "You said you didn't do the parent thing, remember? It's rule number three. Besides, what parent in their right mind would leave their kids with someone they've never met?" I blinked. "Not that you're not trustworthy. I'd trust you with Sutton's life."

"Good, because you're going to. And you forget, just because I've been gone ten years doesn't mean I don't know the parents of every single child in this house. Small towns have long memories, Callie." Another stroke of my hair, and my eyes closed. "Just sleep. I promise the house will still be standing when you wake up tomorrow."

"You don't have to do this," I protested, guilt swamping me worse than the nausea.

"No, but Sutton needs me to," he replied. "Sleep."

I faded off, but not before I heard his footsteps retreat down the stairs.

"Okay, so how many of you have never seen a helicopter?"

The sound of excited cheering carried me right off to sleep.

10

W eston

MY FINGERNAILS WERE PURPLE, and it was going to take at least three showers to scrub the glitter out of my scalp from the insanity of the evening. I'm not sure what I'd expected from a group of eleven-year-old girls, but it definitely hadn't been an all-nighter.

I cracked a yawn and navigated the maze of sleeping bags in our living room, making my way to the kitchen on all three hours of sleep I'd managed to snag between the end of their movie and my alarm clock blaring in my ear.

My thumbs flew over the keyboard of my phone, typing out a text to the only other skier I knew in town who could handle guiding a group of tourists through the backcountry.

"Hey," Callie whispered, and my gaze shot up. She was in the kitchen, dumping bags of pancake mix into a giant mixing bowl.

"What are you doing out of bed?" I skirted the last sleeping girl and strode through the dining room and into the kitchen. She should be sleeping off her night.

"I woke up about a half hour ago, and I'm okay," she said softly.

"But—"

"It's out of my system. No puking since about nine last night, and I slept a good ten hours." She gave me a shy smile and looked away. "I even managed a shower."

"I can tell." Her hair was wet. "You look better."

"I feel better," she promised, taking the eggs out of the refrigerator. "And you need to get to the hangar. I know weekends are busiest for you."

My brow furrowed, because she was right.

"Don't deny it," she challenged, her voice strong but her cheeks pale.

"I was just texting someone to take over for the morning." My thumb hovered over the send button. "Theo will have to fly, anyway. There's no way I'm getting behind the controls on a few hours of sleep."

"I'm so sorry about last night." Guilt sagged her shoulders.

"Don't be." I shrugged. "It was...an experience."

"I bet." She glanced toward the sleeping girls. "Looks like everyone lived. I really can't thank you enough."

"They did. I probably could have gone to sleep once they settled in on a movie, but I didn't want to be the guy who lost one of them because they decided to run amok in the dark or something. I don't have a lot of experience with eleven-year-old girls."

She scoffed, then tilted her head like she was thinking about it. "Yeah, that was probably a good idea. And did I hear something about helicopters last night? I was pretty out of it."

I nodded. "I called up Theo and he brought the minivan over. Sutton thought it was the coolest thing, and between you and me, I think it got Max a few cool points too. The kids had a blast."

Her eyes widened. "Wait. You didn't take them flying, did you? Because I can't even imagine the liability—"

I laughed. "I'm not exactly a parent, but I do have some common sense, Callie. It was dark by the time we got there anyway, and I'm not about to fly instruments around a place with a bunch of lifts just for a joyride."

"Oh, thank God. I'm already the weird single mom in the PTA."

"Your standing is safe," I assured her.

She glanced at her phone on the counter. "It's already seven fifteen. You'd better get down there."

"You're sure you'll be okay?" Leaving her felt wrong. Necessary, but totally and completely wrong.

"It's just pancakes from a box and sending the girls home," she assured me. "I've got—" Her mouth dropped open as her attention snagged on my hands. "I have nail polish remover, and we can get that off in seconds." She pivoted like she was about to start scrubbing my nails right now.

"It can wait."

"They're purple." Her gaze jumped to mine.

That area behind my ribs went tight again, a sensation I was not only starting to expect every time we locked eyes but anticipate. Damn it, I liked the way she made me feel with nothing but a glance, like I wasn't just needed but *wanted*. Like she worried about me.

The feeling was inconveniently addictive.

"I'm secure enough in my manhood to rock the purple nails." I scrubbed my hand over my head and a few pieces of glitter fell to the ground. "Not sure about the sparkles, though."

"Oh, you pull it off." Her mouth curved into a smile, and I battled through the urge to kiss her.

Instead, I lifted one hand and cupped her cheek. "Tell me

you're really okay, and I'll go. But if you're not, I'll figure something out and stay." Her eyes went liquid, and she leaned into my touch.

"I'm fine. If I need backup, I'll call Ava." She put her hand over mine, holding me to her. "I don't know what to say about last night." Her voice dropped to a whisper.

"You don't have to say anything." I bit back a smile at her wording, but she saw it.

"What?"

"I just thought if you said those words, it would be under very different circumstances." Circumstances that had to do with me in her bed, or hers in mine, for more than just sleeping and reading. Circumstances that required way less clothing.

"Oh, really?" She grinned, but it slipped quickly. "Really, though. I'm not used to someone taking care of me."

I stroked my thumb along the flawless skin of her cheek. "Then you're going to have to raise your standards, Calliope." Bending forward, I brushed a kiss over her forehead.

She melted.

I got the hell out of there before I did something even stupider, like move that kiss to her mouth.

———

"So you survived the gaggle of women in your house?" Theo joked as we finished tucking the bird in the next day. "I keep forgetting to ask." The storm had blown through last night, leaving us thirteen new inches of powder, and the skiers we'd taken up this morning had already booked another trip for February, which made for a stellar morning.

"I'm standing here, right?" I rolled my shoulders. My muscles were stiff and sore from the amount of time I'd spent on the mountain in the two weeks since opening. Taking every-other-day shifts with Theo helped, but even the gym time I'd put in over the summer hadn't prepared me for the full-body torture I was putting my body through. Sure was fun, though.

"I'm..." He shook his head as we headed into the office.

"You're what?" I asked, falling into my chair and firing up the computer. "Shocked?"

"Impressed," he said, reaching for his coat. "You're evolving. It's pretty damned intriguing to watch."

"Like I've been a Neanderthal for the seven years we've known each other?" I glanced up over the monitor as the accounting software loaded. I would have called Maria in to my defense, but she'd already gone home for the day. The best part of working our own business was definitely setting our own hours. It was only four p.m., and we were already closing up shop.

"I was going to go for reclusive asshole, but I guess Neanderthal works." He grinned. "How are the books?"

"What makes you think I'm looking at the books?" I clicked the page that showed our bottom line.

"Because I know you." He came around the desk to stand next to me. "And I know you're stressed."

I hadn't been this nervous waiting for the promotion list to come out, but I'd never had so many people's futures riding on my own choices before, either. My eyebrows hit the ceiling when the page loaded.

"Holy shit." Theo grinned and shook the back of my chair. "Look at that!"

"We're in the black." At least for the month we were. We'd more than made enough to cover the payment on the bird, our salaries, and tuck money away for the summer payments. Relief surged through every cell in my body.

"This is going to work. We're going to make this work!"

"Hell yeah, we are." I nodded and clicked over to our scheduling software. The bookings next month were already filling up quickly. We really were taking off. "No regrets?" I asked Theo as he shoved his arms into his coat.

"What? About giving up my military career seven years before retirement to risk it all on this little venture with you?" He zipped his coat. "None."

The tension in my shoulders eased a little. "And the kids? They're settling in? Jeanine?" I didn't just feel responsible for Theo's paycheck but for the stress I'd put on his family with this move.

"Relax, West. Kids are doing great. You saw how well Max gets along with his classmates, and Seline is already harping on us to check out the little dance studio downtown for lessons. And Jeanine is looking to put her nursing license to use in the emergency clinic. They're offering her a more than competitive contract."

"Good." I sighed, leaning back in my chair. It had been hard on Jeanine, moving post to post, constantly changing hospitals, gaining experience but never seniority. "That's good."

"It's better than good." He squeezed my shoulder. "This move wasn't just about you, so stop taking it all on yourself. Jeanine was ready to put down roots, to stop moving the kids, and I agreed. I'm just as committed to making this business work as you are."

"I know." Logically, I did. "And you have to know that I couldn't do any of this without you. There's no one else I'd trust."

He scoffed. "That's because you're a cynical ass."

The bell jingled as Callie walked through the door, her gaze finding mine instantly. "Hi." She glanced between Theo and me as the door shut behind her. "You look busy. I can absolutely make an appointment." She looked oddly nervous.

"Hey," I answered, ignoring that last part and the little jump in my chest that said I was happy to see her. What the hell was wrong with me? I lived with the woman. I was pretty much guaranteed to see her.

"Make an appointment?" Theo balked.

"It's rule number thirteen," Callie explained, taking her blue beanie off and smoothing her hair. "We don't talk about work at home. You're off tomorrow, so it can wait until Tuesday."

Theo shot me a dry look. "So much for evolving." He slapped my back and walked around the desk toward Callie. "That's my cue to leave. It's good to see you up and about, Callie."

"Thank you for helping out Friday night. I can't apologize enough." She fidgeted with her hat.

"Seeing this guy surrounded by shrieking little girls was absolutely worth it." He gave her a smile and headed for the door. "See you Tuesday, West." With one last look and a mouthed *evolve* over Callie's shoulder, he disappeared through the door.

We were alone.

"I really can come back," Callie said.

"We really can talk about work at home." That rule had been designed to keep me from being the *boss* at home, but a few days around Callie had taught me there was no danger of that. She was true to rule number five—she ruled it all. "But since you're already here, what's up?" I glanced behind her, but the door didn't open again. "And where's Sutton?"

"Halley has her until five." She glanced at the clock above the desk. "Which gives me exactly an hour to make my proposal."

Okay, now I was curious. I leaned back in my chair. "And what proposal is that?"

She came around the desk, pulling a folded sheet of paper from the back pocket of her jeans. "This."

I unfolded the paper as she shucked off her jacket and hung it on the coat rack.

"Is this that internship you were talking about?" I looked

over the extreme sport photography section. The pictures were more than impressive.

"Yes, but I'm not entering it or anything." She moved closer, perching her ass on the edge of my desk and facing me. "At least not this year. I just brought that for an example." She white-knuckled the edge of the desk and took a deep breath. "I want to get my work into the local gallery, and I think learning how to take these kinds of shots will get me there."

"I think that's great. How can I help?" The shots were cool. They captured athletes midair, or in the seconds where their movements defied all logic and gravity.

"I was hoping you might take me up with you on days my assistant is shooting the standard 'look, we went skiing' pictures at the top of the lift." She swallowed, slowly dragging her gaze back to meet mine. "I know it's more than the landscapes I'd asked about before, and it would mean you'd have to do some extra flying, since I'm sure you don't exactly hover next to the cliffs your clients jump off—the cliffs *you* jump off."

I examined the only winter photo on the sheet, gauging the distance the photographer had to be to capture the shot. "We usually drop them at the ridgeline and then wait in the valley below, but it wouldn't a big deal to follow them down so you get the shots."

"Really?" Her smile was instant and gorgeous.

My whole body went tight. Damn, I wanted her. *Not the time.*

"Really." I handed the paper back to her.

"You don't even want to know what you'd get out of it?" Her eyebrows rose.

"I don't have to get something out of helping you, Callie."

"But I want you to!" She composed herself with a quick breath. "I mean, this is a business proposal. Yes, I'd need some training, and I've already enrolled in an online seminar for this kind of photography—"

"You know I already said yes, right?" A smile quirked my lips.

"Just let me get this out!" She leaned forward and put a finger across my lips.

I resisted the urge to suck it into my mouth.

"As I was saying." She removed her finger, then folded the *World Geographic* flyer and put it back in her pocket. "I've already invested in some equipment. I would absolutely make sure the skiers signed releases, and you could use whatever photographs we get for marketing. Ava said that might help you out, since I'm not really in a position to pay your hourly fee. See? It's a business proposal." She grinned.

"A good one too." I nodded, my chest going liquid at the joy in her eyes. "If you're taking marketing photos, the extra flight hours would just be a business expense for us." I probably would have agreed to fly her to every resort in Colorado if it made her smile like that at me again. "You know, you could enter that competition this year if you wanted to. It says the deadline is in January. We'd have months to get you ready."

"Oh no. I'm not looking for anything like that. Sutton…" She vehemently shook her head. "Besides, I'd need way more than a couple months," she scoffed, turning slightly so she could see the screen and palming my mouse. "Here, I'll show you." She navigated to the resort's webpage. "I've taken all of these, but they're not the same."

"These are good." The pictures were of skiers and boarders coming down the runs. Some were mid-jump on the little manmade area we had, and others were action shots in the trees.

"Thank you. I just want to up my game. Getting into that gallery, even as small as it is, would make Sutton proud." She shrugged. "It would make me proud too."

"It's a great gallery. They have some of my mom's pieces."

The ones Reed had been able to track down. The ones Dad hadn't pulverized in rage-filled grief.

"Her sculptures are phenomenal," Callie said softly.

"*She* was phenomenal." I pushed away the wave of sorrow that always loomed when it came to missing Mom and leaned in toward the screen, my shoulder brushing Callie's arm. The contact was electric as always. "These say photos are courtesy of Callie Sutton Photography."

"Yeah." She nodded. "Part of the deal when I renegotiated my contract about five years ago was photo credit, even though the resort owns the rights to everything I shoot on property. And I thought combining our names was cute for my LLC." She tensed. "But I'd need you to sign over some of the rights for the photos I'd shoot."

"The ones you'd want to submit to the gallery," I guessed.

"Yes. Assuming you can sign on behalf of Madigan Mountain." Her teeth bit into her lower lip for a second. "And I know that might be abusing the fact that we live together, and I can ask Reed—"

"I can sign for Madigan." I'd never been happier about the deal Reed and I had cut before I came home, and it had nothing to do with the money. This was something I could give Callie. "It's not a problem. I'll handle Reed if he has any questions. And we can start whenever you want. We don't have a trip planned tomorrow, but I'll give you the schedule." Had to admit, I liked the idea of spending time with her outside the house, even if it was for work. I couldn't seem to get enough of her.

She grinned. "That would be amazing."

"Your shots will be amazing, especially once we get you harnessed in so you can lean out the door of the bird." I nodded, already thinking through the safest way to get her a clean view.

Her mouth dropped open. "Harnessed?"

"Oh yeah." I grinned. "We already have a rig."

"You think I should hang out the door of a helicopter?" Her eyes flew wide.

I wanted to kiss the surprise right off her face.

"It's safe," I promised. "Come on, I'll show you." I shut down the computer quickly and locked the front door as I led Callie into the hangar. We were closed for the day, so it wasn't like I was shutting out guests or anything.

She was quiet as I slid the door open to the helicopter and climbed inside. "Come on." I walked back between the seats, and she followed me in, watching as I opened the container near the back row and pulled out the harness. "See?"

"I think I could get some fabulous shots from that chair right there," she said, pointing to the seat nearest the window.

"And you'd get even better ones if you could change your angle. Plus, if I'm flying you, then you have to be strapped in if you've got that door open. I'm not risking you falling. Zero chance." I handed her the harness.

She took it, biting her lower lip. "And it clips in?"

"There's a hook right above the door." A teasing grin tugged at my mouth. "I mean, we can always hook you in on the rescue hoist, but I don't think swinging around out there is really what you had in mind."

Her head snapped up and sputtered. "Absolutely not."

"I figured." I moved forward, my head hunched so I didn't smack it on the roof. Then I guided her hands so the harness was open. "See? You put your legs here and here." I pointed to the openings. "And then we cinch you in tight with this buckle." My fingers brushed hers.

Her breath caught. "And then I won't fall out. Because I'm not a big fan of anything physically reckless, and Sutton only has one parent—"

"I won't let anything happen to you. And I'll be the one flying, so I have no problem making that promise. Not that Theo isn't absolutely capable—"

"No, I want you," she said, her hands gripping the harness as she looked up at me. Tension filled every inch between our bodies.

That was all it took to get me hard.

"I mean...I want you to be the one flying," she whispered, her gaze dropping to my mouth.

"Good." My voice lowered. "Because I want to be the one..." My words trailed off. I was too distracted by her nearness, by the scent of her hair and the way her lips parted to hold a single fucking thought besides *kiss her.*

"Good," she parroted, the harness falling to the seat. "Then I guess we agree." She rested her hands on my chest, her fingers fisting the material of my sweater.

"We agree." My hands found her hips and I squeezed, pulling her against me even though I knew it was a bad idea. Maybe I was just beyond caring.

"Totally agree." She slid one hand up over my shoulder to the back of my neck.

I lowered my head. I was a compass, and she was north. I was powerless to fight whatever this was between us.

My lips brushed hers once. Twice.

"This is a bad idea," I warned her. "We both know it."

"Just kiss me, Weston." She pulled me down, and I went willingly, unleashing weeks of want and need.

I took her mouth without preamble, sweeping inside with my tongue to reclaim everything I'd sworn off touching again in the name of safety.

Fuck that. This was too powerful to ignore.

We both knew it.

My hand tunneled through her hair, gripping just enough to tilt her for a deeper kiss. It wasn't just as good as the first time, it was better. Her nails bit into the back of my neck and the little whimper that caught in her throat was going to be the death of me.

I wanted to hear that sound over and over again.

She sucked on my tongue and I groaned, filling my hand with her ass I shifted us to the bench seat in the center of the helicopter. Lying her down made the most sense if I was going to kiss her in here, so I did it, my mouth never leaving hers as she met each stroke of my tongue. It was all about her comfort.

Liar.

I wanted between her thighs, and that's exactly where I found myself, bracing my weight with one hand on the frame of the bird above her head so I didn't crush her. She locked her legs around my hips, and the need that had been gathering near the base of my spine grew tenfold.

I kissed a path down her neck, pausing at the spot that made her writhe, and grinned when she sucked in a breath, her hands tightening in my hair. "You like that."

"Yes." She rocked up against me, and I cursed the layers of clothing between us even as I thanked God they were there.

"And this?" I flicked open the buttons on her shirt one by one, caressing each inch of bare skin with my mouth as it was revealed.

"Yes."

"What about this?" I kissed the swells of her breasts when the next button opened over her bra, revealing delicate blue lace cups and the creamiest skin I'd ever seen.

"Yes!" She guided my head to her breast, and I took absolute advantage, pushing the peak high above the cup and swirling my tongue over her nipple.

She gasped, and I sucked her between my lips, raking her nipple lightly with my teeth. Then I gave the same treatment to the other as my hand kept the first one warm. The weight of her felt so good in my palm, and the way she responded to every kiss, every touch, had my dick throbbing with its own demand.

I couldn't take her. Not here. Not like this.

But her body was giving me every green light, arching

against mine, trembling under me as I kissed down her stomach. Her breathing went wild as the last of the buttons fell to the side, leaving her bare from the waist up.

"You're gorgeous," I said, lifting my head so I could see her.

Her lips were swollen, her breasts full and rose-tipped from my mouth. She was the picture of every fantasy, looking at me with lust-glazed eyes. "I want you."

"Callie." Her name was a groan I barely recognized.

"Weston," she begged, rolling her hips. "I want you."

"It's too damned cold in here to strip you naked the way I want." My mouth brushed the waistband of her jeans. It was probably only sixty or so in here, even with the heated hangar.

"I don't care what you strip." Her eyes met mine, and the pure desire I saw there echoed every demand my own body was making.

I prowled up her body, taking the same path I had before, buttoning her shirt as I went, torturing us both with what we couldn't have. Then I kissed her breathless, taking her mouth over and over again, until the friction and heat between us was a fire all on its own.

"I can't stop kissing you," I admitted, my hand pinning her hip to the seat so I could grind against her. The pressure was too much and not enough. Everything about this was too much and not enough.

"Then don't." She bit my lower lip and reached between us, palming my dick and squeezing through the fabric of my jeans.

"Calliope." Her name was a strangled mess between my lips.

"Please." She stroked the length of me. "Don't think. Don't reason. Just be here with me, Weston."

I wanted her too damn much to say no, but I wasn't about to give her a quickie in the most uncomfortable setting known to man. But leaving her wanting wasn't an option.

I flicked open the button on her jeans. "You have to let go of me or this isn't going to work," I said against her mouth.

"I don't want to let go." She ran her tongue over my lower lip, then sucked at it.

"I'll make it worth your while," I promised, lowering her zipper.

She rocked against my hand.

If she squeezed me one more time, I was going to throw all my noble ideals right out of this bird and fuck her on the bench. She had my control teetering on the edge of oblivion.

I grazed my fingers along the elastic of her underwear. I glanced down. The sight was the hottest thing I'd ever seen. Blue lace, just like her bra. "You're going to need to say yes if you want my fingers any lower."

"Yes. Yes. Yes." Her eyes locked with mine.

I slid my fingers through the strip of curls and then growled at the feel of her, hot and slick. "Damn, Calliope. You are so ready for me, aren't you?" She felt like liquid fire, and I knew I'd slide inside her with one thrust. *Not here. Not like this.*

She gasped as my fingertips grazed her clit, and she let go of me, both of her hands flying to my shoulders.

I slid down her body, my knees hitting the floorboards.

"What are you doing?" she asked as I slipped out of her reach.

"Keeping my promise." My gaze locked with hers, I angled her hips and lowered my mouth to that scrap of lace, pushing my tongue against the fabric to press against her clit.

She cried out, arching her back. "Take them off!" Her feet planted on the edge of the bench, and she lifted her hips.

I hooked my fingers in the waist of her jeans and the straps of her underwear, then worked the fabric down her legs, leaving them bunched at the top of her boots. Then I dragged her to the edge of the bench, spread her thighs with my hands, and put my mouth on her.

The sound of her moan singed itself into my memory.

I worked her with my tongue, alternating light flicks and circles around her clit. Sweet...she was so fucking sweet.

"Weston!" Her nails raked over my scalp.

That was exactly how I wanted to hear her say my name for the rest of...ever. I used every trick I'd ever learned, pushing her toward orgasm but keeping her on the edge. Every thought revolved around how to make her whimper, cataloging what had her keening, and how to make this last longer. Any second the logic would return and remind me why we shouldn't be doing this—I had to make this last.

Her back arched when I speared my tongue inside her, and her breaths came at ragged intervals. She was close. I could feel it in the tension of her thighs, the higher pitch of the cries she tried to muffle with her own fist.

I replaced my tongue with one finger, then two, thrusting inside her in the same rhythm I would have used with my cock —hard and slow. She squeezed me tight, and I moaned, my lips against her clit, the vibrations making her legs clench.

She was right there.

Her thighs gripped my head, and her hands held me against her. I used the flat of my tongue to press and scrape that sensitive bundle of nerves as her hips rocked, taking what she needed, riding my fingers and mouth. I looked up and our eyes locked.

She was the sexiest woman I'd ever seen, half-clothed, her skin flushed, and the desperation in her eyes had me second-guessing my decision not to take every last inch of her in this helicopter.

She came with a muffled cry, her body arching up as the waves took her over and over.

My body screamed, demanding the same release, but I shut it down, somehow managing to leash what had become an uncontrollable desire. I softened my strokes, bringing her down until she fell limp against the bench, her chest heaving as she sucked in breath after breath.

"Oh. My. God." She propped herself up on her elbows and looked down at me. "What was that?"

"That was...us." I'd never craved anyone the way I did her.

Her body shivered from head to toe, and I cursed. It was too fucking cold for this in here. "Come here." I held out my hands and she took them. Once I had her on her feet, I dragged her underwear and jeans up her incredible legs. There was still so much of her to explore, to taste.

"Weston, let's finish this," she whispered.

"It's too—"

A phone alarm went off, and Callie startled, turning around to find her discarded cell on the bench. "It's my reminder to pick up Sutton."

"See? This is not the time." There was a slight tremble in my hands as I dragged her zipper up and fastened the button of her jeans. Then I found my feet and got out of the helicopter, where I could stand without hunching over. My dick pressed at the fabric of my pants, throbbing in time with my pulse, but I put my hands behind my neck, closed my eyes, and willed it to stop.

It didn't.

"But there is going to be a time, right?" Callie climbed out of the bird, and when I opened my eyes, she was standing in front of me. There was too much going on in her expression, in her eyes, to get a read on what she was feeling. There was satisfaction and want, but a touch of unease that hit me in the stomach.

"This wasn't a quid pro quo thing, Callie," I assured her, taking her face in my hands. "Nothing that happened in there has to be paid back, or anything. You don't owe me, if that's what you're thinking." What had happened in there had been a sweet, reckless form of madness that I could barely explain to myself.

"No." She shook her head. "I mean, I want you." She gripped

my sweater and pulled me closer. "I know all the reasons I shouldn't. I know it could make everything at home awkward as hell, but ignoring it has us going at it in the helicopter. What's next? The lift?"

"Yeah, that was pretty intense." And *shit*, now I was thinking of her straddling me on the lift.

"So tell me we won't ignore it. Tell me I can have you." She rose up on her toes and pressed a soft kiss to my lips. "Even if it's just once."

My control slipped, and I kissed her hard until her hands were around my neck, and mine were on her ass, pulling her closer, forgetting where we were again. "Are you trying to tell me I'm the anything in your 'try anything once' mantra?" I asked against her mouth.

"I think you're the *everything* in that philosophy," she muttered as her cell phone blared again. "Crap. I really have to go."

"Go." I dropped my hands and stepped back.

"Say yes." She silenced the alarm and slid it back into her pocket, raising her chin in challenge as she stared me down. "We can't screw everything up if it's just once, right?"

"Because you think we can stop at only once." I cocked an eyebrow at her. A single taste of her and I was already jonesing for another hit, and she thought we'd make once work? "I swear, if you say it's to get it out of our systems—"

She laughed. "I'm not that foolish, West. But I think we either give into this thing once or we risk spontaneous combustion in the house we happen to share." She started backing away toward the exit. "Say yes. Don't leave me hanging out here on the limb alone. Unless you really don't want me. Then I guess the idea is moot anyway."

I would have traded my wings for a single night with her.

"Once," I agreed.

She grinned and walked away.

allie

"I CAN'T BELIEVE I let you talk me into this," I muttered as the lift climbed the smallest slope at Madigan. It was silent, and not the kind of quiet that was sporadically interrupted by skiers below on an average day—the kind of silence that made me feel like we were the only ones on the slopes, period.

Because we were.

"You can't take the action shots you want to without knowing how to ski," Weston argued next to me, his goggles on his forehead. The early morning sun was behind us, so those golden flecks in his eyes weren't as obvious, but I could still see them as he smiled at me.

"Sure you can. I take pictures of weddings all the time, and yet I've never gotten married. Experience isn't necessary to capture something," I countered.

When he suggested we do this last night, I told him he'd lost his mind.

Then he presented me with skis, poles, boots, bindings—the whole lot—and I wavered. He'd even gotten me shorter skis so I'd have better *control*, as he called it. No one had ever put that kind of care into anything for me before.

Usually, when someone tried to coax me out of my comfort zone, I shoved them fully out of my immediate surroundings. But there had been something in his eyes, a boyish excitement, that I'd been unable to deny.

Or maybe it was just that he'd completely left my brain addled after he devoured me in the helicopter like I was his dinner *and* dessert. The man had a tongue that should have been declared a national treasure. Monuments should have been built. Monuments that only I would have access to, but still.

Don't get possessive. I'd repeated that phrase in my head every few minutes for the past twelve or so hours, and yet it wasn't helping.

Weston was just my roommate. A roommate with a godlike tongue and hands that were made for giving out orgasms like candy, but still...just my roommate. At least in his eyes. Here I was, crushing so hard on the man that I had clipped myself into long, aerodynamic sticks and was about to hurl myself down the mountain just to see him smile.

But he'd promised me I'd be able to do other things I knew would leave him smiling. Even if it was only once, I'd get to have Weston in my bed.

"But think of how it will change your perspective when shooting," Weston said.

Crap, what were we talking about? Skiing. Right. I needed to pull my head out of the orgasmic bliss he'd left me in yesterday and concentrate.

"I somehow doubt you're going to teach me to backcountry ski in a morning," I teased.

"Oh, no, we're strictly bunny-skiing this morning." He motioned to the empty slope beneath us as the lift neared the end. "But if you understand how the skier's body is moving, you'll be able to anticipate for your shots. You'll know what angle you want to be at. You'll be able to tell me exactly where you want me to fly so you can capture what you want."

"I'd like to capture you," I muttered. This was never going to work if I couldn't concentrate on anything but his voice, his hands, his...everything.

He reached toward me, gripped the base of my neck, and tilted my head, swooping in for a hard, fast kiss that left me stunned and a little more than turned on. "Concentrate," he whispered.

Then he lifted the bar as we approached the end of the lift.

"I'm going to fall off this stupid thing."

"No, you're not." He lowered his hand to my waist and gripped. "Just trust me."

I did. That was the only reason I was up here at eight o'clock in the freaking morning on a Monday. We'd dropped Sutton off at school a half hour ago, and now I was getting ready to land on my ass in front of the sole liftie up here, who had the nerve to wave to us as we approached certain doom.

"One, two," Weston started, pulling me closer. "Three. Stand." We stood, but my skis never touched the ground. Weston held me anchored to him, holding me to his side, well off the ground as he skied off the lift effortlessly.

"That's cheating," I muttered as he set me down at the top of the bunny slope.

"Maybe it was just an excuse to get my hands on you." He winked.

The. Man. *Winked*.

"Who *are* you?" The serious guy I'd written our contract for —on the lines—would never have winked.

He simply laughed in response. "Okay, so this is just the bunny bowl."

"More like the slaughterhouse," I muttered.

He rolled his eyes. "And as you can see, we're the only ones up here. There are no children to roll over, no adults to petrify, no one to bear witness to whatever happens."

I stuck my poles in the snow. "So what you're saying is that we're alone for the first time since..." Flames rushed up my cheeks. "And you want to use this time to ski."

He moved behind me, his skis outside mine, and he brought his mouth to my ear, our helmets lightly touching. "The first time since I put my head between your thighs and licked you until you came?" he whispered.

"Weston." Heat flooded my entire body.

"That's what happened, right?" He tugged my earlobe between his teeth. "If I only get you once, Calliope, then there's not going to be any room for shyness."

My lungs filled with a shuddering breath. "And if you keep talking like that, we'll melt the snow on this entire mountain."

He turned my head, angled his, and kissed me. Long, slow, thorough strokes of his tongue had me clutching him in a matter of seconds. "I'm not against that either." He pulled away with another soft kiss. "Though, we're not exactly alone. Jules is over there running the lift for us," he reminded me.

"Right." I shook my head. "Because it's completely logical to shut down an entire mountain so you can teach your...your roommate how to ski."

"First, I didn't shut down the mountain. I asked two lifties to run the lift an hour before opening for the day. Two, if she saw me kiss you, then I highly doubt she thinks you're just my roommate."

"Not helping!" I stared down the hill of death. "And how is this the easiest slope we have?"

"You're going to be okay," he promised me. "I won't let anything bad happen to you."

"And if I land on my ass?" I cocked a brow at him.

He lowered my goggles so they covered my eyes. "Then I'll kiss it and make it all better later."

"Stop distracting me with your sexual promises and your....you-ness."

"But it's fun. And I think I remember someone telling me I needed to smile more." He angled his skis, pushing the fronts together to form a triangle. "This is a snowplow."

"I know it's a snowplow," I grumbled. "Just because I don't ski doesn't mean I don't live here. I've watched Sutton, you know."

"Okay, then you know it's the easiest, slowest way to come down the hill. Pick up your poles."

"Why didn't you bring poles?" I grabbed mine by the handle.

"Because it's the bunny slope. I don't need poles. You don't either, but you wanted them, so here we are." He sounded so calm, so relaxed, like we weren't about to hurl ourselves down a slippery sheet of groomed snow and call it fun. Like we weren't pressed against each other.

I wanted him to feel just as frazzled, as distracted by me as I was by him.

"Now, we're going to start down the hill, but instead of going straight, we're going to cut across the slope side to side, turning at each end, okay?" His hands gripped my waist. "And I'm right here. We'll pause about halfway down and see if you're ready to try it on your own, and if you're not, then that's okay."

So. Freaking. Calm. Didn't anything ruffle Weston Madigan's feathers?

"Let's get this over with." I was resigned to my fate. If I fell and took him down in the process, then that was his own fault.

"Okay." He pushed forward and we leaned slightly to turn,

slowly crossing the slope at an almost perpendicular angle. "See? This isn't so bad, right?"

"We're not going *down* the hill," I reminded him, holding onto my poles like they might save my life.

"All in good time, Callie. Just get comfortable."

He surrounded me in every way. His skis caged mine, keeping them at the appropriate angle. His arms were locked around me, anchoring my back to his chest. His body curved around mine so his mouth was at my ear. I was totally and completely safe because Weston was in total, complete control.

I relaxed.

"Good, now we're going to lift a little with our right foot and lean into the left so we turn."

My ski skidded, but he kept me locked in tight, pivoting to face the direction we came. The turn had eaten up the most vertical distance we'd conquered.

"You're doing great." We glided across the slope, and Weston turned us so we traveled downward a little more, picking up a slight speed but nothing that froze me with fear. "Turn again." We shifted our weight, the opposite of how we'd done the first time, and executed the turn. "Perfect. See? You didn't even slip there."

"Because you're holding me," I argued, but a smile pulled at my lips.

"Perks of the job." We made it across the slope at the same steady speed. "There you go. Lean into it, but keep your balance. You're in full control," he told me as we turned again. His grip loosened slightly. "You have the athleticism for it. You just need to remember that you tell your skis where to go, not vice versa."

"And if I skid out on the turn and go straight down?" I challenged as we approached the edge again.

"Then keep your skis angled just like this, and your rate of descent will slow. If you fall, you fall. Everyone falls. Sutton falls. I fall. Even my little brother falls, and that kid has too many X Games medals to count. You just have to get back up."

We made another turn, and he angled us a little more steeply, his arms loosening even more.

"Ready to try it on your own?" he asked, stopping us midway across the slope.

"Why? I mean, if it's easy with you, then maybe this is just how I ski, with you attached to me."

He laughed softly, the sound spreading through me like a wildfire. I loved the sound of his laugh. If I was being honest, I loved that I was one of the few people he chose to laugh around.

"I'll be right here." He let me go, and I immediately missed the warmth, the security of him. "Not that I'm against being attached to you, but skiing is one of the most empowering things I've ever done besides flying, and I want you to know you're a badass all on your own." He stepped sideways uphill, then maneuvered himself in front of me, angling his skis in a backward version of my own.

"Badass and bunny bowl do not belong in the same sentence," I argued, noting that we were halfway down the hill.

"They do for the first few times."

I scoffed but followed his lead as we made our way across the slope.

"Good," he said. "Now same thing. Lift that left ski a little, lean into the right, and make the turn."

My heart galloped, but I did it and had the added bonus of not falling on my face.

"Excellent!" He grinned at me.

"Says the man who's going backward," I muttered. Every muscle in my body was tense and active. I was hyperaware of everything—my balance, my skis, the very angle of the slope— and he was skiing backward like it was as easy as walking.

"Hey, I learned on this very same hill." He glanced behind him. "Another turn."

"Who taught you?" I leaned and moved, executing the turn. Had to say, it was a lot easier this time without some three-year-old flying past me with the expertise of an Olympian.

"My dad," he answered, his jaw muscle popping. "But I didn't catch on quickly enough for him. Not like Reed. So, my mom took over. That woman had the patience of a saint."

We pivoted through another turn. "So you didn't have that reckless second-son energy I hear so much about from other parents?"

"Oh." He grinned. "I had it. Just took me until the age of five to figure out I could ski out of bounds. Reed wanted speed. Crew liked to flip around. I just wanted to carve my own path, to follow only the rules I set for myself."

"You do like your rules." I somehow found myself smiling through the next turn.

"I keep breaking them for you," he said softly.

"Hey now," I challenged. "So far, we've only broken *my* rules on that list. Well, except I did make you dinner one night. But the rest of the broken ones are all mine."

"You've only seen a fraction of the rules I keep for myself," he replied with a wicked little smile.

We made it through another turn. Weston's arms were at his side, his whole body relaxed like this was a spa trip, his eyes teasing through the tinted shield of his goggles. Nothing phased this man.

"Sutton is spending the night at Betty's tonight," I said as we neared the bottom of the slope.

He cocked his head to the side.

"That means we'll be alone." I smiled. "All night. Alone."

He slipped, his whole body wobbling before he straightened his skis and caught his balance, coming to a complete standstill.

I laughed as I passed by him, then slowly made a turn all on my own. I fought off the urge to fist pump. Like hell was I doing anything to lose my balance now.

He caught up to me easily, moving so quickly I couldn't help but stare in appreciation as he cut down the slope and sprayed snow everywhere in a quick stop a few feet below me but out of my path. So controlled. So precise.

Guess *one* thing got to him, and it was me.

I was more than okay with that.

I LEANED up against the kitchen island in what I hoped was a seductive pose and watched the door. It was five thirty, Sutton was already at Betty's, and I'd just heard Weston's truck pull into our driveway.

My pulse leapt. There wasn't exactly an extensive collection of lingerie at my disposal, but I did have a soft spot for pretty, matching underwear sets, so I'd put on my favorite lavender one and hoped he'd like it.

Fine, I more than hoped. I sent up a prayer to whatever God had made a man as utterly indescribable as Weston. If I only got to have this man once, then I wanted him as completely lost for me as I was for him.

Now I just had to hope that the silk robe Ava had given me for Christmas two years ago was enough to cut through whatever awkwardness there might be after I'd pretty much told him this morning that tonight was the night.

His footsteps sounded outside the door, and I swallowed the knot of anticipation in my throat.

I'd had all day to think about the things I wanted to do to him—the things I wanted *him* to do to me. I felt like a thoroughbred racehorse, just waiting to be let out of the stall, warmed up and ready to be—

Okay, that was enough horse analogies.

The door handle turned and a stab of anxiety tightened my stomach. Had I forgotten anything? I'd shaved my legs. Washed my hair. I'd even taken off an hour early so I could paint my toenails.

What if he had changed his mind? What if he took one look at me and laughed about me trying too hard. Shit. *Was* I trying too hard?

The door opened and Weston walked in, a blustery wave of snow following before he shut the door. Guess the storm had started. He turned, taking off his hat and unzipping his coat while juggling a bottle of wine.

He froze the second he saw me.

His hat fluttered to the tile entry.

Our eyes met across the room and his jaw dropped, then snapped shut and clenched as his gaze raked over me from the top of my head to the tips of my painted toes. The heat there was unmistakable, making my thighs clench.

"I thought you might want to order dinner." His coat hit the floor as he walked toward me.

I shook my head.

"Wine?" He lifted the bottle.

"Nope."

He set it on the dining room table and kept coming. "Anything you do want?"

"Just you." I reached for the belt holding my robe together, but he was already against me, his hands sweeping down my back to grab my ass as he kissed me.

His tongue stroked into my mouth, and I whimpered. He tasted like mint and Weston. My arms wound around his neck, and he lifted me to the counter, setting me at the edge. My thighs parted. He moved between them, the rough denim abrading the sensitive skin of my inner thighs with delicious friction.

"I like you like this." His hands stroked up my thighs, skimming under the satin robe.

"All prepped and waiting for you?" I teased.

"All *mine.*" His hands reached my hips and he yanked me forward, crushing his mouth to mine. It wasn't sweet or slow. It was all tongues and teeth and need left too long unsatisfied. He'd brought me to climax yesterday, but that wasn't enough. I wanted *him.*

I needed to know what it felt like to have him inside me, how he moved, how he sounded when he came. I needed it all.

His hand tangled in my hair, and he moved my head, angling it for a deeper kiss. I pressed flush against him, locking my ankles at the small of his back and gave just as much as he was giving. Every nerve ending in my body was alive, reveling in the glide of his tongue with mine, the press of his fingers into the flesh of my hip, the slight sting at my scalp when he tugged gently.

"Off," I demanded, grabbing the bottom of his Henley.

He reached behind his head and tugged it over and off, dropping it to the side.

"Weston." It was all I could say as my fingers traced the lines of his pecs and down the carved ridges of his abs. For weeks, I'd watched him. For *weeks*, I'd wanted him, stared at him, craved the feel of his skin beneath my fingertips. He was velvet-soft skin over miles of hard muscle, and my mouth watered to taste every inch.

"Keep looking at me like that, and we won't make it upstairs." His voice sounded like it had been scraped over sandpaper.

"I'm okay with that." I didn't care where, only when, and when was *now.*

"I'm not." He ducked his head and kissed my neck, toying with my skin like it was the start button to my sex drive. He didn't know I'd been primed all day, counting down the minutes, waiting for him. "If we're only doing this once, then it's going to be in a bed, Calliope. Where I can stretch you out and take you in every way I've imagined."

"You haven't imagined the kitchen counter?" My fingers toyed with the button of his jeans. "Because I have. Every time you're in here cooking, I think about what it would feel like to have you just like this."

He groaned, his teeth nipping the joint between my shoulder and neck, sending a shiver of pure pleasure down my spine. "Fuck yes, I've thought about it." His hand slid across my back and to my ribs before he brushed his thumb over my nipple. "I've pictured you on this very counter, laid out like a feast."

"See? Counters are good." I flicked open his button.

"Agreed, but I can't feel you under me on a counter." He palmed my breast. "And that's what I want, Callie. I need you under me." His hands retreated to my ass, and he lifted me against him, stepping back and carrying me fully. "Your room or mine?"

"No difference. You can put me against the wall for all I care, as long as I get to have you." I kissed his jaw, his ear, his throat.

"Fuck." His grip tightened. "My room. I have condoms."

"Good idea. And I'm on birth control," I said as we started to move, but I was too busy sucking on the little area right beneath his ear to look where we were going. "And it's been about a year."

"A little less for me, but I'm clean," he promised, and I felt us climbing the stairs.

"I trust you." Our mouths met as he opened the door to his hallway, and then my back was against the wall, as if he couldn't take another step without kissing the breath from my lungs. He rocked against me, and I felt him hard and heavy between my thighs, my robe slipping so it was just his jeans against the fabric of my thong.

I used the wall for leverage and rolled back, grinding down on him.

The sound that came from his throat could only be described as a growl, and I loved it. Gone was the rigid, rule-oriented man who kept everything in its place. This Weston was hard in all the right places, but just as wild and needy as I was.

He yanked me off the wall and kicked open the door to his room. I didn't even have time to look around before I was on my back in the middle of his bed, and he was over me, his hips between my thighs.

A tug, and he had my belt undone, the halves of my robe sliding off me completely.

The heat in his eyes said more than a million words could have as he looked me over, obviously liking what he found. I wanted to purr under that gaze, to stretch and show every curve of my body at its best angle.

"You're incredible," he said, sitting back on his heels to pull me into a sitting position. "I've never wanted anyone this way." He slipped the robe off completely.

"What way is that?" I went for his zipper.

He kissed me hard, setting me back down on the bed. "Like I'll die from needing you. You're a fucking obsession, Calliope. I think about you when I'm flying, when I'm guiding, when I'm lying here in this bed and you're just a wall away. I never stop thinking about you."

I whimpered in reply and kissed him harder because I felt the exact same way.

His boots came off. Then his pants. There were fewer layers between us than ever and still it was too much. I pushed his shoulder, and he got the message, rolling to his back.

Straddling his hips, I let my hands trace every line I'd fantasized about, then followed them with my mouth. His muscles tensed underneath me, and he tunneled his fingers through my hair, his grip light as I kissed down his chest, letting my tongue play across the disks of his nipples before venturing lower.

"I swear, you're photoshopped," I muttered, trailing my tongue down the path of his abs. "No one looks this good—feels this good naturally."

He laughed, but the sound was tense and choppy as I reached the elastic waist of his boxer briefs. I already knew his size, his length, from holding him in the helicopter, but my thighs clenched at the sight of him straining against the material, the head of him pushing at the band.

I lowered my lips and swiped my tongue over that exposed inch.

"Fuck!" His hips bucked.

I'd never felt so powerful in my entire life. I raked my teeth over him through the fabric of his underwear and the result was instant. He grabbed me under my arms and hauled me up the length of his body, then flipped so he was above me.

"You can't do that if you want this to last," he warned, his eyes darker than I'd ever seen them as he pressed into me.

I gasped, angling my hips so he'd rock against the one place I desperately needed friction. "But I want to." If he'd lost it with one lick, what would he do if I took him deep?

"And trust me, I want you to." His hand slid under my back, and he unfastened my bra. "But we said *once*, and I want that once to last all damned night." My bra flew toward the floor. "You put your mouth on me, and this will be over before it begins. I need you too much."

I parted my lips to remind him that he'd had his mouth on *me*, and turnabout was fair play, but then he lowered his head to my breasts, and I forgot every word in my head. He licked and sucked until both peaks were swollen and red, sensitive to even a whisper of air from his lips.

Then he locked eyes with me and reached for my thong.

I nodded and lifted my hips.

He dragged the fabric down my thighs and over my knees and ankles. Then I was completely bare.

"Damn," he muttered, his gaze roaming and lingering. "Just… damn." He kissed a path up my legs, teasing my inner thigh before starting again at the other ankle. He found erogenous zones I didn't even know I had and played there, lighting me on fire one kiss, one touch, at a time.

I was a puddle by the time he made it to the apex of my thighs, and with one lick, I completely melted into the bed.

"Weston," I groaned as sensation took over. My heart beat for the next stroke of his tongue. My lungs drew air only to exhale in moans of appreciation. I existed only at the pleasure of this man.

"Addictive." He slid his fingers inside me. "I knew it from the first taste. You're fucking addictive."

My head thrashed as he worked me over with tongue, teeth, and fingers, building that coiling pleasure with an expert skill that had me grasping at his head, his sheets, looking for something, anything to hold me to the earth. I slammed a hand over my mouth and shouted.

"Not tonight." He reached up and tugged at my elbow. "I want to hear every single scream."

Then he drew those screams from me with the flicks of his tongue and the strokes of his fingers. He constructed my orgasm like an architect and then sent me into oblivion. The first ripple made my entire body arch up for his, the edges of my vision going blurry as I came, and came, and came, each wave pulling me under and drowning me in white-hot pleasure.

Finally, I collapsed under him, but the hunger didn't die, it only grew, and I was ravenous for him.

I reached for him, and his boxer briefs came off.

The nightstand drawer opened, and there was a rip of foil.

Then he was over me, his eyes locked with mine, the head of him resting at my entrance, right where I needed him.

He balanced his weight on one hand and held my face with the other as I drew my knees up to cradle his hips. "Tell me this is what you want."

"And you'll give it to me?" I teased, my fingers tracing his cheeks, his lips, his jaw, memorizing every detail of his features.

"Tell me, Calliope." The muscles in his jaw flexed, and I saw it, the complete and utter restraint he was using in this moment for me.

"I want this, Weston." I leaned up and kissed him. "I want you."

He groaned in answer and thrust forward, stretching me, filling me with one long push of his hips.

I gasped at the feel of him, the slight burn accompanied by a pulsing pleasure.

"Holy shit." He buried his face in my neck, giving me a second to adjust, for my body to ease and accommodate. "You feel so fucking good."

I rocked my hips, and the inch I lost and gained was exquisite.

"You okay?" he asked, lifting up so he could see me.

"I'll be better once you start moving."

He grinned, then withdrew almost to the tip and drove back inside me.

I saw the stars.

"Like that?" He kissed the tip of my nose, then my lips.

"Exactly like that." I scraped my nails down his back, and he moaned.

Then his hips set a rhythm, deep and slow, and my world narrowed to Weston. Only Weston. I rocked back when he withdrew, and arched up to meet every thrust, our bodies colliding over and over. Each thrust was better, sweeter, taking me so deep I felt him from the tips of my fingers to my toes. He owned every part of me, and I loved it.

I loved the wild intensity in his eyes.

I loved the strain of his muscles against mine.

I loved that he watched me, changing his angle, his rhythm, doing whatever made me mindless with pleasure.

Oh God, I was falling for him.

My heart seized and I pulled him down for a kiss, pouring

every feeling into it as if I could siphon the emotions off, bury them in the heat, the lust.

"I want this to last forever," he said, his hips jerking, that coiling tension within me building yet again. "I want you in every way possible."

He slid out of me, and before I could cry at the loss, at the empty feeling he'd left behind, he flipped me to my stomach and pulled me up on my knees.

I arched my back, lifting my ass for him, and he thrust home, taking me even deeper than before. Each stroke had me keening, the sounds from my mouth indecipherable as he drove into me again and again.

"Not. Close. Enough," he said, each word punctuated by the drive of his hips. He reached forward and gripped my waist, pulling me upward until my back rested against his chest, my knees bracketing his, unable to reach the bed.

"Weston!" I cried out at the deeper fit.

"Calliope," he answered, tipping my face toward his with his fingers, then kissing me deep as he moved within me.

His hands were on my waist, my hips, raising and dropping me back onto him in time with his thrusts. I stroked his waist, his neck, whatever I could reach. Our bodies glided, slick with sweat, and he only broke the kiss when we both struggled to breathe, our pulses racing.

"I'm...I'm..." I couldn't even get the words out. Everything within me drew tight, all centered exactly where we were connected, and he brought his fingers to my clit.

"I know. Me. Too." His breath came in pants against my lips, and his fingers pushed me right over the edge, the second orgasm making my body lock, then let go as the pleasure of it blinded me.

I cried out again, but this time it was his name, and I felt him jolt inside me as he found his own release, his mouth on mine.

We breathed the same air as we came down, our chests

heaving as he lowered us to the bed, tucking me against him as the sun set through the window.

"That was..." I shook my head.

"It was," he agreed, his hand stroking up and down my side, soothing and yet inflaming with the same touch.

I wanted to cry when he slid out of me, to demand that time rewind so I could experience that again, so I could live in the moment we'd just surrendered to. But time didn't work like that.

He kissed my shoulder, and I rolled to my back so I could look up at him.

The gold flecks in his eyes caught the light, and my heart ached as I soaked in everything about him. I'd never seen him look so at peace, so happy. "You're beautiful."

"You're drunk on sex and orgasms," he replied with a grin.

And now he was even *more* beautiful.

I drew my tongue across my swollen lower lip, and he groaned, bending down to kiss me.

Just like that, I wanted him again. I wanted everything there could be between us.

"I want you on top of me next time," he growled against my lips. "I want these in my hands as you ride me." He cupped my breast, his thumb flicking over my nipple.

"I thought we were only doing this once." I turned fully to face him.

"Give me one night." The look in his eyes had me arching closer.

"And then what? You'll let me go?" My fingers drifted from his neck down his chest.

Two lines formed between his eyebrows. "I make no promises."

"You can have whatever you want, Weston." I lifted my knee over his hip.

He nodded. Then he started the taking all over again.

eston

WORKING ON THANKSGIVING SUCKED, but there was no rest when it came to a ski resort on a holiday weekend. It was the reason dinner was scheduled for eight p.m. tonight.

I set the bird down on the ridgeline to the south of Madigan Mountain. "Go time," I said through my headset.

Theo opened the sliding door and ushered the guests out onto the snow-covered peak, reminding them to keep their heads low and move away from the helicopter. Once they were out, I headed to the rear, leaving the rotors spinning, and motioned toward Callie, who had taken the farthest seat in the back next to Sutton.

"You ready for this?" I asked through the headset.

She turned toward Sutton. "Promise me you won't leave that seat."

"Promise!" Sutton said through a headset of her own.

Callie sucked in a deep breath as she brought her eyes to mine, moving past the center bench to where I waited.

She was already wearing the harness, which had taken minutes for me to buckle her into back in the hangar. Minutes where I'd used it as an excuse to caress the curve of her waist and brush the insides of her thighs with my fingers.

I'd held true to our *one night* promise and kept my hands off her for three days.

Three very long days and torturously eternal nights.

The problem—and the perk—of fucking Callie all night long in my bed? It still smelled like her. I'd gone to sleep with a hard-on for two nights and woken up the same way.

We'd gone at it four times, and it hadn't been enough. There was a small but infinitely loud part of me that wouldn't stop screaming it would never be enough. I'd taken her in my bed twice, in the shower once—that turned into against the wall— and back to my bed. And yet I still found myself staring at every surface I came across, making plans for how I'd bend her over it.

And the worst part was that she looked at me like she was thinking the exact same way.

We hadn't gotten it out of our systems, or even fallen into awkwardness...we'd just cranked up the heat on a chemistry experiment we both knew was going to explode.

"You promise you won't dump me out of this helicopter?" she asked, her eyes wide and nervous.

"I'd never dump you out of anything," I said before I could stop myself.

Her eyebrows rose.

"Here." I clipped one end of the strap into the hook above the door and locked it into place, yanking hard. "See? That's not going anywhere." Then I wrapped my arm around her waist and pulled her forward. Our lower bodies collided, and I clipped her in at the ring in the back of the harness. "You're not going anywhere you don't want to."

She swallowed and leaned into me, only her camera between our bodies.

Every nerve in my body zinged.

Yeah, one night was an appetizer with this woman.

"This is going to be so cool!" Sutton said.

I cleared my throat and stepped back. "We have five skiers out there, including Theo, and they'll all take turns dropping in. You just tell me if you want to go higher or lower, and I'll make that happen for you."

"I have no doubt you will." She gifted me with a flirtatious smile and picked up her camera from where it hung on her neck strap.

I shook my head at her and looked out the window. Theo had cleared the gear from the basket and was waiting with the others. It took a second or two to climb back behind the controls and buckle in. "You ready out there?" I asked Theo.

"Whenever you are," he replied.

"Hold on, Callie," I warned, my hands on the controls and my feet resting on the pedals.

"Already holding. Been holding. Not going to stop holding," she muttered.

I grinned as I took off, pitching us down to the left, then leveling out. Flying at altitude was a bitch, but this bird had the power needed to hold the hover in the thinner air. A helicopter needed two out of three elements to pull off a maneuver: power, speed, and/or altitude.

Hovering left us with zero speed, but I had both the power and altitude on my side if something went wrong.

"We're dropping in," Theo said through the radio.

I looked over to see the first skier taking his chosen fall line. There was a twenty-foot drop a little way down, so I lowered us to that marker and held her steady.

Callie clutched the frame of the helicopter with one hand for the first skier, clicking away as he took the cliff.

She leaned against it on the next, the strap giving her about a half foot of leeway.

She stood in the doorway for the third.

By the time Theo came down, she was leaning out of the door, the strap carrying her slight weight as she snapped picture after picture.

She came back in and grinned at me over her shoulder. "That's incredible!"

"We'll have to get you a longer strap."

"You're a badass, Mom!" Sutton exclaimed.

"Language!" Callie shouted, but there was laughter in her tone.

"I want to do that run next time!"

"We'll work up to it," I promised.

"Then I can compete in big mountain?" Her voice practically bubbled with excitement.

"Stop pushing the envelope, Sutton," Callie warned.

"Had to try," Sutton muttered.

We landed at the bottom of the valley, and I made my way back to Callie as Theo and the skiers muddled our way, keeping as low as possible.

"You are a phenomenal pilot," Callie said as I pulled her against my chest, her eyes bright when I swept my hand down her back to the loop at the rear of the harness.

"That was absolutely nothing. And Sutton's right, you know." I glanced over the seats and saw Sutton's back to us as she stared out the window, watching the skiers approach. I took blatant advantage of the millisecond and stole a kiss. "You are a badass."

I unclipped her and headed back to the controls before either of us could question me crossing that boundary.

But I didn't regret it.

"WE CAN LEAVE the second you're uncomfortable," Callie promised later that night, cradling a bottle of wine over her coat as she rang the doorbell at Reed's house. The second I'd gotten a peek at the dark-blue wrap dress she was rocking, we nearly had to cancel our dinner plans. It came to just above her knees, and the sight of her bare legs had me hard in about two heartbeats.

I was in major trouble if I got turned on by the sight of her calves.

"I mean it," Callie repeated.

"I've been uncomfortable since we pulled into the driveway," I told her honestly, juggling the crockpot of mashed potatoes I'd made from scratch a half hour ago. Uncomfortable was an understatement. Stepping foot on this property again after eleven years was like casually ripping scabs off wounds I'd never taken the time to heal.

Callie flinched. "I never should have asked you to do this."

"It's okay." Fuck, was my collar actually tightening?

Right there, next to the walkway, was where Dad had thrown Mom's things into a pile after the funeral.

This porch? This was where I'd watched Reed walk away, leaving me with an alcoholic father who couldn't stand the sight of us and a devastated fourteen-year-old little brother. This was where I'd transformed from a grief-stricken sixteen-year-old boy into an angry sixteen-year-old adult in the span of a heartbeat.

"We can go—" Callie started, concern etching two lines in her brow.

The door swung open, and Ava smiled at us. "Welcome!"

"Hey, Ava!" Sutton walked right in, unzipping her coat as she went.

Ava glanced between Callie and me, her dark brow furrowing. "Need me to give you guys a second?"

I took a deep breath. Callie had given up half her house and almost all her privacy for me. The least I could do was eat Thanksgiving in the house I'd grown up in. "Nope. We're all good. After you, Callie."

Callie shot me a look of pure apology that wasn't needed and followed Sutton inside, walking past Ava.

"I brought the potatoes," I told Ava. Then I took my first step inside for over a decade.

It didn't smell like her, not anymore. Mom had always preferred the scent of apples and cinnamon in the fall, but there was only pumpkin pie in the air.

The faded red curtains Mom had made when I was ten were gone, replaced by cheerful checkered ones, and the hallway runner was new too. But it was the same house. It was *her* house, the one he'd wrecked, then let fall into disrepair when he'd been too self-absorbed to show up for anyone else, even his sons.

The same photos lined the entry, but there were a couple new additions too. The brunette in the first picture was Dad's new wife, Melody. I didn't know her. I honestly didn't want to. I didn't hate her, or even dislike her...there was just apathy where she was concerned. Had to admit, though, she won a point for hanging pictures of my mom along the hallway. Dad had made it a point to remove everything that reminded him of Mom those first few months, so Melody must have found them where I'd hidden them away in the garage for safe keeping.

"You have her eyes," Callie said quietly, coming to stand next to me. She'd lost her coat and the bottle of wine, which told me I'd been standing here lost in my thoughts for far too long.

"Yeah." I tried to force a smile, but there was nothing there. The usual lightness I felt around her, the peace that made it easier to breathe, had been replaced by a fifty-pound sack of concrete in my stomach. "I'd better take these in."

I walked into the center of the A-frame house, where a vaulted ceiling rose to the roofline, and stared at the dining area. Ava had set the table for five, complete with linens and a centerpiece.

The last Thanksgiving I'd spent here had been a crockpot turkey breast on our laps because Crew had a competition that morning and Dad was nowhere to be found. It was the only Thanksgiving Reed hadn't come home from college for.

"I'll take those," Ava said with a smile, reaching for the crockpot. I surrendered it only because I didn't know where she was putting everything.

The jingling of piano keys sounded, and I pivoted, seeing Sutton at the bench of Mom's piano.

"Sutton, honey. No." Callie shook her head.

"She's fine," I told her. "Mom would hate that it wasn't being used." I shucked off my jacket and hung it on the coatrack.

Callie jumped into helping Ava.

And I...I stared.

I couldn't tell which was the bigger anachronism—me or the decor. There was a new couch. New television. New pillows. New art. None of it was Mom's style, even though the house had been her love. Everything looked like it didn't belong here, but maybe I was the one out of place, out of time.

"Can you play, Weston?" Sutton asked me.

"A little." My feet took me to her, and I sat on the empty space on the leather bench, my fingers finding their places on the keys like it hadn't been fifteen years since I'd touched them.

Play for me, Weston. I heard Mom's voice in my head as clearly as if she were laying there on the couch behind us. She'd spent most of her time there that last year, an invisible illness stealing her away before they could even diagnose what was wrong with her.

"I don't know how," Sutton said, poking at one of the keys.

"I'm not sure I remember," I admitted, but then my hands moved over the keys, and before I could warn my heart not to let it happen, the keys gave way under my fingers, and a song I'd had memorized since childhood drifted through the upright. A note here and there was off, but I played anyway, reaching across Sutton to strike the lower keys.

The G was hopelessly out of key.

"Moonlight Sonata" echoed through the house, filling the cavernous space of the chalet in a way nothing else could have, filling it with her, even though she wasn't here. She'd never hear it again, never ask me to play it just one more time.

I stared at where the music would have been during the days she taught me, the ghost of her memory turning the pages as I played on, going through the motions with pure muscle memory. How many times had I played this for her after she'd taught me? Hundreds? Thousands?

The last chord sounded, reverberating through every bone in my body, and I sat there, letting it work its way through me, like it would magically make everything better.

"Mozart?" Sutton asked.

"Beethoven," I answered.

"Jesus, Weston." Reed's voice snapped me out of whatever trance I'd been in, and I jerked my head toward him, yanking my fingers off the keys like they'd burned me. "I didn't know you could still play." He was at the foot of the staircase, disbelief etched into every line of his face.

I got up as quickly as I could, moving away from the bench. What the hell had come over me?

Ava and Callie stood by the dining room table, and while Ava smiled, Callie stared at me with wide eyes and something like awe shaping her features.

I ripped my eyes from hers, from the unspoken praise I

didn't deserve, and looked back at Reed. "The piano is out of tune."

His eyebrows shot up. "Been a little busy saving this place from being sold and getting the whole expansion thing up and going. And besides, I don't think anyone has touched it since you."

"It's her piano," I bit out. "Have. It. Tuned."

His eyes narrowed, but he didn't fight me on it. He just nodded.

"That was beautiful," Callie said as I walked toward her. "I didn't know you played piano."

"I don't." The words came out clipped.

Her brow puckered, and I immediately felt a pang of guilt. This place brought out the absolute worst in me and she didn't deserve it. The sooner we were out of here, the better.

Ava cleared her throat. "So, dinner is ready, if you guys want to eat."

"Let's get it over with," I muttered.

We sat down to the table, Ava and Reed at one corner, and Callie on the end, with Sutton in between us. It was weird as hell seeing Reed in Dad's seat, but whatever. This wasn't my table anymore.

Ava apologized for not cooking, saying she'd had everything but the potatoes brought up from the resort.

"Trust me, after a couple Thanksgivings in Afghanistan, you don't really care where the food comes from," I said, heaping potatoes onto my plate and then helping Sutton.

I should have accepted Theo's offer. No doubt he, Jeanine, the kids, Maria, and Scott were having a blast, not silently fighting for the self-control not to burn down the place they swore they'd never go to again.

Callie and Ava made small talk as we tucked in, and I did my best to focus on the food and include Sutton in the conversation whenever she chimed in. I'd been in forward operating bases with less tension, but that didn't stop me from eating.

I kept my gaze away from the empty shelf, the one high up on the wall Dad had built to display Mom's pottery. The one he'd ransacked, fracturing almost every piece in a drunken fit of...assholery.

"It's been nice having the place to ourselves," Ava said. "But they're due back pretty soon, so we'll have to decide if we're going to live here or find somewhere on our own."

Which meant pretty soon I'd have to deal with Dad. Fucking *awesome*. My throat tightened and another thread of the control I'd carefully constructed over the last decade frayed. I started tapping my foot beneath the table, needing some kind of outlet.

"It's a beautiful house," Callie said with a little sigh, her gaze taking it in with the kind of unbiased eye I'd never had.

"It's our mother's," Reed said in explanation. "Pretty much everything about it is Mom."

"Except all the stuff that isn't." I took a drink. "She would hate that couch." Mom had always chosen comfort over style. Always. That thing looked like it slid right off the pages of a magazine.

Reed sighed. "You can hardly expect them to keep it as a mausoleum."

"I don't." I shrugged. "But it's not Mom."

"You know, all your stuff is upstairs," Ava tried. "You have a ton of big mountain trophies in your closet."

Sutton's wide eyes snapped my way. "I didn't know you competed!"

"I didn't. Not really." I offered her the softest smile I could, and I was still pretty sure it came out like a gargoyle. "I stopped competing when my mom got sick."

"You were really great," Reed said, his tone full of pride he had no right to. "You shouldn't have quit."

"Mom got sick." I shrugged.

His brow puckered. "We would have made it work if you wanted to keep competing."

The look I gave him stopped that line of conversation cold.

He sighed so deeply it should have moved the house off its foundation, but he kept eating.

Fuck, I wished Crew were here, but he'd texted earlier today that he was in Aspen. Knowing him, it was the closest he'd come to this place.

Reed laughed at something Ava said, and he looked so much like our dad that my jaw locked and my blood pressure rose. This was wrong. Sitting here, laughing, pretending like we weren't the world's most dysfunctional family was fucking *wrong*.

"He wouldn't care if you sat there anyway," Reed went on, and I tried my best to tune into the conversation. "That's always been Crew's seat."

"Well, that makes me feel better," she replied, her laughter easy.

I shook my head and my blood rose to the boiling point.

"And it's not like Crew would care, right, Weston?" Reed asked.

"Since Crew hasn't sat there since he broke his hand in that accident March of his junior year, I highly doubt he'd care," I snapped, letting my silverware fall to the plate.

"What?" Reed drew back as if I'd punched him in the face.

"March. His junior year in high school," I clarified. "He fell—"

"I know that," Reed argued.

"Breaking six bones in his hand," I continued. "He couldn't cut his food, and we could see the TV from this side better, anyways, so he moved here," I pointed to Sutton's seat. "Where he sat for the next fifteen months until he graduated."

Reed's face fell. "He couldn't cut his own food?"

"His hand was broken. And you would have known just how

bad it was if you'd actually *been here*. But we both know you weren't, so stop acting like you were."

Reed's jaw unhinged.

I didn't apologize or look away, just kept him pinned to his seat with a stare that said he wasn't about to change my opinion on this.

Tension rose to a breaking point.

"Sutton, why don't you go upstairs to Weston's room," Callie suggested.

"It's the second door on the left," Ava added.

"And count just how many big mountain trophies he has," Callie finished.

"But Mom—"

"*Now.*"

I heard Sutton push away from the table and saw her move up the stairs in my peripheral vision.

"Is this how we're going to do this?" Reed asked, his voice lowering. "You've been home for two months and now you want to have it out at the Thanksgiving table?"

I'd had it up to my fucking eyeballs with him telling me what he thought was appropriate, and what he thought I should do about *anything*. "You lost the right to chastise me like an older brother when you stopped acting like one."

"I'm sorry?"

"You should be!" I hissed, keeping my voice low so Sutton wouldn't hear. "You want to know why I quit competing? Because you were off racing every goddamn weekend, and Dad checked out the minute Mom got sick. Who was going to take care of her?"

"Racing was the only way I had to get a scholarship," he said defensively, dropping his silverware like he'd just now noticed I was coming for blood.

"Oh, I noticed. You packed up and moved to the east coast like life wasn't going to shit around here."

"I knew you were angry at Dad, and I got it, but..." He blinked. "This is why you're so pissed at me? Because I made a life for myself?"

"Fuck, Reed, it's not always about you!" I shoved away from the table and stood.

"You could have left!" he fired back, standing to face me.

"I was sixteen when she died."

"You're right." His jaw flexed. "You were too young, then. But you had every opportunity to leave after graduation, just like me." He tapped his chest. "Honestly, I was shocked as hell when you didn't, considering how much you hate our father."

"And what the fuck would Crew have done?"

Reed opened his mouth and then closed it. "He could drive by the time you graduated. He wasn't some helpless baby that needed looking after."

"He needed someone to *contain* him so he didn't get himself killed. He needed someone to sign his permission slips. He needed someone to make his excuses to the office when he skipped school or needed to miss for some half-pipe in Utah. He needed someone to bribe him to graduate from high school when he decided that dropping out was a better plan. I'm the one that kept him in high school, because that's what Mom wanted. I'm the one that said I'd only take him to competitions if he kept his grades passing. Did you really think Dad was going to do any of that? News flash, Reed. Dad didn't give a shit about us after Mom died. He threw himself into a bottle, and then into this damn resort the same way you are right now, with single-minded focus."

He glanced at Ava. "I'm not single-minded."

"No, thank God you have a woman you love to keep your priorities straight, but Dad did too, until he didn't." I glanced at Reed's fiancée. "No offense, Ava. I'm glad you make him happy."

"Are you really?" Reed challenged. "Because it feels like you want everyone to be just as miserable as you are. You've had a stick up your ass since you landed here. I'm not going to apologize for being happy, not after the hell we've been—"

"The hell *we've* been through?" I backed up, scared that if I got any closer, I might actually put my fist through his face.

"My mother died too!"

"And you weren't here!" I jabbed my finger in his direction. "Oh sure, you may have shown up for the holidays, been here when she finally found peace over Christmas, but you weren't here when she got bad, and you sure as hell weren't here when it got worse. You visited hell on vacation, but you sure didn't live here."

"What do you want me to do, Weston? Go back in time and make different decisions?"

"I want you to stop pretending that you actually *would.*" I threw up my hands, lacing them behind my neck as I pulled air in through my nose and shoved it out of my mouth, trying like hell to keep calm, and failing. "I want you to acknowledge that while you remember it as being the same, you and I had very different teenaged years."

"I did everything I could," he argued. "I sent money. I bought groceries when I was home—"

"You didn't do the *one* thing that would have made a difference, and stuck around to actually do the whole big brother role you're so proud of," I seethed.

"Stop acting like an asshole. It's impossible to talk to you when you're like this." Reed folded his arms across his chest. "I don't know what you want from me."

"I want you to stop needing things from *me.*" My hands fell to my sides. "I need you to acknowledge that while you got off the Titanic, some of us went down with the ship."

"And I'm here now!" He gestured to the house around us. "Righting the damned ship!"

"And you forced me back here to right it with you!"

Reed took a step back. "I never *forced* you."

"You're right. You just said that you *needed* me." I glanced up at the ceiling, recalling the conversation. "What was it you said? You *needed* a way to bring in high-end clientele. You *needed* a new income stream because you were spending some major money. What the hell was I supposed to do? Let you fail and then blame it on me?"

"We were far from failing. I offered you a business opportunity and you took it, with some pretty hefty financial gains if I read that profit sharing plan correctly. Sue me if I wanted to save this place from the god-awful deal Dad had structured." He shook his head. "Hell, sue me if I just wanted to spend some time with my brothers, to try and make this place the home it used to be before Mom died. I want my family back, Weston."

"Did you think we'd be right where you left us?" I lifted my hand toward the front door. "Standing on that porch?"

His lips flattened.

"You don't get it because you've never had to give anything up. You've always done exactly what you wanted exactly when you wanted to. But I gave up my future so everyone else could have theirs, and that apparently wasn't enough for you—for this place. You called me up and told me you needed me to give up the career I love, the promotion I'd worked my ass off for, the career I've thrown my entire life into, and I did it. Hell, you know I can't stand the thought of stepping foot inside this house, and yet, here I am, just like you asked." I threw out my arms. "What else do *you* want from *me*, Reed? Do you want me to call up Crew and tell him he has to come back and use his fame to make the expansion successful too?"

Reed paled.

"You're kidding me, right?" My eyes flared.

"He hasn't answered, but that's not why I want to talk to him!" Reed blustered.

I shook my head and laughed. "Holy shit. You actually want

me to call up Crew. What's wrong, big brother? Little bro not taking your calls?"

"Like he answers you either," Reed snapped.

"He answers *whenever* I call." I didn't give a shit that he looked like a wounded puppy. "I just know better than to call him unless it's life or death."

Silence stretched between us, so thick it strangled any positive feelings and so fragile I knew the next words could break us past any chance of repair.

"You made a life for yourself," I said softly. "Good for you. We're all proud. But some of us had little brothers to take care of. If you want to call me an asshole, fine. I am what you and Dad made me. Every choice the two of you made shaped me, and you should be glad about that because I'm here now. I came when you called. But would you *ever* have done the same for me?" My words lost their fight. I looked at Callie. "I need air."

She nodded, her face pale and her eyes wider than the dinner plates on the table.

I grabbed my jacket and walked straight out of the house, closing the door softer than I ever thought possible. Then I stalked to the side of the driveway and looked out over the Madigan property, the land we'd managed to save while the family fell apart.

The door opened and shut, and I cringed. "I'm going to need a little space, Reed."

"Good thing I'm not Reed." Callie shoved her arms into her coat and zipped it as the first flakes started to fall, making her way toward me. She put her hand on my arm and my head hung.

"I'm so damned sorry," I muttered. "I only came here so you could have Thanksgiving with Ava, and then I just blew it all up."

"It was pretty nuke-tacular," she joked with a sad smile. "But I don't blame you. It was bound to happen sometime. If not now, then Christmas, or even worse—their wedding. I mean, could you imagine that going down in front of a full audience?"

I pulled her to me and wrapped my arms around her, resting my chin on the top of her head. "I didn't mean for that to happen." Guilt gnawed at my stomach for the way I'd lost control, but there was a small part of me that was glad I did, glad that at least Reed knew how I felt.

"I know." She linked her arms around my back and held tight. "I just wish for your sake that you'd said it before now."

"So I didn't ruin dinner?"

"So you didn't carry it for all these years." She turned her head to the side and put her ear against my heart. "But I understand you a little better now. Why you show up when you're needed. You're an incredible man, Weston."

"There was nothing flattering about what went on in there." I sighed. "I just lost it."

"Losing it would have been hitting him."

"What about wanting to?" I tilted my face and pressed a kiss to the top of her head.

"If the world starts judging people on what they want to do instead of what they actually do, we're in trouble." She squeezed me tight and stepped away, and I let her. "How about I get Sutton out of your room and we head home?"

"You should stay. I'll go." I felt like shit for ruining her evening.

She shook her head. "I want to be wherever you are."

The words punched me in the stomach and somehow jump-started my heart all at once.

"Give me two minutes." She backed away and then turned, walking up the steps to the front porch.

"Callie," I called out.

She turned, her hand on the front door.

"Steal their pie."

A grin flashed across her face and my heart raced double time.

I'd spent fifteen years building up my defenses, but when it came to Callie?

Fuck, I could fall for that woman, and that was...unthinkable.

allie

THE SHOTS WERE PHENOMENAL. The way the sunlight caught the bride's veil? Absolutely scrumptious. Lighting was on point, the colors were heavenly, and the look in the groom's eyes sent a stab of straight-up yearning through my chest.

I wanted Weston to look at me that way.

Like I was the only woman in the world he'd ever want.

When the hell had that happened? I knew I'd been falling for him last week, and if I was being honest with myself, I never would have slept with him if I hadn't. Not when there was so much on the line.

But watching him shred himself in front of Reed a couple of nights ago had gutted me in a way I hadn't expected. He'd raised his voice, and yet had controlled his temper in a way I'm not sure I could have if I'd been dragged into Thanksgiving with my parents. My stomach turned just thinking about facing them again. He'd made it an hour longer than I would have.

And yet Weston was here at Madigan, facing down his demons because his family said they needed him. He'd known the cost and paid it anyway.

He'd shown up, just like he had for Sutton with skiing and me when I was sick or needed help shooting action shots.

And I loved him for it.

I, Calliope Thorne, was head over heels in love with Weston Madigan, fully knowing he avoided attachment like the plague, knowing loving him would eventually break my heart. But there was nothing I could do about it. It wasn't the sweet, childhood love I'd had for Gavin, either. No, this love was messy, inconvenient, and worse...unrequited.

I shut my laptop and stood, rolling my neck with a sigh. It was midnight, and Sutton was long since asleep upstairs, but Weston hadn't come home yet from a night out with Theo... assuming he was planning on coming home tonight. A knot formed in my throat, and I shook it off. Weston and I had agreed to one night, not a relationship.

It wasn't his responsibility that I'd gone and fallen in love with him. Snagging a spoon from the drawer, I opened the freezer and took out one of the pints of Orange Dreamsicle I'd picked up for him. Then I hopped up onto the end of the island and shamelessly dug into it.

It was sweet yet understated, citrusy without being tart. Kind of like Weston himself. Man, I had it bad if I was comparing that man to freaking ice cream.

As if he'd read my mind, a key turned in the lock and the front door swung open. Weston walked in, rubbing the snow out of his hair.

He saw me as he shut the door. "You're still awake?" He kicked off his boots and put them away with his jacket in the hall closet. The routine of it made me smile.

"Just finished editing the first set of pictures from a wedding this morning." I took another bite of ice cream.

"First set?" He came over to me, pushing up the sleeves of his dark-gray Henley. God, I loved when he did that. There was something undeniably sexy about it.

"Only about three hundred and forty pictures to go." I forced a smile and concentrated on the ice cream. Had he met someone while he was out? Was I going to have to watch him date another girl? Or bring someone home? The jealousy was a hundred percent absurd, and yet, just like loving him, I couldn't seem to control it.

"Good choice." He motioned to my ice cream.

I raised my gaze to his and blatantly took another bite, licking the back of the spoon. "It's pretty yummy." His eyes darkened and he moved forward, caging me between his arms but not touching me. "I figured it wasn't quite a violation of rule number four since there's another pint in there if you want it. Plus, I'm the one who bought them for you, so..." I shrugged.

A soft smile tugged at his lips. "You bought them for me?"

"You said you liked it." I spooned a small bite of the ice cream.

"I do." He leaned forward. "Just didn't realize you noticed. Feel like sharing?" He parted his lips.

I fed him a bite, and my thighs clenched at the way his mouth moved over the spoon. I'd had that mouth on me, knew exactly what it was capable of doing. An ache settled low in my stomach. One night hadn't been enough. I wanted every night.

He reached over and plucked our contract off the refrigerator. "You know, I think we've pretty much broken most of these already."

"Really?" My breath caught as he shifted closer, the taut muscles of his stomach brushing my bare knees. Maybe I should have dressed a little sexier—especially if I wanted *another* night, but it wasn't the first time he'd seen me in oversized pajama shorts and a hoodie, even if these shorts barely covered my ass. There was probably room for two of me in here, but more importantly, they were comfortable.

"No one upstairs," he recited. "Think we crossed that one off earlier this week." The smirk he gave me was hot enough to melt the whole pint in my hands. "And from what I remember— which is every single second—you weren't exactly a quiet, *respectful* guest."

"It's not my fault you made me scream." I cocked an eyebrow at him and took another bite of his ice cream.

He leaned in and I fed him another spoonful, stealing the contract out of his hand. "You did supervise Sutton's party, so I guess that one's moot." I skipped number four since we'd just covered it with the ice cream. "We're sticking to rule five." My brow furrowed. "Well, except the way you and Sutton are on me for her to join the big mountain team. Don't think I didn't notice the registration paperwork on the counter yesterday."

"All her." His smile turned sheepish. "But I did print it out at her request."

"Hmm." Sutton had her sleepover, we'd been sharing the housework, and I was at about ninety-five percent when it came to picking up after ourselves, though he was still the cleanest guy I'd ever been around.

"I'd never question you in front of Sutton, but what's your reasoning there? If you know she's good enough, and that they wouldn't start her on something too extreme, why not let her go for the team?"

"It's not that I don't want her to experience everything life has to offer. It's just…" I searched for the right words that wouldn't make me sound like a helicopter mom. "We're only given one body. One. And there are some injuries that medicine can't heal."

"Ahh." He looked at me like he was trying to see past the surface, to decipher some puzzle I wasn't aware of. "Gavin."

I swallowed, then nodded slowly. "I guess. I just wish her dreams were a little safer. And I only have a few more years before all those choices are hers. Her dad only made it to eighteen. I didn't realize it then, but he was still a kid. We both were."

"Every dream risks a broken heart, you know. There's nothing completely safe in this world."

I scooped another bite and fed it to him. "I'd rather she break her heart a dozen times and learn to dust herself off than break her body beyond repair."

"Hmm." He gave me that look again, like he was trying to understand me, then looked away, his brow knitting.

"What are you thinking?"

"It's nothing." He shook his head.

"It's not nothing," I said softly, stabbing the spoon into the pint so I could smooth the concerned lines of his forehead. "Tell me." *Trust me. Let me in.*

"You said Gavin was a kid," he said slowly. "And it just reminded me that Reed was too. He was eighteen." His gaze shot to mine. "Not that the two situations are anything alike—"

"I know what you're saying." I slipped my hand to his cheek and savored the feel of his scruff against my palm. "And yeah, you were both just...kids, even if you were the one forced to grow up entirely too fast."

"But you were too. You were only eighteen when he died, and what? Nineteen when Sutton was born? And yet, there's not a drop of anger in you about the cards you were dealt." He sighed. "And then there's me."

"I was absolutely angry about losing Gavin, about how unfair it was, not just for me but for Sutton." Weston's skin was warm to the touch as I slid my fingers to cup the side of his neck. "But I was mad at fate, and then I was..." I searched for the right words. "Heartbroken that my parents chose not to support my pregnancy. I was devastated when they threw me out. You saw me. I was a mess."

He nodded, his lips flattening.

"And the truth is that I'm still angry. I just haven't seen my parents since they threw me out, so I haven't had the chance to blow up on them. I honestly don't know if I'll ever have the strength or the grace to see them again, even if they actually wanted us. But I chose Sutton, and I have no regrets." My eyebrows rose as I looked into his eyes so he'd know I meant it, that he wasn't the only one with mixed emotions about his family. "Sometimes I think we spend our adulthoods trying to heal whatever cut us as kids." I took a steadying breath. "And maybe that's what both you and Reed are doing here at Madigan. Trying to heal what sliced you open."

Weston's gaze shuttered, and my heart clenched in protest as I watched his shoulders straighten, as I watched him put his walls back up. He cleared his throat and stepped away, setting our contract on the counter. "You know, we've definitely busted leaving work at the door, but we've done very well with keeping shoes off the couch and pets out of the house."

"Heaven forbid you attach to a hamster," I muttered.

He raised a sardonic eyebrow. "I've done most of the cooking, but you're way better than you led on when I moved in."

"It's more a of a quantity issue with me than quality," I teased, swirling the spoon around the pint to scoop another bite. "And I think I've done well with rule number fourteen."

His brow lowered as he studied the page. "There's no rule fourteen."

"Oh, it's just on the draft. I removed it from the final copy to spare your tender feelings." I batted my eyelashes with false innocence. "It says to remove the stick from Weston's ass."

He laughed.

"See?" I lifted the spoon between us. "You're still pretty

uptight outside the house, but in here? You're absolutely stickless."

"Is that so?" His eyes took on a flirtatious sparkle.

"It is." I swept the spoon across his lips and then stole it back, taking the bite for myself. "Mmm." I gave an exaggerated roll of my eyes. "So good."

He palmed the back of my neck and pounced, kissing me deep. The chill of the ice cream melted with the heat of his tongue. My hands fell to my sides, abandoning the spoon and pint on the counter.

I tilted my head to give him better access, then parted my knees so I could get closer to him. He took the invitation, and I reached for his shoulders, his neck, the back of his head, any part I could get my hands on.

"So good," he said against my mouth, and I could feel his smile before he swept back in, stealing every thought as he turned me into a boneless heap of want.

His hand drifted under my hoodie and up my rib cage to cup my breast.

I sucked in a breath, arching into his hand. More. I needed more.

"I can't get you out of my head," he admitted in a harsh whisper, his mouth sliding to my neck.

My fingers bit into his shoulders. "I can't stop thinking about it—about you and me. The bed. The shower. The wall. It's on constant repeat in my brain."

He groaned, and our mouths met in a blatantly carnal kiss. My body hummed with need, coming alive under his touch. When he gripped my hips and hauled our bodies flush, I felt exactly how the kiss had affected him too.

"It's not going to be just one night." His fingers flexed on my upper thighs.

"No, it's not." My hands slid up his shirt, caressing the hard ridges of his abs.

"I want you." His fingers stroked my inner thigh, dipping under the fabric of my glorified boxer shorts. There was more than enough room for his hand, and he delved beneath my thong. "I want whatever this is between us."

"Weston." I jolted forward, moaning against his shoulder at the first touch. I melted at the second and my hips rocked against his hand with the third. He knew exactly how to turn me on and was using that knowledge to set me on fire. "Wait. How much did you drink while you were out?" I couldn't even taste any alcohol in his kiss, but if sober Weston said we were only happening once, then I wasn't listening to drunk Weston just because it suited my needs.

"One beer about three hours ago," he answered. "I'm completely in my right mind, if that's what you're getting at. The only thing I'm drunk on is you." Then he kissed me, and I forgot every single reason we shouldn't do this. Who cared if we went down in flames and things got awkward? Having him for however long I could was worth the risk.

The damage was done—I was already in love with him, so how much further could I fall?

"Let me take you upstairs." He kissed my jaw, then the edge of my mouth as his fingers stroked and teased my clit.

I was going to die if we waited any longer. "Here. Now. Right now."

He stiffened. "Sutton—"

"Sleeping." I reached for the button of his jeans, flicking it open. "And we'd hear if she wasn't." A simple tug had him unzipped, and then my hand was around him. He was hot and thick against my palm, and so very, very hard.

"Fuck, Callie." He ripped his wallet out of his back pocket and put it on the counter, his hand leaving me to pull out a condom.

I took it from his hand, tearing open the packet. Then I looked him straight in the eye as I rolled it over him, my hand stroking down his length until I reached the base of him, my other hand tugging his jeans and underwear to just below his ass. The groan that rumbled through his chest only made me more frantic.

"You're sure?" He pulled me to the edge of the counter and shoved the opening of my shorts to the side.

"Never been more sure," I whispered.

His fingers tugged the fabric of my underwear aside with my shorts, and then they were inside me, pumping and curling as his thumb worked my clit. When I parted my lips, he swallowed my whimpers with his mouth, his tongue thrusting with the same rhythm of his fingers. "You're so ready for me."

"I need you," I said, the only thing I knew would break his control.

"Calliope." Then his fingers were gone and he was at my entrance, hard and urgent. He thrust at the same time he pulled me to him, his hand at my lower back while the other held the back of my neck.

I gasped as I took every inch, my body molding around his as he moved within me.

Hard, deep strokes had me keening, and I muffled the sound against his neck as my hips rocked to meet every drive of his hips.

"So. Damned. Hot." He punctuated every whispered word with a thrust.

"More." It was the only word I could say as I wrapped my legs around his waist, locking my ankles. I held onto his shoulders as he pulled me into every stroke, our hips meeting again and again.

The tension within me wound tighter, but I hung on, even when my thighs trembled and my breath came in stuttered gasps.

"Right. Fucking. There." He reached between us and stroked

me over the edge with tight little swirls of his fingers and the most glorious pressure.

I flew apart, muffling the sound of my cry between his neck and shoulder as wave after wave of absolute bliss swept over me. He followed right after, his moan low as he shuddered against me.

It took us a couple minutes to get our breathing back under control, and he kissed me gently, sucking on my lower lip as we came down.

It was the most reckless thing I'd done since having Sutton eleven years ago, and I felt absolutely wonderful.

He smiled, caressing my lips with his thumb. "Now that we've taken the edge off, can I convince you to come upstairs with me?"

I laughed quietly, smiling right back at him. "We're really doing this?"

"Yeah. I think we are." He nodded.

"Exclusively?"

"Exclusively." He cupped my cheek and pushed back a strand of my hair that had fallen from my messy bun. "There's no one else."

It wasn't a declaration of love, but it was a start.

"What about you?" Two lines appeared between his eyebrows.

"Only you." *Only ever you.* I told my foolish heart to shut it. Then I blinked, realizing it wasn't only my heart on the line here. "We can't tell Sutton. Not until we know exactly what this is." Breaking my heart was one thing. Crushing hers was unacceptable.

"Whatever you want," he agreed.

I leaned in and kissed him, scraping my teeth along his lower lip just how he liked. "I want you to take me upstairs."

He did. It was almost dawn when I finally crept back to my own bed.

14

Weston

TUESDAYS WERE OUR DAYS. Theo and I had noticed we had the heaviest bookings between Thursday and Mondays, so we declared that Tuesdays would be our day off, no matter what.

They also happened to coincide with one of the days Callie took, which meant Tuesdays belonged to us, especially when Sutton was at school.

Rule number ten, respecting quiet time, flew out the window, and we were as loud as we wanted to be. I took her in my bed and hers. She rode me on the couch. I laid her out on the dining room table. Each time we were together was better than the last, and even now, just a couple hours after we'd climbed out of bed, I was debating taking her right back there.

"I'm still not sure about putting it there," Callie said, staring at the five-foot-tall Christmas tree we'd picked up and decorated over the weekend. "We've always put it against that wall." She motioned to the living room wall that rose with her staircase.

"You've also always had a three-footer that fit on an end table." I walked up behind her and kissed the side of her neck.

"It was easy." She leaned back against me. "And I could always cover my tracks if I heard Sutton coming on Christmas Eve." There was a definite glare as she looked at our bigger tree. "If she comes out of her room, I'll be busted with the tree there. She has a direct line of sight from the landing."

"Well, then I'll sit at the top of the steps and play watch dog for you," I offered, wrapping my arms around her. I couldn't remember feeling this content in my entire life. Was it hard sneaking around behind Sutton? Sure, but it was so worth it to have Callie as my friend during the days when Sutton was at home, and my lover at night. And I understood her reasoning. I wasn't keen on getting attached to anyone either, and the last thing I wanted was to be responsible for hurting Sutton if her expectations weren't...meetable. "And remember, I wanted the eight-footer. So that's a compromise."

She scoffed.

The doorbell rang.

"Go away!" I shouted, half kidding. The plans I had for Callie this afternoon had absolutely nothing to do with anyone at the door.

"Weston!" Callie shook her head at me and laughed, pushing out of my arms and walking to the door.

She opened it and tensed.

"Hey, Callie." Reed forced the fakest smile I'd ever seen and then looked over her at me. "Can we talk?"

Callie looked back at me, raising her eyebrows slightly.

I knew she'd shut the door in his face if that's what I wanted, and it meant everything to me. My chest went all warm at knowing she'd take my side, no questions asked.

"Yeah," I begrudgingly answered. "Come on in."

Callie stepped out of the way so Reed could enter, then shut the door behind him. "I'm...um...going somewhere else." She mouthed *play nice*, around his back, then headed upstairs to her room.

Reed rocked back on his heels, clutching a small box as the awkwardness set in.

It had been almost two weeks since I'd blown up at him on Thanksgiving, and we'd done a damn good job of avoiding each other ever since. But were going to have to deal with what had happened at some point. *Might as well be today.*

At least I'd had time to cool off and really think.

"Want some coffee?" I offered.

"Promise not to throw it in my face?" He ran his hand over his hair.

"No." A corner of my mouth rose.

"Fair enough." He half smiled, but it was genuine. "Look, I was going to wait until Christmas, but after the way things went at Thanksgiving..." He shook his head. "Well, I figured I'd just give it to you now, not that it's mine to give. It's yours." He held out the box and I took it.

"It's mine?" My brow knit in confusion as I opened the top of the cardboard box. Then my heart hit the fucking floor. "It's mine," I whispered, taking the handmade ceramic mug out with exquisite care. Its weight in my palm was familiar and alien all at once. It was a relic from another time, when there had been three Madigan boys doted on by their mother. Its lines were unique, shaped by Mom's hands, and there were only two others in the world like it—one for Reed and one for Crew—a different color for each of us. Holding it put a lump into my throat. "I thought he'd broken them."

"I thought so, too, but Ava found them in a random box." He shoved his hands into his front pockets. "I figured you'd want it."

"Yeah." I nodded slowly. "I want it. Thank you." My eyes squeezed shut as I fought through a wave of grief. It had been fifteen years, and I swore I could still smell her perfume, hear her laugh. I missed everything about her, but most of all, her astute advice.

She would have hated what my relationship with Reed had become. She would have been more than disappointed with me for losing my temper.

I turned around, heading for the kitchen. "Leave your boots on. We're going for a walk."

"Wait a minute. So I'm the one who extends the hand and comes to *your* place, but you're the one setting the terms here?"

"Yep." I set my childhood mug on the counter and prepped two stainless steel travel mugs with black coffee, then put my boots and coat on while he waited by the door, his gaze sweeping over the space I shared with Callie. "Let's go."

He took the cup I offered, and we walked out into the frigid December air. We hadn't had fresh snow in a couple days, but we were due for a dumping tonight.

"How are bookings?" he asked as we walked out of the cul-de-sac and onto the worn path that led toward the slopes. The snow was compact here, and I could even make out Sutton's boot prints from skiing yesterday afternoon.

"You have the same access to the software that I do, so you know we're doing great. We've already made enough to make the summer payments on the bird." I looked over at him. "You really want to talk business?"

"No." He shook his head and yanked his zipper from his collar to all the way up his throat. "I actually came to your house so that you'd know it wasn't about business."

"And yet..." I shot him a pointed look and took a sip of my scalding hot coffee as we hiked through the pines.

"You know, seeing that I spent sixteen years of my life with you after the two-year bliss of being an only child, you'd think I'd know how to talk to you by now," he muttered.

"It wasn't the first sixteen that confused you, it was the fifteen after." I ducked under a pine branch and Reed followed suit.

"Touché."

"Just say what you need to say, Reed. I've never been one for small talk." The snow crunched under my boots and the noon sunlight filtered down through the trees, checkering the path.

"I was really pissed at you for wrecking Thanksgiving."

I laughed at the bewilderment in his voice. "Were you now?"

"Fucking livid." He walked beside me and shot a glare in my direction. "Ava had been stressed about it, especially since we've been living in Mom and Dad's house—"

"It's not her house. Not anymore." That was my problem with going there.

"Fine. Dad and Melody's house, but I get the point." He sighed. "I thought it would be the perfect time for you and me to put shit behind us. Not to mention it was the first time you've agreed to have dinner with me since you got back."

"Your first mistake was putting your expectations on my reactions." I took another drink and willed my temper to stay asleep. If Reed had the balls to make the first move, then I could at least refrain from yelling.

Reed blinked and lifted his eyebrows at me. "Okay, I guess that's fair."

"It is," I assured him. "My first mistake was thinking I could sit there for a couple of hours and *not* fly off the handle." I looked over and waited until we made eye contact. "Ava has my most sincere apology for ruining her dinner. I've already apologized to Callie and Sutton."

A smile tugged at Reed's mouth. "Why do I have the feeling that you're not offering me an apology?"

"Because I'm not." I shrugged. "Can you honestly tell me that you thought a family dinner would be the best place for us to spend a little quality time together, knowing we haven't made it through a full conversation in about fifteen years?"

Reed clenched his jaw, and his gaze jumped from tree to tree as he thought. "I knew it was a risk. My hope just outweighed my logic."

"That will get you every time." We made it to the end of the path, and it opened up to the slope. We were fifty feet or so from the original lift, but skiers almost never took this path, and a small rise in the landscape along the lift hid most of the tourists from our line of sight, leaving our view as pristine as it got down to the lodge, if we ignored the skiers riding the lift. "I am sorry I ruined dinner, though. If I'd realized just how close I was to that breaking point I never would have gone."

"But I wanted you there." Reed turned to face me. "I don't want whatever this rift is between us to get even wider. Maybe it's being back here, or even just being in that house, but I'd like my brother back."

I ripped my hand over my hair, wishing I'd brought my hat. "I know that has to be incredibly hard to say, Reed, but a few words aren't going to change the last fifteen years."

"I know that." A cloud of steam rose as he sighed. "I thought about what you said. It's pretty much *all* I've thought about since Thanksgiving."

"Me too." I shoved my free hand in my pocket and concentrated on the motion of the lift.

"I am so very sorry for leaving you guys to fend for yourselves," he said softly. "I knew how bad it was. Not the part about Crew wanting to drop out of high school, but the rest of it...I had a good idea."

I looked his way and waited, knowing that couldn't be all of it.

"It just hurt so damn much to be here. Mom was gone, and everything was fucked-up, and the way people looked at me—at us?" He shook his head. "At college, I was Reed Madigan, but I wasn't Reed *Madigan*."

"I get that. It's the same way I felt going through basic."

"I still can't believe you joined the damn army," he muttered.

"I always liked those seconds when you drop in and then hit the jump, the cliff, the freefall. That moment when it's just you and gravity, there's nothing like it. The army offered me flight school for free, a chance to serve something greater than myself, and got me the hell out of here. I have no regrets."

"It took me a while to realize you were staying for Crew," Reed admitted. "I just thought you didn't know what to do with your life after graduation so you were hanging here. I didn't want to pressure you about college."

"And once you did figure it out?"

Reed looked away. "It was right around when he graduated, and you left for the army the next week. Wasn't much I could do at that point." He kicked at the snow. "Fucking lame, I know."

I laughed. "That's a word for it." The snow glittered in the sunlight, and when I looked down the slope, my stomach didn't drop. My blood didn't boil. I no longer felt the need to salt the earth. "Bottom line is that we were kids." *Thank you, Callie.*

"I wasn't."

"You were." I took another drink, the coffee going down easier now that it had chilled some. "We all were. As much as I resent the hell out of you for having a life and getting to experience everything I wanted, I can't blame you for going."

"You never would have gone." He shifted his weight. "You *didn't* go."

"You and I aren't the same," I said as gently as I could. "Mom was my favorite person on this earth, even if I wasn't hers."

"She loved—"

"Yeah, I know. She loved me. She loved all of us. She was the most incredible mother I've seen and, honestly, Callie's the only woman I've ever seen give her a run for her money. But you and I both know Crew was Mom's baby."

Reed huffed a laugh. "Yeah, he could pretty much do no wrong."

"Right. So how was I supposed to leave him, knowing she was watching me? Knowing she'd asked me to get him through school?" I shook my head. "I didn't just stay because Dad was an alcoholic, self-absorbed asshole, or even because Crew needed someone to keep his ass in line. I stayed for her." I swallowed the boulder in my throat. "And that decision is on me, Reed. Not you. No matter how much solace I've taken in blaming you, it was my choice. No one tied me to a tree. I shackled myself." It had taken Callie's comments about choosing Sutton for me to really see it.

"I'm sorry. And I know it doesn't change the last fifteen years, but I really am." He put his hand on my shoulder. "It was too much to leave on a sixteen-year-old kid."

"Thanks." That was enough emotion for me for the day. "Let's head back, my hands are freezing."

Reed nodded, and we turned around, walking the path back toward the house.

"So you and Callie..." He lifted his eyebrows.

"None of your business." I sipped my coffee.

"Not a denial."

"Not your business."

He laughed. "Yeah, okay. Point made. But you have to know that when you start elevating her to the same level as our mom, it's a dead giveaway."

"Why? Callie's a fantastic mom. She's dedicated to Sutton in every single way. She's carved out a life here for them, and there's not a decision she makes that doesn't have Sutton's best interest at heart." *Except for being with me.*

"Tell me more about this paragon." Reed grinned and we ducked under a branch.

"She's none of your business." There were a thousand ways to describe Callie. Perfect. Loving. Hot as hell. Kind. Smart. Fierce. But none of that was anything Reed needed to know. "You and Ava are getting married, right?" Fuck, here I was with the small talk.

"Next November. We're planning for the week before opening."

"Good. I'm glad she makes you happy." We neared the end of the path.

"And what makes you happy, Weston?"

"Not talking about what makes me happy," I muttered.

"Says the emotionally evolved male," he joked.

We walked into the cul-de-sac and headed up my driveway.

"Listen..." he started.

I turned my back on the house to face him.

"I really am sorry for not being here. I need you to know that. I need you to understand that if I could go back—"

"Don't," I interrupted. "Don't say you would go back and change it, because what's done is done. Look at all this." I motioned around the little circle of employee duplexes. "Okay, imagine we're still looking down on the resort, that's a little more impressive."

Reed snorted.

"None of this would be ours right now if you hadn't left and gone off to college. Dad would have sold it. We still have Madigan Mountain because you went to school for business and have the expertise to run this place. I can't be sorry about that."

"Thought you hated it here?" His smirk looked a little too much like mine.

"It's growing on me." I shrugged. "And it's home."

"Good, because I wasn't going to say I would have changed anything," he said gently.

Now I was the one raising my brows.

"If I'd stayed here, I would never have met Ava back in Vermont. And as much pain as there is to go around when it comes to our pasts, she's the one thing I can't live without. I wouldn't be me without her. I can't regret anything that brought me to her."

I smiled. "Good. That's what love is supposed to be like, right? The whole *nothing matters but her* mentality?"

"I guess." His eyes drifted over my shoulder.

"I'm happy for you, I really am." I smacked his shoulder. "I also won't be joining you in that emotion…ever."

Reed's face fell.

"Oh, come on, like that's a big surprise. Sorry, but you're braver than I am, Reed. The only woman I've ever loved is our mom, and losing her? I'm never fucking feeling that ever again. Period."

"Weston," Reed hissed, his gaze jumping to mine and back over my shoulder.

I turned to see what he was worried about, and my heart leaped into my throat.

Callie stood on our porch, well within hearing distance, and the look on her face hit me straight in the chest. It was complete and total devastation. I moved toward her, and she blinked it away, leaving only a welcoming smile and bright eyes. I almost wouldn't have believed I'd seen the heartbreak, but it had been there, sharp enough to cut through me.

"Enjoy your walk?" she asked. "I was just thinking about going to the store." She spun her key ring around her finger.

"We both survived," Reed said.

"Good." She nodded. "Excellent." Then she turned on her heel and walked into the house.

"I thought she was going to the store," Reed muttered.

"Guess not." I stared at our front door like I could see through it.

"Okay, well, thanks for the coffee." Reed pressed the travel mug into my empty hand. "And good luck with that."

"Good luck with what?" I shot him a look.

"Women you're sleeping with typically don't like it when you proclaim that you're never going to join them in the four-letter-word department, and no, I don't mean the fun one that starts with F." He slapped me on the back.

"That's not the problem," I muttered. "Trust me, Callie knows the score." I'd told her from the get-go that I was against attachments, period. But the look on her face...

"Right." He waved at me and climbed into his car. "I'll see you later."

Reed drove off and I headed inside. Callie was nowhere to be seen, so I got out of my winter gear, put it away, and set the coffee mugs in the sink. They could wait.

"Hey," she said, skipping down the steps. Her cheeks looked a little blotchy, but she was smiling.

"Everything okay?" I met her at the base of the steps and palmed her waist.

"Everything is great," she promised. "Especially since we have another two hours before Sutton gets home." She rose on her toes and kissed the hell out of me.

My thoughts scattered.

allie

CHRISTMAS CAME AND WENT. We spent New Year's Eve at home, and it was absolutely *perfect*. That was the only way to describe the last six weeks since Weston and I had gotten together.

Well, except for the fact that he'd made it perfectly clear he wasn't going to fall in love with me, and I was falling harder for him every day. That part sucked.

But the rest? It was easier than breathing. There was no pressure with Weston. I didn't have to be perfect. Didn't have to rush to see if my makeup was fresh. Didn't have to coordinate my outfit to see him. The man had seen me at my actual worst and hadn't batted an eye.

He also saw me every single day.

I finished editing my last batch of pictures I'd taken on this morning's heli-skiing trip and uploaded them to Weston's portion of the Madigan site so the guests could download. My butt was going to be numb if I spent much more time at the dining room table. Turned out that people would pay top dollar for photos of themselves hurtling down a mountain, dodging trees, and risking their necks on twenty-foot drops. Reed had hired another photographer, bringing our team up to three, and I'd spent most of my mornings on the helicopter this last month. To be honest, once I swallowed past the anxiety that threatened to eat me alive whenever it was Weston doing the hurtling, I had to admit that the pictures came out pretty cool.

The man had no sense of caution, at least not that I could tell, and Theo was just as bad.

I opened the last picture I'd taken of Theo and shook my head. The shot itself was gorgeous—he was mid-flip off one of the bigger cliffs, and I'd positioned myself somewhat to the side and beneath him, capturing not only the jagged, exposed rock of one outcropping but the pristine fall of new snow spraying against the crystal blue sky as Theo rotated midair. Gorgeous picture.

Reckless stunt.

"That's a good one," Weston said, looking over my shoulder and kissing me on the cheek quickly. Kisses were never slow until Sutton went to bed. Then all bets were off. His hair was damp, and he smelled like bodywash and shampoo, fresh out of the shower. "Is Sutton still out on the slopes?" He glanced over at the clock.

It was a little after four.

"Nope. She said she had to stay after school for some project, but she's due home any second. She asked Halley to bring her home."

"Halley?"

"She, Ava, and Raven are the closest she has to aunts, so I stay out of their way. With my luck, she'll come home with pink streaks in her hair." I grinned at the thought. Sutton would look pretty fierce with pink streaks.

"Well, since she's not here..." He leaned in and kissed me, long, slow, and thorough. It was enough to send heat racing through every one of my veins, and I wasn't nearly satisfied when he pulled back. "Was that yesterday?" He motioned to my laptop screen.

I blinked and tried to pull my head out of his pants. The man had some serious skills. "A couple days before." I pulled my knee to my chest and studied the photo. It was the first picture I'd taken out there where I didn't immediately think of something I would have done better. It was the perfect picture to submit to the gallery...once I was brave enough to chance rejection again.

"It's really incredible." He stood. "You could enter it in that internship competition, you know."

I tilted my head and really examined the photo. Was it good enough to enter in something that big? What if it was? What if I won? My stomach sank. I'd have to choose between doing what I wanted and doing what was best for Sutton.

And Sutton would always win. Choice made.

"Callie?" Weston asked, his hand on my shoulder.

"I'll think about it," I answered. Maybe next year, or the year after, or when Sutton turned eighteen.

"Did you get any new shots of our girl?" He walked to the refrigerator and pulled out two sports drinks.

I loved that he called her *our* girl when he talked about her skiing. It was only because he was the one coaching her, I knew that, but the word still took my heart and blew it up another size.

"I did on Tuesday," I answered, scrolling through my folders to open the one I kept just for Sutton. Her pink hat and gloves were always a fun contrast against the snow. She was getting braver up there with Weston, taking bigger jumps, choosing harder lines. "She's getting..."

"Good?" he teased, cracking the top on one of the bottles and putting it down in front of me. The fact that he knew my hands ached after taking pictures all morning and editing them all afternoon was just another reason to love him.

There were too many reasons.

"Reckless," I countered. "Just like you."

"I take full credit." He laughed. "I could always have Theo take over her training."

I scoffed and clicked through the pictures. "He's just as reckless. You and your best friend are quite the match made in heaven."

"Hey, it's not reckless if you're skilled, baby." He flashed me a grin.

I rolled my eyes but flushed at the endearment. It made me want to shout from the top of the mountain that he was mine and I was his, but there was still Sutton to think about. She adored Weston, loved having him coach her, too, and if something went wrong between us, she'd be devastated.

Loving Weston meant knowing I'd be heartbroken eventually, but I couldn't accept the same fate for Sutton.

"Skill isn't luck," I muttered as the front door opened hard, blowing into the doorstop.

Both Weston and I looked over. *What the hell?*

"Hi!" Sutton stumbled through the door with an enormous cage in her arms.

"Oh, merciful God," I whispered, pushing back from the table to stand, but Weston was across the room before I'd even gotten my feet under me.

He plucked the plastic-bottomed cage out of her grip with one arm and caught her with the other, saving her from a face-plant on the tile.

"What is that?" I squawked, my voice pitching opera high.

Weston steadied Sutton, then carried the cage to the dining room table and set it down on the surface. "It looks like a gerbil."

"Guinea pig, actually." Sutton stripped out of her coat and

boots, hanging them in the closet like it was no big deal that she'd just brought a guinea pig home.

I sent my daughter a glare for good measure, and then my gaze flew to Weston to gauge his reaction.

He'd stepped back from the cage and crossed his arms over his chest. The man was a master at being unreadable sometimes.

"And why, dear daughter, is there a guinea pig in my house?" I asked, my voice dropping to the I-mean-business tone.

"His name is Wilbur, and he's our class pet." She brushed the remnants of this morning's French braid out of her face.

"Still not an answer to my question." I put myself in between her and *Wilbur*. "That's a direct violation of rule eleven!" My arm swung as I pointed in the direction of the contract on our refrigerator. I was *soooo* not mentioning all the rules Weston and I had already broken.

"It was Piper's weekend to take Wilbur, but she got sick, so I said he could stay with us," Sutton replied, her chin lifting in a manner I knew all too well.

"You didn't even ask," I retorted, trying like hell to keep my cool. "It's not just you and me here, kid."

"Weston won't care." Sutton turned those big eyes on him. "Right? I mean, I know you said no pets, but it's just the weekend, and I can keep him in my room."

Weston's gaze jumped between Sutton and me like the conversation was a ball in a tennis match. "Not getting in the middle of this." He put his hands up.

"You couldn't have called and asked?" What the hell was the solution here?

"We didn't realize it until the end of the day, and I didn't want him left all alone at school over the long weekend." She pressed her lips in a thin line.

"The long weekend." Right. Because I'd forgotten it was Martin Luther King, Jr. Day on Monday.

Sutton nodded.

"Did you know about this yesterday? Is this why you asked if Halley could pick you up?" I stared her down.

"No!" She shook her head vehemently. "I swear. That was just...luck." She shrugged.

"Because you knew I'd say no."

Sutton's gaze hit the floor and she nodded slowly. "I just didn't want him to be alone."

The pig chose that moment to scurry though his box, sending wood shavings flying all over the dining room table. Weston was going to melt down.

I looked over at him to find that he was already watching me. "It's your rule," I said softly. "I'll call every single guardian on the PTA roster and find him another home for the weekend."

"Mom!" Sutton whined. "It's just three days. Well, three and a half. Please don't make me the weird kid who can't have a guinea pig for three days."

I kept my attention on Weston. I knew his cues pretty well by now. The set of his jaw said he wasn't happy, but there was a touch of laughter in the tiny lines at the corner of his eyes. "West?"

"This is between you and Sutton." A corner of his mouth lifted. "I refer to rule number five." *Callie rules all.*

An exasperated sigh ripped through my lips as I cocked my head at my daughter. "Who is going to feed him?"

"Me! His food is in my bag, and I know the schedule." Hope bloomed in her eyes.

"And what about cleaning his cage?"

"Me! I have a bag of shavings in my backpack too." She bounced up on her toes.

"And water?"

"Every morning. I know how. We do it at school."

I glanced at the black-and-white pig. "Fine. But three days, Sutton. Do you hear me? Three days."

"Thank you!" She launched at me, hugging my waist, and then skipped away to hug Weston too.

"What's that for? I wasn't the one who said yes," he said with a chuckle.

"That's me hoping you'll carry his cage upstairs for me. It's *really* heavy." She grinned up at him.

"That, I can do." He lifted the massive cage into his arms and followed after Sutton as she walked up the stairs.

There went rule number eleven.

———

"WHAT ARE WE DOING?" I asked Sunday evening as Weston led me to the couch. Dinner was done, showers had been taken, and I was exhausted. I'd manage to edit all of today's heli-skiing photos, but Charles, one of the assistant photographers, had severely mislighted the group ones from the top of the lift, and I probably had another two hours at my computer before I could call it a night.

"Sit right here," Weston said, gesturing to the couch.

"What is going on?" I sat, my eyes narrowing slightly.

"Just wait right here," he answered, a hint of a smile on his lips. "And remember that I'm just the facilitator here."

Now my curiosity was piqued.

"Sutton, you're up!" Weston called up the stairs.

She skipped down the stairs in dress pants and a blouse, her hair perfectly combed and held back by a black headband. "Do you have it set up?" she asked as she skidded around the end of the banister, marching straight for the kitchen.

"Almost," he answered, plugging his laptop into the television.

A Presentation by Sutton filled the flatscreen.

"Is that a PowerPoint?" My eyebrows hit the roof.

"She made it." He grabbed a small black remote off the coffee table as Sutton came back into the living room, her hands full as she balanced a tray.

"Chocolate chip cookies and milk," she said, putting the tray on the coffee table. "Because every good presentation has snacks."

"It does?" I leaned forward, snatching one of the cookies. PowerPoint or no, there was no reason to waste chocolate chip cookies.

"It does." Sutton turned to Weston, and he handed her the remote.

"Good luck, kid." He took the seat directly next to mine, and I crossed my legs under me just so I'd have an excuse to rest my knee against him.

"Is this for school?" I stared at the PowerPoint. "Are you practicing on me?"

"Oh no." Sutton shook her head, standing just off to the side of the television. "This is just for you." She looked at Weston, swallowing nervously, and he nodded.

What the heck were the two of them up to?

"Have you seen this?" I asked him.

"Nope." He settled in and stretched his arm across the back of the couch, just behind my head.

"Mom," Sutton began, straightening her posture. "You've raised me here at Madigan Mountain from the time I was born." She clicked the remote, and the next slide appeared. It was a set of pictures from when she was a baby, one of her standing in the snow after her first birthday, her snowsuit bigger than she was. The second showed us both, me with my photographer parka on and her strapped in on my back under a shaded canopy.

Man, those days had been tough. I'd worked with her on my back, in my arms, or on the ski slope right beside me until she'd been old enough to spend part of her day in the resort kid's club.

"The slopes are my second home." She clicked through the next slide. It was another collection of pictures, this time of her in ski gear from the time she was three all the way to nine or so.

I took a bite of my cookie and chewed, my suspicions rising.

"As you know, I've been training with an expert backcountry skier for the last two months." She clicked and the slide changed to pictures of her with Weston up on the mountain. They were some of my favorite new photos I'd taken.

I lifted an eyebrow at my daughter, clearly seeing where this was headed.

She fidgeted nervously but clicked again. This slide displayed a quote. "Sutton Thorne is a remarkably gifted young skier with a rare combination of raw talent, determination, and good judgment," Sutton read. "The quote is from Weston."

I gave him a slow, sideways glare.

He glanced between us. "I mean, it was just for the application."

"With that in mind"—she clicked again—"I propose that you, my mother, sign the following permission slip for me to join the county's big mountain team." She scurried forward and picked up a manila envelope I hadn't noticed, putting it into my hands.

I sighed but opened the folder. The entire application had been filled out, and sure enough, there was Weston's quote in his own handwriting. "Et tu Brute?" I whispered with more than a little side-eye.

"Hey, I just helped her get her ducks in a row. Nothing more." His arm shifted down and I leaned back, his forearm supporting my neck.

"My proposal has been well researched, and I believe I have eliminated all but a few reasons to say no." She clicked. The cost was on the next slide. I wanted to vomit. "Because I'd be starting two months later, the coach of the team has already dropped my fee to this much more manageable one." A new number popped up.

My daughter and I had very different views on manageable.

"I've also spoken to the"—she glanced at the screen—"Director of Madigan Mountain's Heli-skiing Division," she read right off the television, "who has told me that if I'm the only big mountain skier from Madigan Mountain, I might be able to secure a sponsorship."

My jaw dropped. "Ducks in a row, huh?"

"And what was the caveat?" Weston asked.

Sutton's brow furrowed.

"Conditions," he said. "What were the conditions?"

"Oh!" She clicked the remote for the next slide. "I, Sutton Thorne, will keep my grades up, my equipment well cared for, and get my mother's permission."

I set the folder on the end table and shoved the rest of the cookie in my mouth. It tasted like defeat.

"I know you have concerns." She clicked again, and a picture of caution tape filled the screen. "My dad died before I could even meet him, which has made you worried about my safety my whole life."

I choked on the cookie. Weston pounded my back and handed me the glass of milk. Two swallows later, my airway was clear. "That's rather inappropriate, don't you think?"

"Not really." She shrugged. "He was *my* dad." She clicked and stats slid onto the page. "You see, only eleven skiers were killed last year in Colorado, and none were under the age of fourteen. That makes the chance of death point-eight-nine per million..." She started shaking her head as she looked at Weston, a perplexed look on her face, and I turned to see Weston shaking his head vehemently.

"Not helping," he muttered.

Okay, this was on the ridiculous side.

"Oh. Right." She clicked. "As you see here, the rate of car crashes is way higher, so I'd be far more likely to be hurt or killed on my way to practice—"

"Not helping either," he mumbled.

"I mean, to *school*, than I would on the mountain."

The fact that my daughter thought statistics played into any part of my fear was so ludicrous that I laughed.

She took this as a good sign and smiled, clicking again. "Because Weston trains with me in the afternoons when he can, the county coach said I only had to come once a week."

My eyebrows shot up. That was a serious concern. Breckenridge was forty minutes away, and I wasn't exactly swimming in free time over here.

"I've already solved that problem by securing a ride." She glanced at Weston.

I stared at him with a cocked eyebrow.

He shrugged. "She asked. I said yes. It's once a week."

"And when it comes to competing"—she pressed the remote —"there are only two competitions I'd have time to qualify for this year. One is at Breck, and the other, Steamboat, and that's not until the end of March, so you'd have plenty of data by then to make a choice." She clicked. "And my last point. You should try everything once, just to know if you like it." Her eyes landed on me. "I'm quoting you there, Mom."

Well. Shit.

She clicked one last time. The sign read *please*.

I breathed out a sigh. The days of keeping her tucked away and safe in the little snow globe I'd created just for her were over. I could say no, but she'd be back next year, asking again. Or worse, she'd just stop asking and start doing.

"You care about this so much that you made a PowerPoint?" I asked.

She nodded. "It's all I want."

Man, did I know that feeling well.

I sagged back against the couch, leaning my head on Weston's shoulder. "You think she'll be safe?"

"I think safety is a relative term," he answered gently.

I looked up into his eyes, and they softened. Weston had been up there on the mountain with her. If he didn't think she was safe, he would have told me.

"Okay." I leaned forward and snagged the conveniently placed pen on the cookie tray. "You win." It took less than thirty seconds to scrawl my signature across the permission line.

"Thank you!" Sutton grabbed the folder and hugged me extra tight, knocking me back into the couch. Then she ran upstairs, no doubt needing to secure her paperwork.

"She's tenacious," I muttered, hoping I hadn't just made the biggest mistake of my life.

"She's you," Weston said.

I turned my head and kissed him, my hand cupping the back of his neck.

Footsteps sounded on the stairs, and I jumped back, but it was too late. Sutton had already flown around the banister, headed in our direction like a missile.

"Sutton," I said softly. Oh God, she was going to freak out. She was going to—

"I forgot to say thank you to you!" she said to Weston, lunging at him in a hug.

He caught her easily and squeezed right back. No double pat on the back. No awkwardness. My heart melted.

"You can go back to kissing my mom now," she said, pushing up and whirling away, back toward the steps.

"Sutton!" My mouth dropped.

"I live here too! You guys are so obvious." She raced back up the stairs.

Weston and I stared at each other in shock for a few seconds. Then he smiled, and mine followed. "Obvious? Really?"

"I do really like to look at you," he noted.

Sutton shrieked, the sound filling the house.

"What's wrong?" I fumbled but found my feet.

Weston beat me up the steps and down the hallway to

Sutton's room. I ducked under his shoulder and saw Sutton staring at Wilbur's cage.

Wilbur's *empty* cage.

"Oh, fuck," Weston muttered.

"Language!" I whispered.

"There's a guinea pig missing somewhere in this house and you're—" He paused, then lunged for the end of Sutton's bed.

Wilbur squealed and disappeared.

I snorted a laugh as Weston crawled halfway under the bed.

Wilbur raced out from the other side, and I was the one lunging this time, falling to my knees. My fingers touched rough fur, but he was gone again.

Weston and I locked eyes under the bed. "I'm so sorry," I said.

"At least it's never boring around here," he answered with a grin.

"He's down the hall!" Sutton shouted, already moving.

Twenty minutes later, we had him trapped under a laundry basket in the living room, and my sides hurt from laughing so much.

"I declare victory," Weston announced as the doorbell rang.

"I'll get it," I said, rising to my feet. "Sutton, you'd better put him back in his cage and *lock* it." I gave her a stern look, but it was hard keeping a straight face.

"Got it!" She snagged the laundry basket from Weston.

I opened the door and my stomach hit the floor. I'd never worked directly with him, but eleven years at Madigan meant I knew exactly who I was looking at. This was going to go so bad so quickly.

"Weston," I whispered over my shoulder.

The man on front steps ran his hand over his salt-and-pepper hair and shifted his weight nervously.

Weston appeared at my back, his entire body rigid against mine as he looked over my shoulder.

"When Reed told me you were back, I had to see for myself," Weston's dad said, apprehension etched in every line of his face. "You've always been a man of your word, Weston, and when you swore you'd never speak to me again that night, I never imagined I'd have this chance—"

Weston slammed the door in his face.

eston

My phone rang, buzzing in the cupholder of my truck.

I took one look and hit the decline button.

Callie glanced my way but didn't say a word as we drove down the mountain toward the resort. She hadn't said a word about it since I'd shut the door on my father four weeks ago.

I fucking *loved* that about her.

Watch that word.

"I keep waiting for you to suggest I take the call," I said quietly, well aware that Sutton was in the back. Kids didn't need to know that parents had the potential to suck...not that I was Sutton's parent.

Callie startled, her head whipping toward mine. "I'm the last person who would ever suggest that."

I reached across the console and laced my fingers with hers, holding her hand all the way to Sutton's school. Too bad I wouldn't have Callie with me this morning. I was getting a little too used to spending my work time with her too.

Which reminded me.

"Did you think about that internship contest?" I asked. "The photo one?"

Her eyes flew to mine as we moved forward in the drop-off line.

"No pressure if you don't feel like you're ready. I just remembered that the deadline is tomorrow." I squeezed her fingers in what I hoped was reassurance. "No big deal, really. I just didn't want you to miss the opportunity if you wanted it this year."

"The application form for photo release is on the fridge," Sutton said from the back seat. "You should do it, Mom! You've always wanted to work for *World Geographic*."

"I'll...um... I'll think about it tonight, okay?" Her smile was flustered.

Shit. Had I pressured her by bringing it up? "I don't want you to feel obligated," I said, pulling up to the font of the school. "I just think the world should know how fantastic you are."

"Ditto! See you guys later!" Sutton jumped out, waved good-bye, and ran off toward her friends. I muttered a curse as the neon-orange lunch box in the back seat caught my attention.

"Lunch box," I told Callie.

She unrolled the window and called Sutton's name as I bent to the side, my entire body reaching for the damn thing. "Got it." I handed it to Callie.

"Good luck on your math quiz," Callie said, dangling the box out the window.

"Thanks!" Sutton took it.

"And don't forget, we have practice this afternoon, so you've got to get out here right after the bell so we can make it." I leaned forward, making eye contact with Sutton and lifting my brows. We'd been fifteen minutes late to last week's practice, which wasn't going to fly with the coach, no matter how talented she thought Sutton was.

"I will this time, I promise!" She bounced backward. "Love you!"

"Love you!" Callie responded.

The words came so easily to both of them.

Callie rolled up the window, and I pulled out of the drop-off line and back into traffic so we could both get to work.

"I still can't believe you've been taking her all the way to Breck for practice." Callie looked at me with a mix of wonder and a tenderness I wasn't about to label.

"She's good. She deserves a chance." I shrugged. "Besides, I don't have skiers today, just a private helicopter tour, and we land at two. That's plenty of time to run down the bird and get here, and it will give you time to finish up your edits." We were in a mid-February lull, but we'd be inundated with spring breakers soon enough.

"Why, Weston Madigan, I do believe you've gone domestic on me." Her smile made my chest tighten and warm all at the same time.

I picked up her hand and kissed the back of it. "Only for you." The truth of the words sent a chill down my spine, and I couldn't decide if that was good or bad.

"Even better."

An hour later, I finished up some of the paperwork and made sure our flight plan was filed while Theo ran up the bird.

"You good on supplies?" I asked Maria as she popped her head into the office, snagging one of the turnovers Theo had brought in with him. "I'm making an order next week."

"Solid. I'll take a quick inventory and let you know." She gave me a thumbs-up and disappeared into the hangar.

I was zipping up my Madigan Mountain embroidered vest when Theo walked in.

"Your guy is locked and loaded," he said. "You sure you don't want some company?"

"You have that meeting for Seline, right?" I tugged my baseball cap on and molded the brim.

"True, but I feel like shit skipping out on you."

"Ah, now I understand the reason for the turnovers." I smacked him on the shoulder as I walked by. "Go. Get your kid enrolled into all the gifted stuff. I'll be the one ditching you when I leave early for Sutton's practice."

"Never thought I'd see the day when you settled down," he said with a chuckle.

I spun, my eyes narrowing. "Who said I'm settled down?"

"It's all over you, West." He grinned. "Looks good, too. Never seen you this happy."

My brow furrowed. "I guess I've never been this happy before."

"Don't look so ecstatic about it." He laughed. "She's good for you. They both are. Now you'd better get out there. The guy seems like the real quiet type. He's briefed, strapped in at the bench, and has his headset tuned to the right frequency. Go be the best tour guide you can be."

"Thanks." I nodded and headed out toward the bird. *She's good for you. They both are.* He was right...as usual. The peace that had stolen over me in the last few months could only be because of them. I was changing, bending boundaries I thought were rigid but actually weren't. I didn't mind Sutton's shoes in the middle of the floor, and the usual quiet I needed at the end of the day had been replaced by an insatiable craving for Callie. We still slept in our own beds for the most part, but there was no sneaking back and forth if we fell asleep on the "wrong" side of the house. And maybe they weren't the ones changing me, maybe I was *evolving*, as Theo called it, but I knew the girls were certainly the catalysts.

Ducking my head, I walked under the swirling rotors and

opened the driver's door, climbing in with practiced ease. I slipped the headset on and glanced over my shoulder. Well, that was odd. The guest was on the bench like Theo said, but not the one facing forward. "You sure you don't want to move up front?" I asked through the headset. "It's a better view."

"Nope. This is good." The guest's voice was gruff.

"Okay then, here we go." Hands on the controls and feet on the pedals, I took off, and the earth fell away as we rose into the clear blue sky. "It's a great day for flying. Not a cloud in sight."

The guy grunted.

Theo hadn't been kidding about the quiet-type comment.

I started in on what I hoped was a sufficient tour, pointing out the resort, the original lift, and the new expansion Reed had busted his ass on. We were up and over the Madigan peak before I realized I hadn't even asked the guy's name.

Fantastic helicopter pilot? Check.

Great skier? You bet.

But I was not cut out for this scenic helicopter tour bullshit.

"I'm so sorry, but I didn't catch your name," I said into the headset as we skimmed down the backside of the mountain. There was a mumble that I didn't quite catch.

I flew us through the valley and up to the ridgelines we usually used for the backcountry tours. If the guy wanted a photo op, there was no better place. I set the skids down on the hardpack. We hadn't had new powder in three days. "Feel free to change seats to get a picture. It's completely safe while we're stopped."

"You're a hell of a pilot, aren't you?" he asked, his voice clear as day through the headset.

No fucking way.

I held completely still as the guy moved up to the front bench, hoping I was wrong.

"I wish I'd realized that sooner," he said. "Wish I'd realized a lot of things sooner."

"We're not doing this here." Anger and disbelief mixed in my head until I couldn't separate the emotions.

"Well, it's the only place I could nail you down to do it."

I turned, looking over my shoulder as Dad tugged off his skull cap and unzipped his jacket from where he'd fastened it all the way to his nose. "The things I would say to you, if I even *wanted* to say them, shouldn't be said in a helicopter while I'm flying it."

"Seems like you're not flying it right now." Dad shrugged, the gesture so like mine that my jaw locked.

"You know I could just walk out, right? I don't mind hiking back up for the bird later, if that's what it takes." I was just stubborn enough to do it too.

Dad lounged against the backrest. "From what Reed tells me, this helicopter is your baby. I don't think you'd abandon it on a windy peak. Plus, I'm paying you for the tour, so from where I'm sitting, you're mine for the next"—he checked his watch—"thirty-eight minutes."

Fuck him.

"So tell me, Weston. Are you a mature businessman? Or are you the rebellious teenager who walked away without so much as a goodbye eleven years ago? Because I'm the weathered, aging father who just needs the chance to apologize, if you'll give it to me."

Fine, as lines went, that was a good one. Plus, I had to hand it to him, he'd shelled out a ridiculous sum of money just to get me alone. *And if you leave him up here to die, you'll spend the rest of your life in jail instead of Callie's bed.*

Logic won.

"I'm not going to have this conversation with you in the back like I'm some sort of chauffeur." I motioned to the copilot's seat.

"You actually want me that close to you?" His silvery brow furrowed.

"It's easier to push you out midair if you're up here," I deadpanned.

"I can't tell if you're serious or not. That was always the hardest part about you, not being able to get a read on what you were thinking."

"Guess you'll have to chance it." I looked forward, leaving the choice up to him.

"Damn it," he muttered, but unbuckled and moved between our seats, taking the copilot's position.

"Don't touch any of the controls," I warned.

"Or what?" He fumbled with the belt but got strapped in.

"Or you risk the chance of killing us both, and while you might be done with your life, I'm just starting to like mine." I looked out over the snow-tipped peaks and thought about Callie's smile, her hands, her laugh—anything to keep me focused on my future and not the past that was dredging itself up beside me.

"It's the girl, isn't it?" he asked. "The love of a good woman will do that for you."

"Rule one. She's not up for discussion." Callie didn't love me. She had to know better than that.

"Okay." He put his hands up like he was under arrest. "Damn. Reed said you were prickly—"

"Down to thirty-two minutes." And I was going to count every single one of them.

"I haven't had a drink in a year," he said.

"Good." It was. I couldn't deny that.

"I've somehow managed to keep the love of a good woman," he continued. "She's not your mom, but...I love her."

"Good." Sticking with the one-word answers was easy.

"And I'm damn proud of the man you've become."

That had me swiveling my head toward him. "You had *nothing* to do with the man I've become."

"I'm even prouder of you because of that." His smile was

close-lipped and sad. "I was always proud when you'd bring home a trophy, or when you made your mother smile. But knowing that you've spent a decade serving your country, watching you fly this helicopter like it's nothing more complicated than a car...I'm speechless."

My jaw locked and unlocked, then repeated the process.

"Just let me have it, Weston." He shoved his hands into the pockets of his coat. "Whatever you need to say, just say it."

"I don't need to say shit to you. Thought I made that clear by *not* taking your calls. This"—I motioned between us—"isn't a relationship you can repair. And it's not something I need closure on, either. You were dead to me a long time ago."

"You forgave Reed." The plea in his eyes only loosened the tether I had on my temper.

"Reed was a *child*. Did I resent the hell out of the fact that he got to go do whatever the hell he wanted? Got to have a life? Absolutely. But he was a kid. *You* were the adult." I jabbed my finger in his direction.

"I know, and I'm sorry." His face fell.

"You checked out when she got sick!" I snapped. "She was scared, and confused, and dying, and you decided the bottom of a bottle was a better place to be than at her side."

Memories assaulted me, pulling me back to the sight of the frozen ground being excavated for her body. Crew's tears that he hadn't been able to hide. The absolute terror in Reed's eyes. The weight of everyone's needs settling on my shoulders because I knew I was the only one who could handle it all. Because I knew Mom needed me to handle it all.

"I know, and I'm sorry." Shame washed over his features.

"You abandoned us. You threw yourself into the fucking resort and *abandoned* Crew and me. You left us to raise ourselves. I was sixteen years old when she died, you asshole. *Sixteen.* You were drunk while Reed and I tried to plan the funeral. You were drunk when we buried her. You didn't give a shit about the fact that your sons' worlds were disintegrating. You only cared about yourself, you selfish fuck." The words tasted bitter, and yet I couldn't seem to stop them from flying out of my mouth, and each truth only made me realize just how fucked-up it all really had been.

Because if something happened to Callie, I would have made damn sure Sutton was okay. My chest clenched painfully at the thought, but it was true. I would never leave Sutton to her own grief the way Dad had left us to ours.

"I know, and I'm sorry," he said, softer this time.

"Stop fucking saying that!" I shook my head. "I was the adult in that house for years, Dad. Not days while you got through the shock, or weeks while you processed your grief. Years. You didn't show up to my high school graduation. You couldn't be bothered to get to the ER when the doctors had to set Crew's hand. You sure as hell didn't watch him compete or give a damn when I *stopped* competing."

"I know. And. I'm sorry." His shoulders fell.

"Is that all you have to say? Eleven years, and all you can say is *I know and I'm sorry?*" It wasn't enough, but I wasn't sure anything would ever be enough.

"I won't make any excuses, Weston." He shook his head. "I stopped acting like your father the day we lost your mom, and it's inexcusable."

"You quit before that." The muscles in my jaw ticked. "And maybe if it had just been me, or even Crew that you'd neglected, I could get past it. But the way you abandoned her when she got sick?" My throat closed up. I could still feel her hand squeezing mine, her eyes going cloudy with confusion because she couldn't figure out what day it was. "I'll never forgive you for that."

"I'm not asking you to." He looked away. "I'll never forgive myself. I'm just glad you're here, Weston. I'm thankful you came when Reed called. I'm in awe of what you've done, how successful you've made your side of the business in such a short time."

Silence stretched between us for a minute or two, so tense that every breath was a struggle.

"It took a long time for me to learn how to live with myself," he said slowly. "It was long after you boys were grown. And I guess that's what I'm asking you for."

My gaze clashed with his.

"I won't ever ask your forgiveness, but I will ask that you learn to live...around me." Misery lined his face, but hope flashed in his eyes. "It's a small mountain, Weston. We're bound to see each other."

It was on the tip of my tongue to tell him that we'd managed not seeing each other just fine in the last two weeks he'd been home.

"I just want the chance to be in your life. Whatever that looks like to you, I'm fine with. Just...the chance."

The angry sixteen-year-old boy that still lived within me wanted to tell him to fuck off. But the fifteen-year-old? He was tempted to say yes. "Time's up."

Dad nodded, his back falling against the seat in defeat.

I took off and managed to keep my head clear enough to fly back to the helipad. It was the longest flight of my life, and I'd survived being shot at in the air before.

I ran the bird down in silence while Dad waited for the rotors to come to a complete stop.

It felt like forever, but they finally did.

"Thanks for the flight. It was worth every penny." He reached for the handle.

"Why?" I asked, unable to let it go. "Why now? Because you managed to fall in love and Melody changed you? Because Reed swooped in and saved the resort? Because it's convenient now that I'm home and you don't have to track me down across the world to apologize?" My grip tightened on the laminated check-list. "Why. Now."

He closed his eyes for a second, and then looked my way. "Because I'm finally in a place where I can say I'm sorry without any of those excuses you were looking for, and because despite my lack of showing it, I've always loved you, Weston. Always will." He climbed out of the helicopter and left me sitting on the pad.

———

CALLIE CLIMBED into bed with me later that night, long after Sutton was asleep.

"You were off tonight," she said, laying her head on my chest.

"I'm sorry." My hand stroked up and down her back over her tank top.

"Nothing to be sorry about." She rolled, lacing her fingers over my chest and propping her chin on them. "You weren't mean, or short. Just...off."

Any other woman, and I would have gotten up and left. Hell, any other person on the planet and I would have walked out of the conversation. Then again, I'd never felt this way about a woman before. It was more than respect and friendship. I lived for the moments I was with her. As terrifying as it was, I adored her.

"I got into it with my dad today." I kept making small circles on her back, touching her because it brought me comfort.

Her eyebrows shot up.

I gave her the Cliffs Notes version of what happened, and she listened silently.

"And then he said he loved me." I scoffed. "Like that word could even remotely pair with his actions. Like that word could erase the last fifteen years."

"I'm so sorry," she said softly, her eyes liquid in the moon-light that came in through the window.

"Gavin died." My hand slid to the small of her back. "And yet you didn't fall apart. You took care of Sutton."

A sad smile tipped her lips. "You saw me on one of the many nights I fell apart. I was a damn wreck most of that year. If anything, Sutton was what pulled me through it. She gave me purpose, a reason to live. Every time she'd smile, I'd see him." She didn't look away. She let me see everything she was feeling without reservation. "Sometimes I still do."

My hand stilled. "You still love him."

"Yes." She tilted her head. "But it's faded with time. It doesn't hurt in the same way it used to either. The waves don't pull me under when I think about him anymore. I'm less angry that he died and more thankful that I had those years with him." Her smile brightened. "And I'm infinitely thankful that he gave me Sutton."

"You're an incredible mom, Calliope." I forced a smile, but it slipped. "And my mom would have loved you."

"And I'm sure I would have loved her."

I looked up at the ceiling. "She never would have done what he did. I just don't understand what the hell made us so unlov-able that he couldn't show up for us." I shook my head. "We were kids. Fine, teenagers, and unruly ones at that, but still... just kids."

"Nothing." She sat up on her knees and cupped my face. "Weston, nothing about you is unlovable. Not now, and I'm sure not then."

A wry laugh escaped. "There are about a million things I could list."

She leaned in, hovering close and filling my vision. "And there are a million things I could list, because I love you."

My heart stopped. "You can't." It was impossible...and yet,

she was the most emotionally reckless person I'd ever known. She threw her heart into *everything*.

"I can, and I do." She nodded, her face scrunching before she smiled again. "I love how you take care of everyone around you. I love to watch you with Sutton. I love how you handle a helicopter. I love how you force me to the edge of my comfort zone. I love that you like everything in its place, and I love that you make exceptions for me, for us." She stroked her thumbs over my cheeks. "I love how you worry about your friends. I love that you can't keep your hands off me. I love how you touch me, how you make me feel Like there's nowhere safer to be than in your arms."

"Callie," I whispered. My heart was thundering now, panic creeping into my veins. I wasn't capable of returning the emotion, and it would wreck her. I would destroy her. "Don't love me. Please, don't love me. I'm nowhere near good enough." She deserved someone who could love her back just as fiercely.

I already hated whomever it was.

"Too late." She shrugged. "I love everything about you, Weston Madigan, even when you're driving me up the wall with your rules and your silence. I love you."

"Fuck." My grip shifted to her waist, and she slid her knee over me, straddling my lap.

"I love you." She kissed my forehead. "I love you." My cheek. "I love you." My jaw. "And I'll say it as many times as you need to believe it." My lips.

I should have pushed her away, set her free before I could do any more damage, but instead, I kissed her right back. For the first time in my life, I needed someone more than I needed solitude. I needed Callie.

"I love you," she whispered with every kiss. Every touch. She said it when I slid inside her and when she came. And it wasn't just her words. She said it with her hands, her eyes, her entire body.

I fell asleep with those words engraved in my fucking soul.

She loved me, and I didn't deserve it because I'd never risk loving her back, but I wasn't capable of letting her go, either.

Guess I was the selfish asshole now.

It was dawn when I crept out of bed after kissing her forehead.

If I wasn't going to let her go, then I had to find a way to make loving me worth her while.

Sutton was in the kitchen when I came down the stairs.

"You're up early," I said.

She startled, backing away from the kitchen island. "I was just...thirsty." She went to the refrigerator and pulled out the carton of orange juice.

"Okay." It was more than weird, but what did I really know about the early morning drinking habits of eleven-year-old girls? The thumb drive on top of the internship application I'd left out for Callie at the corner of the counter caught my attention. It had to be whatever photo she'd chosen. "She's going to enter?" Pride had me smiling ear to ear.

"Looks like it," Sutton said, pulling a glass from the cabinet.

I flipped the application over and ran my thumb over the signature required for the photo release. "Guess she is, since she signed it." But there was something a little off about the E in her name.

"She's going to place, maybe even win the amateur division," Sutton said, nodding her head as she poured the juice into the small glass. "We both know it. She's so good, and she shouldn't hide it."

Apprehension slid down my spine. "Sutton, did you sign this?"

She put the carton of orange juice away.

"Sutton?"

"Do you really want to know?" She faced me head on, tilting

her chin in the same way Callie did when she'd made up her mind on a subject.

"This is a big deal," I said slowly. "It's not a pretend contract on our refrigerator, or some note to get you out of trouble at school." *Shit.* What was I supposed to do with this?

"You have to enter for her," Sutton whispered. "Everything is signed. The picture is right there. And the deadline is in a couple hours."

"If she doesn't want to enter, we can't make her enter." Even if it would skyrocket her personal portfolio. If she even touched the top twenty-five, she'd have national attention, the kind she deserved, the kind that would get her into the local gallery she'd set her sights on…if she'd just get out of her own way.

"Fine." Sutton tensed. "If you won't do it, then I will." She reached for the application, and I jerked it back.

"Is that why you're up this early? So you could just enter for her?"

"If it was your mom, wouldn't you want the whole world to know how special she was?"

Ouch. She hit the nail on the fucking head.

"I'm not a little kid. I'm *eleven*. I know how hard it's been for her to raise me all on her own. She should get to have this." She must have seen me wavering, because she came toward me, the plea evident in her eyes. "Please let her have this."

"If she doesn't want it, we can't make her," I argued. Even if I agreed with Sutton, which I did, if Callie hadn't been the one to sign this, and I couldn't do it behind her back.

"She's *my* mom. I know her. She won't say it, but I'm the reason she's not entering, just like I'm the reason she couldn't finish college. She's always been too busy taking care of me."

I shook my head. "No. Sutton, you can't blame yourself for—"

"If she doesn't place, she'll never have to know," she argued, running me over. "And if she does? If she makes the finals or wins? Everyone will see her pictures." She did the chin-tilt thing again. "And I'm going to enter her."

Callie would be furious with Sutton if she did it against her wishes...but how happy would she be if her photo was chosen? If she had the validation of just how good she was? But I was the adult here. I couldn't let Sutton take the blame.

If the choice was between Callie being pissed at Sutton for something she was obviously going to do with or without my permission, or pissed at me, then it was a no-brainer.

And Callie deserved her shot. She deserved to shine, even if she didn't think she did. Maybe I couldn't give her the words she wanted, the ones she'd given me last night, but I could give her this.

"I'll do it." I uploaded the signed release and the photo of Theo from the thumb drive.

World, meet the incredible Calliope Thorne.

allie

"IT'S NOT on the market yet, but I think we might be able to get in to see it before it even hits the MLS," Shannon, my realtor, said through the phone.

"Really?" I glanced at Weston in the driver's seat as we pulled into the venue at Steamboat. Crap, why was my first instinct when talking to *my* realtor about *my* potential house to look at Weston?

Because you love him.

Yeah, well, it had been a month since I'd dropped that bomb on him, and other than telling me *not* to love him that first night, I hadn't even gotten a gun-shot level response. I hadn't given him those words just to hear them back, but it would have been nice. It would have been *perfect*.

"So, what do you think?" Shannon asked.

"It's two bedrooms? Two baths?" I repeated the details she'd given me.

Weston glanced my way, but his expression was unreadable as he found a parking spot.

"Yep. In that new development. I know it's a condo, so it wouldn't fit your exact wish list, but it's in your price range."

It was at the top of my price range, but a condo would still be *mine*. It would still be someplace Sutton and I could call our own. "Go ahead and see if we can get in tomorrow."

"You're set with the down payment, right?"

"Yep." My stomach swirled. It would wipe out my savings, but wasn't this what I'd been building it for?

"Good. I'll text you with the details." Shannon and I hung up as Weston put the truck into park.

"Good news?" he asked.

"Shannon found another place she wants me to look at." It had been weeks since the last call. "It's a condo that's about to go on the market, and it's within my price range."

"That's good...right?" Was that a flicker of panic in his eyes? Maybe I just *wanted* it to be. Maybe I wanted him to tell me we'd look for something together, that he saw a future for us outside employee housing.

Or maybe I was just being needy.

"Yeah, it's great. Let's get this show started." I forced a smile, and we all piled out of the truck in various states of readiness. I helped Sutton into her snow pants in the cab and then wiggled my way into my own in the front seat. We were here. Against my better judgment, I'd agreed to let her compete. It was the last event of the season, and her coach promised me she was ready.

"I can't believe this is real!" Sutton was a bundle of excitement as Weston grabbed her equipment from the back. She practically thrummed with nervous, joyful energy.

"Believe it, kid." He ruffled the top of her hat. "Time to put your focus hat on, or your mother might get even more nervous and withdraw her consent."

"Ha." I rolled my eyes as we walked toward the registration table under the *Welcome to the Steamboat IFSA Extreme Freeride Qualifier* banner. "And what exactly are we qualifying for?"

"Some of the kids are trying to qualify for nationals," Sutton answered. "I'm just hoping to place. Don't worry, Mom, I'm just in the U12 division."

"Right." I gripped the release in my hands as the line moved forward and read it over again. *The Undersigned understands that taking part in the Activity can be HAZARDOUS AND INVOLVES THE RISK OF PHYSICAL INJURY AND/OR DEATH.*

"She'll be okay," Weston assured me, wrapping his arm around my shoulders.

"Because you've signed one of these before?" I lifted my brows at him.

"Actually, yeah. I took on guardianship for Crew and signed more than my fair share of those." He kissed my temple. "But I totally understand that you're nervous."

Nervous didn't begin to explain the riot of emotions galloping through my heart like a herd of unwanted horses.

"Name?" the registrar asked.

"Sutton Thorne. Team Summit." Sutton beamed a smile, and my nerves lessened. If this was what made her glow with happiness, then I'd learn to live with the anxiety.

"Here you go." The registrar handed over a bib with a number on it. "Waiver?"

I had to trust that Weston knew her capabilities and that her coach wouldn't put her into a competition she wasn't ready for. Inwardly cringing, I handed the paper over.

We met up with the rest of the team, then split for the gondola ride. Weston laced my fingers with his, rubbing his thumb over the back of my hand as Sutton talked with a few of the other girls.

"She's trained," he said softly, so only I could hear. "It's going to be the easier of the courses, not the extreme stuff you can see over there." He pointed to the ridge above, where the course looked like a straight-up cliff. "And she's smart, Callie. She'll pick a good line."

"Distract me."

He squeezed my hand. "How would you feel about getting the condo?"

I looked at him as the gondola made its steady climb. "How would *you* feel about me getting the condo?"

"I want whatever makes you happy." His mouth tightened. "But I would be lying if I said I wouldn't miss seeing you every day. I've gotten so used to being with you all the time that I honestly can't imagine *not* being with you."

My heart freaking soared. "You could always come look at it with me."

His eyes flared, and the struggle I saw written in the lines of his face made my chest ache. He wasn't ready. Weston may have been a daredevil when it came to physical risk, but he moved with the emotional speed of a turtle. We were polar opposites that way.

"But you don't have to," I assured him. "Just because Sutton and I would be moving out doesn't mean we wouldn't still be together."

"Just in different houses." His brow furrowed.

"There's that whole thing called dating. We just kind of jumped into this all backward." I leaned into him. "You know I love you, right?"

"I know." He kissed my forehead. "And you know I'm wild about you."

"I know." I grinned. Wild wasn't love, but I'd take it.

Ten minutes later, we were at the base of the competition area, which looked like nothing but untamed backcountry to me as I surveyed the face of the ridge.

"What are you thinking?" Weston asked Sutton as they studied the lay of the land.

"That one looks pretty tame," Sutton said, pointing up to the ridge.

Compared to the rocky cliffs and dramatic falls on the left, she was right.

"I can drop into that keyhole right there." Her eyes narrowed as she studied the path. "And it's got a couple good drops. That one looks like an eight-footer."

"Solid choice." He put out his fist and she bumped it. "Use your head."

"Thorne!" her coach called out.

"Bye, Mom!" She hugged me quickly and headed off with her team to hike to the top of their runs.

"Have to admit, it's not as bad as I thought," I said to Weston as we picked our way through the small crowd of spectators. "I kinda thought that was their area." I motioned toward the right.

Weston laughed. "In the under twelve division? No way."

I watched her neon-pink hat as the group climbed. "Explain it to me. She picks her own path?"

He nodded. "They're kind of set. There's a score for the line she chooses, based on how steep it is, the snow conditions, exposure, and air."

"Air." I didn't take my eyes off Sutton.

"The little jumps." He rubbed his hand over my back.

"The little *cliffs*."

He laughed. "Then she can earn up to three points more depending on how she skis that line. How fluid she is, her technique, style, control."

The announcer called a name over the portable loudspeaker, and I watched one of the competitors come down, holding my breath the whole time. The crowd clapped as she made it to the bottom.

A dozen more went after her, all choosing different lines.

One girl walked away crying, holding an arm at a morbid angle that was obviously broken.

What the hell had I been thinking?

"From Team Summit, number eight eight two, Sutton Thorne," the announcer said.

I lifted my camera from the strap around my neck, zooming in as my heart threatened to beat right out of my chest. Sutton's pink hat appeared, and then the rest of her came into view at the edge of the line.

"Think smart, kid," Weston whispered.

Sutton dropped into her line. She looked controlled and confident as she hit the first jump, but I didn't exactly have the most experienced eye to judge as I clicked picture after picture. She landed it and continued down, cutting back and forth through a chute before taking the next jump.

"Land it, land it," I begged.

She did.

Then she tucked her legs up on the last, biggest cliff, crossing her skis...

And landed it.

The crowd clapped and I took my first breath. I didn't give a shit what the judges thought of her run. To me, she'd nailed it.

It took another few minutes before she found us in the crowd. "Did you see me?"

"Of course I did!" I yanked her into a hug, uncaring if it wasn't cool to have your mom basically smother you in public. "You were amazing!"

"Solid run! You nailed it!" Weston threw up his hand, and Sutton high-fived it.

She sat with us as the rest of her team made their runs, and my shoulders finally lost their tension. I'd signed the waiver. She'd made the run. It had all worked out. And even better? I wouldn't have to deal with this stress again until next season— and I wasn't about to borrow tomorrow's trouble.

"You made round two!" Sutton's coach told us a half hour after that, waving a paper.

"Wait." My head snapped toward Weston. "There are *two* rounds?"

An hour later, I emptied the last of my water bottle, trying to dislodge the boulder in my throat.

Sutton was at the top of the competition zone with the other finalists—twelve in total—and since she'd scored the lowest in the initial round, she was up first.

She's going to be fine. She just showed you she can do this.

But then her pink hat appeared a little to the left of where she'd begun last time.

"What are you doing, kid?" Weston whispered, his eyes narrowing.

"What is she doing?" I had his fingers in a vise grip.

"Not taking the same line," he muttered. "She wants the higher run score." He shook his head, and Sutton dropped in.

Higher run score meant she'd upped her difficulty.

Her posture was just as confident, her moves just as controlled as the first run, which helped ease my blood pressure as she hit the first jump. She tucked her knees, crossing her skis just like she had with the final jump before, but she barely got them back under her before landing, and she wobbled.

"Come on, Sutton," Weston whispered. "Think smart."

She carved left, then right, coming down the steeper chute, and she skidded right before the jump. She pulled the same maneuver, crossing her skis for what I guessed had to be style points.

She tipped backward.

My heart froze as the backs of her skis hit the terrain. One went flying. Her butt hit. Her back hit. Her head bounced.

I muffled my cry with the back of my hand.

She slipped right off the edge of the highest jump...and fell... and fell.

We were too far away to hear the impact, but she slid down the rest of the run like a limp doll, her arms above her head, her equipment everywhere.

Weston dropped my hand and bolted, dodging spectators as he raced across the snow. I took off after him, but I was no match for his longer legs as he sprinted forward through the silent crowd.

I ran my heart out over the open terrain once we were beyond the ropes. *Be okay. Just be okay.* Ski patrol was already there, hovering over her, their snowmobiles parked just off the side at the end of the slope.

Weston stood close enough to see her but far enough to keep out of the way.

This wasn't happening. It couldn't happen. Not to her.

"Can you hear us?" one of the ski patrol asked. "What's her name?"

"Sutton," Weston responded, his voice tenser than I'd ever heard as I got there, my lungs burning and legs screaming.

"Is she okay?" I pushed past Weston. "I'm her mother."

I'm the one who let her fling herself off a mountain.

"We're checking her out." One of the ski patrol guys looked up at me while the other peeled back Sutton's eyelids.

"You there, Sutton?"

She moaned, and I went limp. She was alive. Weston's arms came around me, holding me upright.

"Can you move your legs?" the guy asked.

She whimpered in pain.

"We need to board her," the other patrol member said. Four people jumped into action, collaring Sutton's neck and putting her onto a backboard. "We can take her down the mountain on the board, or we can call the helicopter up."

Buzzing filled my ears. They had her strapped to a board.

"Callie, it's up to you," Weston said, but he sounded miles

away. "They can pull her on the board, and take her down with the gondola, or they can call the helicopter up."

One body. She only had one body. "Whatever's fastest."

"Call the bird."

"Hey." Weston pushed open the door to Sutton's hospital room, juggling two cups of coffee. "Thought you might need some caffeine."

"Thanks." I took a cup and set it next to my cell phone on the rolling table beside the chair I'd been in for the last nine hours. Weston leaned against the wall—the position he'd mostly been in since he got here—but I couldn't look at him.

The fear had ebbed after the CT scan and X-rays had come back, but the anger had taken root in my stomach and spread until I couldn't think around it.

"Where did they take her this time?" he asked.

"To splint her arm." I stared blankly at the pile of discharge paperwork in my lap.

"Better than her neck," he said softly.

"Better than her neck," I agreed, a bite to my tone. A concussion and broken arm were the worst of it.

"Are you going to talk to me?" he asked. "You've been quiet since I got here."

I'd flown with Sutton. Weston had driven into downtown Steamboat.

"What would you like me to say?" I managed to drag my gaze up to meet his, but I couldn't hold it for long.

"Whatever you need to." God, his tone was so reassuring, so comforting. And I'd been a lovesick fool to trust him, to listen when he told me she'd be fine.

"I'm never going to forget the sight of her on that board." I gripped the paperwork, and it gave way, crinkling. "Is that what you want me to say?"

"Yes." He pushed off the wall. "I want you to scream at me."

I shook my head.

"Yell at me." He crouched down in front of me, right where Sutton's bed belonged. "Because it's more than obvious that you blame me for this."

"She never would have been on that mountain if it wasn't for you."

He flinched.

"You told me she was ready. You told me she'd be fine!"

"I know it was scary, but it's just a broken arm and a concussion," he said softly.

"She could have broken her neck!" I snapped. "They thought she'd broken her neck!"

"They were cautious." So calm. So controlled. So...Weston.

"I never should have listened to you!" I lifted the papers. "Do you know what these say?"

"Why don't you tell me?" He never looked away.

"They say that while this hospital is in network, the helicopter ambulance wasn't." I laughed, the sound bitter and harsh. "How ironic is that? I spend almost every day flying around in your helicopter, taking pictures of foolish, reckless people risking their bodies for an adrenaline rush, and yet when I need a helicopter to bring Sutton to the hospital, it's not covered because her life wasn't in danger."

"What exactly are you saying?" Weston's jaw ticked.

"I'm saying that the guy from the billing department just told me that it's up to my insurance to decide if they'll cover the helicopter ride, and since nothing was life-threatening, I need to be prepared for up to a thirty-thousand-dollar bill." I drew in a shaky breath. "Thirty. Thousand. Dollars." I understood the number when the billing department told me, but the full ramifications were just now hitting me. "Don't get me wrong. I would do it again. Standing there over her, not knowing if that fall had broken her neck or caused internal bleeding, I would make the same decision. Sutton is worth everything to me."

"I know she is." He reached for my knee, and I dodged his hand, pivoting in my seat.

"I don't have my down payment anymore," I whispered.

He blanched. "Shit. Callie, I'll pay for it."

"You're not paying my kid's medical bills." I stood, sidestepping away from him so I could get some space. "Why did I listen to you? Why? I knew better. I knew it was putting her at unnecessary risk, but I was so blinded by my love for you, by my trust in you, that I ignored every instinct in my body!"

"I'm so sorry she got hurt. If I could do anything to change it, I would," he said softly.

My cell phone dinged, and I marched past Weston and plucked it off the table, expecting to see a new text from Ava or Raven. Instead, it was an email alert.

YOU'VE BEEN CHOSEN AS THIS YEAR'S WINNER—

"What the hell?" I touched the notification, and my inbox filled the screen. I tapped on the first unread email. "Congratulations, Calliope Thorne, your photograph has been selected as this year's winner for the *World Geographic* amateur photography division," I read aloud. I blinked, trying to get my brain to compute. "Our article will go live later tomorrow, and I'll reach out to you regarding the details of your internship."

"Holy shit!" Weston grinned and swept me against him, holding me tight and pinning my arms between us. "I'm so proud of you!"

I read the email again. "But I didn't enter the competition." Using my hands, I shoved out of Weston's arms, backing up enough to process the joy on his face. "Weston, I *didn't* enter the competition," I repeated.

I couldn't have won. It was impossible. There had to be a mistake.

His face fell, and he shoved his hands into the front pockets of his jeans. "I uploaded the photo and the release."

"You *what?*" My whole body went numb, as if all the sensation had been drained out of me.

"I'm the one who entered you in the competition." He swallowed, and for the first time since I'd met him, he looked uncertain. Unsteady.

Oh God. I'd won. It was real.

I'd. WON. My mind whirled, and a jolt of pure, unadulterated joy coursed through me for a heartbeat. Reality swiftly tugged me back to earth. I couldn't leave Sutton for a year, and taking her with me wasn't exactly an option. A whimper bubbled out of my throat.

I was going to have to decline the internship.

Never allowing myself to dream was one thing, but touching it, brushing my fingertips along everything I'd ever wanted just to have to walk away was an acute form of torture. My cheeks heated as fury took hold.

"I told you I was thinking about it!" I shouted at Weston. "You had no right!"

"I wanted you to know how good you are," he said, leaning forward like he wanted to cross the distance between us but knew better. "And you *are.* Callie, you won! Think of all the exposure your work is going to get. The gallery is going to be begging you for photos! I'm sorry I did it without telling you, but you won! You get to intern with them, or not...it's your choice now." His eyes searched mine, and I saw it, the certainty that what he'd done had been for my own good.

"I never wanted to *choose!*" I snapped, shoving my phone into my back pocket. "Don't you get it? I didn't *want* to enter, and it wasn't because I was scared I wouldn't be chosen, it was because I was petrified that I would be! I'm a single mom. I don't have the luxury of running all over the world for a year! What the hell am I supposed to do now, Weston?" Panic warred with anger. This was everything I'd avoided.

He opened his mouth and then shut it.

"You had no right to do this." My hands curled into fists. "No right to make me choose between my dream and Sutton. No right!" Oh God. Sutton. "And don't you *dare* tell Sutton about the internship."

"What?" His eyes flared. "You're going to keep this from her? Turn it down without even asking what your options are?"

I nodded. "She'll blame herself if she knows I won and had to decline. It would destroy her. Why do you think I never wanted to enter?"

"You can't—"

"I can, Weston. She's *mine*. I'm the one who makes decisions for my daughter. Not you." I glanced around the hospital room. "Look where we end up when I go against my instincts."

His face went blank, as if he'd pulled a mask down. He looked like he had in that first week we'd lived together, before I'd gotten to know him.

He looked like a stranger. A stranger I loved but would never love me back.

"Promise me you won't say a thing to her about this." I narrowed my eyes at him.

"As you told me when we moved in together, Callie rules all."

18

C allie

"YOU SURE YOU don't need anything?" I asked Sutton, smoothing her hair back from her forehead as I settled her into her bed the next evening, being sure to elevate her splinted arm. Hopefully the swelling would go down enough to cast her tomorrow.

"I'm okay, Mom." she said, her eyes already closing. No doubt the pain meds were kicking in.

"Okay. Just shout if you need anything." I bent down and kissed her forehead, then backed out of her room, shutting the door quietly.

I made my way down the stairs and into the empty living room. Weston wasn't home from work yet, but would be any minute, and there were exactly five of those minutes before *World Geographic* was scheduled to call.

Wrapping my arms around my chest, I stared at the pictures I'd framed more than eleven years ago. My cell phone felt like a ticking time bomb in my pocket. But this was what I'd always wanted, wasn't it? The chance to learn from the best photographers, the opportunity to make a name for myself, doing exactly what I loved.

But I loved Sutton more. There really was no choice to make.

My home was here. *Our* home was here. I couldn't leave her for a year, even if I knew Gavin's parents would dote on her for the full twelve months. Not only could I never do that to her, but I wasn't sure I'd even make it a couple of weeks before breaking down without her. We'd never been apart for more than a day since she'd been born.

And Weston? As pissed as I was that he'd submitted my photo, I still loved him, and I couldn't imagine walking away from him for a year either. Sure, we were in a fight. A pretty big one. But in the scheme of things, it was just a fight, and I knew his heart had been in the right place.

I pulled my phone from my back pocket and checked the time.

Three minutes. That's all the time I had before I needed to decline. Before my fingertips slipped off my dream.

For those three minutes, I stared at the sunset pictures of the Serengeti and the midair jump of lemurs in Madagascar and let myself soak it in. I had won an internship. In another life, my eyes would be prickling with joy as I scurried to pack my life into a rucksack.

But this was the life I'd chosen.

Sutton hadn't, and she was what mattered.

My phone rang, and I swiped to answer it. "Hello?"

"Ms. Thorne?" a feminine voice said through the line.

"This is she." My heart clenched. Was I really about to turn down the chance of a lifetime?

"Hi! I'm Maggie Brettwell from *World Geographic*, and I'm so excited to chat about your internship!"

My eyes slid shut as my throat tied itself into a knot. "Maggie, before we get too far into this, I'm so sorry, but I'm going to have to decline." Somehow, I got the words out.

"Oh?" She sounded as stunned to hear it as I felt having to say it.

"I—" What the hell could I say? That my boyfriend conspired to enter me behind my back? "I have an eleven-year-old daughter. And as much as I have dreamed about being chosen for one of your incredible internships, I just can't leave her. Not for a year." The idea of it was unbearable.

"Oh!" She laughed. "You had me worried there for a moment. That's not a problem, Calliope. Our business model changed a few years ago, and we're very kid-friendly. Just bring her with you!"

My jaw hit the floor. "I'm sorry?" Did she just say what I thought she did?

"You're more than welcome to bring your daughter with you."

"I am?" My mind spun and I backed up a few steps to lean against the couch for balance.

"Absolutely." She sounded like this was a normal occurrence. Maybe it was. Maybe I'd been wrong about this all along.

The front door opened and Weston stepped in, accompanied by a gust of cold air. He had on his favorite baseball cap despite the temperature and shot me an inquisitive look from under the brim.

World Geographic, I mouthed, pointing to the phone.

He nodded and proceeded to take off his winter gear, storing it in the closet.

"Let me get this right," I said into the phone, my pulse skyrocketing at the possibility of actually holding my dream. "You're okay with me bringing my eleven-year-old daughter for a year-long internship around the world?"

Weston's head snapped up and his wide eyes met mine.

"That's exactly what I'm saying. You'll be with a full staff of our photojournalists and a few others travel with their kids too. Of course we already have next year's publications mapped out, so we know exactly where you'd be, and in my opinion, the itinerary is one of our best yet."

"But school…" My brow puckered.

"You would have to homeschool," Maggie said. "But there are some great online programs the other photographers can tell you about, and we make sure to have Wi-Fi at our base locations, so the kids don't fall behind. Oh, but there's one thing."

"I figured there had to be a catch," I replied with a slightly panicked laugh.

"While the company pays for all your expenses—and it's a paid internship, of course—we don't cover family members, which can eat into your check."

I blinked. "So that's it? The catch is I wouldn't get paid as much?"

Maggie chuckled. "Well, it can take up a *lot* of your check, especially for those who travel with two kids, but of course our staffers get paid a bit more than our interns."

World Geographic photojournalists made *bank*.

"But if you're okay with less pay and homeschooling for a year—or longer, if you choose to stay on as freelance or maybe even staff, depending on how the year goes—then your daughter is more than welcome. From what I hear, the kids love the travel."

Sutton could go with me. Holy crap. I had enough money in my savings account, even if the insurance didn't cover her helicopter ambulance. We'd have to save up again for a house, and we'd be gone for a year, but the things she would see? The opportunities we'd have?

I'd never once imagined it was possible, and now that it was—

"Callie?" Maggie prompted.

"Sorry." I shook my head to clear my thoughts. "I'm just a little shocked. How soon would we need to leave?"

The sound of a mouse clicking came through the phone. "We could have you meet the team in as little as a couple of days, or give you a month or so to get everything straight if you need to. Most of our interns need a couple weeks. You're in Colorado, right?"

"Yes." A couple of *days?*

"The team is in Paraguay right now, and they're not set to move to the next location for another few weeks, so it's really up to you."

Paraguay. We could be in freaking Paraguay.

I locked eyes with Weston and my stomach twisted. He was as unreadable as always. "How long do I have to decide?"

"The article is going live tonight," she said quietly. "And if you know you aren't interested, we'd offer the internship to the second-place finisher. But you'd still be our winner, of course. How long do you think you need to make a decision?"

"I don't…" How long *did* I need?

"How about I give you a call tomorrow just to see where you're at? I can put you in touch with one of the other staff that travels with their kids so you can make a more informed decision about homeschooling and what it costs for her travel."

"That sounds great."

We hung up and I slid my phone into my pocket, my eyes never leaving Weston's as he came toward me. "I can take Sutton. On the internship. For *World Geographic.* I can take her."

"That's what I gathered." He smiled, but it wasn't a real one. "When do you leave?"

"It would probably be a couple of weeks…but I don't know if I can do it," I whispered, my heart at war with my mind.

"Sure you can." He cupped my face and caressed my cheek with his thumb. "And you should."

I shook my head. "It would probably eat my savings. I'd have to pay for Sutton's travel, and I won't know until tomorrow how much that will be."

"Do it anyway." He brushed his mouth over mine and heat rushed through me, just like it always did. It was soft, lingering, and even when I rose on my tiptoes, he didn't deepen the kiss. He lifted his head, and there was a resolve in his eyes that made my thoughts trip.

"We can't go. Sutton has a broken arm—"

"And I'm sure they have doctors wherever you're going." His gaze moved over my features like he needed to memorize them.

"But I'm just starting to get my feet under me with the heli-skiing photography and I really love it." Every excuse not to go flooded my brain, but I refused to acknowledge the biggest one.

"It will be here when you get back. If you choose to come back." His hand slid away from my face, and he stepped away, turning his back on me and heading for the kitchen.

"I'd have to homeschool her." I followed him, dread growing, filling my chest.

"She'd do just fine in online school." He took a glass from the cabinet and then moved to the refrigerator.

"You really think I should go, don't you?" It came out like an accusation.

"I do." He grabbed the orange juice from the fridge and poured it into the glass, his hands and words steady.

"I would be gone for a year, Weston!"

He put the juice back and closed the refrigerator. "Those have always been the terms, right?"

"You don't care that I'd be gone for a *year?*"

He leaned back against the counter and sipped the juice before answering. "This is your dream, Callie. I don't factor in." He shrugged.

He fucking *shrugged.*

"You don't..." I shook my head, fumbling for words.

"You were pissed because, by entering you, I'd forced you to choose between your dream and Sutton." He lifted his brows. "Now you don't have to choose."

"But I'd be leaving *you*." My heart ached in protest at the thought. I needed him. Didn't he need me too? Wasn't there some part of him that cared?

"That would be the logical conclusion, yes." He took another drink and set the glass on the counter.

A fissure opened under my ribs. "Is that all you have to say?"

"I think you're a fool if you let this chance pass you by, because you won't get another one. Not like this. It's all you've ever wanted." His features were flat. His walls were up. I got the sinking feeling he'd shut me out for good.

"I don't want to leave you," I whispered.

"You sure about that?" He arched a brow. "Because yesterday, it sure seemed like you did."

My cheeks heated. "I was really angry about Sutton getting hurt, and I lashed out. I know it wasn't your fault—"

"Sure it was. I'm the one who taught her. I'm the one who put her up there." He looked away, his jaw tensing. "You can't make a decision like this based on what you think we have between us."

I stared at his stoic, gorgeous face and forced my lungs to inhale. "Of course I have to think about us, Weston. I love you!"

He flinched, his gaze pinned on the island ahead of him. "And yesterday, you told me that love had blinded you. That love had gotten Sutton hurt, right? You said your trust in me had been misplaced, so why would you care about my opinion today?"

Because I thought we were forever.

"It was never going to work between us, anyways," he continued. "You want the things I can't give you."

Like his love.

"The things you *won't* give me," I snapped.

"Same thing." He shrugged again. "I'm not capable of it."

Seeing him like this sent ice trickling down my spine. This was how he talked to Reed. How he *used* to talk to Reed, at least.

"You have every reason to go, Callie." He finally lifted his gaze to mine, and I thought there was a flash of pain there for a second, but it was gone in a heartbeat. "And I can't give you a reason to stay."

"You care about me," I argued, putting myself in front of him. "I *know* you care about me!"

He sidestepped. "Look, it's been fun, and you're a great woman—"

"Fuck that!" My heart screamed, agony pumping through me with every beat. "I love you, Weston. I am in love with you! That's worth fighting for!"

His gaze met mine. "But I never said I was in love with *you*, did I?"

I inhaled sharply. There was no lie in those cool brown eyes. "No," I whispered, the word like acid on my tongue. "You never said that." Could I really have been so blind? Was I so deeply in love with this man that I'd made more of his touch, his mannerisms, his consideration than I should have? "You made it clear to Reed that you are *never* going to love me. And I've been so stupid, so foolish, to think that I could change your mind, that I could win your heart. But that's the thing about you. You have no problem risking your life on the regular, but you draw the line at your heart."

He nodded once. "Right. I'm going to pack a bag and head out for a few days. I really, truly hope you're not here when I get back." He didn't so much as wait for a response before walking away.

"And what if I'm still here? What if I don't go?" I knew how to get him to stay. All I had to tell him was that I needed him, and he'd never go. But if he didn't need me, what the hell was the point of all of this?

"Then I'll find somewhere else to stay," he said over his shoulder.

"But there is nowhere else," I snapped. "Remember? That's why we're both here in the first place."

"I still have a room with Reed and Ava." He trudged up the stairs.

Holy shit. The man would rather go live in a house he hated than be with me? How had things gone so wrong in twenty-four hours?

You blamed him for Sutton's accident.

No. That wasn't it. Weston wasn't a quitter. If he wanted to stay, to fight for us, he would.

Fifteen minutes later, he was gone.

"You're sure you have everything you need?" Ava asked, her voice practically dripping with sympathy through the phone.

"Yep," I answered, yanking a Pop-Tart from the box and ripping open the wrapper. Who needed healthy breakfasts when you had brown sugar and cinnamon? "I bought some rucksacks from the outdoor store downtown, and everything personal is almost boxed up for storage."

The rest I'd left for Weston, who'd been true to his word and hadn't been home in three days.

"How do you feel? At least a little excited?"

Heartbroken. Angry. Betrayed. Confused. Right back to heartbroken. I seemed to be following a pattern every few hours. Heartbroken was winning.

"I honestly don't know." My shoulders sagged, and I dropped the Pop-Tart onto its wrapper on the counter. Sutton and I had a week before we were set to leave, and yet I knew Weston wouldn't want to say goodbye. When he was done, he was done, and it was more than clear he was finished with me.

"You sure you don't want me to come over? I can be there in a few minutes. There's something I need to tell you."

"No. You're way too busy." I shook my head. "Just tell me now."

"I think Weston's…gone. Reed told him he could leave," Ava whispered.

"What?" I stood up straight.

"I shouldn't say anything, but I overheard Reed on the phone this morning. He told Weston that he's glad he got away from the mountain, that he'll find someone else to run the heli-skiing operation if that was what he wanted. That he wasn't going to force him to stay again."

"Weston's gone? Reed gave him an out?" My heart thundered in my ears. Guess I'd been right about the goodbyes. Weston had only been here because Reed had said he'd needed him, and if that need was gone…

"Yeah. He said that Weston got them off the ground, and he shouldn't feel like he's chained to his hangar."

"And he's already gone?" I asked.

"I…" She took a deep breath. "I saw the new hire forms for another guide for the heli-skiing department. He started today. But I haven't had a chance to ask Reed about it yet. He's been in meetings all day, so I don't know for certain."

I stared at the contract Weston had left on the fridge. If Reed had given him the all-clear, then he was finally free.

My stomach sank. Weston hated it here. Hated how much it reminded him of his mom and the grief he still struggled with. Hated that he'd been obligated, yet again, to save his family. Hated that his dad was prying his way back into his life…and hated that he might actually have to let some of his anger go when it came to his father. He hated all of it.

"Maybe you should call down to the hangar. If it were Reed, I'd want to know for certain."

"Reed loves you." My eyes burned. "And we both know that

Weston doesn't love me. God, what is wrong with me, Ava? The first guy I fall for has the biggest heart but his body can't survive, and the second guy has a body that won't quit and a heart that refuses to actually live."

"Mom! I can't get this box taped!" Sutton shouted from upstairs. She'd been a buzz of energy for the last few days since I'd told her we were going.

"I'll be there in a second!" I said up the stairs. "I have to help Sutton," I told Ava. "We'll chat later?"

"You bet," she promised.

We hung up and I stared at my phone. There was no way he was really gone, right? I punched the number for the hangar.

It rang twice.

"Mountain Madigan Heli-skiing, this is Simon. Can I help you?" a guy answered.

The new hire.

"Hi. I was just looking for Weston." My voice shook.

"Oh, he's gone, but if you're looking for a ski trip, I'm happy to book you."

I swallowed. "No. But thank you." I ended the call.

He was gone.

I headed upstairs to help Sutton finish the last of her boxes, her bright orange cast standing out in the strangely colorless room. We'd packed up her pretty curtains and taken down her artwork, boxing up the last eleven years of our lives and choosing only the most essential items for our packs.

We'd be nomads for the next year.

"You sure you want to do this, sugar?" I asked her. "We can still choose to stay."

She wrapped her arms around me and squeezed tight. "No way. We're going. And don't be sad, Mom. It's just a year. Everything will be here when we get back."

Everything but Weston.

"What do you think about leaving a little early?" I asked, resting my chin on the top of her head.

"Really?" She smiled up at me.

"Really."

I made a call.

eston

I WALKED into the hangar at two p.m. on Monday and found a twenty-year-old kid with his feet on my desk. "Who the hell are you?"

"Simon Matthews," the kid sneered. "Who the fuck are you?"

"Weston-fucking-Madigan." I cocked an eyebrow.

The kid's eyes blew wide.

"Now get your feet off my damn desk."

He moved so fast the chair came out from underneath him and he tumbled to the floor.

This was the expert backcountry guide Reed had hired to fill in while I'd been at the Army Aviation Association of America conference for the last four days. When they'd called, asking me to fill in for a speaker last minute, I'd almost said no, but the topic had been on transitioning from military to civilian aviation careers, and honestly, I'd just needed out of Penny Ridge for a couple of days.

Anything to keep me from throwing myself at Callie's door and begging her to forgive me for lying, for not telling her exactly how much I cared about her, for letting her think I didn't want her. It had been a little over a week since Sutton had been injured, since I'd told her to take the internship, and I was in hell.

But I never said I was in love with you, did I? Fuck. I was never going to get those words out of my head.

Simon scurried to stand. "Sorry, I didn't know it was you."

"Obviously." I yanked my coat off and hung it on the rack. "How was today's tour?"

"They were okay. A bunch of suits from Kansas who needed to spend a little more time on the groomed areas of the slope, if you know what I mean." He rolled his eyes.

"Unfortunately, I know exactly what you mean." I moved around him and took my seat back, firing up the computer. "How old are you, anyway?"

"Twenty-one," he replied. "Moved here about three years ago. You're kind of a legend around here."

"Thanks, but I think you're talking about my brother, Crew." Twenty-one? The kid looked like a baby. Man, I was getting old. I logged in and immediately checked our bookings. We were pretty solid until the third week in May. We'd only take reservations on an if-we're-still-open basis after that. Typically, we were closed by Memorial Day, but the new area was at a slightly higher elevation, so there was a chance the season would be extended.

"No. He's pretty awesome. I've actually seen him live once. But I was talking about your freeskiing skills. Some of the townies say that you've skied every part of these mountains."

"Just about," I answered honestly.

The door from the inside of the hangar burst open and Theo spread his arms wide. "The public speaker has returned!"

I scoffed.

"My favorite part was when you tried to draw the analogy to carrying troops into battle with ferrying the spoiled-ass rich people up the mountain to ski." He grinned, flashing his bright white teeth at me.

"You were watching?" I clicked over to see our financials. Damn, we were solid.

"Online, of course. Like I'd miss it." He leaned back and kicked his feet up on the desk. "I also enjoyed the part where you almost knocked your entire glass of water over."

"Public speaking is not my strong suit." I glared at him.

"Why does he get to put his feet on the desk?" Simon whined.

"Because he's my business partner and my best friend."

"We both know you didn't go there to speak, anyway." Theo started throwing his tennis ball into the air and catching it. "You were running away."

"What?" Simon asked.

I bit back a growl at my best friend. "Did the kid hold his own?"

Theo glanced at Simon. "He wasn't too bad."

I grunted in approval. "Why don't you head home, Simon. We'll call you if we need you. If you're interested."

"Absolutely interested!" He took his jacket off the rack, knocking mine to the ground. "Oh, sorry." He hung it back up. "Thanks for the chance!" He waved on his way out the door.

"You're telling me that clumsy oaf held his own?" I asked Theo.

"I'd give him a solid eight." Theo threw the ball up and caught it. "So tell me, how did running away work for you?"

I shot him a look that told him to drop it.

He sat up straight and pinned me with a single stare. "Because I'm thinking it didn't work out so well."

"I couldn't be here." I rubbed my hands over my face. Shit, I was exhausted. Turned out, I'd forgotten how to sleep through the night without Callie. "Not after I told her to go. One look at her and I'd cave. I'd beg her to stay, and I'll be damned if I'm going to be the reason she misses out on her dream." Not when I knew exactly how it had broken my heart to lose mine.

So, I'd done the only respectable thing and cut the tether between us. God, I hoped she'd chosen to go, otherwise all this pain would be for nothing.

Reed told me the day I'd left for the conference that Callie was set to leave a week later, which meant I only had to avoid her for three days.

"Seriously, West? That's how you want to leave things with her?" He lifted his brows at me. "With some bullshit where you force her into a choice because you don't give her all the information she needs to make a real decision?" He shook his head. "You're better than that."

"What am I supposed to do, Theo? Ask her not to go?"

He scoffed. "You do what Jeanine has done through every deployment and you tell her you'll wait. That you'll be here when she gets back. A year sucks, but it's nothing in the scheme of things."

"Even if she wasn't about to leave—which I hope she is—for this incredible internship, I can't be what she deserves, man. It's not that I wouldn't wait a year for her, because I would. I'd wait for as long as she wanted me to, but I can't give her what she wants." The sooner she realized that, the better.

"And what exactly is that?"

"She wants me to love her." The admission came out gruff.

"And the problem is?"

"You know what happens when you love people? They leave.

They die. Losing them makes you fucking miserable, and you never get over it. Who signs up for that?"

He stared at me in pure exasperation.

"What?"

"You're an idiot." He snorted.

"I'm sorry?"

"She wants you to love her. Damn, I mean, that's a pretty heavy demand. Next thing you know, she'll be asking you to be faithful to her and to come home every night. Then you'll really have a problem." He threw the ball and caught it again.

"I'm already faithful and already come home every night." I grimaced. "At least I did before we ended things." Before *I* ended things.

"And you're already in love with her, so I guess I just don't see the point you're trying to make."

I stared at him.

"Please." He shook his head. "Like you don't already know that. Somewhere deep down, you do. I've never seen you look at someone the way you watch her. Never seen you smile so much. Never seen you lose your damn mind over a woman either." He caught the ball and looked me in the eyes. "You don't have to admit to something for it to be true."

Fuck.

"I'm going for a drive." I pushed back from the desk and grabbed my coat on the way out the door.

"Maybe you should drive by your house so you can stop sleeping on my couch," he called after me. "Even if she's leaving, she should know how you feel. Evolve, West!"

A growl rumbled in my chest as I climbed into my truck and turned the ignition. I wanted to run, to drive as far and as fast as I could. I wanted to go back to last month or the month before and tell Sutton she couldn't compete. I wanted to go back to that fight in the kitchen and tell her that I was so wrapped up in her that I couldn't see a future without her.

Damn it. More than anything, I wanted her to go, to have her chance at living out her dream. But I wasn't sure I'd survive losing her.

I ended up at the duplex.

I just really wanted to talk it out with Callie.

Guilt gnawed at the edges of my stomach. If I told her how I felt, and she chose to stay, I'd never forgive myself. But the lie didn't sit right either. Theo was right. Callie deserved all of the information. She deserved to know I'd wait. She deserved to know how badly I wanted her.

She could do whatever she wanted with the information.

Taking the deepest breath possible, I climbed out of the truck and walked up the steps to the little porch. Then I put my key in the lock and opened the door.

There was something off.

The house didn't smell like oranges, and the art was missing from the walls. My stomach churned, and I ran up Callie's steps, throwing open her bedroom door. Her furniture was there, but everything else was gone. Her bed was stripped, her windows were bare, and it was...empty.

I yanked out my phone and called the only person I knew who might know what the fuck was going on.

"Hey, Weston," Ava answered, sadness saturating her voice.

"Where's Callie?"

"Did you just get back?"

"Yeah, about an hour ago. Where's Callie?"

She sighed. "So, please don't hate me, but I made a mistake."

"About what?"

"I heard Reed tell you that he was glad you'd left the mountain, and I told Callie."

"Okay? You overheard us talking about the conference. No big deal." That didn't explain why Callie's room was empty.

"Right, so from this end of the conversation, it sounded like you'd *left*...left. And I was asleep by the time Reed got home so I didn't get to talk to him until the next morning, and that's when he told me that you were only gone for a few days and he was glad you were getting the break because of what you and Callie were going through, but by the time I tried to call Callie, her phone was off—"

"Where. Is. Callie?"

"She left for the internship three days ago, Weston. I'm so sorry."

Whatever was left of my heart shattered.

eston

THREE MONTHS later

DEAR WESTON,

We're in Ecuador now. It's hot, but the flowers are pretty, and I like being so close to the ocean. I get to go to the beach on days Mom isn't shooting. But she shoots a lot. Yesterday we spent the whole day in one tiny area of the forest while she took pictures of flowers. I think we messed up. She's not happy. Not like I thought she would be. I know you can't write back. Mom gets sad when I say your name, but I wanted you to

know we made it here, and we'll be here for a
few weeks. I'll ask Carmen to sneak me out
another letter when we get to Panama next
month.

    Love,
    Sutton

YOU'RE ALREADY *in love with her.* Theo's words and Sutton's
monthly letters were my only companions in the empty house.

They were gone. The house smelled like...nothing, which
was why I couldn't stand to be there. I loathed every part of my
day, from the second I woke up without her beside me, through
the mornings I spent flying when she wasn't strapped in behind
me, to the nights when there was no laughter at dinner. No
Sutton cracking jokes. No Callie helping her with her
homework.

Everything in my life felt...empty, and whatever wasn't
empty was just pain.

You're already in love with her.

"Are you listening to me?" Reed asked as we walked downtown, dodging early June tourists who darted in and out of the
shops that lined the street.

"Expansion, blah blah. Profits, blah blah. Missing an entire
demographic, blah blah." I finished my overpriced coffee and
threw the cup into the trash on the corner of Hudson and Main.

"This is your family business, too, you know." Reed shot me
a glare.

"Well aware." I stared at the light, willing the crosswalk
symbol to illuminate. The fact that Dad respected my boundaries, leaving Reed and me to make the decisions about our
various responsibilities, was the only reason I was willing to call
it a *family* business.

Reed and my relationship wasn't perfect, but it was a hell of a lot better than when I'd come home nine months ago.

"You can go, you have to know that," he said softly.

I turned to face him. "You've said that twice in the last three months."

"Yeah, well, this time I don't mean for the weekend." He blew out a breath. "You're miserable here, Weston. For a while there, I thought you were happy, but..."

I was miserable without Callie. We both knew it. I wasn't sure how I was still managing to breathe, how I kept forcing air through my lungs.

"I'm just saying that if you need an out, I'm giving you one. I know you came back because I needed you."

"And you don't need me anymore?" I looked over his shoulder and saw Mrs. Rupert a block away, fighting with a fallen tree branch. Late spring snows were the worst, and last week's dumping had been the heavy kind that took down trees and a couple power lines.

"I need you to be happy. I need to not be the cause of your misery."

You're already in love with her.

And yet, if this pain had anything to do with that emotion, I couldn't understand why everyone was so hell-bent on feeling it. Hell, even Callie was sad according to Sutton, and she was out there living her dream.

Damn it, I hated that she was sad. She was supposed to be happy. That was the only saving grace of this whole cursed situation. She was supposed to thrive, and there wasn't a thing I could do about it.

Except maybe there was.

I'd let her go so she could be happy, but if she wasn't, then all bets were off.

"You're not the cause of my misery." My eyes narrowed on

Mrs. Rupert. Shit, she was struggling. I started walking in her direction.

"You could call her. I'm sure she has international service." He sighed. "Are you seriously walking away right now?"

"Give me a second," I called back over my shoulder as I walked up the incline toward Vine Street. "Hey, Mrs. Rupert. Need a hand?"

The older woman was currently at war with what looked like an entire trunk of an Aspen tree.

"Every year, Edward Baker just lets his branches tumble into our yard, and every year I have to yank them out." She grumbled.

"I've got you." I gripped the thick branch with both hands and she let go.

"It's been a few years since I've seen you around, Weston Madigan."

"Yes, ma'am." I made quick work of hauling it to the street, where other limbs were gathered for pickup.

"I swear, I'm getting too old for this kind of upkeep. I've been asking my husband to downsize for the last year, but he refuses to sell to Airbnb vacation rental people." She shook her head, her silver curls wobbling.

"But you'd sell to a local?" A knot threatened to form at the base of my throat. What would it mean if Callie wasn't even here? But she'd be back in nine months…if she chose to return to Madigan.

My chest constricted. I wasn't going to make it that long without seeing her, without telling her the truth. And if exposing my emotional jugular was what it took to ensure she'd come back here when she was done with her internship…

"Maybe." She lifted her brows under her lavender hat. "You know anyone who might be interested?"

I nodded.

Five minutes later, I made my way back down to where Reed was waiting.

"How is Mrs. Rupert?" he asked as we started walking, heading across the street.

"She's good." My smile stretched from ear to ear.

"It scares me when you smile."

I laughed.

"That's fucking terrifying." He glanced sideways at me.

"I know how we hit that demographic you're so worried about," I said, yanking out my phone.

"Okay. I'm all ears."

I looked over to see if he was being sarcastic, but he wasn't. He honestly wanted my opinion. "We need a new terrain park with a world-class half-pipe."

"He isn't going to come home for that."

"No, but he'll know someone who can help design it." I lifted my brows. "Besides, that's not the only reason to call him, is it?"

His eyebrows rose. "You're going to ask?"

"Yep." I dialed the number and lifted my phone to my ear. "Oh, and I'm going to need some time off," I said to Reed as the line rang and rang. "Starting tomorrow. We only have scenic tours booked, and Theo can fly, so it's not like I need a temp or anything."

"Have somewhere to be?" he asked.

"Actually, yes," I answered as he finally picked up.

"Are you dying?" Crew sounded winded, and I wondered where he was, who had snow this time of year. Chile? Argentina? I never knew when it came to him.

"Nope."

"Reed dying?"

"Nope."

"Okay, now you have my curiosity piqued. What's up?"

"I need a favor. Well, Reed needs a favor." I caught Reed's glare. "Fine, we both need a favor."

"What is it?"

"What does your schedule look like for coming home?"

"You're kidding, right?" I could almost see him rolling his eyes from here.

"Nope. Reed is getting married."

allie

I BENT low and captured the picture of Sutton running through the surf with a couple other kids. The lighting was gorgeous this time in the afternoon.

Then again, everything about Ecuador was gorgeous.

Paraguay, Brazil, and Peru had been the same. Breathtaking views. Rare wildlife. Exquisite florals.

"Do you ever take a break?" Carmen asked, a slight smile on her lips as she watched our kids in the water, her sandals clutched in one hand with a manila folder.

"Did you get where you are by taking breaks?" I asked, clicking another shot.

Carmen was everything I wanted to be. Well, everything eighteen-year-old me had wanted to be. She was a wildly successful photographer on the full-time staff at *World*

Geographic, and in her forty-four years had taken some of the best landscape shots I'd ever seen in my life.

Including the lemur picture I'd had on my wall back in Colorado.

"I didn't have Milo back then," she said, waving to her son as he ran beside Sutton.

"I just have to balance both." I shrugged, crouching in the sand for a better angle and taking another series of pictures. "I never thought I'd have this opportunity, so I have to make the most of it." This experience had to be worth everything we'd gambled, from my savings account to my job back at Madigan.

And losing Weston.

My chest tightened. If he were here, he'd be out there in the water with Sutton, throwing her into the ocean, playing in the waves while I swallowed my protests that they were out too far.

If Weston were here, Sutton would be grinning, not just smiling. She loved the way he pushed the envelope because, as much as I hated to admit it, she was just like him. Always looking for the zip line, for the harder route to hike, for the biggest waves to bodysurf.

"You're good at the action shots," Carmen said as I stood again, grabbing for my sun hat so it didn't blow away. "It's something I've noticed when we're in camp."

Camp right now was a series of houses *World Geographic* had rented for the twenty of us who traveled to get the shots the magazine needed.

"Thank you." I lifted my lens to grab another shot, then lowered it, letting my camera hang from its neck strap so I could watch Sutton for a few minutes without the lens between us. "They're some of my favorite to take, actually."

"I can see that." She studied me for a second before turning her gaze to her son. "You've grown remarkably over the last few months."

"Thank you," I said again. Coming from her, the compliment was priceless.

"But there's an element you're missing in your landscapes. You don't enjoy them, do you? The stills? The nature shots?" There was no judgment in her voice.

"I…" What was the right thing to say to the woman who was mentoring me? "I prefer the action shots," I admitted. "There's something riveting about capturing a moment that won't happen again."

She nodded. "I'm glad you're honest. You know I don't have much to teach you here about action shots. We primarily focus on nature photography. And honestly, from the shot you won with, there's not much for you to learn. You're a natural."

"Thank you." God, why couldn't I think of something else to say?

"George needs you to sign a few releases for some of your Peru shots for the September issue." She handed me the manila file.

"No problem. I'm just honored there are some shots worth publishing in there." I took the file and twisted the tie on the top so it wouldn't blow open in the wind.

"Is it what you thought it would be?" she asked, looking over her sunglasses at me. "Working for the magazine?"

I thought about the incessant travel, the beautiful locations, and the assignments that hadn't quite held my interest like I thought they would. Sure, a hillside in Brazil was breathtaking, but I found it way more rewarding to photograph people and animals…anything that moved. "It's exactly what I dreamed of," I said quietly.

And it was all happening because Weston had submitted the picture.

I picked up my camera and snapped another shot of Sutton.

Sutton offered me a smile, but the light had dimmed in her

eyes about a week after we'd gotten to Paraguay. The first month had been almost magical.

But then the novelty had worn off. Even getting her cast off in Peru hadn't made her happy, though she'd stopped complaining about the constant itch. Humidity was horrible in a cast and our treks through the jungle hadn't helped.

We'd been in so many different locations that I'd stopped counting. And while Sutton had finished fifth grade through her online program, her grades had tanked. Turned out my girl was an in-person learner. But that didn't matter, right? It was only a year, and we could make up anything she didn't quite grasp once we were back in the States.

"She really is beautiful," Carmen said.

"Yeah, she is." I waved at Sutton, and she returned the gesture, heading back into the water.

"She's also unhappy." Carmen lifted her sunglasses to the top of her head, her forehead scrunching as she watched Sutton.

"I know." I lowered my camera so I could see her with my own eyes instead of through the lens.

Sutton hunted for shells. It was the wrong time of day for it, but I wasn't about to interrupt the first peaceful moment I'd seen her have in the past couple of weeks.

"Is she homesick?" Carmen asked. "It can be hard for some of the kids to adjust. It's why most of us only travel a year at a time. Not everyone is cut out for this kind of life."

"I think she misses Colorado." I sucked in a lungful of salty, oxygenated air and felt a pang of longing for the sharp, crisp scent of the snow. Maybe I was the one who missed Colorado and our small mountain town.

I knew we both missed Weston.

Sutton asked about him every few days at first, and I would gently remind her that adults have problems kids aren't responsible for, but that I knew he cared about her and I bet he missed her just as much as she missed him. Slowly, her inquiries dropped to about once a week.

I held it together every single day for her, but when the night came, all bets were off. I'd cried myself to sleep too many times to count. And it didn't matter that I could list off all the reasons we shouldn't be together. I was well aware he'd violated my trust by submitting that photo, and I was still pissed. I knew he was reckless with every part of him except his heart. I even knew the probability of him ever letting me in enough to love me was somewhere between zero and negative one.

But I also knew he'd been the catalyst for me taking control of my life and my career. He'd unknowingly made this very moment possible. He was the reason Sutton's confidence had shot sky high, and the reason I had received at least a dozen offers for contract photography work. He was the reason the local gallery in Penny Ridge had requested four pictures for display after the curator had seen my win for *World Geographic*. That moment alone had been better than winning the internship.

Weston had completely altered my comfort zone and made me better for it. I simply hadn't managed to do the same for him.

God, I missed him.

"You said you've been dreaming of this program since you were eighteen," Carmen said.

That was among the dozen things I'd awkwardly blurted during our first meeting in Paraguay. "Yes. It was all I wanted."

She nodded, watching her son. "When I was eighteen, I wanted to be a war correspondent."

"You what?" My gaze snapped toward her. Carmen was known for her nature photography, period.

"I know, right?" She laughed, the skin around her eyes crinkling. "But at eighteen, I wanted the drama and the tragedy. I wanted to shoot the moments of pain and anguish so everyone could see just how cruel we are to each other."

"What changed?" The two different specialties were worlds apart.

"Me." She shrugged. "After a few years of documenting misery, I realized I wanted to showcase the beauty in the world instead." Her gaze found mine. "The dreams we have at eighteen aren't the same dreams we have at forty, or thirty"—she arched a brow—"or twenty-nine. We change. We evolve. Imagine how boring our lives would be if we didn't."

"What did you do when your dream changed?" I asked Carmen.

"I corrected course to my new goal." She offered me a knowing smile. "There's nothing wrong with admitting that dreams change, that plans change, that our tastes change. There's only something wrong if we *don't* admit it. And I only say this because while you're an excellent, talented photographer, Callie, your daughter isn't the only one who is unhappy."

I swallowed the knot in my throat that had been lodged there since our first week in Paraguay. Logically, this was the right choice. It was a once-in-a-lifetime opportunity to learn nature photography from the best in the business.

But there was part of me that wouldn't stop internally screaming that all of this was wrong. I was slowly realizing I didn't want to *be* a nature photographer. Carmen had simply seen it through my photographs before I'd allowed myself to admit it.

I'd been happy, not just with Weston, but taking pictures of extreme athletes at Madigan. Once I'd stopped shaking, I'd loved hanging off the side of the helicopter to capture the perfect shot. I'd loved the thrill of watching through the lens, like I was the one on that slope.

To be honest, I couldn't even imagine which nature shots had been good enough from Peru to publish. There wasn't any passion in those pictures, no heart-stopping imagery. Holding the file, I turned my back against the wind and slid the papers out, noting which pictures were mentioned.

"I accidentally grabbed your whole file, so don't let it blow away," Carmen said. "Just sign the top ones and drop everything off to George once you get back in camp."

I nodded, flipping through the stack of releases. The last one caught my eye. It was my entry form from the competition.

My chest tightened. That wasn't Weston's handwriting. And the signature...

I spun toward the water, shoving the releases back into the file. Why hadn't I thought to ask about it sooner? I'd assumed the release had been one of those typed entries—those on-your-honor signatures, but it wasn't. My name had been scrawled across the form in a familiar slant.

Sutton ran out of the water, and I grabbed a beach towel from the bag, wrapping it around her to dry her off.

"Having fun?" I asked her, keeping the rest of my questions behind my teeth. If she had a reason, I wanted her to tell me on her own.

"I like the ocean." She smiled, but it felt forced, like she was putting on a show for me. "I mean, it's not as great as the mountains, but I like it. Can we go back to the house now?"

I stared into my daughter's eyes and nodded. "Sure. We can go back to the house."

She didn't call it home, and I couldn't blame her. Home was thousands of miles away.

"I want to go home."

"I'm sorry?" My gaze jumped across the wooden kitchen table to Sutton a couple of days later, and I squeezed the syrup bottle a little too hard, flooding her pancakes with way too much sugar. She'd wanted waffles, but it wasn't like we were carting a waffle iron around with us in our packs. Then again, she'd been grumpy since waking up this morning, probably because we were due to pack up again tomorrow and move, this time inland.

We shared this house with three other photographers, two of whom had brought their kids, but no one else was up yet, so at least I could handle this in relative privacy.

"I want to go home," she repeated.

I stared at her and she stared right back, lifting her chin an inch. There may as well have been a black cloud hanging above my daughter's head.

She fisted her fork like she was preparing for battle.

"Are you having trouble making friends?" I pushed a glass of orange juice at her, which only reminded me of Weston. Freaking *everything* reminded me of Weston. "I thought you and Milo were getting along pretty well."

"I don't want to make friends." The fork hit the plate.

"Okay." I pushed the sleeves of my Madigan Mountain hoodie up my forearms. It would be too hot for it in a few hours, but it was still my favorite piece of clothing. "Want to talk about it?"

"I don't want to make friends because I don't want to stay here." She shoved her hair out of her face. "And you don't have to come with me, Mom. I know this is your dream job, but I want to go home. Back to our house, and my friends, and everything I love."

I tried not to take that last part personally.

"Are you that unhappy?" I shifted my weight on the stool, my pajama shorts catching on the white upholstery.

"I miss my friends," she admitted, her gaze falling from mine. "And I miss the mountains. And I feel horrible because this is everything you've wanted, and I don't want to be the reason you don't have it."

"Oh, Sutton." I shook my head and reached to tuck her hair behind her ear, but she dodged me.

"You can just send me back," she pleaded, so much misery in her eyes that my chest clenched. "I can live with Halley or Ava, or even Weston. I know he'd take care of me until you got home."

"Sugar, I'm not going to ship you off. Whatever we do, we do together." But if she was this forlorn, was it even an option to stay?

Did I even want to stay?

Callie, your daughter isn't the only one who is unhappy. Carmen was right, and Sutton had noticed too.

"Then let's go home," she whispered. "I know you're as unhappy as I am. I hear you crying at night."

My stomach fell through the floor. Home. Is that what it would even feel like without Weston? How could I go back to Penny Ridge—Weston's home town, and not be *with* him? There was no way I'd survive seeing him and not being able to touch him.

"We agreed to try everything once, Mom, and we've tried. You don't even smile while you're taking pictures anymore, and wasn't that what this was all about?"

It was on the tip of my tongue to argue that I was learning too much here to go, but I wasn't learning anything I wanted to use once we'd leave.

This wasn't my dream anymore. Eighteen-year-old Callie would have relished every second of this, but I wasn't that girl anymore.

"Let's go home." Sutton got off the stool and tugged her Team Summit T-shirt down. It was too big for her, but she loved it.

"It's not that simple," I said quietly.

"Why?" Her face scrunched. "Because you got so mad at Weston that we couldn't live with him anymore?"

My mouth dropped open. "That...happened before we moved here. He had already left, remember?"

"Because you got in a fight." She folded her arms across her chest.

"Because adults have issues that kids don't need to worry about."

"It was because of me, wasn't it?" The worry in her eyes killed me.

"No. Never. Weston adores you. You know that." I laced my fingers together, gripping them tight.

"That's not what I mean. You fought because I got hurt! Because I picked the harder line and crashed." She shook her head. "It wasn't his fault, Mom. He wanted me to take the other one. It's my fault!"

"Sutton," I whispered, standing, wishing I could pull her into my arms and hug her, but that wasn't what she wanted, what she needed, right now. She needed to yell, to scream, to let it out.

"Can we go home if I promise not to compete anymore?" Her lower lip trembled.

I hit my knees in front of her. "It's not that. You aren't the reason. Sometimes things just don't work out between people because they're too different, or because they want different things."

"Like you didn't want to enter the picture contest."

"That's true." Just because I wasn't about to unload heavy adult emotions on my eleven-year-old didn't mean I was going to lie to her either. "I didn't want to enter. And sometimes when someone makes a choice for you, it can be the wrong one." I arched a brow at her.

"Don't blame him for it!" She shook her head, panic pressing her mouth tight.

"This isn't something you have to worry about, sugar."

"You can't blame Weston when I'm the one who wanted you

to enter!"

"Is that why you signed the waiver?" I asked quietly, keeping my voice as calm as possible so this didn't escalate. "Did Weston ask for your help?" The thought had been in my head since yesterday, spreading like poison.

Her arms fell to her sides.

"Sutton, it's okay. Just tell me the truth. I've already seen the waiver. I know you signed it. You're good, kiddo, but you're not that good."

"It was me," she whispered. "I signed it, and I was going to upload it, but Weston caught me."

I blinked. "What?"

"I told him that if he didn't do it, I would." Her gaze hit the floor. "I said that if you were his mom, he'd want everyone to know you were special too."

"Oh God." I covered my mouth with my hand. The way Weston loved his mom…that must have sliced him to the quick. "Tell me you're kidding. Tell me you didn't really say that."

"I did." She nodded, her lower lip trembling. "And I told him that I knew I was the reason you didn't try to do this years ago. And I didn't want to be the reason you lost your dream again."

She'd hit him with a one-two punch, nailing both his trigger points. *Damn it. Poor Weston.*

And Sutton… I'd worked so hard to make sure she never felt like she was anything but the biggest blessing in my life, yet here we were. My stomach turned to lead. "Sutton, listen to me. You have never been the reason for *anything* bad in my life. You're the best part of it."

She took two deep breaths and looked me in the eyes. "He didn't tell you it was me?"

"No," I whispered, shaking my head. "But you wouldn't have been able to do it. You didn't have a picture of me to submit with the application."

She cocked her eyebrow. "I was just going to scan your pass

and then crop it. I'm not five, Mom." Her lips pressed in a thin line and her shoulders dipped. "So, can we go home?"

I reached forward and brushed the back of my hand across her cheek. "You need to know that not everything with Weston was about you falling, or the contest. None of this is your fault, Sutton. None of it." How was I supposed to teach her not to accept less than she deserved if I stayed with a man I loved, who would never love me back?

But how could I keep her here when we were obviously both miserable?

There was a knock at the door. It was probably time to start tearing down our equipment to prepare for tomorrow's move.

"Some of it is," she muttered.

"None of this is on you. Adults make the decisions, not the kids." I stood, struggling to get my thoughts into coherent order as I headed for the front door. Weston hadn't told me that he'd caught Sutton with the application. He hadn't told me she was going to upload it if he didn't.

He'd covered for her.

He'd still made the absolutely wrong decision, but he'd covered for her.

I crossed through the living room and opened the door.

Then I stopped breathing.

Weston stood on the front steps.

 eston

CALLIE ANSWERED THE DOOR, and I took my first full breath in almost a month. Her hair was up off her neck in a messy bun that told me she'd only been awake for an hour or two, and she was wearing her Madigan hoodie, the one with the frayed cuffs, and pajama bottoms.

She'd never looked better to me.

Heartbeats passed as we stood there, our eyes locked, neither of us saying a word. I drank in the sight of her, and my heart started to pound.

I'd flown all this way, rented a car, and driven to this remote little village, and now that I was standing here, everything I'd planned out on the flight seemed...lame. I shoved my hands into the front pockets of my shorts and opened my mouth. *You have to say something.*

"Weston!" Sutton slipped under Callie's arm and flung herself at me.

"Hey, kid." I caught her easily and hugged her tight, lifting her feet off the ground. The scent of cherry shampoo filled my lungs, and I breathed in deep, rocking her slightly. "I've missed you too." That was the understatement of the year.

"You found us!" She pulled back, and I set her down on her feet, grinning at her shirt. Guess you could take the girls out of Colorado, but they'd still sleep in the merch.

"I had a little help." I took the worn envelope out of my back pocket and pointed to the return address she'd penned.

"Sutton, why don't you give us a minute?" Callie said.

Sutton turned toward her mother, and whatever face she made had Callie raising her eyebrows.

"Now." Callie motioned into the house.

Sutton sighed but marched inside, muttering something I couldn't hear but had Callie shaking her head as she passed by.

Then it was just us on the doorstep.

"Weston," she whispered, and there were so many emotions skipping across her face that I couldn't catch them all.

"Calliope." I cleared my throat. Somehow getting on the plane had been easier than getting words out of my mouth.

"Do you want to come in?" She stepped back and held the door open.

"Sure." I walked in behind her, noting the serviceable furniture and photography equipment on a nearby table.

"No one else is up yet, which is saying something since we usually sleep so late." She laughed awkwardly as she shut the door, and I turned as she leaned back against it.

I wanted to close the distance between us, press my body against hers, and kiss her until she remembered why we were right for each other. I wanted to throw her over my shoulder caveman-style and carry her back to Colorado where she belonged. But what I wanted didn't matter if she didn't want the same.

I took a fortifying breath. "You're probably wondering why I'm here."

"Yes, but why did you cover for Sutton?" She slipped her hands into the pocket of her hoodie, a gesture so familiar I almost forgot where we were, and what we *weren't* at the moment. "I have to know."

"What do you mean?" I shoved the envelope back in my pocket.

"Other than the fact that she's apparently been writing you letters, she signed the competition release. I saw it." Her eyebrows rose slightly. "You know, the one I yelled at you about in Steamboat."

"Ah. That waiver." I sighed and icy fear slid down my spine. Maybe the way I'd submitted her picture was too big of an issue for her to forgive, for us to get past.

"She said she told you she was going to enter it in the competition if you didn't." She huffed a laugh. "We were actually talking about it when you knocked."

"You were talking about me?" I cracked a smile.

"Weston." She lifted a brow.

"Right. The release. Sutton was pretty determined, but I'm the one who uploaded and hit enter. If you're looking for someone to blame, it's me." I squared my shoulders, ready for her to toss me out.

"Why didn't you tell me she'd already signed it? Why didn't you tell me she was going to submit it?" Two lines crinkled between her brows.

"Would it have made a difference?" I shrugged. "In that moment, under those circumstances, would it really have changed anything?"

"Maybe!" Her shoulders rose. "I don't know."

"There was no point causing drama between you and Sutton.

I was the one who submitted it. I'm the adult. I'm not about to blame a kid, and I sure as hell wasn't going to do anything that came between you two."

"You are so incredibly frustrating." She sagged against the door and glared at me.

"Not the first person to tell me that." I ripped my hand over my hair. "And I didn't come here to fight with you."

"Then why are you here?" she snapped. The same agony that had taken up residence in my chest shone in her eyes.

"I'm here because I'm in love with you!" There. The words I hadn't even let myself think, let myself accept, were out and hers to do whatever she wanted with.

Her lips parted and her eyes flared.

A breath passed, then two.

"I said I'm in love with you," I repeated. "I flew all this way just to tell you that."

"I heard you," she whispered, but there was disbelief in her eyes.

"I can't breathe without you, Callie. And I thought maybe that's what this feeling was." I touched the center of my chest. "Dependency. Addiction. And it grew with every day I spent with you, slowly consuming me. So I shoved it away and told myself it was okay to want you, to spend all my time with you, to think about you constantly, as long as I didn't need you." Those last words came out as a whisper. "Because when you need someone, and they leave you, that's when you're fucked."

"Weston," she whispered, her face falling.

"I've spent my entire adult life avoiding attachments. I have some great friends who put up with my bullshit, but that's it. And then I move in with you, and suddenly I'm eating ice cream on the counter and getting up early just so I can be there when you come down the steps in the morning. I'm finding any excuse to touch you, to just be around you, and that feeling…" I shook my head. "It starts to make decisions for me. And the truth is, I didn't even recognize how much I needed you until you weren't there. Until I came home to an empty house because you left for Paraguay early."

"When Ava told me you'd left, that Reed had pretty much given you permission to leave Madigan and go live your life, I figured maybe it was for the best. You've always done what people needed, Weston, not what you wanted." She pressed her lips in a tight line.

"Ava misheard what was going on. Reed told me I could take a few days off for an aviation conference. I needed some space... some kind of physical barrier so I didn't crawl back to you on my knees and beg you not to leave, so I went to the conference. And yes, Reed did tell me I could leave Madigan, that I didn't have to stay and run the operation if I wanted out, but that was just a couple of days ago, and I'm pretty sure it was only because he saw how miserable I am without you." It took everything I had to keep my feet planted where they were, but I did it, even though the palms of my hands itched to feel the soft skin of her cheeks, the silky strands of her hair.

She blinked. "Wait...so you didn't leave?"

"Not like you thought. I was gone four days, and you had left for Paraguay by the time I got back."

Her blue eyes went wide. "You aren't leaving Madigan?"

"No." I shook my head. "The exact opposite. And I need you to know that I'll be there, waiting for you, if you still want me."

"If I still..." She sucked in a shaky breath. "Weston, you deserve to go find whatever your new dream is. You hate being at Madigan."

"I hate being at Madigan without *you*," I corrected her. "And somewhere in the last season, I realized that I have everything I dreamed about as a kid. I get to ski the backcountry every day and fly helicopters. It doesn't get much better than that. And when I dream, Calliope Thorne, I dream about *you*. When Sutton wrote and told me you were unhappy—"

"Traitor," she muttered, her cheeks flushing.

I cracked a smile. "She has your best interest at heart."

"She wants to go home, and I didn't know what to say to her." She bit her lower lip. "Because I couldn't admit that I've felt that way for weeks, but…"

I moved, leaving only inches between us as I tilted her chin up with my thumb and forefinger. "But what?"

"But I didn't know how to live there, to work there, and to see you every day if you weren't mine." Her eyes watered. "And I couldn't handle living with the ghost of you if you had left, either. And I told myself that you were never going to love me back, and that I could make a future here, carve out the career I thought I wanted, but we're both so wretchedly unhappy. And bored, Weston. I'm so damn bored. Do you have any idea how many flowers I've photographed at every possible angle?"

"You're bored?" My eyebrows shot up.

"So. Many. Flowers." She nodded. "And hills, and trees, and landscapes. The occasional wildlife is keeping me somewhat sane, but it's nothing like doing the kind of work I do with you. There's no adrenaline, no moment where I hold my breath. And it took me *months* to realize that this isn't my dream anymore." She forced a smile. "It turns out eleven years can really change a person."

I thought back to the night she'd shown up at Madigan, rain-soaked and sobbing. "Yeah. It does. So what *do* you want, Calliope?" Whatever it was, I'd do my damnedest to give it to her.

"I want to be the best extreme sports photographer in the Rockies." She said it with the kind of confidence that made me grin. "And I want you."

"You have me." She could have whatever she wanted from me.

"Don't say that if you don't mean it, Weston." She tilted her chin even higher. "And don't tell me that you flew all this way and that should prove it, because I know that if Sutton wrote to you and told you she needed freaking toothpaste, you'd be on the next plane—"

"You have every part of me. I love you." I let my forehead rest against hers, and my heart seemed to slow and steady. "I know it's love because I don't just want you. I need you, Callie. I need you more than air, or flying, or skiing, or anything else that makes me...me. I *need* you to survive, and yet I will walk away if that's what you want. I'll do whatever makes you happy." I picked up her hand and put it on my chest. "You just have to know that this is yours. You don't have to want it, or need it, or accept it. It belongs to you, no matter what."

She sucked in a breath, and her fingers moved, gripping my shirt and tugging me closer. "You love me."

"I. Love. You." My hand curled around the back of her neck. "And I'm praying that you still love me too. Because I swear, if you do—if you need me the way I need you—I'll never let another day go by where I don't tell you what you mean to me."

"I won't say that I need you, because I never want you to feel that kind of obligation. But I do want you. God, do I want you." She grinned. "I love you, Weston. It's kind of impossible to stop."

I kissed her, and the world fell back into place. It was as simple as that. This is where everything made sense, where I saw my future—with Callie...which reminded me.

"I bought you a house," I said against her mouth.

"What?" She pulled back, her eyes wide with shock, and I lifted my head to give her space, since she couldn't retreat past the door.

"Technically, I'm under contract on a house." I grinned. "You might know it. It's a cute little Victorian on the corner of Hudson and Vine."

Her mouth hung open.

"Right now, the contract is only in my name, since Sutton wasn't around to forge your signature, but we'll add you as soon as you want. Or I'll assign the whole contract to you and find somewhere else to live. I don't care, as long as you're happy, as long as you get what you need. Owning it would mean nothing if I didn't have you and Sutton living there with me." I shifted my hand and stroked my thumb along her jaw.

I was never going to stop touching her. Ever.

"The Rupert place?" she whispered.

"That's the one." The corners of my mouth pulled into a smile. "Someone told me it's her dream house, and it turns out the Ruperts are more than happy to sell to a local."

"I'm not a local." Her arm wound around my neck.

"You've lived there over ten years—" I smirked. "With a little vacation to South America. Trust me, you're local enough." Slowly, I bent and brushed a kiss over her lips. "What do you say, Calliope?"

She kissed me right back, nipping my bottom lip. "I say take us home, Weston."

EPILOGUE

allie

THE LODGE WAS GORGEOUS, decorated in pinks and florals for Reed and Ava's wedding. Family and friends filed in, filling the chairs in the ballroom. They'd chosen the week before the resort was scheduled to open to tie the knot, and even the snow had cooperated, leaving the roads clear so everyone could get here.

And as much as I loved photography, I was more than grateful I got to be a bridesmaid instead of the photographer for today. Sometimes life was even better outside the lens. I'd debated leaving my camera at home, perched on the table beside the piano Reed had given us, but brought it just in case Ava wanted some special shots. Reed had the piano delivered from their parents' house the day we closed on our dream home.

Weston had it tuned within a couple of weeks, and I'd even caught him playing it once or twice.

Our home was exactly what I'd dreamed of. It was a little too organized for me and a little too cluttered for Weston. And though we never abided by it, our roommate contract was framed on the wall in the kitchen. Plus, it was only a block away from the studio space I'd just signed the lease on.

I'd still freelance for Madigan Mountain and planned to spend most my winter days with Weston, but now I'd be able to take other extreme clients, and with the publicity from the *World Geographic* competition, I'd already booked my first half-dozen.

I leaned into the doorway and noted Sutton had taken her seat next to Melody, Weston's stepmother. The relationship between Weston and his dad was still pretty rocky, but at least we could all be together in the same room without it coming to blows, especially on a day like today. I knew it would take time, but time was something we had now.

Smoothing the lines of my dress, I retreated, then turned to head back to the bride's room, where Ava was putting the finishing touches on the vows she'd edited at least sixteen times already. Of course they were perfect.

I ran smack into a hard chest in the darkened hallway, and the hands that steadied my hips made me smile. I'd know that scent, that body anywhere. "You're supposed to be dragging Reed to the altar."

"Trust me, Reed is chomping at the bit." Weston dipped his head and kissed my neck. "We're just waiting for the clock to chime four. What are you doing out here?"

I shivered at the feel of his lips on my skin. "Checking to make sure Sutton is where she's supposed to be." My brow puckered. "Pretty sure I saw someone who looks a lot like your brother wandering the halls, too."

"He's upstairs changing." I felt him smile as his lips grazed my jaw. "It's great to have him here."

"I bet it is." I swayed in his arms when his mouth moved toward my ear. "You are going to wrinkle me, Weston Madigan."

"Sounds like a good time." He ghosted his lips across mine.

"Lipstick," I warned him. It had taken a professional an hour to paint me up this way, and if he smeared me before the pictures, Ava was going to lose it.

"Who said I was kissing your mouth?" His lips hovered, and I leaned into him, my hands gripping his shoulders.

My pulse raced as he kissed the corner of my lips, my jaw, and the side of my neck. "We cannot make out in the hallway like a couple of teenagers," I protested, but my hands pulled him closer. He was never close enough.

"You feel incredible in this dress." His hands swept over my ass. "I can't wait to take it off you later. Or maybe I'll just lift the hem for dessert. I've never been too keen on cake."

I whimpered and heat flushed my skin. It was always like this with him. The electric connection never fizzled, it only grew stronger. The man could turn me on with nothing but a look. Hell, sometimes I didn't even need that.

He tilted his head to kiss my fingertips, then took my hand in his, lifting it to his mouth. He kissed the inside of my wrist, then my palm, then the diamond I'd spun around to face inward for today. "Still glad you said yes?"

"Every day." I grinned.

"It's only been two days." He chuckled.

He'd proposed after flying us to the top of the ridge behind the resort, his words stealing my breath just as effectively as the altitude. The sight of him on one knee was something I'd never forget.

It was also something we were keeping to ourselves for the next few weeks so Reed and Ava could have the spotlight.

"I'm going to be glad next week, and the week after, and the year after that," I promised, happiness filling every cell in my body.

"God, I love you," he whispered, and the admission hit me just like it did the first time, humbling me to my toes while simultaneously making me want to climb him at the next opportunity. I'd never get tired of hearing him say it.

"Good thing, because I love you too."

He ran his thumb over the diamond. "Can't we at least tell Sutton soon?"

"Yeah. Soon." I nodded.

He lifted his head and our lips met.

The door to the bridal room opened and Ava's head peeked out. "Oh no you don't, Weston. No smearing her up until after pictures!"

"I'm coming," I said to Ava. "Get back in there before Reed sees you!"

She disappeared, shutting the door.

"You'd better go," Weston said, his hands skimming over the satin of my dress.

"I'll see you in a few minutes." I grazed my fingers along his jaw.

"I'll be the one at the end of the aisle, next to the guy getting married," he teased, turning his head and kissing my fingers.

I took a step backward, but he caught my wrist before I could turn away completely. There was just enough light for me to see his eyes, and my heart raced at all the emotion I saw there.

This man. This difficult, stubborn, reckless man had become the epicenter of my dreams. And I knew that a lot could change in the years ahead, but that never would. We'd build our family, our life, around each other, and I'd make sure every single one of his dreams came true.

"We're next, Calliope," he whispered, his fingers slipping through mine.

"Hell yes, we are."

And I couldn't wait.

ACKNOWLEDGMENTS

First and foremost, thank you to my Heavenly Father for blessing me beyond my wildest dreams.

Thank you to my husband, Jason. You've always been the man I chose above all others and the man I choose every day. I couldn't ask for a better partner in this life. Thank you to my children, who keep me on my toes and laughing every day. You guys teach me more about life than I could ever hope to teach you.

Thank you to Devney Perry and Sarina Bowen for teaming up for another collaboration. It's an honor to work with such talented, hard-working women. You've both taught me so much!

Thank you to Karen Grove, for dealing with my squirrel of a brain. I never worry when I know you're coming behind me with edits. To Jenn Wood for dropping everything to copy edit, and to Sarah Hansen for the delicious cover. To my phenomenal agent, Louise Fury, who makes my life easier simply by standing at my back.

Thank you to my wifeys, our unholy trinity, Gina Maxwell and Cindi Madsen, who always pick up the phone. To Jay Crownover for being my safe place and the wolf to my rabbit. To Shelby and Cassie for putting up with my unicorn brain. To every blogger and reader who has taken a chance on me over the years. To my reader group, The Flygirls, for giving me a safe space on the wild west of the internet.

Lastly, because you're my beginning and end, thank you again to my Jason. None of this would be possible without your love and support. There's a little of you in every hero I write.

A LITTLE TOO LATE

BY SARINA BOWEN

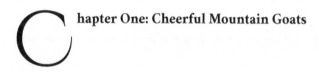

C hapter One: Cheerful Mountain Goats

REED

There's snow on the ground in Colorado. It must be fresh, because it's still white and fluffy, and it coats every pine bough at the side of the road.

I haven't seen snow in a while. And I haven't seen snow on *this* road in ten years.

"Reed?" my assistant's voice prompts. "Are you still there?"

"Yeah, sorry. Go ahead. I'm listening." *Sort of.*

"What do you want me to do about the lunch tomorrow with those friends from Stanford?" Sheila asks as I coast down the two-lane highway in my rental SUV.

"Just postpone it." The curve of the road is so familiar, even after all this time. It's trippy.

"You postponed that lunch already," she points out. "So I'm

going to tell them to go ahead without you. That reservation at Four Palms shouldn't go to waste."

"Then why did you even bother asking me?"

"I thought I'd give you the chance to do the right thing."

I roll my eyes. Sheila is a pain in my ass, but I'll be lost when she goes back for her MBA next year.

She knows it, too, which is problematic.

"Next up—Prashant is concerned that Deevers hasn't signed the paperwork for this new round of funding."

"Deevers will sign. He's a contemplative guy. Likes to sit a moment with big decisions. Give him a couple more days before you nudge."

"All right. Last thing," Sheila chirps as I slow down in antici- pation of the final turn. "I'm *not* telling Harper that you have to cancel Friday's dinner. You have to call her yourself."

Fuck. "Uh... I'd forgotten about that dinner. Couldn't you just..."

"Reed Madigan!" Sheila yells. "Don't even finish that sentence. Just man up and call her. And if you forget, just know you'll be walking to Starbucks yourself for two weeks after you return."

"Two weeks, huh? That's hardcore." Honestly, I could just fire Sheila and find an assistant who'll robotically do whatever I need. But I'm not going to, and we both know it. "I'll call Harp- er," I grumble.

"Okay, boss. That's about all I need from you. What are you doing in Colorado, anyway? Is this some top-secret investment?"

"No. Just some personal stuff to take care of."

"Personal stuff?" she asks, her young voice going high with disbelief. "You have a personal life?"

"Shut up."

She laughs.

"My father decided to sell the family business." I try to keep the irritation out of my voice, but it isn't easy. I'm the only one in the family with an MBA. But did my father consult me? No way. He just dropped an email bomb into my inbox yesterday. In four lines of text, he let my two brothers and me know that A) he'd gotten remarried and B) he's planning to sell the mountain property that's been in our family for several generations.

I'm really not sure how I feel about it.

"What kind of family business?" Sheila asks.

"It's a ski resort."

Sheila says nothing for a moment, and I wonder if the call got dropped. That happens a lot in the mountains. But then she gasps. "Wait, really? Do you mean Madigan Mountain?"

"That's the one. Doesn't make you Sherlock Holmes, though, seeing as it's named after us."

"*God,* you're a freak," Sheila says suddenly.

"Hey—haven't we talked about boundaries?"

"Oh, please. There's such a thing as respecting boundaries. And then there's you. I've been keeping your calendar for two years, and you never mentioned your family owns the coolest boutique ski mountain in the country. I've never even booked you on a flight to Colorado before this morning. I didn't even know you were from there."

I don't try to argue, because she's right—it's weird that I never go home, and that I don't spend a lot of time thinking about this place. But if she knew what hell it had become after my mother died, she'd understand.

"I mean, you went skiing at *Whistler* last year. That condo you rented was two thousand bucks a night, Reed. *Why?*"

"It's complicated," I grumble.

"What? You're breaking up."

"It's *complicated!* You'll lose me in a second." The narrow mountain road passes between two tall ledges of rock.

"I c... hear... at all. BUT CALL HARPER DAMMIT!"

The phone makes those two high-pitched beeps that tell you

the call has been dropped. Sheila naturally got the last word. Of course she did.

I put on my blinker and prepare to take the turn onto Old Mine Road. That's when I spot the sign. *Two Miles to Madigan Mountain*. But it's not the low-profile, carved wooden sign that used to stand here at the roadside. This one is new and bright and about three times larger than the old one.

And I hate it on sight.

A car behind me leans on the horn, and I realize I'm stopping traffic. So I make the final, familiar turn onto the steep and twisty road to my family's resort. The SUV downshifts as I begin the climb. There are rocky outcroppings on either side, alternating with stands of tall pines. It's only November, but the forest floor is white with snow.

Hell, this road is still as familiar as my own hand. The sight of it puts an ache right into the center of my chest. It's like heartburn, I guess—inconvenient, but ultimately survivable.

I hadn't planned to reschedule my whole life in order to suddenly fly to Colorado and face down my past, and the higher the car climbs, the worse this idea gets. Even though the windows of the SUV are rolled up all the way, I could swear I smell the scent of pine, and I hear the snap the needles make underfoot when you walk through these woods.

Almost a hundred years ago, my great-grandfather bought this spot at the end of a challenging old logging road. He passed it on to my grandfather, who build one of the first ski resorts in the Rockies.

The location is a challenge, though. When it snows, the road is difficult to plow. In weekend traffic, if someone takes a turn too fast and skids, the resulting fender bender can stop the flow of cars for hours while the tow truck does its job hauling the unfortunate victim away.

That's why Madigan Mountain never became a sprawling international destination, like Aspen or Whistler. Our vibe was

—and still is, I guess—a smaller, family ski mountain. Our customers like it that way. The regulars often book next year's vacation before they've even left the premises.

It's heartbreakingly easy to picture my mom waving them off with a happy smile. "See you next year!"

Even that brief memory stings. She's been gone more than a decade, and it still hurts me. That's why my brothers and I avoid this place.

And it's not like my dad ever gave his three sons a good reason to visit. After Mom's death, he became a surly beast. We all fled. Ain't nobody got time for his bitterness.

But here I am anyway. Dad may be a decent hotelier, but he wouldn't know a financing contract if it bit him in his grumpy ass. I'm here to make sure he doesn't get fleeced.

You could argue that Dad's finances are none of my business. After all, I've already made my own tidy fortune. But I have two younger brothers. Weston is a military pilot, and Crew is busy being famous. His daredevil ass could literally be on any continent right now, as long as there's snow there. He doesn't like to check in or return phone calls. Who knows if he even *saw* Dad's crazy email?

I haven't always been a great brother. After my mom died, I didn't stick around for Weston and Crew. I hightailed it back to Middlebury College in Vermont. After graduation, I settled in Silicon Valley, where I made a career for myself with a Stanford MBA and a lot of ambition.

So I'm showing up because they can't. Or won't, in Crew's case. I need to hear what the hell Dad is thinking. I need to know if he's serious about selling a property that's been in our family all this time.

It's also the place where my mother is buried. If nothing else, I can put flowers on her grave one last time.

The road makes a final turn, and the resort comes into view. I find myself slowing down to take a good look.

The sprawling resort footprint hasn't changed much in decades. The stone lodge my grandfather constructed in the fifties is connected to a three-story hotel that was added on later. That original lodge holds the hotel lobby, restaurants, and offices. And there are fifty rooms in the hotel.

The resort follows a half moon shape, with most buildings facing the mountain. Slanted, late afternoon sunlight paints the snowy peaks a golden color. Down the slope is the big wooden ski lodge my grandfather built in the eighties. That's where the day skiers go to rent their skis, book a lesson, or buy a bowl of chili.

And in the other direction—behind the hotel, and beyond my current view—there's a spa, a heated pool, and a couple of hot tubs. There's an outdoor pavilion where weddings are held during the warmer months.

All the buildings have peaked roofs and about a million shutters painted a color called Heritage Red. The summer after eighth grade, I painted a bunch of those damn shutters myself. For weeks, my hands were splattered with Heritage Red, and so were my shoes. But a guy has to earn money somehow, and there was a sweet pair of Rossignol skis that I just had to have.

The rest of the resort spreads farther along the mountain's base. The foothills are dotted with fifty or so condo units that my family sold in the nineties. They have red shutters, too, which gives everything a unified appearance.

I'm a little stunned by how gorgeous everything is. I'd honestly forgotten just how striking the rugged mountain range looks against the blue sky. The resort looks well kept, too. The shutters are as fresh as ever. The gravel parking lot is well graded and carefully plowed.

My father had been such a wreck after my mother died that I wasn't sure what to expect. If the place had crumbled to the ground, I wouldn't have been shocked.

There are no indications of crumbling, though. Two new

signs direct visitors to Skier Parking or Hotel Check-In. Each sign features a cheerful mountain goat—on the first, he's driving a SUV with skis mounted on top, and on the other, he's carrying a backpack toward the lodge.

I stare at these signs a little longer than necessary, because there's something vaguely familiar about the art. I can't quite put my finger on why.

But I'm not here to see the sights, so I pull up to the hotel. A young man hurries outside to greet me. He's wearing a Madigan Mountain jacket in a snappy design. That's new, too.

"Checking in, sir?" he asks.

"Uh, yes." I haven't given much thought to where I'll sleep tonight. When your family owns a ski resort, you don't have to plan ahead. It's only November, so there's no way the place is booked.

I suppose I could sleep in my old bedroom if I have to. Although my father just got remarried to a stranger, so I don't know if that's my best option.

"Name, sir?" the young man asks. He holds out his hand for my rental car key.

I let out a snort and toss him the fob. "The name is Reed Madigan. Thanks, pal."

He makes the catch in spite of the shocked look on his face. "Whoa, really?"

But I'm already turning my back and headed for the door to the lodge. My father had better be in his office. We've got some talking to do.

* * *

Ava

How about trivia night at the Broken Prong? I text to my girl-friends. *It's been a few weeks since we made the other tables cry.*

I don't have a babysitter, Callie replies. *Could we do drinks at my place? I'll make frosé.*

Sure, I reply immediately.

I'm sorry! Callie says. *I know it's more fun to get off the mountain!*

She isn't wrong. I spend entirely too many hours on this property. I haven't had a real vacation in years. That's the first thing I'm going to do when the sale of Madigan Mountain goes through—book a trip somewhere and put my two-week vacation on the calendar. It doesn't matter where, just as long as I'm not responsible for calling a plumber if a pipe breaks or soothing a finicky guest when all the spa appointments are booked up.

In the meantime, Tuesday night is always girls' night, no exceptions. And it wouldn't be the same without Callie. *Don't worry about it*, I assure her. *We always have fun. What can I bring?*

How about brownies? Callie suggests.

Then our friend Raven chimes in. *I love Ava's brownies! And so do my hips. I'm down for frozen pink wine at Callie's.*

"Ava!" my boss calls from the inner office. "Can you make my keys sing? I can't find them!"

"Yep!" I yell back. "Hang on." I wake up my computer and pull up the app I use to keep Mark Madigan organized. I hit a big orange button on the screen, and a moment later I hear the telltale chime of the hotelier's keys in the other room.

"Found 'em!" he yells.

Of course he did. I pick up my hot chocolate mug and drain the last of my afternoon treat. In the text thread, Raven has sent us a funny gif of a woman drinking wine from a fishbowl. So I'm grinning down at my phone when a deep voice says. "Excuse me, is he in there?"

Before I can even look up, my heart skips a beat. *That voice.* It's straight from my past. And by the time I turn my head to find him in the doorway, I'm already trembling.

Holy crap.

Holy.

Crap.

Reed Madigan is standing there. *Right there* on the carpet in front of my desk. I'm so startled that my hot chocolate mug slips out of my hands. It hits the slate coaster on my desk hard, and at a bad angle. And then my favorite mug—my *lucky* mug—makes an unholy cracking noise, before splitting into two pieces right in front of me.

Oh my God. Now I don't even know where to look—at the ooze of chocolate spreading toward my keyboard? Or up into the startled eyes of the only man I've ever loved.

"*Ava?*" Reed says slowly. Like he can't believe his eyes, either. "What the *hell* are you doing here?"

A LITTLE TOO WILD

BY DEVNEY PERRY

 hapter 1

CREW

"The plane is crashing. I gotta go."

"Crew." I could practically hear Sydney's eyes roll on the other end of our phone call. "Stop being overdramatic."

"What if it really was crashing? And your last words to me were an insult?"

"You're not even on a plane," she barked as the whirl of my wheels on the highway's pavement hummed in the background. "Focus."

No, I didn't want to focus. I wanted to skip the lecture she'd started five minutes ago, then turn my army-green G-Wagon around and drive back to Utah.

"You need to be back in Park City on Monday for that photo shoot with GNU."

"I know." This was the fifth time she'd reminded me about that photo shoot. "I'll be back in time."

"You cannot be late. They are flying in from Washington just for this shoot."

Also something she'd told me five times. "Don't worry. I'll be there. Trust me." The last place in the world I wanted to be this weekend was Colorado.

"This trip couldn't fall at a worse time." Sydney sighed. "This sponsorship is huge. I don't want to risk anything happening to screw it up."

"Relax, Syd. It'll be fine. I'll be there Monday."

"Is this trip one hundred percent necessary?"

"What would you like me to do? Skip my brother's wedding?"

"Yes."

I chuckled. "You are ruthless."

"Which is why you love me."

"True."

Sydney had been my agent for the past three years and had made it her personal mission in life to make me, Crew Madigan, the face of snowboarding in America. So far, she'd done a hell of a job.

Her ruthlessness padded my bank account. As well as her own.

This Mercedes was my latest purchase, thanks to my recent sponsorship contracts. Syd had spent her commission on the same model, but in black.

"I'll see you Monday." There was no chance I'd linger in Colorado. My only obligation was the actual wedding tonight, and first thing tomorrow morning, I'd be on the road.

"Expect a phone call on Monday morning," Sydney said. "Early. I don't trust you to set your alarm."

"One time, Syd. I was late for one photo shoot."

She'd scheduled it for six in the morning because the photographer had wanted a sunrise shot, and when I'd set the hotel alarm the night before, I'd accidentally chosen p.m., not a.m.

Though Syd loved to rub that in my face, the shoot itself had worked out fine. The photographer was cool, and instead of worrying about a morning shoot, we'd just spent the day together, freestyling the Big Sky slopes in Montana.

With nothing staged or faked, the photos he'd taken had been epic. He'd captured a picture of me as I'd come off a cliff and bent for a grab, the afternoon sky at my back with mountain ranges and clouds in the distance.

That photo had landed on the cover of *Snowboarder Magazine*.

"Be on time, Crew."

"I cross my heart."

"And hope to die if you disappoint me."

Why did I always feel like saluting Sydney at the end of a phone call? "See ya."

She hung up without a goodbye.

I sighed, shifting my grip on the wheel. The drive from Park City was seven hours, and with every passing minute, the throb behind my temples intensified. For the past hundred miles, I'd begun to squirm.

Nagging as it was, at least Sydney's call had been a brief distraction from the anxiety rattling through my bones. I had been in knots for weeks, dreading this trip.

Why couldn't Reed have gotten married in Hawaii or Cabo?

My stomach churned as I neared the outskirts of Penny Ridge. For twelve years, I'd avoided returning to my hometown. Over a decade. After all that time, shouldn't this be easier? After the life and career I'd built, shouldn't twelve years have dulled the painful memories of home?

I was no longer the eighteen-year-old kid who'd run away from anything and everything in his life. Except as the speed limit dropped, the town coming into view, it was like being blasted into the past.

My heart beat too fast as I approached a sign with an arrow that hadn't been there when I'd left.

Madigan Mountain

A new access point to my family's ski resort. The entrance to a place I would have happily avoided until the end of my days.

The turnoff to town approached, so I slowed, hit my turn signal and pulled off the highway to Main Street. Buildings with red-brick faces sprouted up on both sides of the road, like walls —or jail-cell bars.

Another sign came into view, this one familiar and built into the median of the road.

Welcome to Penny Ridge

Located seventy miles from Denver along the ridgeline from Keystone, Penny Ridge had been my family's home for generations. But the day I'd left town, I hadn't looked back once. Not for friends. Not even for family.

As a professional snowboarder, there was no way to entirely avoid Colorado, not with its famed ski slopes and resorts. But I'd limited my time in the state, spending the bulk of it at alternative mountains.

Park City had become home. Montana was a favorite vacation destination. So were Canada, New Zealand and Japan. I'd travel anywhere in the world, especially if it meant distance from Penny Ridge.

Maybe I should have skipped my brother's wedding. Except I hadn't seen Reed in years. Hell, I hadn't even met his fiancée. Weston and I hadn't caught up lately either, and the only time I'd seen his fiancée, Callie, had been over FaceTime.

When both of my brothers had called about the wedding, asking me to come, I'd had a hard time finding an excuse not to show.

There was a suit in the back seat, pressed and ready for

tonight's ceremony and reception. My overnight bag was packed with a single change of clothes, limited toiletries and nothing more. I'd do this wedding, make an appearance, then disappear from Penny Ridge for another decade. Maybe two.

As I drove down Main, I took in the changes as I rolled down the blocks. Flip's Gold and Silver was now Black Diamond Coffee. The Dive Bar was gone, replaced with a craft brewery. Mom's favorite bookstore was a Helly Hansen franchise.

The coffee shop and brewery, she would have loved. The demise of her bookstore, not so much.

Her ghost walked these sidewalks. Mom haunted this town, these streets.

Tomorrow. I only had to stick this out through tomorrow. Then I'd get out of Penny Ridge.

People meandered the sidewalks. Half of the parking spaces were taken. It was fairly quiet this afternoon, something I suspected would change when the resort opened for the season next weekend. Then downtown would be clamoring with tourists.

As much as I longed to retreat to the highway, I headed for the winding Old Mine Road and started up the mountain.

My ears popped as I climbed and weaved past towering evergreens. With the new access point, I doubted this old road got as much traffic as it had in years past. Probably a good thing. It was too narrow for decent shuttles, and on icy days, the drive down could be treacherous.

Mom had always hated this road in the winter, given the sharp drop-off. She'd love that Reed had put in a safer road.

My oldest brother had been working hard for the past two years to expand Madigan Mountain. The new access road. More terrain. New residential and commercial properties. Not that I'd seen any of it firsthand, but Weston had told me that it was becoming a next-level resort. He'd even moved home last year to help Reed by starting a heliskiing operation.

They had more plans, some of which they'd shared, but whatever they had in store for the mountain was not my problem. I was here for one night and one night only.

I turned one final corner and the lodge and hotel came into view. The mountain stood tall and proud at its back.

It looked the same. It looked different.

It was home. Yet it wasn't.

"I don't want to be here," I muttered as I drove past the parking lots.

The signage was new, branded with mountain goats. Beyond the hotel, a condo development hugged the mountain base. The new chairlift stretched toward the summit, leading to new runs that snaked white through the trees. And past the lodge, in a forest clearing, was a helipad. Weston's helicopter was likely stowed in the adjacent hangar.

I pulled into a parking spot outside the hotel and hopped out, breathing the mountain air as I stretched my legs. It smelled like my childhood, snow and pine and sunshine. It smelled like good memories. And bad.

With my bag looped over a shoulder and my suit bag draped over an arm, I walked toward the hotel's stone entrance. My grandfather had constructed this wooden A-frame in the fifties as the original ski lodge. Years later, a new lodge had been built and this had become the lobby to the connected three-story hotel.

At least with all the changes Reed had made lately, he'd left the red shutters on the windows. Mom had loved those shutters.

I dropped my eyes to the sidewalk. The less I took in, the better. The more I looked around, the more I saw Mom.

"Good afternoon, sir." The bellhop opened the door, waving me inside.

The lobby smelled like vanilla and cedar. Tall, gleaming windows along the far wall gave guests a sweeping view of the mountain. As a kid, my brothers would chase me around the lobby in the summers, when there weren't many guests and my parents were busy. The long-time front desk clerk, Mona, would snap at us whenever we got too loud. But Mom would always laugh it off, telling her we were simply testing the acoustics, then shooing us outside to play.

More memories.

"Excuse me."

A man walked past me, snapping me out of my stupor. I unglued my feet from the floor and walked toward the front desk, passing a couple as they came out of the bar. The woman was dressed in a black gown. The man was in a gray suit. Each was carrying a cocktail.

They were most likely going to the wedding. There was a good chance Dad was in the bar, holding a tumbler of his favorite whiskey, and since that reunion was one I'd delay for as long as possible, I headed for the reception desk.

"Good afternoon, sir." The clerk smiled, her eyes flaring slightly. She was young. Pretty. Blond hair with big hazel eyes. If this were any other resort, any other mountain, maybe I'd let her flirt. Maybe I'd get an extra key to my room and hand it over with an invitation.

But I was leaving first thing in the morning and had no time to play with my brothers' employees.

"Crew Madigan," I said. "Checking in."

"Madigan. Oh, um, of course." She stood taller, a flush creeping into her cheeks as she focused on the computer's screen. "You're in a suite, staying for two nights."

"No, just the one." I dug out my wallet from my jeans pocket, fishing out a credit card.

"There's no charge, Mr. Madigan." Reed's doing, no doubt.

"You're on the third floor. Room 312. It's the Vista Suite. How many keys would you like?"

"Also just the one." This trip wasn't pleasure. It wasn't business either. It was family.

She worked quickly to get me my key card, sliding it across the counter. "Can I help you with anything else?"

"No, thanks." With a nod, I walked away, heading straight for the elevators and the third floor.

The hallway greeted me with fresh paint, clean carpets and the scent of laundry soap. These hallways used to be racetracks for us. Reed, Weston and I had played hide-and-seek throughout the hotel until the time I'd hidden in a storage closet for an hour. By the time Weston had found me, every staff member and my parents had been in a panic.

That was back when Dad had actually cared about his kids' whereabouts. When he'd been more than the cold, heartless widower who'd forgotten his three sons had just lost their mother.

I unlocked the door to my suite, letting it close behind me as I strode into the living room, plopping my things on the leather sofa.

The updates from the hallway extended into the rooms, making them feel up-to-date with that rustic ski resort vibe. It was a nice room, with a fireplace and sprawling view of the mountain. Perfect for one night and one night only.

I unzipped my bag, wanting to take a quick shower to wash off the road trip before the wedding started in an hour. But the moment I had my toiletry case in the bathroom, a knock came at the door.

Probably someone with the last name Madigan. Hopefully a brother, not a father. I checked the peephole, grinning at the man wearing a black suit on the other side.

"Hey," I said, opening the door.

"Hi." Weston smiled, pulling me into a hug and slapping me

on the back. "About time you got here. I was starting to worry you weren't going to show."

"Tempting, but I figured you'd bust my ass, so here I am."

"How are you?" he asked, coming inside.

I shrugged. "All right. It's good to see you."

"Yeah." He put his hand on my shoulder. "You too."

Weston was two years older, and when our family had fallen apart after Mom's death, he'd been the one to see me through the darkest days. Instead of moving away to start his own life, he'd stayed in Penny Ridge until I'd graduated high school. He'd made sure that a fourteen-year-old kid hadn't drowned in his grief.

He'd done what Dad should have.

Those four years, I couldn't repay him for that. For all he'd done. I wasn't here because Reed had called, even though it was his wedding.

I'd come because Weston had asked me to.

Not that I didn't love Reed. But our relationship was different. After Mom, he'd gone away to college. He'd left us behind. For those first few years, I'd blamed Reed for abandoning us. But over time, that resentment had faded.

We'd all been devastated. We'd all needed to escape.

But unlike my brothers, I had no intention of returning home.

"You look good," I told Weston as we moved into the living room, each taking a chair in the sitting area next to the windows that overlooked the mountain.

He seemed . . . lighter. Happy. There was a twinkle in his brown eyes.

"I am good," he said. "Glad you're here. Nice to talk to you face-to-face for a change."

Conversation between us had been limited over the years. He'd been busy with his career in the military. I'd been consumed with professional sports.

Mostly, we'd talked via voicemail. The last time I'd actually seen him in person had been three years ago. Our travel schedules had coincided and we'd met for dinner in the Seattle airport.

"How do you like living here?" I asked.

"It's been good. Retirement took a bit of an adjustment but I've managed to keep myself out of trouble."

"Saw a helipad on my way in."

He grinned. "This expansion has been amazing. The new terrain is insane. We've got decent snow already too. The base is solid. If you want to go up tomorrow—"

"Can't." I cut him off before he could talk me into it. "I've got to get back to Park City. There's a sponsor flying in for a meeting."

"Oh." His smile faltered. "Thought we'd get you for a couple days at least."

"Not this time." *Not any time.* "Besides, I didn't bring a board," I lied.

I didn't go anywhere in the winter without a snowboard, not that I'd be tempted to ride here. The memories . . .

The hotel, the lodge, the town were bad enough. I wasn't sure I could handle being on the mountain.

"We do have snowboards here," Weston said. "A whole rental shop full of them, in fact."

"Next time." There would be no next time.

Weston studied my face, undoubtedly spotting the lie. Once upon a time, he'd been both brother and keeper. When I'd told a bullshit lie to do something stupid, like go to a party or skip school to ride, those lies had gone to Weston, not my father.

Disappointment clouded his gaze as he dropped it to the floor before standing. "I'd better let you get ready. And I need to go pick up Callie and Sutton."

"I'm looking forward to meeting them."

"Yeah." His face softened. "They're excited to meet you too."

Just to warn you, Sutton is going to ask you for your autograph. She found one of your old Olympic posters at a shop downtown. She wants to take it to school next week to show her friends."

"I'll sign whatever she wants."

"Appreciate it." Weston clapped me on the shoulder again, his version of another hug. "See you in a bit? I'll save you a seat."

"Sounds great." I forced another smile, then waited for him to leave before I returned to the bathroom, taking a long look in the mirror.

Damn, I didn't want to be here. But it was just one night.

I'd congratulate Reed and meet Ava. I'd meet Weston's fiancée, Callie, and her daughter, Sutton. I'd ignore my father and his new wife, Melody. Then come dawn . . .

"I'm getting the hell off this mountain."

After a quick shower, I styled my hair and dressed in my black suit. With my shoulders squared, I headed to the main floor, following a stream of people through the lobby.

"Crew."

I turned at my name. Reed crossed the space, wearing a tux and an ear-to-ear grin. "Hey."

"Thanks for being here." He closed the space between us, pulling me into a hug, holding me so tight it took me off guard.

"Congratulations."

"Thanks." He gulped, then fussed with the boutonniere pinned to his lapel.

"Nervous?" I asked.

"Yes. No. I just want everything to go smoothly. But I'm more than ready to make Ava my wife. And I'm glad you could be here."

"Me too." It was even slightly true. For Reed, I was glad to be here. "You'd better go. I'll be here afterward. We'll catch up. Have a drink."

"There's a lot to talk about." He laughed. "So I'll hold you to that drink."

He strode past me for the entrance to the ballrooms, greeting people as he walked.

I followed, in no rush. I fell in line with the other guests, shuffling into the ballrooms, taking in more of the changes. Structurally, the hotel was exactly as I remembered. But with the updated décor and style, it rivaled larger, glitzier Colorado resorts.

A new crystal chandelier illuminated the foyer between the ballrooms. The old industrial tile had been removed and replaced with a plush burgundy carpet. The elk and moose mounts had been swapped for wall art.

The line filtered through double doors to a room decked out in flowers and glimmering lights. An aisle, flanked by two sections of white chairs, led to an arched altar adorned with greenery and roses.

Reed stood chatting with Pastor Jennings, the man who'd busted me at thirteen for making out with his daughter at a middle school dance.

Familiar faces jumped out from all directions, including one that wasn't all that different from my own.

Dad stood not far from Reed, laughing with the woman on his arm. She was tall and thin. Pretty, with a big smile and graying blond hair.

It wasn't fair that she was here. Mom should have been here on her oldest son's wedding day.

I clenched my teeth, my molars grinding, as a hand smacked my back.

"Hey, man."

"River." I relaxed instantly, letting my best friend from high school pull me into a quick hug. "How are you?"

"Can't complain."

River was one of the few people in Penny Ridge I'd kept in

touch with over the years. Mostly because he was good about texting and had met me a few times to ride.

We'd both grown up with dreams of professional snow-boarding. While I'd gone on to become a world champion, his career had fizzled. But there'd been trips when I'd invited him along. River was always good at providing levity in heavy moments and irritating the shit out of Sydney and my manager.

"What's new?" I asked.

"Not much. Looking forward to another season. Think this is gonna be my year."

It wasn't. But I didn't have the heart to break it to River that he just wasn't good enough. Maybe he could have been, but he didn't have the discipline to hone his skill and take it to the next level.

"I'm sure it is," I lied. "Did you come with a date?"

"Nah. I'm here with my sister."

"Raven's here?"

"Yeah." River searched the crowd. "She's around here somewhere."

But before he could find her, another man appeared at my side. "Crew."

Fuck. So much for avoidance. "Dad."

"How are you, son? Glad to see you."

I nodded, holding his gaze for a moment. He looked . . . different. Maybe because he was missing his standard scowl.

"Oh, hello!" The woman he'd been standing with earlier swept past him, coming straight into my space for a hug. "Crew, I'm Melody. It is so good to finally meet you."

"Uh . . ." I looked down at her, then to Dad, who just beamed at his new wife.

"You must sit with us," Melody said. "The front row is for family."

Family. That word felt like a knife to my spine spoken from a woman who hadn't been around when my real family had disintegrated.

"Actually, I'm sitting with River." I took my friend's elbow, practically shoving him out of the line. "Nice to meet you."

Melody's smile faltered.

Dad put his arm around her shoulders, hauling her into his side. He bent to murmur something in her ear, but I didn't stick around.

I pushed River along toward the middle of the groom's section.

"Take it you haven't talked to your old man lately?" River asked.

"No." And I didn't plan on changing that tonight.

"I got you. I'll run interference."

"Appreciated."

River knew all about what had happened in high school. He'd had my back then and still had it now.

We lingered beside the aisle, standing between huddles of people all chatting before the ceremony started.

A swish of black hair caught my eye. I did a double take and the air was sucked out of my lungs.

Raven.

River's sister had always been pretty. When I'd left here, she'd been a sophomore. Twelve years later, she'd grown into a woman who wasn't pretty.

She was devastating.

Long, silky hair fell nearly to her waist. A handful of freckles dusted her nose. Her soft lips were painted a sultry red. A sleeveless, black dress hugged her lithe body.

The dress had a swath of leather around her torso, giving it a sexy edge. That and the slit that ran up her thigh. She had mile-long legs accentuated with a pair of strappy heels.

Goddamn. She was stunning.

Then again, she'd always snagged my attention.

There wasn't much that River didn't know about me. Mostly because we'd been friends for so long, but also because he'd been my confidant in high school.

But not once had I let it show how much I'd crushed on his sister.

"Raven." He jerked up his chin, waving her over.

"Oh, there you are." She smiled at him, then turned to me, flashing me those arctic-blue eyes framed by sooty lashes. "Oh." Her smile dropped. "Hey, Crew."

"Hey, Raven."

"I'm going to go find a seat," she told River.

"'Kay. I'm sitting with Crew."

Without another word, she walked away, taking a chair on the bride's side of the room.

Twelve years and all I got was a *Hey, Crew*.

Why did that surprise me? Raven had never seemed even slightly interested. The only girl at Penny Ridge High I'd wanted was the only girl who couldn't have cared less. I was a world champion, an Olympian, and she still stared straight through me.

Maybe some things around here had changed. But not enough.

I needed to get the fuck off Madigan Mountain.

ALSO BY REBECCA YARROS

ABOUT THE AUTHOR

Rebecca Yarros is a hopeless romantic and an incurable coffee addict. She is the *Wall Street Journal* and *USA Today* bestselling author of over ten novels, including *The Last Letter* and *The Things We Leave Unfinished*. She is also the recipient of the Colorado Romance Writer's Award of Excellence for *Eyes Turned Skyward* from her *Flight and Glory* series.

Rebecca loves military heroes and has been blissfully married to hers for twenty years. She's the mother of six children and is currently surviving the teenage years with two of her four hockey-playing sons. When she's not writing, you can find her at the hockey rink or sneaking in some guitar time. She lives in Colorado with her family, their stubborn English bulldogs, Maine Coon cat, and feisty chinchillas who loves to chase the aforementioned bulldogs. Having fostered then adopted their youngest daughter, Rebecca is passionate about helping children in the foster system through her nonprofit, One October.

Want to know about Rebecca's next release? Join her mailing list! Or check her out online at www.rebeccayarros.com.

Printed in the USA
CPSIA information can be obtained
at www.ICGtesting.com
LVHW090505230224
772587LV00005B/774